GRIMM'S FAIRY TALES

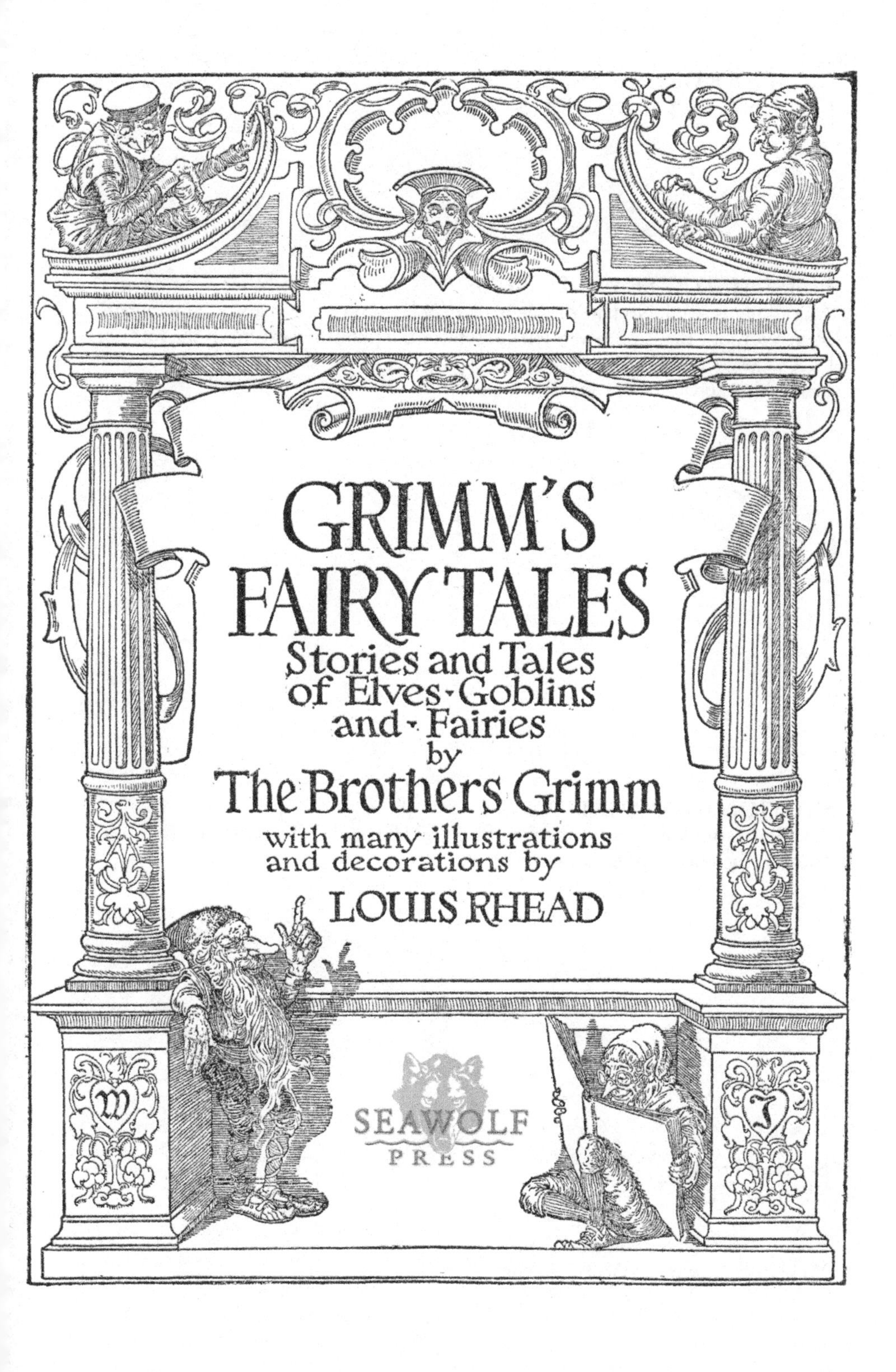
GRIMM'S
FAIRY TALES
Stories and Tales
of Elves - Goblins
and - Fairies
by
The Brothers Grimm
with many illustrations
and decorations by
LOUIS RHEAD
SEAWOLF
PRESS

GRIMM'S FAIRY TALES

PUBLISHED BY SEAWOLF PRESS

Printed in the U.S.A. on acid-free paper.

EDITION INFORMATION
The illustrations and cover are taken from the Harper Brothers 1917 edition. The tales are the tales covered in that edition.

SeaWolf Press
P.O. Box 961
Orinda, CA 94563
Email: support@seawolfpress.com
Web: http://www.SeaWolfPress.com

CONTENTS

CONTENTS

IT is more than one hundred years ago, to be exact, in the year 1812, that a first selection of stories appeared in book form under the title of *Children's and Household Tales*, chosen from a large number obtained from the mouths of German peasants by the indefatigable exertions of the brothers Jacob and Wilhelm Grimm. The first translation published in the English language in 1823 was a selection made by Mr. Edgar Taylor, accompanied with twelve wonderful etchings by George Cruikshank, which John Ruskin very eloquently describes in detail in his *Elements of Drawing*. A second collection of these stories was issued three years later by the same translator, with ten more etchings by the same great artist, whose power in depicting fairyland has no equal.

These world-famous stories are by no means of one nationality, for we find counterparts of them in the literature of Scandinavia, Russia, England, and in other sources. The two brothers, both learned in other branches of the literature of their own country, gained enduring fame, mostly from these stories--ostensibly written for the education of the young. Like the tales of the great Danish story-teller, Hans Andersen, the stories have an equal fascination for boys and girls.

A work of art is often more easily understood when a comparison is made with some masterpiece of another age and country, and the difference between the Grimms and Andersen is that the former, as it seems to me, have an advantage in their cheerful humor and their many mirth-provoking situations. A pathetic sadness runs through many stories of Andersen, and the endings of some are very mournful, often tragic. It is not so with the Grimms. However fearful a

PREFACE

calamity may be, they deftly develop dire situations into a most laughable and pleasing climax. So true, so natural do they seem, that not only the young, but those of graver years read "these gay creations of the imagination" with keenest pleasure. Many of the comic situations are produced by the introduction of wild or domestic animals and birds. Even commonplace objects about the house take the part of characters that talk and move about in the most natural, and yet most ludicrous, manner. Pins and needles, sausages, a cudgel, or a table--all are made to do things by the magic of "make-believe," together with the assistance of some kind goblin, fairy, or good-natured elf, and this is done in such a way that the reader is fairly convinced that the situation is real.

This sense of reality must have influenced one dear little girl of nine, who was asked by her grandmother to mark the stories which she preferred to have read to her. She gravely set to work to cut sixty-seven pieces of paper in order to mark every story in the book: which she had read several times before. "But, Marion," said Grandma, "which one shall we start with?" "Oh !" said the child. "Begin at the first and go right through. Every one of them is the best, so I cannot make a choice." It is to be regretted that some later translators of these inimitable stories have made numerous changes in the titles of various tales, venerated through so many years of affectionate usage. In some versions "Red Ridinghood" is called "Little Redcap," "Snow-White" becomes "Snowdrop," "Sleeping Beauty" is transformed into the "Briar Rose," and many other changes in titles have been made. The well-known story of "Hansel and Grethel," which in its original form found a worthy and appreciative place in opera and on the stage, has been altered by a modern translator into a story far inferior to the original and unworthy of the Grimms. The present edition has retained the favorite old titles.

LOUIS RHEAD

(from 1917 edition)

LITTLE RED RIDINGHOOD

THERE was once a sweet little maid, much beloved by everybody, but most of all by her grandmother, who never knew how to make enough of her. Once she sent her a little riding hood of red velvet, and as it was very becoming to her, and she never wore anything else, people called her Little Red Ridinghood.

One day her mother said to her, "Come, Little Red Ridinghood, here are some cakes and a flask of wine for you to take to grandmother; she is weak and ill, and they will do her good. Make haste and start before it grows hot, and walk properly and nicely, and don't run, or you might fall and break the flask of wine, and there would be none left for grandmother. And when you go into her room, don't forget to say good morning, instead of staring about you."

"I will be sure to take care," said Little Red Ridinghood to her mother, and gave her hand upon it. Now the grandmother lived away in the wood, half an hour's walk from the village; and when Little Red Ridinghood had reached the wood, she met the wolf; but as she did not know what a bad sort of animal he was, she did not feel frightened.

"Good day. Little Red Ridinghood," said he.

"Thank you kindly, wolf," answered she.

"Where are you going so early Little Red Ridinghood?"

"To my grandmother's."

"What are you carrying under your apron?"

"Cakes and wine; we baked yesterday; and my grandmother is very weak and ill, so they will do her good, and strengthen her."

"Where does your grandmother live, Little Red Ridinghood?"

"A quarter of an hour's walk from here; her house stands beneath the three oak trees, and you may know it by the hazel bushes," said Little Red Ridinghood.

The wolf thought to himself, "That tender young thing would be a delicious morsel, and would taste better than the old one; I must manage somehow to get both of them."

Then he walked by Little Red Ridinghood a little while, and said, "Little Red Ridinghood, just look at the pretty flowers that are growing all round you; and I don't think you are listening to the song of the birds; you are posting along just as if you were going to school, and it is so delightful out here in the wood."

Little Red Ridinghood glanced round her, and when she saw the sunbeams darting here and there through the trees, and lovely flowers everywhere, she thought to herself, "If I were to take a fresh nosegay to my grandmother she would be very pleased, and it is so early in the day that I shall reach her in plenty of time"; and so she ran about in the wood, looking for flowers. And as she picked one she saw a still prettier one a little farther off, and so she went farther and farther into the wood.

But the wolf went straight to the grandmother's house and knocked at the door.

"Who is there?" cried the grandmother.

"Little Red Ridinghood," he answered, "and I have brought you some cake and wine. Please open the door."

"Lift the latch," cried the grandmother; "I am too feeble to get up."

So the wolf lifted the latch, and the door flew open, and he fell on the grandmother and ate her up without saying one word. Then he drew on her clothes, put on her cap, lay down in her bed, and drew the curtains.

Little Red Ridinghood was all this time running about among the flowers, and when she had gathered as many as she could hold, she remembered her grandmother, and set off to go to her. She was surprised to find the door standing open, and when she came inside she felt very strange, and thought to herself, "Oh dear, how uncomfortable I feel, and I was so glad this morning to go to my grandmother!"

And when she said, "Good morning," there was no answer. Then she went up to the bed and drew back the curtains; there lay the grandmother with her cap pulled over her eyes, so that she looked very odd.

"O grandmother, what large ears you have!"

"The better to hear with."

"O grandmother, what great eyes you have!"

"The better to see with."

"O grandmother, what large hands you have!"

"The better to take hold of you with."

"But, grandmother, what a terrible large mouth you have!"

"The better to devour you!" And no sooner had the wolf said it than he made one bound from the bed, and swallowed up poor Little Red Ridinghood.

Then the wolf, having satisfied his hunger, lay down again in the bed, went to sleep, and began to snore loudly. The huntsman heard him as he was passing by the house, and thought,

"How the old woman snores – I had better see if there is anything the matter with her."

Then he went into the room, and walked up to the bed, and saw the wolf lying there.

"WHAT A TERRIBLE LARGE MOUTH YOU HAVE GOT!"

"At last I find you, you old sinner!" said he; "I have been looking for you a long time." And he made up his mind that the wolf had swallowed the grandmother whole, and that she might yet be saved. So he did not fire, but took a pair of shears and began to slit up the wolf's body. When he made a few snips Little Red Ridinghood appeared, and after a few more snips she jumped out and cried, "Oh dear, how frightened I have been! It is so dark inside the wolf." And then out came the old grandmother, still living and breathing. But Little Red Ridinghood went and quickly fetched some large stones, with which she filled the wolfs body, so that when he waked up, and was going to rush away, the stones were so heavy that he sank down and fell dead.

They were all three very pleased. The huntsman took off the wolfs skin, and carried it home. The grandmother ate the cakes, and drank the wine, and held up her head again, and Little Red Ridinghood said to herself that she would never more stray about in the wood alone, but would mind what her mother told her.

It must also be related how a few days afterwards, when Little Red Ridinghood was again taking cakes to her grandmother, another wolf spoke to her, and wanted to tempt her to leave the path; but she was on her guard, and went straight on her way, and told her grandmother how that the wolf had met her, and wished her good day, but had looked so wicked about the eyes that she thought if it had not been on the high road he would have devoured her.

"Come," said the grandmother, "we will shut the door, so that he may not get in."

Soon after came the wolf knocking at the door, and calling out, "Open the door, grandmother, I am Little Red Ridinghood, bringing you cakes." But they remained still, and did not open the door. After that the wolf slunk by the house, and got at last upon the roof to wait until Little Red Ridinghood should return home in the evening; then he meant to spring down upon her, and devour her in the darkness. But the grandmother discovered his plot. Now there stood before the house a great stone trough, and the grandmother said to the child, "Little Red Ridinghood, I was boiling sausages yesterday, so take the bucket, and carry away the water they were boiled in, and pour it into the trough."

And Little Red Ridinghood did so until the great trough was quite full. When the smell of the sausages reached the nose of the wolf he snuffed it up, and looked round, and stretched out his neck so far that he lost his balance and began to slip, and he slipped down off the roof straight into the great trough, and was drowned. Then Little Red Ridinghood went cheerfully home, and came to no harm.

FAIRY TALES

THE GOLDEN GOOSE

THERE was a man who had three sons, the youngest of whom was called Dunderhead, and was despised, mocked, and put down on every occasion.

It happened, that the eldest wanted to go into the forest to hew wood. Before he went his mother gave him a beautiful sweet cake and a bottle of wine, that he might not suffer from hunger or thirst.

When he entered the forest, there met him a little old Gray Man who bade him good-day, and said, "Do give me a piece of cake out of your pocket, and let me have a draught of your wine. I am so hungry and thirsty."

But the prudent youth answered, "If I give you my cake and wine, I shall have none for myself. Be off with you," and he left the Little Man standing and went on.

But when he began to hew down a tree, it was not long before he made a false stroke, and the axe cut him in the arm. So he had to go home and have it bound up. And this was the little Gray Man's doing.

After this, the second son went into the forest, and his mother gave him, like the eldest, a cake and a bottle of wine. The little old Gray Man met him likewise, and asked him for a piece of cake and a drink of wine. But the second son, too, said with much reason,

"What I give you will be taken away from myself. Be off!" and he left the Little Man standing and went on.

His punishment, however, was not delayed. When he had made a few strokes at the tree, he struck himself in the leg. So he had to be carried home.

Then Dunderhead said, "Father, do let me go and cut wood."

The father answered, "Your brothers have hurt themselves doing so. Leave it alone. You do not understand anything about it."

But Dunderhead begged so long that at last he said, "Go then. You will get wiser by hurting yourself."

His mother gave him a cake made with water and baked in the cinders, and with it a bottle of sour beer.

When he came to the forest the little old Gray Man met him likewise, and greeting him said, "Give me a piece of your cake and a drink out of your bottle. I am so hungry and thirsty."

Dunderhead answered, "I have only cinder-cake and sour beer. If that pleases you, we will sit down and eat."

So they sat down, and when Dunderhead pulled out his cinder-cake, it was a fine sweet cake, and the sour beer had become good wine.

So they ate and drank, and after that the Little Man said, "Since you have a good heart, and are willing to divide what you have, I will give you good luck. There stands an old tree. Cut it down, and you will find something at the roots."

Then the old man took leave of him.

Dunderhead went and cut down the tree; and when it fell there was a Goose sitting in the roots, with feathers of pure gold. He lifted her up, and taking her with him, went to an inn, where he thought he would stay the night. Now the host had three daughters, who saw the Goose and were curious to know what such a wonderful bird might be. And each wanted one of its feathers.

The eldest thought, "I shall soon find an opportunity of pulling out a feather," and when Dunderhead was gone out, she seized the Goose by the wing. But her finger and hand remained sticking fast to it.

The second came in soon afterward, thinking only of how she might get a feather for herself, but she had scarcely touched her sister than she was held fast.

"AND SO THEY MADE SEVEN, ALL RUNNING TOGETHER AFTER DUNDERHEAD AND HIS GOOSE."

At last, the third came with the like intent, and the others screamed out, "Keep away! For goodness' sake keep away!"

But she did not understand why she was to keep away. "The others are there," she thought, "I may as well be there too," and ran to them. But as soon as she had touched her sister, she remained sticking fast to her. So they had to spend the night with the Goose.

The next morning, Dunderhead took the Goose under his arm and set out, without troubling himself about the three girls who were hanging on to it. They were obliged to run after him, now left, now right, just as he was inclined to go.

In the middle of the fields, the parson met them, and when he saw the procession he said, "For shame, you good-for-nothing girls! Why are you running across the fields after this young man? Is that seemly?" At the same time he seized the youngest by the hand in order to pull her away. But as soon as he touched her, he likewise stuck fast, and was obliged to run behind. Before long, the sexton came by and saw his master, the parson, running on foot behind three girls. He was astonished at this, and called out, "Hi! your Reverence! Whither away so quickly? Do not forget that we have a christening to-day!" and running after him he took him by the sleeve, but was also held fast.

While the five were trotting thus one behind the other, two laborers came with their hoes from the fields. The parson called out to them and begged that they would set him and the sexton free. But they had scarcely touched the sexton, when they were held fast. And now there were seven of them running behind Dunderhead and the Goose.

Soon afterward, he came to a city, where a King ruled who had a daughter who was so serious that no one could make her laugh. So he had put forth a decree that whosoever should make her laugh should marry her. When Dunderhead heard this, he went with his Goose and all her train before the King's Daughter.

As soon as she saw the seven people running on and on, one behind the other, she began to laugh very loudly as if she would never leave off. Thereupon Dunderhead asked to have her for his wife, and the wedding was celebrated.

After the King's death, Dunderhead inherited the Kingdom, and lived a long time contentedly with his wife.

THE WISHING-TABLE, THE GOLD ASS, AND THE CUDGEL

A LONG time ago there lived a tailor who had three sons but only one goat. As the goat supplied the whole family with milk, she had to be well fed and taken daily to pasture. This the sons did in turn. One day the eldest son led her into the churchyard, where he knew there was fine herbage to be found, and there let her browse and skip about till evening. It being then time to return home, he said to her, "Goat, have you had enough to eat?" and the goat answered,—

"I have eaten so much,
Not a leaf can I touch, Nan, Nan."

"Come along home then," said the boy, and he led her by the cord round her neck back to the stable and tied her up.

"Well," said the old tailor, "has the goat had her proper amount of food?"

"Why, she has eaten so much, not a leaf can she touch," answered the son.

The father, however, thinking he should like to assure himself of this, went down to the stable, patted the animal and said caressingly, "Goat, have you really had enough to eat?" The goat answered,—

"How can my hunger be allayed?
About the little graves I played
And could not find a single blade, Nan, Nan."

"What is this I hear!" cried the tailor, and running upstairs to his son, "You young liar!" he exclaimed, "to tell me the goat had had enough to eat, and all the while she is starving." And overcome with anger, he took his yard-measure down from the wall, and beat his son out of doors.

The next day it was the second son's turn, and he found a place near a garden hedge, where there were the juiciest plants for the goat to feed upon, and she enjoyed them so much that she ate them all up. Before taking her home in the evening, he said to her, "Goat, have you had enough to eat?" and the goat answered,—

"I have eaten so much,
Not a leaf can I touch, Nan, Nan."

"Come along home then," said the boy, and he led her away to the stable and tied her up.

"Well," said the old tailor, "has the goat had her proper amount of food?"

"Why, she has eaten so much, not a leaf can she touch," answered the boy.

But the tailor was not satisfied with this, and went down to the stable. "Goat, have you really had enough to eat?" he asked; and the goat answered,—

"How can my hunger be allayed?
About the little graves I played
And could not find a single blade, Nan, Nan."

"The shameless young rascal!" cried the tailor, "to let an innocent animal like this starve!" and he ran upstairs, and drove the boy from the house with the yard-measure.

It was now the third son's turn, who, hoping to make things better for himself, let the goat feed on the leaves of all the shrubs he could pick out that were covered with the richest foliage. "Goat, have you had enough to eat?" he said, as the evening fell, and the goat answered,—

"I have eaten so much,
Not a leaf can I touch, Nan, Nan."

"Come along home then," said the boy, and he took her back and tied her up.

"Well," said the old tailor, "has the goat had her proper amount of food?"

"Why, she has eaten so much, not a leaf can she touch," answered the boy.

But the tailor felt mistrustful, and went down and asked, "Goat, have you really had enough to eat?" and the mischievous animal answered,—

"How can my hunger be allayed?
About the little graves I played
And could not find a single blade, Nan, Nan."

"Oh! what a pack of liars!" cried the tailor. "One as wicked and deceitful as the other, but they shall not make a fool of me any longer." And beside himself with anger, he rushed upstairs, and so belaboured his son with the yard-measure, that the boy fled from the house.

The old tailor was now left alone with his goat. The following morning he went down to the stable and stroked and caressed her. "Come along, my pet," he said, "I will take you out myself to-day," and he led her by the green hedgerows and weed-grown banks, and wherever he knew that goats love to feed. "You shall eat to your heart's content for once," he said to her, and so let her browse till evening. "Goat, have you had enough to eat?" he asked her at the close of the day, and she answered,—

"I have eaten so much,
Not a leaf can I touch, Nan, Nan."

"Come along home then," said the tailor, and he led her to the stable and tied her up. He turned round, however, before leaving her, and said once more, "You have really had enough to eat for once?" But the goat gave him no better answer than her usual one, and replied,—

"How can my hunger be allayed?
About the little graves I played
And could not find a single blade, Nan, Nan."

On hearing this, the tailor stood, struck dumb with astonishment. He saw now how unjust he had been in driving away his sons. When he found his voice, he cried: "Wait, you ungrateful creature!

it is not enough to drive you away, but I will put such a mark upon you, that you will not dare to shew your face again among honest tailors." And so saying, he sprang upstairs, brought down his razor, lathered the goat's head all over, and shaved it till it was as smooth as the back of his hand. Then he fetched the whip,—his yard-measure he considered was too good for such work,—and dealt the animal such blows, that she leapt into the air and away.

Sitting now quite alone in his house, the tailor fell into great melancholy, and would gladly have had his sons back again, but no one knew what had become of them.

The eldest had apprenticed himself to a joiner, and had set himself cheerfully and diligently to learn his trade. When the time came for him to start as a journeyman, his master made him a present of a table, which was of ordinary wood, and to all outward appearance exactly like any other table. It had, however, one good quality, for if anyone set it down, and said, "Table, serve up a meal," it was immediately covered with a nice fresh cloth, laid with a plate, knife and fork, and dishes of boiled and baked meats, as many as there was room for, and a glass of red wine, which only to look at made the heart rejoice.

"I have enough now to last me as long as I live," thought the young man to himself, and accordingly he went about enjoying himself, not minding whether the inns he stayed at were good or bad, whether there was food to be had there or not. Sometimes it pleased him not to seek shelter within them at all, but to turn into a field or a wood, or wherever else he fancied. When there he put down his table, and said, "Serve up a meal," and he was at once supplied with everything he could desire in the way of food.

After he had been going about like this for some time, he bethought him that he should like to go home again. His father's anger would by this time have passed away and now that he had the wishing-table with him, he was sure of a ready welcome.

He happened, on his homeward way, to come one evening to an inn full of guests. They bid him welcome, and invited him to sit down with them and share their supper, otherwise, they added, he would have a difficulty in getting anything to eat.

But the joiner replied, "I will not take from you what little you have, I would rather that you should consent to be my guests," whereupon they all laughed, thinking he was only joking with them. He now put down his table in the middle of the room, and said, "Table, serve up a meal," and in a moment it was covered with a variety of food of better quality than any the host could have supplied, and a fragrant steam rose from the dishes and greeted the nostrils of the guests. "Now, friends, fall to," said the young man, and the guests, seeing that the invitation was well intended, did not wait to be asked twice, but drew up their chairs and began vigorously to ply their knives and forks. What astonished them most was the way in which, as soon as a dish was empty, another full one appeared in its place. Meanwhile the landlord was standing in the corner of the room looking on; he did not know what to think of it all, but said to himself, "I could make good use of a cook like that."

The joiner and his friends kept up their merriment late into the night, but at last they retired to rest, the young journeyman placing his table against the wall before going to bed.

The landlord, however, could not sleep for thinking of what he had seen; at last it occurred to him that up in his lumber-room he had an old table, which was just such another one to all appearance as the wishing table; so he crept away softly to fetch it, and put it against the wall in place of the other.

When the morning came, the joiner paid for his night's lodging, took up his table, and left, never suspecting that the one he was carrying was not his own.

He reached home at mid-day, and was greeted with joy by his father. "And now, dear son," said the old man "what trade have you learnt?"

"I am a joiner, father."

"A capital business," responded the father, "and what have you brought home with you from your travels?"

"The best thing I have brought with me, father, is that table."

The tailor carefully examined the table on all sides. "Well," he said at last, "you have certainly not brought a master-piece back with you; it is a wretched, badly-made old table."

"But it is a wishing-table," interrupted his son, "if I put it down and order a meal, it is at once covered with the best of food and wine. If you will only invite your relations and friends, they shall, for once in their lives, have a good meal, for no one ever leaves this table unsatisfied."

When the guests were all assembled, he put his table down as usual, and said, "Table, serve up a meal," but the table did not stir, and remained as empty as any ordinary table at such a command. Then the poor young man saw that his table had been changed, and he was covered with shame at having to stand there before them all like a liar. The guests made fun of him, and had to return home without bite or sup. The tailor took out his cloth and sat down once more to his tailoring, and the son started work again under a master-joiner.

The Wishing Table, the Gold Ass and the Cudgel

The second son had apprenticed himself to a miller. When his term of apprenticeship had expired, the miller said to him, "As you have behaved so well, I will make you a present of an ass; it is a curious animal, it will neither draw a cart nor carry a sack."

"Of what use is he then?" asked the young apprentice. "He gives gold," answered the miller, "if you stand him on a cloth, and say 'Bricklebrit,' gold pieces will fall from his mouth."

"That is a handsome present," said the young miller, and he thanked his master and departed.

After this, whenever he was in need of money, he had only to say "Bricklebrit," and a shower of gold pieces fell on the ground, and all he had to do was to pick them up. He ordered the best of everything wherever he went, in short, the dearer the better, for his purse was always full.

He had been going about the world like this for some time, when he began to think he should like to see his father again. When he sees my gold ass, he said to himself, he will forget his anger, and be glad to have me back.

It came to pass that he arrived one evening at the same inn in which his brother had had his table stolen from him. He was leading his ass up to the door, when the landlord came out and offered to take the animal, but the young miller refused his help. "Do not trouble yourself," he said, "I will take my old Greycoat myself to the stable and fasten her up, as I like to know where she is."

The landlord was very much astonished at this; the man cannot be very well off, he thought, to look after his own ass. When the stranger, therefore, pulled two gold pieces out of his pocket, and ordered the best of everything that could be got in the market, the landlord opened his eyes, but he ran off with alacrity to do his bidding.

Having finished his meal, the stranger asked for his bill, and the landlord thinking he might safely overcharge such a rich customer, asked for two more gold pieces. The miller felt in his pocket but found he had spent all his gold. "Wait a minute," he said to the landlord, "I will go and fetch some more money." Whereupon he went out, carrying the table-cloth with him.

This was more than the landlord's curiosity could stand, and he followed his guest to the stable. As the latter bolted the door after him, he went and peeped through a hole in the wall, and there he saw the stranger spread the cloth under his ass, and heard him say, "Bricklebrit," and immediately the floor was covered with gold pieces which fell from the animal's mouth.

"A good thousand, I declare," cried the host, "the gold pieces do not take long to coin! it's not a bad thing to have a money-bag like that."

The guest settled his account and went to bed. During the night the landlord crept down to the stable, led away the gold-coining ass, and fastened up another in its place.

Early the next morning the young miller went off with his ass, thinking all the time that he was leading his own. By noonday he had reached home, where his father gave him a warm welcome.

"What have you been doing with yourself, my son?" asked the old man.

"I am a miller, dear father," he answered.

"And what have you brought home with you from your travels?"

"Nothing but an ass, father."

"There are asses enough here," said the father, "I should have been better pleased if it had been a goat."

"Very likely," replied the son, "but this is no ordinary ass, it is an ass that coins money; if I say "Bricklebrit" to it, a whole sackful of gold pours from its mouth. Call all your relations and friends together, I will turn you all into rich people."

"I shall like that well enough," said the tailor, "for then I shall not have to go on plaguing myself with stitching," and he ran out himself to invite his neighbors. As soon as they were all assembled, the young miller asked them to clear a space, and he then spread his cloth and brought the ass into the room. "Now see," said he, and cried "Bricklebrit," but not a single gold piece appeared, and it was evident that the animal knew nothing of the art of gold-coining, for it is not every ass that attains to such a degree of excellence.

The poor young miller pulled a long face, for he saw that he had been tricked: he begged forgiveness of the company, who all returned home as poor as they came. There was nothing to be done now but for the old man to go back to his needle, and the young one to hire himself to a miller.

The third son had apprenticed himself to a turner, which, being a trade requiring a great deal of skill, obliged him to serve a longer time than his brothers. He had, however, heard from them by letter, and knew how badly things had gone with them, and that they had been robbed of their property by an innkeeper on the last evening before reaching home.

When it was time for him to start as a journeyman, his master, being pleased with his conduct, presented him with a bag, saying as he did so, "You will find a cudgel inside."

"The bag I can carry over my shoulder, and it will no doubt be of great service to me, but of what use is a cudgel inside, it will only add to the weight?"

"I will explain," said the master, "if any one at any time should behave badly to you, you have only to say, 'Cudgel, out of the bag,' and the stick will jump out, and give him such a cudgelling, that he will not be able to move or stir for a week afterwards, and it will not leave off till you say, 'Cudgel, into the bag.'"

The young man thanked him, hung the bag on his back, and when any one threatened to attack him, or in any way to do him harm, he called out, "Cudgel, out of the bag," and no sooner were the words said than out jumped the stick, and beat the offenders soundly on the back, till their clothes were in ribbons, and it did it all so quickly, that the turn had come round to each of them before he was aware.

It was evening when the young turner reached the inn where his brothers had been so badly treated. He laid his bag down on the table, and began giving an account of all the wonderful things he had seen while going about the world.

"One may come across a wishing-table," he said, "or an ass that gives gold, and such like; all very good things in their way, but not all of them put together are worth the treasure of which I have possession, and which I carry with me in that bag."

The landlord pricked up his ears. "What can it be," he asked himself, "the bag must be filled with precious stones; I must try and get hold of that cheaply too, for there is luck in odd numbers."

Bed-time came, and the guest stretched himself out on one of the benches and placed his bag under his head for a pillow. As soon as the landlord thought he was fast asleep, he went up to him, and began gently and cautiously pulling and pushing at the bag to see if he could get it away and put another in its place.

But the young miller had been waiting for this and just as the landlord was about to give a good last pull, he cried, "Cudgel, out of the bag," and the same moment the stick was out, and beginning its usual dance. It beat him with such a vengeance that the landlord cried out for mercy, but the louder his cries, the more lustily did the stick beat time to them, until he fell to the ground exhausted.

"If you do not give back the wishing-table and the gold ass," said the young turner, "the game shall begin over again."

"No, no," cried the landlord in a feeble voice, "I will gladly give every thing back, if only you will make that dreadful demon of a stick return to the bag."

"This time," said the turner, "I will deal with you according to mercy rather than justice, but beware of offending in like manner again." Then he cried, "Cudgel, into the bag," and let the man remain in peace.

The turner journeyed on next day to his father's house, taking with him the wishing-table and the gold ass. The tailor was delighted to see his son again, and asked him, as he had the others, what trade he had learnt since he left home.

"I am a turner, dear father," he answered.

"A highly skilled trade," said the tailor, "and what have you brought back with you from your travels?"

"An invaluable thing, dear father," replied the son, "a cudgel."

"What! a cudgel!" exclaimed the old man, "that was certainly well worth while, seeing that you can cut yourself one from the first tree you come across."

"But not such a one as this, dear father; for, if I say to it, "Cudgel, out of the bag," out it jumps, and gives any one who has evil intentions towards me such a bad time of it, that he falls down and cries for mercy. And know, that it was with this stick that I got back the wishing-table and the gold ass, which the dishonest innkeeper stole from my brothers. Now, go and call them both here, and invite all your relations and friends, and I will feast them and fill their pockets with gold."

The old tailor was slow to believe all this but nevertheless he went out and gathered his neighbors together. Then the turner put down a cloth, and led in the gold ass, and said to his brother, "Now, dear brother, speak to him." The miller said "Bricklebrit," and the cloth was immediately covered with gold pieces, which continued to pour from the ass's mouth until everyone had taken as many as he could carry. (I see by your faces that you are all wishing you had been there).

Then the turner brought in the wishing-table, and said, "Now, dear brother, speak to it." And scarcely had the joiner cried, "Table, serve up a meal," than it was covered with a profusion of daintily dressed meats. Then the tailor and his guests sat down to a meal such as they had never enjoyed before in their lives, and they all sat up late into the night, full of good cheer and jollity.

The tailor put away his needle and thread, his yard-measure and his goose, and he and his three sons lived together henceforth in contentment and luxury.

Meanwhile, what had become of the goat, who had been the guilty cause of the three sons being driven from their home? I will tell you.

"THE LANDLORD CRIED OUT FOR MERCY."

She was so ashamed of her shaven crown, that she ran and crept into a fox's hole. When the fox came home, he was met by two large glittering eyes that gleamed at him out of the darkness, and he was so frightened that he ran away. The bear met him, and perceiving that he was in some distress, said, "What is the matter, brother Fox, why are you pulling such a long face?" "Ah!" answered Redskin, "there is a dreadful animal sitting in my hole, which glared at me with fiery eyes."

"We will soon drive him out," said the Bear, and he trotted back with his friend to the hole and looked in, but the sight of the fiery eyes was quite enough for him, and he turned and took to his heels.

The bee met him and noticing that he was somewhat ill at ease, said, "Bear, you look remarkably out of humour, where have you left your good spirits?" "It's easy for you to talk," replied the bear, "a horrible animal with red goggle-eyes is sitting in the fox's hole, and we cannot drive it out."

The bee said, "I really am sorry for you, Bear; I am but a poor weak little creature that you scarcely deign to look at in passing, but, for all that, I think I shall be able to help you."

With this the bee flew to the fox's hole, settled on the smooth shaven head of the goat, and stung her so violently, that she leaped high into the air, crying, "Nan, nan!" and fled away like a mad thing into the open country; but no one, to this hour, has found out what became of her after that.

THE MOUSE, THE BIRD, AND THE SAUSAGE

ONCE upon a time, a mouse, a bird, and a sausage, entered into partnership and set up house together. For a long time all went well; they lived in great comfort, and prospered so far as to be able to add considerably to their stores. The bird's duty was to fly daily into the wood and bring in fuel; the mouse fetched the water, and the sausage saw to the cooking.

When people are too well off they always begin to long for something new. And so it came to pass, that the bird, while out one day, met a fellow bird, to whom he boastfully expatiated on the excellence of his household arrangements. But the other bird sneered at him for being a poor simpleton, who did all the hard work, while the other two stayed at home and had a good time of it. For, when the mouse had made the fire and fetched in the water, she could retire into her little room and rest until it was time to set the table. The sausage had only to watch the pot to see that the food was properly cooked, and when it was near dinner-time, he just threw himself into the broth, or rolled in and out among the vegetables three or four times, and there they were, buttered, and salted, and ready to be served. Then, when the bird came home and had laid aside his burden, they sat down to table, and when they had finished their meal, they could sleep their fill till the following morning: and that was really a very delightful life.

Influenced by those remarks, the bird next morning refused to bring in the wood, telling the others that he had been their servant long enough, and had been a fool into the bargain, and that it was now time to make a change, and to try some other way of arranging the work. Beg and pray as the mouse and the sausage might, it was of no use; the bird remained master of the situation, and the venture had to be made. They therefore drew lots, and it fell to the sausage to bring in the wood, to the mouse to cook, and to the bird to fetch the water.

And now what happened? The sausage started in search of wood, the bird made the fire, and the mouse put on the pot, and then these two waited till the sausage returned with the fuel for the following day. But the sausage remained so long away, that they became uneasy, and the bird flew out to meet him. He had not flown far, however, when he came across a dog who, having met the sausage, had regarded him as his legitimate booty, and so seized and swallowed him. The bird complained to the dog of this bare-faced robbery, but nothing he said was of any avail, for the dog answered that he found false credentials on the sausage, and that was the reason his life had been forfeited.

He picked up the wood, and flew sadly home, and told the mouse all he had seen and heard. They were both very unhappy, but agreed to make the best of things and to remain with one another.

So now the bird set the table, and the mouse looked after the food and, wishing to prepare it in the same way as the sausage, by rolling in and out among the vegetables to salt and butter them, she jumped into the pot; but she stopped short long before she reached the bottom, having already parted not only with her skin and hair, but also with life.

Presently the bird came in and wanted to serve up the dinner, but he could nowhere see the cook. In his alarm and flurry, he threw the wood here and there about the floor, called and searched, but no cook was to be found. Then some of the wood that had been carelessly thrown down, caught fire and began to blaze. The bird hastened to fetch some water, but his pail fell into the well, and he after it, and as he was unable to recover himself, he was drowned.

THE FOX'S BRUSH

THE King of the East had a beautiful garden, and in the garden stood a tree that bore golden apples. Lest any of these apples should be stolen, they were always counted; but about the time when they began to grow ripe, it was found that every night one of them was gone. The king became very angry at this, and told the gardener to keep a watch under the tree all night.

The gardener set his eldest son to watch, but about twelve o'clock he fell asleep, and in the morning another of the apples was missing.

Then the second son was set to watch, and at midnight he too fell asleep, and in the morning another apple was gone.

Then the third son offered to keep watch: but the gardener at first would not let him, for fear some harm should come to him. However, at last he yielded, and the young man laid himself under the tree to watch. As the clock struck twelve he heard a rustling noise in the air, and a bird came flying and sat upon the tree. This bird's feathers were all of pure gold; and as it was snapping at one of the apples with its beak, the gardener's son jumped up and shot an arrow at it. The arrow, however, did the bird no harm, it only dropped a golden feather from its tail, and flew away. The golden feather was then brought to the king in the morning, and all his court were called together. Every one agreed that it was the most beautiful thing that had ever been seen, and that it was worth more than all the wealth of the kingdom: but the king said, "One feather is of no use to me, I must and will have the whole bird."

Then the gardener's eldest son set out to find this golden bird, and thought to find it very easily; and when he had gone but a little way, he came to a wood, and by the side of the wood he saw a fox sitting. The lad was fond of a little sporting, so he took his bow and made ready to shoot at it. Then Mr Reynard, who saw what he was about, and did not like the thought of being shot at, cried out, "Softly, softly! do not shoot me, I can give you good counsel. I know what your business is, and that you want to find the golden bird. You will reach a village in the evening, and when you get there you will see two inns, built one on each side of the street. The right-hand one is very pleasant and beautiful to look at, but go not in there. Rest for the night in the other, though it may seem to you very poor and mean." "What can such a beast as this know about the matter?" thought the silly lad to himself. So he shot his arrow at the fox, but he missed it, and it only laughed at him, set up its tail above its back, and ran into the wood.

The young man went his way, and in the evening came to the village where the two inns were. In the right-hand one were people singing, and dancing, and feasting; but the other looked very dirty, and poor, "I should be very silly," said he, "if I went to that shabby house, and left this charming place:" so he went into the smart house, and ate and drank at his ease; and there he stayed, and forgot the bird and his country too.

Time passed on, and as the eldest son did not come back, and no tidings were heard of him, the second son set out, and the same thing happened to him. He met with the fox sitting by the roadside, who gave him the same good advice as he had given his brother: but when he came to the two inns, his eldest brother was standing at the window where the merry-making was, and called to him to come in; and he could not withstand the temptation, but went in, joined the merry-making, and there forgot the golden bird and his country in the same manner.

Time passed on again, and the youngest son too wished to set out into the wide world, to seek for the golden bird; but his father would not listen to him for a long while, for he was very fond of his son, and was afraid that some ill-luck might happen to him also, and hinder his coming back. However, at last it was agreed he should go; for, to tell the truth, he would not rest at home. As he came to

THEY TRAVELLED "SO QUICKLY THAT THEIR HAIR WHISTLED IN THE WIND"

the wood he met the fox, who gave him the same good counsel that he had given the other brothers. But he was thankful to the fox, and did not shoot at him, as his brothers had done. Then the fox said, "Sit upon my tail, and you will travel faster." So he sat down: and the fox began to run, and away they went over stock and stone, so quickly that their hair whistled in the wind.

When they came to the village, the young man was wise enough to follow the fox's counsel, and, without looking about him, went straight to the shabby inn, and rested there all night at his ease. In the morning came the fox again, and met him as he was beginning his journey, and said, "Go straight forward till you come to a castle, before which lie a whole troop of soldiers fast asleep and snoring; take no notice of them, but go into the castle, and pass on and on till you come to a room where the golden bird sits in a wooden cage: close by it stands a beautiful golden cage; but do not try to take the bird out of the shabby cage and put it into the handsome one, otherwise you will be sorry for it." Then the fox stretched out his brush again, and the young man sat himself down, and away they went over stock and stone, till their hair whistled in the wind.

Before the castle gate all was as the fox had said: so the lad went in, and found the chamber, where the golden bird hung in a wooden cage. Below stood the golden cage; and the three golden apples, that had been lost, were lying close by its side. Then he thought to himself, "It will be a very droll thing to bring away such a fine bird in this shabby cage;" so he opened the door and took hold of the bird, and put it into the golden cage. But it set up at once such a loud scream, that all the soldiers awoke; and they took him prisoner, and carried him before the king.

The next morning the court sat to judge him; and when all was heard, it doomed him to die, unless he should bring the king the golden horse, that could run as swiftly as the wind. If he did this he was to have the golden bird given him for his own.

So he set out once more on his journey, sighing, and in great despair; when, on a sudden, he met his good friend the fox taking his morning's walk. "Heyday, young gentleman!" said Reynard; "you see now what has happened from you not listening to my advice. I will still, however, tell you how you may find the golden horse, if you will but do as I bid you. You must go straight on till you come to the castle, where the horse stands in his stall. By his side will lie the groom fast asleep and snoring; take away the horse softly; but be sure to let the old leathern saddle be upon him, and do not put on the golden one that is close by." Then the young man sat down on the fox's tail; and away they went over stock and stone, till their hair whistled in the wind.

All went right, and the groom lay snoring, with his hand upon the golden saddle. But when the lad looked at the horse, he thought it a great pity to keep the leathern saddle upon it. "I will give him the good one," said he: "I am sure he is worth it." As he took up the golden saddle, the groom awoke, and cried out so loud, that all the guards ran in and took him prisoner; and in the morning he was brought before the king's court to be judged, and was once more doomed to die. But it was agreed that if he could bring thither the beautiful princess, he should live and have the horse given him for his own.

Then he went his way again very sorrowful; but the old fox once more met him on the road, and said, "Why did you not listen to me? If you had, you would have carried away both the bird and the horse. Yet I will once more give you counsel. Go straight on, and in the evening you will come to a castle. At twelve o'clock every night the princess goes to the bath: go up to her as she passes, and give her a kiss, and she will let you lead her away; but take care you do not let her go and take leave of her father and mother." Then the fox stretched out his tail, and away they went over stock and stone till their hair whistled again.

As they came to the castle all was as the fox had said; and at twelve o'clock the young man met the princess going to the bath, and gave her the kiss; and she agreed to run away with him, but begged with many tears that he would let her take leave of her father. At first he said, "No!" but she wept still more and more, and fell at his feet, till at last he yielded; but the moment she came to her father's door the guards awoke, and he was taken prisoner again.

So he was brought at once before the king, who lived in that castle. And the king said, "You shall never have my daughter, unless in eight days you dig away the hill that stops the view from my window." Now this hill was so big that all the men in the whole world The princess going to the bath

could not have taken it away: and when he had worked for seven days, and had done very little, the fox came and said, "Lie down and go to sleep! I will work for you." In the morning he awoke, and the hill was gone; so he went merrily to the king, and told him that now it was gone he must give him the princess.

Then the king was obliged to keep his word, and away went the young man and the princess. But the fox came and said to him, "That will not do; we will have all three,—the princess, the horse, and the bird." "Ah!" said the young man, "that would be a great thing; but how can it be?"

"If you will only listen," said the fox, "it can soon be done. When you come to the king of the castle where the golden horse is, and he asks for the beautiful princess, you must say, 'Here she is!' Then he will be very glad to see her, and will run to welcome her; and you will mount the golden horse that they are to give you, and put out your hand to take leave of them; but shake hands with the princess last. Then lift her quickly on to the horse, behind you; clap your spurs to his side, and gallop away as fast as you can."

All went right: then the fox said, "When you come to the castle where the bird is, I will stay with the princess at the door, and you will ride in and speak to the king; and when he sees that it is the right horse, he will bring out the bird: but you must sit still, and say that you want to look at it, to see whether it is the true golden bird or not; and when you get it into your hand, ride away as fast as you can."

This, too, happened as the fox said: they carried off the bird; the princess mounted again, and off they rode till they came to a great wood. On their way through it they met their old friend Reynard again, and he said, "Pray kill me, and cut off my head and my brush!" The young man would not do any such thing to so good a friend: so the fox said, "I will at any rate give you good counsel: beware of two things! ransom no one from the gallows, and sit down by the side of no brook!" Then away he went. "Well," thought the young man, "it is no hard matter, at any rate, to follow that advice."

So he rode on with the princess, till at last they came to the village where he had left his two brothers. And there he heard a great noise and uproar: and when he asked what was the matter, the people said, "Two rogues are going to be hanged." As he came nearer, he saw that the two men were his brothers, who had turned robbers. At the sight of them in this sad plight his heart was very heavy, and he cried out, "Can nothing save them from such a death?" but the people said "No!" unless he would bestow all his money upon the rascals, and buy their freedom, by repaying all they had stolen. Then he did not stay to think about it, but paid whatever was asked; and his brothers were given up, and went on with him towards their father's home.

Now the weather was very hot; and as they came to the wood where the fox first met them, they found it so cool and shady under the trees, by the side of a brook that ran close by, that the two brothers said, "Let us sit down by the side of this brook and rest a while, to eat and drink." "Very well!" said he, and forgot what the fox had said, and sat down on the side of the brook: and while he thought of no harm coming to him they crept behind him, and threw him down the bank, and took the princess, the horse, and the bird, and went home to the king their master, and said, "All these we have won by our own skill and strength." Then there was great merriment made, and the king held a feast, and the two brothers were welcomed home; but the horse would not eat, the bird would not sing, and the princess sat by herself in her chamber, and wept bitterly.

The youngest son fell to the bottom of the bed of the stream. Luckily, it was nearly dry, but his bones were almost broken, and the bank was so steep that he could find no way to get out. As he stood bewailing his fate, and thinking what he should do, to his great joy he spied his old and faithful friend the fox, looking down from the bank upon him. Then Reynard scolded him for not following his advice, which would have saved him from all the troubles that had befallen him. "Yet," said he, "silly as you have been, I cannot bear to leave you here; so lay hold of my brush, and hold fast!" Then he pulled him out of the river, and said to him, as he got upon the bank, "Your brothers have set a watch to kill you if they find you making your way back." So he dressed himself as a poor piper, and came playing on his pipe to the king's court. But he was scarcely within the gate when the horse began to eat, and the bird to sing, and the princess left off weeping. And when he got to the great hall, where all the court sat feasting, he went straight up to the king, and told him all his brothers' roguery. Then it made the king very angry to hear what they had done, and they were seized and punished; and the youngest son had the princess given to him again; and he married her; and after the king's death he was chosen king in his stead.

After his marriage he went one day to walk in the wood, and there the old fox met him once more, and besought him, with tears in his eyes, to be so kind as to cut off his head and his brush. At last he did so, though sorely against his will, and in the same moment the fox was changed into a prince, and the princess knew him to be her own brother, who had been lost a great many years; for a spiteful fairy had enchanted him, with a spell that could only be broken by some one getting the golden bird, and by cutting off his head and his brush.

THE FISHERMAN AND HIS WIFE

THERE was once a fisherman who lived with his wife in a pigsty, close by the seaside. The fisherman used to go out all day long a-fishing; and one day, as he sat on the shore with his rod, looking at the sparkling waves and watching his line, all on a sudden his float was dragged away deep into the water: and in drawing it up he pulled out a great fish. But the fish said, "Pray let me live! I am not a real fish; I am an enchanted prince: put me in the water again, and let me go!" "Oh, ho!" said the man, "you need not make so many words about the matter; I will have nothing to do with a fish that can talk: so swim away, sir, as soon as you please!" Then he put him back into the water, and the fish darted straight down to the bottom, and left a long streak of blood behind him on the wave.

When the fisherman went home to his wife in the pigsty, he told her how he had caught a great fish, and how it had told him it was an enchanted prince, and how, on hearing it speak, he had let it go again. "Did not you ask it for anything?" said the wife, "we live very wretchedly here, in this nasty dirty pigsty; do go back and tell the fish we want a snug little cottage."

The fisherman did not much like the business: however, he went to the seashore; and when he came back there the water looked all yellow and green. And he stood at the water's edge, and said:

"O man of the sea!
Hearken to me!
My wife Ilsabill
Will have her own will,
And hath sent me to beg a boon of thee!"

Then the fish came swimming to him, and said, "Well, what is her will? What does your wife want?" "Ah!" said the fisherman, "she says that when I had caught you, I ought to have asked you for something before I let you go; she does not like living any longer in the pigsty, and wants a snug little cottage." "Go home, then," said the fish; "she is in the cottage already!" So the man went home, and saw his wife standing at the door of a nice trim little cottage. "Come in, come in!" said she; "is not this much better than the filthy pigsty we had?" And there was a parlour, and a bedchamber, and a kitchen; and behind the cottage there was a little garden, planted with all sorts of flowers and fruits; and there was a courtyard behind, full of ducks and chickens. "Ah!" said the fisherman, "how happily we shall live now!" "We will try to do so, at least," said his wife.

Everything went right for a week or two, and then Dame Ilsabill said, "Husband, there is not near room enough for us in this cottage; the courtyard and the garden are a great deal too small; I should like to have a large stone castle to live in: go to the fish again and tell him to give us a castle." "Wife," said the fisherman, "I don't like to go to him again, for perhaps he will be angry; we ought to be easy with this pretty cottage to live in." "Nonsense!" said the wife; "he will do it very willingly, I know; go along and try!"

The fisherman went, but his heart was very heavy: and when he came to the sea, it looked blue and gloomy, though it was very calm; and he went close to the edge of the waves, and said:

"O man of the sea!
Hearken to me!
My wife Ilsabill
Will have her own will,
And hath sent me to beg a boon of thee!"

"Well, what does she want now?" said the fish. "Ah!" said the man, dolefully, "my wife wants to live in a stone castle." "Go home, then," said the fish; "she is standing at the gate of it already." So

"DO GO BACK AND TELL THE FISH WE WANT A SNUG LITTLE COTTAGE"

away went the fisherman, and found his wife standing before the gate of a great castle. "See," said she, "is not this grand?" With that they went into the castle together, and found a great many servants there, and the rooms all richly furnished, and full of golden chairs and tables; and behind the castle was a garden, and around it was a park half a mile long, full of sheep, and goats, and hares, and deer; and in the courtyard were stables and cow-houses. "Well," said the man, "now we will live cheerful and happy in this beautiful castle for the rest of our lives." "Perhaps we may," said the wife; "but let us sleep upon it, before we make up our minds to that." So they went to bed.

The next morning when Dame Ilsabill awoke it was broad daylight, and she jogged the fisherman with her elbow, and said, "Get up, husband, and bestir yourself, for we must be king of all the land." "Wife, wife," said the man, "why should we wish to be the king? I will not be king." "Then I will," said she. "But, wife," said the fisherman, "how can you be king—the fish cannot make you a king?" "Husband," said she, "say no more about it, but go and try! I will be king." So the man went away quite sorrowful to think that his wife should want to be king. This time the sea looked a dark grey color, and was overspread with curling waves and the ridges of foam as he cried out:

"O man of the sea!
Hearken to me!
My wife Ilsabill
Will have her own will,
And hath sent me to beg a boon of thee!"

"Well, what would she have now?" said the fish. "Alas!" said the poor man, "my wife wants to be king." "Go home," said the fish; "she is king already."

Then the fisherman went home; and as he came close to the palace he saw a troop of soldiers, and heard the sound of drums and trumpets. And when he went in he saw his wife sitting on a throne of gold and diamonds, with a golden crown upon her head; and on each side of her stood six fair maidens, each a head taller than the other. "Well, wife," said the fisherman, "are you king?" "Yes," said she, "I am king." And when he had looked at her for a long time, he said, "Ah, wife! what a fine thing it is to be king! Now we shall never have anything more to wish for as long as we live." "I don't know how that may be," said she; "never is a long time. I am king, it is true; but I begin to be tired of that, and I think I should like to be emperor." "Alas, wife! why should you wish to be emperor?" said the fisherman. "Husband," said she, "go to the fish! I say I will be emperor." "Ah, wife!" replied the fisherman, "the fish cannot make an emperor, I am sure, and I should not like to ask him for such a thing." "I am king," said Ilsabill, "and you are my slave; so go at once!"

So the fisherman was forced to go; and he muttered as he went along, "This will come to no good, it is too much to ask; the fish will be tired at last, and then we shall be sorry for what we have done." He soon came to the seashore; and the water was quite black and muddy, and a mighty whirlwind blew over the waves and rolled them about, but he went as near as he could to the water's brink, and said:

"O man of the sea!
Hearken to me!
My wife Ilsabill
Will have her own will,
And hath sent me to beg a boon of thee!"

"What would she have now?" said the fish. "Ah!" said the fisherman, "she wants to be emperor." "Go home," said the fish; "she is emperor already."

So he went home again; and as he came near he saw his wife Ilsabill sitting on a very lofty throne made of solid gold, with a great crown on her head full two yards high; and on each side of her stood her guards and attendants in a row, each one smaller than the other, from the tallest giant down to a little dwarf no bigger than my finger. And before her stood princes, and dukes, and earls: and the fisherman went up to her and said, "Wife, are you emperor?" "Yes," said she, "I am emperor." "Ah!" said the man, as he gazed upon her, "what a fine thing it is to be emperor!" "Husband," said she, "why should we stop at being emperor? I will be pope next." "O wife, wife!" said he, "how can you be pope? there is but one pope at a time in Christendom." "Husband," said she, "I will be pope this very day." "But," replied the husband, "the fish cannot make you pope." "What nonsense!" said she; "if he can make an emperor, he can make a pope: go and try him."

So the fisherman went. But when he came to the shore the wind was raging and the sea was tossed up and down in boiling waves, and the ships were in trouble, and rolled fearfully upon the tops of the billows. In the middle of the heavens there was a little piece of blue sky, but towards the south all was red, as if a dreadful storm was rising. At this sight the fisherman was dreadfully frightened, and he trembled so that his knees knocked together: but still he went down near to the shore, and said:

"O man of the sea!
Hearken to me!
My wife Ilsabill
Will have her own will,
And hath sent me to beg a boon of thee!"

"What does she want now?" said the fish. "Ah!" said the fisherman, "my wife wants to be pope." "Go home," said the fish; "she is pope already."

Then the fisherman went home, and found Ilsabill sitting on a throne that was two miles high. And she had three great crowns on her head, and around her stood all the pomp and power of the Church. And on each side of her were two rows of burning lights, of all sizes, the greatest as large as the highest and biggest tower in the world, and the least no larger than a small rushlight. "Wife," said the fisherman, as he looked at all this greatness, "are you pope?" "Yes," said she, "I am pope." "Well, wife," replied he, "it is a grand thing to be pope; and now you must be easy, for you can be nothing greater." "I will think about that," said the wife. Then they went to bed: but Dame Ilsabill could not sleep all night for thinking what she should be next. At last, as she was dropping asleep, morning broke, and the sun rose. "Ha!" thought she, as she woke up and looked at it through the window, "after all I cannot prevent the sun rising." At this thought she was very angry, and wakened her husband, and said, "Husband, go to the fish and tell him I must be lord of the sun and moon." The fisherman was half asleep, but the thought frightened him so much that he started and fell out of bed. "Alas, wife!" said he, "cannot you be easy with being pope?" "No," said she, "I am very uneasy as long as the sun and moon rise without my leave. Go to the fish at once!"

Then the man went shivering with fear; and as he was going down to the shore a dreadful storm arose, so that the trees and the very rocks shook. And all the heavens became black with stormy clouds, and the lightnings played, and the thunders rolled; and you might have seen in the sea great black waves, swelling up like mountains with crowns of white foam upon their heads. And the fisherman crept towards the sea, and cried out, as well as he could:

> "O man of the sea!
> Hearken to me!
> My wife Ilsabill
> Will have her own will,
> And hath sent me to beg a boon of thee!"

"What does she want now?" said the fish. "Ah!" said he, "she wants to be lord of the sun and moon." "Go home," said the fish, "to your pigsty again."

And there they live to this very day.

THE TWELVE BROTHERS

ONCE upon a time there lived a King and Queen very peacefully together; they had twelve children, all boys. Now the King said to the Queen one day,

"If our thirteenth child should be a girl the twelve boys shall die, so that her riches may be the greater, and the kingdom fall to her alone."

Then he caused twelve coffins to be made; and they were filled with shavings, and a little pillow laid in each, and they were brought and put in a locked-up room; and the King gave the key to the Queen, and told her to say nothing about it to any one.

But the mother sat the whole day sorrowing, so that her youngest son, who never left her, and to whom she had given the Bible name Benjamin, said to her,

"Dear mother, why are you so sad?"

"Dearest child," answered she, "I dare not tell you."

But he let her have no peace until she went and unlocked the room, and showed him the twelve coffins with the shavings and the little pillows. Then she said,

"My dear Benjamin, your father has caused these coffins to be made for you and your eleven brothers, and if I bring a little girl into the world you are all to be put to death together and buried therein." And she wept as she spoke, and her little son comforted her and said,

"Weep not, dear mother, we will save ourselves and go far away." Then she answered,

"Yes, go with your eleven brothers out into the world, and let one of you always sit on the top of the highest tree that can be found, and keep watch upon the tower of this castle. If a little son is born I will put out a white flag, and then you may safely venture back again; but if it is a little daughter I will put out a red flag, and then flee away as fast as you can, and the dear God watch over you. Every night will I arise and pray for you—in winter that you may have a fire to warm yourselves by, and in summer that you may not languish in the heat."

After that, when she had given her sons her blessing, they went away out into the wood. One after another kept watch, sitting on the highest oak tree, looking towards the tower. When eleven days had passed, and Benjamin's turn came, he saw a flag put out, but it was not white, but blood red, to warn them that they were to die. When the brothers knew this they became angry, saying,

"Shall we suffer death because of a girl! we swear to be revenged; wherever we find a girl we will shed her blood."

Then they went deeper into the wood; and in the middle, where it was darkest, they found a little enchanted house, standing empty. Then they said,

"Here will we dwell; and you, Benjamin, the youngest and weakest, shall stay at home and keep house; we others will go abroad and purvey food."

Then they went into the wood and caught hares, wild roes, birds, and pigeons, and whatever else is good to eat, and brought them to Benjamin for him to cook and make ready to satisfy their hunger. So they lived together in the little house for ten years, and the time did not seem long.

By this time the Queen's little daughter was growing up, she had a kind heart and a beautiful face, and a golden star on her forehead. Once when there was a great wash she saw among the clothes twelve shirts, and she asked her mother,

"Whose are these twelve shirts? they are too small to be my father's." Then the mother answered with a sore heart,

"Dear child, they belong to your twelve brothers." The little girl said,

"Where are my twelve brothers? I have never heard of them." And her mother answered,

"God only knows where they are wandering about in the world." Then she led the little girl to the secret room and unlocked it, and showed her the twelve coffins with the shavings and the little pillows.

"These coffins," said she, "were intended for your twelve brothers, but they went away far from home when you were born," and she related how everything had come to pass. Then said the little girl,

"Dear mother, do not weep, I will go and seek my brothers."

So she took the twelve shirts and went far and wide in the great forest. The day sped on, and in the evening she came to the enchanted house. She went in and found a youth, who asked,

"Whence do you come, and what do you want?" and he marvelled at her beauty, her royal garments, and the star on her forehead. Then she answered,

"I am a king's daughter, and I seek my twelve brothers, and I will go everywhere under the blue sky until I find them." And she showed him the twelve shirts which belonged to them. Then Benjamin saw that it must be his sister, and said,

"I am Benjamin, your youngest brother."

And she began weeping for joy, and Benjamin also, and they kissed and cheered each other with great love. After a while he said,

"Dear sister, there is still a hindrance; we have sworn that any maiden that we meet must die, as it was because of a maiden that we had to leave our kingdom." Then she said,

"I will willingly die, if so I may benefit my twelve brothers."

"No," answered he, "you shall not die; sit down under this tub until the eleven brothers come, and I agree with them about it." She did so; and as night came on they returned from hunting, and supper was ready. And as they were sitting at table and eating, they asked,

"What news?" And Benjamin said,

"Don't you know any?"

"No," answered they. So he said,

"TWELVE RAVENS CAME FLYING DOWN"

"You have been in the wood, and I have stayed at home, and yet I know more than you."

"Tell us!" cried they. He answered,

"Promise me that the first maiden we see shall not be put to death."

"Yes, we promise," cried they all, "she shall have mercy; tell us now." Then he said,

"Our sister is here," and lifted up the tub, and the king's daughter came forth in her royal garments with her golden star on her forehead, and she seemed so beautiful, delicate, and sweet, that they all rejoiced, and fell on her neck and kissed her, and loved her with all their hearts.

After this she remained with Benjamin in the house and helped him with the work. The others went forth into the woods to catch wild animals, does, birds, and pigeons, for food for them all, and their sister and Benjamin took care that all was made ready for them. She fetched the wood for cooking, and the vegetables, and watched the pots on the fire, so that supper was always ready when the others came in. She kept also great order in the house, and the beds were always beautifully white and clean, and the brothers were contented, and lived in unity.

One day the two got ready a fine feast, and when they were all assembled they sat down and ate and drank, and were full of joy. Now there was a little garden belonging to the enchanted house, in which grew twelve lilies; the maiden, thinking to please her brothers, went out to gather the twelve flowers, meaning to give one to each as they sat at meat. But as she broke off the flowers, in the same moment the brothers were changed into twelve ravens, and flew over the wood far away, and the house with the garden also disappeared. So the poor maiden stood alone in the wild wood, and as she was looking around her she saw an old woman standing by her, who said,

"My child, what hast thou done! why couldst thou not leave the twelve flowers standing? they were thy twelve brothers, who are now changed to ravens for ever." The maiden said, weeping,

"Is there no means of setting them free?"

"No," said the old woman, "there is in the whole world no way but one, and that is difficult; thou canst not release them but by being dumb for seven years: thou must neither speak nor laugh; and wert thou to speak one single word, and it wanted but one hour of the seven years, all would be in vain, and thy brothers would perish because of that one word."

Then the maiden said in her heart, "I am quite sure that I can set my brothers free," and went and sought a tall tree, climbed up, and sat there spinning, and never spoke or laughed. Now it happened that a King, who was hunting in the wood, had with him a large greyhound, who ran to the tree where the maiden was, sprang up at it, and barked loudly. Up came the King and saw the beautiful Princess with the golden star on her forehead, and he was so charmed with her beauty that he prayed her to become his wife. She gave no answer, only a little nod of her head. Then he himself climbed the tree and brought her down, set her on his horse and took her home. The wedding was held with great splendor and rejoicing, but the bride neither spoke nor laughed. After they had lived pleasantly together for a few years, the King's mother, who was a wicked woman, began to slander the young Queen, and said to the King,

"She is only a low beggar-maid that you have taken to yourself; who knows what mean tricks she is playing? Even if she is really dumb and cannot speak she might at least laugh; not to laugh is the sign of a bad conscience."

At first the King would believe nothing of it, but the old woman talked so long, and suggested so many bad things, that he at last let himself be persuaded, and condemned the Queen to death.

Now a great fire was kindled in the courtyard, and she was to be burned in it; and the King stood above at the window, and watched it all with weeping eyes, for he had held her very dear. And when she was already fast bound to the stake, and the fire was licking her garments with red tongues, the last moment of the seven years came to an end. Then a rushing sound was heard in the air, and twelve ravens came flying and sank downwards; and as they touched the earth they became her twelve brothers that she had lost. They rushed through the fire and quenched the flames, and set their dear sister free, kissing and consoling her. And now that her mouth was opened, and that she might venture to speak, she told the King the reason of her dumbness, and why she had never laughed. The King rejoiced when he heard of her innocence, and they all lived together in happiness until their death.

But the wicked mother-in-law was very unhappy, and died miserably.

SLEEPING BEAUTY

IN times past there lived a king and queen, who said to each other every day of their lives, "Would that we had a child!" and yet they had none. But it happened once that when the queen was bathing, there came a frog out of the water, and he squatted on the ground, and said to her,

"Thy wish shall be fulfilled; before a year has gone by, thou shalt bring a daughter into the world."

And as the frog foretold, so it happened; and the queen bore a daughter so beautiful that the king could not contain himself for joy, and he ordained a great feast. Not only did he bid to it his relations, friends, and acquaintances, but also the wise women, that they might be kind and favorable to the child. There were thirteen of them in his kingdom, but as he had only provided twelve golden plates for them to eat from, one of them had to be left out. However, the feast was celebrated with all splendor; and as it drew to an end, the wise women stood forward to present to the child their wonderful gifts: one bestowed virtue, one beauty, a third riches, and so on, whatever there is in the world to wish for. And when eleven of them had said their say, in came the uninvited thirteenth, burning to revenge herself, and without greeting or respect, she cried with a loud voice,

"In the fifteenth year of her age the princess shall prick herself with a spindle and shall fall down dead."

And without speaking one more word she turned away and left the hall. Every one was terrified at her saying, when the twelfth came forward, for she had not yet bestowed her gift, and though she could not do away with the evil prophecy, yet she could soften it, so she said,

"The princess shall not die, but fall into a deep sleep for a hundred years."

Now the king, being desirous of saving his child even from this misfortune, gave commandment that all the spindles in his kingdom should be burnt up.

The maiden grew up, adorned with all the gifts of the wise women; and she was so lovely, modest, sweet, and kind and clever, that no one who saw her could help loving her.

It happened one day, she being already fifteen years old, that the king and queen rode abroad, and the maiden was left behind alone in the castle. She wandered about into all the nooks and corners, and into all the chambers and parlours, as the fancy took her, till at last she came to an old tower. She climbed the narrow winding stair which led to a little door, with a rusty key sticking out of the lock; she turned the key, and the door opened, and there in the little room sat an old woman with a spindle, diligently spinning her flax.

"Good day, mother," said the princess, "what are you doing?"

"I am spinning," answered the old woman, nodding her head.

"What thing is that that twists round so briskly?" asked the maiden, and taking the spindle into her hand she began to spin; but no sooner had she touched it than the evil prophecy was fulfilled, and she pricked her finger with it. In that very moment she fell back upon the bed that stood there, and lay in a deep sleep. And this sleep fell upon the whole castle; the king and queen, who had returned and were in the great hall, fell fast asleep, and with them the whole court. The horses in their stalls, the dogs in the yard, the pigeons on the roof, the flies on the wall, the very fire that flickered on the hearth, became still, and slept like the rest; and the meat on the spit ceased roasting, and the cook, who was going to pull the scullion's hair for some mistake he had made, let him go, and went

"AND THERE SHE LAY FAST ASLEEP ON A COUCH"

to sleep. And the wind ceased, and not a leaf fell from the trees about the castle.

Then round about that place there grew a hedge of thorns thicker every year, until at last the whole castle was hidden from view, and nothing of it could be seen but the vane on the roof. And a rumor went abroad in all that country of the beautiful sleeping Rosamond, for so was the princess called; and from time to time many kings' sons came and tried to force their way through the hedge; but it was impossible for them to do so, for the thorns held fast together like strong hands, and the young men were caught by them, and not being able to get free, there died a lamentable death.

Many a long year afterwards there came a king's son into that country, and heard an old man tell how there should be a castle standing behind the hedge of thorns, and that there a beautiful enchanted princess named Rosamond had slept for a hundred years, and with her the king and queen, and the whole court. The old man had been told by his grandfather that many king's sons had sought to pass the thorn-hedge, but had been caught and pierced by the thorns, and had died a miserable death. Then said the young man, "Nevertheless, I do not fear to try; I shall win through and see the lovely Rosamond." The good old man tried to dissuade him, but he would not listen to his words.

For now the hundred years were at an end, and the day had come when Rosamond should be awakened. When the prince drew near the hedge of thorns, it was changed into a hedge of beautiful large flowers, which parted and bent aside to let him pass, and then closed behind him in a thick hedge. When he reached the castle-yard, he saw the horses and brindled hunting-dogs lying asleep, and on the roof the pigeons were sitting with their heads under their wings. And when he came indoors, the flies on the wall were asleep, the cook in the kitchen had his hand uplifted to strike the scullion, and the kitchen-maid had the black fowl on her lap ready to pluck. Then he mounted higher, and saw in the hall the whole court lying asleep, and above them, on their thrones, slept the king and the queen. And still he went farther, and all was so quiet that he could hear his own breathing; and at last he came to the tower, and went up the winding stair, and opened the door of the little room where Rosamond lay. And when he saw her looking so lovely in her sleep, he could not turn away his eyes; and presently he stooped and kissed her, and she awaked, and opened her eyes, and looked very kindly on him. And she rose, and they went forth together, and the king and the queen and whole court waked up, and gazed on each other with great eyes of wonderment. And the horses in the yard got up and shook themselves, the hounds sprang up and wagged their tails, the pigeons on the roof drew their heads from under their wings, looked round, and flew into the field, the flies on the wall crept on a little farther, the kitchen fire leapt up and blazed, and cooked the meat, the joint on the spit began to roast, the cook gave the scullion such a box on the ear that he roared out, and the maid went on plucking the fowl.

Then the wedding of the Prince and Rosamond was held with all splendor, and they lived very happily together until their lives' end.

THE RAVEN

THERE was once a queen who had a little daughter, still too young to run alone. One day the child was very troublesome, and the mother could not quiet it, do what she would. She grew impatient, and seeing the ravens flying round the castle, she opened the window, and said: "I wish you were a raven and would fly away, then I should have a little peace." Scarcely were the words out of her mouth, when the child in her arms was turned into a raven, and flew away from her through the open window. The bird took its flight to a dark wood and remained there for a long time, and meanwhile the parents could hear nothing of their child.

Long after this, a man was making his way through the wood when he heard a raven calling, and he followed the sound of the voice. As he drew near, the raven said, "I am by birth a king's daughter, but am now under the spell of some enchantment; you can, however, set me free." "What am I to do?" he asked. She replied, "Go farther into the wood until you come to a house, wherein lives an old woman; she will offer you food and drink, but you must not take of either; if you do, you will fall into a deep sleep, and will not be able to help me. In the garden behind the house is a large tan-heap, and on that you must stand and watch for me. I shall drive there in my carriage at two o'clock in the afternoon for three successive days; the first day it will be drawn by four white, the second by four chestnut, and the last by four black horses; but if you fail to keep awake and I find you sleeping, I shall not be set free."

The man promised to do all that she wished, but the raven said, "Alas! I know even now that you will take something from the woman and be unable to save me." The man assured her again that he would on no account touch a thing to eat or drink.

When he came to the house and went inside, the old woman met him, and said, "Poor man! how tired you are! Come in and rest and let me give you something to eat and drink."

"No," answered the man, "I will neither eat not drink."

But she would not leave him alone, and urged him saying, "If you will not eat anything, at least you might take a draught of wine; one drink counts for nothing," and at last he allowed himself to be persuaded, and drank.

As it drew towards the appointed hour, he went outside into the garden and mounted the tan-heap to await the raven. Suddenly a feeling of fatigue came over him, and unable to resist it, he lay down for a little while, fully determined, however, to keep awake; but in another minute his eyes closed of their own accord, and he fell into such a deep sleep, that all the noises in the world would not have awakened him. At two o'clock the raven came driving along, drawn by her four white horses; but even before she reached the spot, she said to herself, sighing, "I know he has fallen asleep." When she entered the garden, there she found him as she had feared, lying on the tan-heap, fast asleep. She got out of her carriage and went to him; she called him and shook him, but it was all in vain, he still continued sleeping.

The next day at noon, the old woman came to him again with food and drink which he at first refused. At last, overcome by her persistent entreaties that he would take something, he lifted the glass and drank again.

Towards two o'clock he went into the garden and on to the tan-heap to watch for the raven. He had not been there long before he began to feel so tired that his limbs seemed hardly able to support him, and he could not stand upright any longer; so again he lay down and fell fast asleep. As the raven drove along her four chestnut horses, she said sorrowfully to herself, "I know he has fallen asleep." She went as before to look for him, but he slept, and it was impossible to awaken him.

The following day the old woman said to him, "What is this? You are not eating or drinking anything, do you want to kill yourself?"

He answered, "I may not and will not either eat or drink."

But she put down the dish of food and the glass of wine in front of him, and when he smelt the wine, he was unable to resist the temptation, and took a deep draught.

When the hour came round again he went as usual on to the tan-heap in the garden to await the king's daughter, but he felt even more overcome with weariness than on the two previous days, and throwing himself down, he slept like a log. At two o'clock the raven could be seen approaching, and this time her coachman and everything about her, as well as her horses, were black.

She was sadder than ever as she drove along, and said mournfully, "I know he has fallen asleep, and will not be able to set me free." She found him sleeping heavily, and all her efforts to awaken him were of no avail. Then she placed beside him a loaf, and some meat, and a flask of wine, of such a kind, that however much he took of them, they would never grow less. After that she drew a gold ring, on which her name was engraved, off her finger, and put it upon one of his. Finally, she laid a letter near him, in which, after giving him particulars of the food and drink she had left for him, she finished with the following words: "I see that as long as you remain here you will never be able to set me free; if, however, you still wish to do so, come to the golden castle of Stromberg; this is well within your power to accomplish." She then returned to her carriage and drove to the golden castle of Stromberg.

When the man awoke and found that he had been sleeping, he was grieved at heart, and said, "She has no doubt been here and driven away again, and it is now too late for me to save her." Then his eyes fell on the things which were lying beside him; he read the letter, and knew from it all that had happened. He rose up without delay, eager to start on his way and to reach the castle of Stromberg, but he had no idea in which direction he ought to go. He travelled about a long time in search of it and came at last to a dark forest, through which he went on walking for fourteen days and still could

THE RAVEN SAID, "I AM BY BIRTH A KING'S DAUGHTER"

not find a way out. Once more the night came on, and worn out he lay down under a bush and fell asleep. Again the next day he pursued his way through the forest, and that evening, thinking to rest again, he lay down as before, but he heard such a howling and wailing that he found it impossible to sleep. He waited till it was darker and people had begun to light up their houses, and then seeing a little glimmer ahead of him, he went towards it.

He found that the light came from a house which looked smaller than it really was, from the contrast of its height with that of an immense giant who stood in front of it. He thought to himself, "If the giant sees me going in, my life will not be worth much." However, after a while he summoned up courage and went forward. When the giant saw him, he called out, "It is lucky for that you have come, for I have not had anything to eat for a long time. I can have you now for my supper." "I would rather you let that alone," said the man, "for I do not willingly give myself up to be eaten; if you are wanting food I have enough to satisfy your hunger." "If that is so," replied the giant, "I will leave you in peace; I only thought of eating you because I had nothing else."

So they went indoors together and sat down, and the man brought out the bread, meat, and wine, which although he had eaten and drunk of them, were still unconsumed. The giant was pleased with the good cheer, and ate and drank to his heart's content. When he had finished his supper the man asked him if he could direct him to the castle of Stromberg. The giant said, "I will look on my map; on it are marked all the towns, villages, and houses." So he fetched his map, and looked for the castle, but could not find it. "Never mind," he said, "I have larger maps upstairs in the cupboard, we will look on those," but they searched in vain, for the castle was not marked even on these. The man now thought he should like to continue his journey, but the giant begged him to remain for a day or two longer until the return of his brother, who was away in search of provisions. When the brother came home, they asked him about the castle of Stromberg, and he told them he would look on his own maps as soon as he had eaten and appeased his hunger. Accordingly, when he had finished his supper, they all went up together to his room and looked through his maps, but the castle was not to be found. Then he fetched other older maps, and they went on looking for the castle until at last they found it, but it was many thousand miles away. "How shall I be able to get there?" asked the man. "I have two hours to spare," said the giant, "and I will carry you into the neighborhood of the castle; I must then return to look after the child who is in our care."

The giant, thereupon, carried the man to within about a hundred leagues of the castle, where he left him, saying, "You will be able to walk the remainder of the way yourself." The man journeyed on day and night till he reached the golden castle of Stromberg. He found it situated, however, on a glass mountain, and looking up from the foot he saw the enchanted maiden drive round her castle and then go inside. He was overjoyed to see her, and longed to get to the top of the mountain, but the sides were so slippery that every time he attempted to climb he fell back again. When he saw that it was impossible to reach her, he was greatly grieved, and said to himself, "I will remain here and wait for her," so he built himself a little hut, and there he sat and watched for a whole year, and every day he saw the king's daughter driving round her castle, but still was unable to get nearer to her.

Looking out from his hut one day he saw three robbers fighting and he called out to them, "God be with you." They stopped when they heard the call, but looking round and seeing nobody, they went on again with their fighting, which now became more furious. "God be with you," he cried again, and again they paused and looked about, but seeing no one went back to their fighting. A third time he called out, "God be with you," and then thinking he should like to know the cause of dispute between the three men, he went out and asked them why they were fighting so angrily with one another. One of them said that he had found a stick, and that he had but to strike it against any door through which he wished to pass, and it immediately flew open. Another told him that he had found a cloak which rendered its wearer invisible; and the third had caught a horse which would carry its rider over any obstacle, and even up the glass mountain. They had been unable to decide whether they would keep together and have the things in common, or whether they would separate. On hearing this, the man said, "I will give you something in exchange for those three things; not money, for that I have not got, but something that is of far more value. I must first, however, prove whether all you have told me about your three things is true." The robbers, therefore, made him get on the horse, and handed him the stick and the cloak, and when he had put this round him he was no longer visible. Then he fell upon them with the stick and beat them one after another, crying, "There, you idle vagabonds, you have got what you deserve; are you satisfied now!"

After this he rode up the glass mountain. When he reached the gate of the castle, he found it closed, but he gave it a blow with his stick, and it flew wide open at once and he passed through. He mounted the steps and entered the room where the maiden was sitting, with a golden goblet full of wine in front of her. She could not see him for he still wore his cloak. He took the ring which she had given him off his finger, and threw it into the goblet, so that it rang as it touched the bottom. "That is my own ring," she exclaimed, "and if that is so the man must also be here who is coming to set me free."

She sought for him about the castle, but could find him nowhere. Meanwhile he had gone outside again and mounted his horse and thrown off the cloak. When therefore she came to the castle gate she saw him, and cried aloud for joy. Then he dismounted and took her in his arms; and she kissed him, and said, "Now you have indeed set me free, and tomorrow we will celebrate our marriage."

FRITZ AND HIS FRIENDS

HONEST Fritz had worked hard all his life, but ill luck befell him; his cattle died, his barns were burned, and he lost almost all his money. So at last he said, "Before it is all gone I will buy goods, and go out into the world, and see whether I shall have the luck to mend my fortune."

The first place he came to was a village, where the boys were running about, crying and shouting. "What is the matter?" asked he. "See here!" said they, "we have got a mouse that we make dance to please us. Do look at him; what a droll sight it is! how he jumps about!" But the man pitied the poor little thing, and said, "Let the poor mouse go, and I will give you money." So he gave them some money, and took the mouse and let it run: and it soon jumped into a hole that was close by, and was out of their reach.

Then he travelled on and came to another village: and there the boys had got an ass, that they made stand on its hind legs, and tumble and cut capers. Then they laughed and shouted, and gave the poor beast no rest. So the good man gave them too some of his money, to let the poor thing go away in peace.

At the next village he came to, the young people were leading a bear, that had been taught to dance, and were plaguing the poor thing sadly. Then he gave them too some money, to let the beast go; and Master Bruin was very glad to get on his four feet, and seemed quite at his ease and happy again.

But now our traveller found that he had given away all the money he had in the world, and had not a shilling in his pocket. Then said he to himself, "The King has heaps of gold in his strong box that he never uses; I cannot die of hunger: so I hope I shall be forgiven if I borrow a little from him, and when I get rich again I will repay it all."

So he managed to get at the King's strong box, and took a very little money; but as he came out the guards saw him, and said he was a thief, and took him to the judge. The poor man told his story; but the judge said that sort of borrowing could not be suffered, and that those who took other people's money must be punished; so the end of his trial was that Fritz was found guilty, and doomed to be thrown into the lake, shut up in a box. The lid of the box was full of holes to let in air; and one jug of water and one loaf of bread were given him.

Whilst he was swimming along in the water very sorrowfully, he heard something nibbling and biting at the lock. All on a sudden it fell off, the lid flew open, and there stood his old friend the little mouse, who had done him this good turn. Then came the ass and the bear too, and pulled the box ashore; and all helped him because he had been kind to them.

But now they did not know what to do next, and began to lay their heads together; when on a sudden a wave threw on the shore a pretty white stone, that looked like an egg. Then the bear said, "That's a lucky thing! this is the wonderful stone; whoever has it needs only to wish, and everything that he wishes for comes to him at once." So Fritz went and picked up the stone, and wished for a palace and a garden, and a stud of horses; and his wish was fulfilled as soon as he had made it. And there he lived in his castle and garden, with fine stables and horses; and all was so grand and beautiful, that he never could wonder and gaze at it enough.

After some time some merchants passed by that way. "See," said they, "what a princely palace! The last time we were here it was nothing but a desert waste." They were very eager to know how all this had happened, and went in and asked the master of the palace how it had been so quickly raised. "I have done nothing myself," said he; "it is the wonderful stone that did all." "What a strange stone that must be! " said they. Then he asked them to walk in, and showed it to them.

They asked him whether he would sell it, and offered him all their goods for it; and the goods seemed so fine and costly, that he quite forgot that the stone would bring him in a moment a thousand better and richer things; and he agreed to make the bargain. Scarcely was the stone, however, out of his hands before all his riches were gone, and poor Fritz found himself sitting in his box in the water, with his jug of water and loaf of bread by his side.

However, his grateful friends, the mouse, the ass, and the bear, came quickly to help him; but the mouse found she could not nibble off the lock this time, for it was a great deal stronger than before. Then the bear said, "We must find the wonderful stone again, or all we can do will be fruitless."

The merchants, meantime, had taken up their abode in the palace; so away went the three friends, and when they came near, the bear said, "Mouse, go in and look through the keyhole, and see where the stone is kept: you are small, nobody will see you." The mouse did as she was told, but soon came back and said, "Bad news! I have looked in, and the stone hangs under the looking-glass by a red silk string, and on each side of it sits a great black cat with fiery eyes, watching it."

Then the others took counsel together, and said, "Go back again, and wait till the master of the palace is in bed asleep; then nip his nose and pull his hair." Away went the mouse, and did as they told her; and the master jumped up very angrily, and rubbed his nose, and cried, "Those rascally cats are good for nothing at all; they let the mice bite my very nose, and pull the hair off my head." Then he hunted them out of the room; and so the mouse had the best of the game.

Next night, as soon as the master was asleep, the mouse crept in again; and (the cats being gone) she nibbled at the red silken string to which the stone hung, till down it dropped. Then she rolled it along to the door; but when it got there the poor little mouse was quite tired, and said to the ass, "Put in your foot, and lift it over the threshold." This was soon done; and they took up the stone, and set off for the waterside. Then the ass said, "How shall we reach the box?" "That is easily managed, my friend," said the bear: "I can swim very well; and do you, donkey, put your fore feet over my shoulders;—mind and hold fast, and take the stone in your mouth;—as for you, mouse, you can sit in my ear."

Thus all was settled, and away they swam. After a time, Bruin began to brag and boast: "We are brave fellows, are not we?" said he; "what do you think, donkey?" But the ass held his tongue, and said not a word. "Why don't you answer me?" said the bear; "you must be an ill-mannered brute not to speak when you are spoken to." When the ass heard this, he could hold no longer; so he opened his mouth, and out dropped the wonderful stone. "I could not speak," said he; "did not you know I had the stone in my mouth? Now it is lost, and that is your fault." "Do but hold your tongue and be easy!" said the bear; "and let us think what is to be done now."

Then another council was held: and at last they called together all the frogs, their wives and families, kindred and friends; and said, "A great foe of yours is coming to eat you all up; but never mind, bring us up plenty of stones, and we will build a strong wall to guard you." The frogs hearing this were dreadfully frightened, and set to work, bringing up all the stones they could find. At last came a large fat frog, pulling along the wonderful stone by the silken string; and when the bear saw it he jumped for joy, and said, "Now we have found what we wanted." So he set the old frog free from his load, and told him to tell his friends they might now go home to their dinners as soon as they pleased.

Then the three friends swam off again for the box, and the lid flew open, and they found they were but just in time, for the bread was all eaten and the jug of water almost empty. But as soon as honest Fritz had the stone in his hand, he wished himself safe in his palace again; and in a moment he was there, with his garden, and his stables, and his horses; and his three faithful friends lived with him, and they all spent their time happily and merrily together as long as they lived. And thus the good man's kindness was rewarded; and so it ought, for—One good turn deserves another.

THE ELFIN GROVE

AS an honest woodman was sitting one evening, after his work was done, talking with his wife, he said, "I hope the children will not run into that grove by the side of the river; it looks more gloomy than ever; the old oak tree is sadly blasted and torn; and some odd folks, I am sure, are lurking about there, but who they are nobody knows." The woodman, however, could not say that they brought ill luck, whatever they were; for every one said that the village had thriven more than ever of late, that the fields looked gayer and greener, that even the sky was of a deeper blue, and that the moon and stars shed a brighter light. So, not knowing what to think, the good people very wisely let the new comers alone; and, in truth, seldom said or thought anything at all about them.

That very evening, the woodman's daughter Roseken, and her playfellow Martin, ran out to have a game of hide-and-seek in the valley. "Where can he be hidden?" said she; "he must have gone towards the grove; perhaps he is behind the old oak tree": and down she ran to look. Just then she spied a little dog that jumped and frisked round her, and wagged his tail, and led her on towards the grove. Then he ran into it, and she soon jumped up the bank by the side of the old oak to look for him; but was overjoyed to see a beautiful meadow, where flowers and shrubs of every kind grew upon turf of the softest green; gay butterflies flew about; the birds sang sweetly;

"AND SO, PRETTY ROSEKEN, YOU ARE COME AT LAST TO SEE US?"

and what was strangest, the prettiest little children sported about like fairies on all sides; some twining the flowers, and others dancing in rings upon the smooth turf beneath the trees. In the midst of the grove, instead of the hovels of which Roseken had heard, she could see a palace, that dazzled her eyes with its brightness.

For a while she gazed on the fairy scene, till at last one of the little dancers ran up to her, and said, "And so, pretty Roseken, you are come at last to see us? We have often seen you play about, and wished to have you with us." Then she plucked some of the fruit that grew near, and Roseken at the first taste forgot her home, and wished only to see and know more of her fairy friends. So she jumped down from the bank and joined the merry dance.

Then they led her about with them, and showed her all their sports. One while they danced by moonlight on the primrose banks, at another time they skipped from bough to bough, among the trees that hung over the cooling streams, for they moved as lightly and easily through the air as on the ground: and Roseken went with them everywhere, for they bore her in their arms wherever they wished to go. Sometimes they would throw seeds on the turf, and little trees would spring up; and then they would set their feet upon the branches, and rise as the trees grew under them, till they danced upon the boughs in the air, wherever the breezes carried them, singing merry songs.

At other times they would go and visit the palace of their queen: and there the richest food was spread before them, and the softest music was heard; and all around grew flowers, which were always changing their hues, from scarlet to purple, and yellow, and emerald. Sometimes they went to look at the heaps of treasure which were piled up in the royal stores; for little dwarfs were always employed in searching the earth for gold. Small as this fairy land looked from without, it seemed within to have no end; a mist hung around it to shield it from the eyes of men; and some of the little elves sat perched upon the outermost trees, to keep watch lest the step of man should break in and spoil the charm.

"And who are you?" said Roseken one day. "We are what are called elves in your world," said one whose name was Gossamer, and who had become her dearest friend: "we are told you talk a great deal about us. Some of our tribes like to work you mischief, but we who live here seek only to be happy; we meddle little with mankind, and when we do come among them it is to do them good." "And where is your queen?" said Roseken. "Hush! hush! you cannot see or know her: you must leave us before she comes back, which will be now very soon, for mortal step cannot come where she is. But you will know that she is here, when you see the meadows gayer, the rivers more sparkling, and the sun brighter."

Soon afterwards Gossamer told Roseken the time was come to bid her farewell; and she gave her a ring in token of their friendship, and led her to the edge of the grove. "Think of me," said she; "but beware how you tell what you have seen, or try to visit any of us again: for if you do, we shall quit this grove and come back no more." Turning back, Roseken saw nothing but the old oak and the gloomy grove she had known before. "How frightened my father and mother will be!" thought she, as she looked at the sun, which had risen some time. "They will wonder where I have been all night, and yet I must not tell them what I have seen."

Then she hastened homewards, wondering, however, as she went, to see that the leaves, which were yesterday so fresh and green, were now falling dry and yellow around her. The cottage, too, seemed changed; and when she went in, there sat her father, looking some years older than when she saw him last, and her mother, whom she hardly knew, was by his side. Close by was a young man. "Father," said Roseken, "who is this?" "Who are you that call me father?" said he; "are you—no, you cannot be—our long-lost Roseken?" But they soon saw that it was their Roseken; and the young man, who was her old friend and playfellow Martin, said, "No wonder you had forgotten me in seven years; do not you remember how we parted, seven years ago, while playing in the field? We thought you were quite lost; but I am glad to see that some one has taken care of you, and brought you home at last." Roseken said nothing, for she could not tell all; but she wondered at the strange tale, and felt gloomy at the change from fairy land to her father's cottage.

Little by little she came to herself, thought of her story as a mere dream, and soon became Martin's bride. Everything seemed to thrive around them; and Roseken thought of her friends, and so called her first little girl Elfie. The little thing was loved by every one. It was pretty and very good-tempered. Roseken thought that it was very like a little elf; and all, without knowing why, called it the fairy-child.

One day, while Roseken was dressing her little Elfie, she found a piece of gold hanging round her neck by a silken thread; and knew it to be of the same sort as she had seen in the hands of the fairy dwarfs. Elfie seemed sorry at its being seen, and said that she had found it in the garden. But Roseken watched her, and soon found that she went every afternoon to sit by herself in a shady place behind the house. So one day she hid herself to see what the child did there, and to her great wonder Gossamer was sitting by her side. "Dear Elfie," she was saying, "your mother and I used to sit thus when she was young and lived among us. Oh, if you could but come and do so too! But since our queen came to us it cannot be; yet I will come and see you, and talk to you whilst you are a child; when you grow up we must part for ever." Then she plucked one of the roses that grew around them, and breathed gently upon it, and said, "Take this for my sake! it will now keep fresh for a whole year."

Then Roseken loved her little Elfie more than ever; and when she found that she spent some hours of almost every day with the elf, she used to hide herself and watch them without being seen; till one day, when Gossamer was bearing her little friend through the air from tree to tree, her mother was so frightened lest her child should fall, that she could not help screaming out; and Gossamer set her gently on the ground, and seemed angry, and flew away. But still she used sometimes to come and play with her little friend; and would soon, perhaps, have done so the same as before, had not Roseken one day told her husband the whole story: for she could not bear to hear him always wondering and laughing at their little child's odd ways, and saying he was sure there was something in the grove that brought them no good. So, to show him that all she said was true, she took him to see Elfie and the fairy; but no sooner did Gossamer know that he was there (which she did in an instant), than she changed herself into a raven, and flew off into the grove.

Roseken burst into tears, and so did Elfie, for she knew she should see her dear friend no more; but Martin was restless and bent upon following up his search after the fairies, so when night came he stole away towards the grove. When he came to it nothing was to be seen but the old oak, and the gloomy grove, and the hovels; and the thunder rolled, and the wind whistled. It seemed that all about him was angry, so he turned homewards, frightened at what he had done.

In the morning all the neighbors flocked around, asking one another what the noise and bustle of the last night could mean; and when they looked about them, their trees seemed blighted and the meadows parched, the streams were dried up, and everything seemed troubled and sorrowful.

But yet they all thought that, somehow or other, the grove had not near so forbidding a look as it used to have. Strange stories were told: how one had heard flutterings in the air, another had seen the grove as it were alive with little beings, that flew away from it. Each neighbor told his tale, and all wondered what could have happened. But Roseken and her husband knew what was the matter, and bewailed their folly; for they foresaw that their kind neighbors, to whom they owed all their luck, were gone for ever.

Among the bystanders none told a wilder story than the old ferryman, who plied across the river at the foot of the grove. He told how at midnight his boat was carried away, and how hundreds of little beings seemed to load it with treasures: how a strange piece of gold was left for him in the boat as his fare; how the air seemed full of fairy forms fluttering around; and how at last a great train passed over, that seemed to be guarding their leader to the meadows on the other side; and how he heard soft music floating around; and how sweet voices sang as they hovered overhead,—

Fairy Queen!
Fairy Queen!
Mortal steps are on the green;
Come away!
Haste away!
Fairies, guard your Queen!
Hither, hither, Fairy Queen!
Lest thy silvery wing be seen;
O'er the sky.
Fly, fly, fly!
Fairies, guard your lady Queen!

O'er the sky,
Fly, fly, fly!
Fairies, guard your Queen!
Fairy Queen!
Fairy Queen!
Mortal steps no more are seen;
Now we may
Down and play
O'er the daisied green.
Lightly, lightly, Fairy Queen!
Trip it gently o'er the green!
Fairies gay,
Trip away,
Round about your lady Queen!
Fairies gay,
Trip away,
Round about your Queen!

Poor Elfie mourned their loss the most; and would spend whole hours in looking upon the rose that her playfellow had given her, and singing over it the pretty airs she had taught her: till at length, when the year's charm had passed away, and it began to fade, she planted the stalk in her garden, and there it grew and grew, till she could sit under the shade of it, and think of her friend Gossamer.

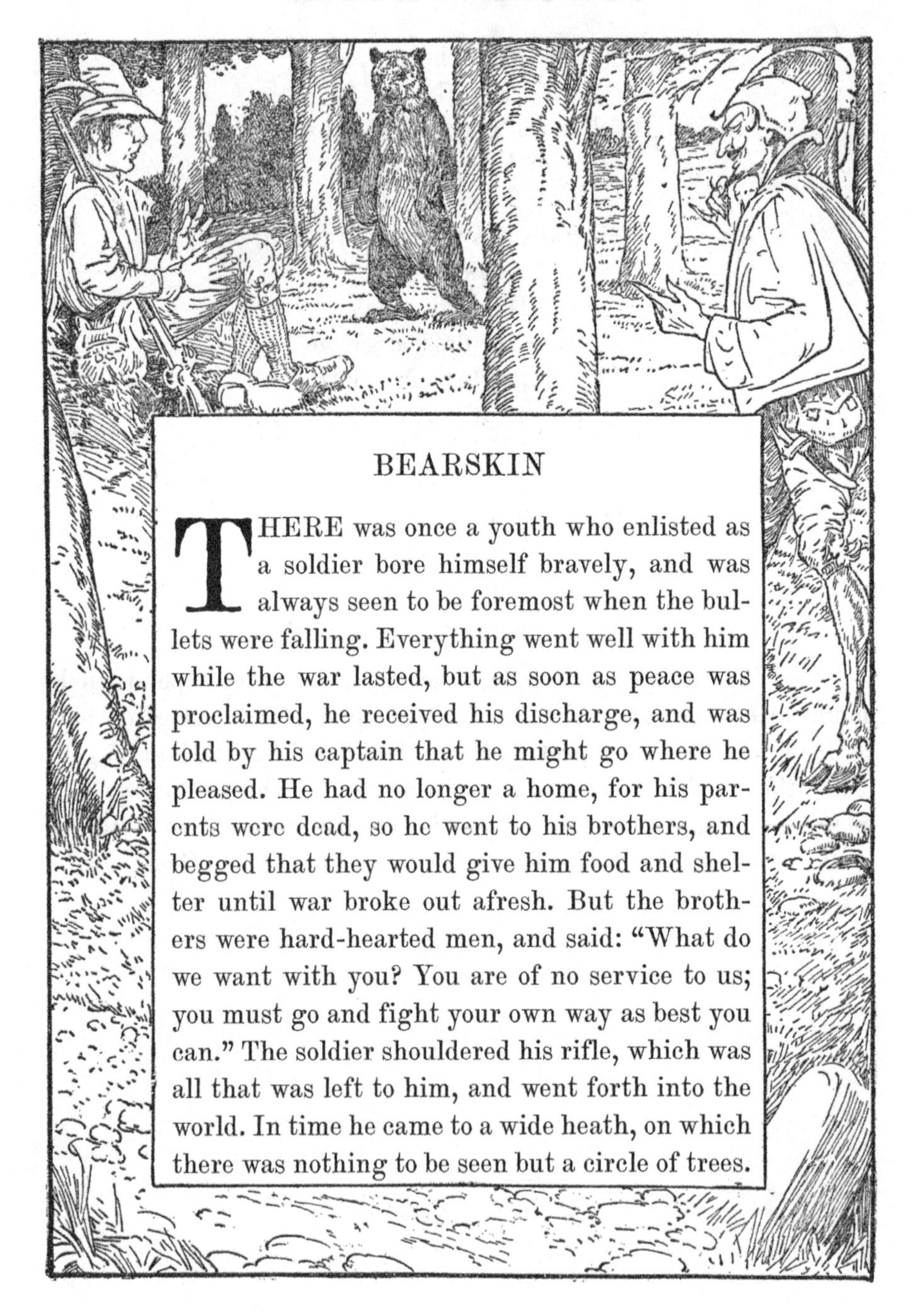

BEARSKIN

THERE was once a youth who enlisted as a soldier bore himself bravely, and was always seen to be foremost when the bullets were falling. Everything went well with him while the war lasted, but as soon as peace was proclaimed, he received his discharge, and was told by his captain that he might go where he pleased. He had no longer a home, for his parents were dead, so he went to his brothers, and begged that they would give him food and shelter until war broke out afresh. But the brothers were hard-hearted men, and said: "What do we want with you? You are of no service to us; you must go and fight your own way as best you can." The soldier shouldered his rifle, which was all that was left to him, and went forth into the world. In time he came to a wide heath, on which there was nothing to be seen but a circle of trees.

Full of sorrowful thoughts, he sat down under one of these and began meditating on the sadness of his lot. "I have no money," he said to himself, "and I have learnt no trade but that of fighting, and for this I am no longer wanted since peace was declared; I see nothing left for me to do but to starve." All at once he heard a sound as of the wind blowing, and looking up, he saw a stranger standing in front of him, dressed in a green coat. He was of stately appearance but had a nasty cloven-foot. "You have no need to tell me of what you are in want," said the stranger, "I know already; both money and property I am prepared to give you, as much as you can make use of, spend what you will, but I must be first assured that you are a man without fear, for I do not wish to waste my money on a coward."

"A soldier and fear!" he answered, "when were they ever found together? You can put me to the proof." "Good," replied the stranger, "turn and look behind you." The soldier turned, and saw, trotting towards him, a great bear, growling as it came along. "Ho! ho!" cried he, "I will tickle your nose for you in such a way that you will not want to growl any more," and so saying, he aimed at the bear and shot it through the muzzle, and the animal fell over and did not move again. "I see that you are not wanting in courage," said the stranger, "but there is yet another condition that you will have to fulfil."

"I will consent to anything that does not endanger my salvation," answered the soldier, who was perfectly aware with whom he had to deal. "Otherwise I will have nothing to do with it."

"You shall judge for yourself," continued Greencoat; "during the next seven years you must neither wash, shave, comb your hair, or cut your nails, nor say a paternoster. I will give you a coat and cloak which you must wear the whole time. Should you die before the end of the seven years, you will be mine; but if you survive, you will be a free man, and a rich one, as long as you live." The soldier thought of the great poverty and distress in which he now found himself, and of how often he had before faced death, and he made up his mind to brave it once again, and so gave his consent to the proposed conditions. The Devil then drew off his coat, handed it to the soldier, and said, "When you are wearing this coat, you have only to thrust your hand into the pocket and you will find it full of gold."

He then went and cut off the bear's skin. "This," he said, "is to be your cloak and your bed; on this must you sleep and on no other bed must you lie, and on account of your apparel, you shall be called Bearskin." And with these words the Devil disappeared.

The soldier put on the green coat, thrust his hand at once into the pocket, and found he had not been deceived. Then he threw the bearskin over his shoulders and started again on his travels, but he now enjoyed himself, and denied himself nothing that did him good and his money harm.

In the first year his appearance was tolerable, but in the second year he already looked more like a monster than a man. His face was nearly covered with hair, his beard was like a piece of coarse felt, there were claws at the ends of his fingers, and cress might have been grown in the dirt that had collected on his face. Everyone who saw him fled before him; he was still, however, able to find shelter for himself, for, in whatever place he stayed, he always gave largely to the poor, begging them in return to pray for him, that he might not die before the close of the seven years, and he always paid handsomely for everything he ordered.

It was in the course of the fourth year that he came to an inn, the landlord of which refused to take him in, or even to allow him a place in the stables, for he was afraid that even the horses would take fright.

But when Bearskin put his hand in his pocket and then held it out to him full of gold pieces, the landlord thought better of it, and gave him a room in one of the back parts of the house, making him promise, however, not to let himself be seen, as it would give his house a bad name.

As Bearskin sat alone that evening, wishing with all his heart that the seven years were over, he heard sounds of lamentation in the adjoining room. He was a man of a kind and sympathizing heart, and he therefore went to the door and opened it, and there he saw an old man flinging up his arms in despair and weeping bitterly.

Bearskin stepped nearer, but at first sight of him, the old man sprang up and was about to escape from the room. He paused, however, when he heard a human voice, and finally, so persuasively did Bearskin speak to him, he was induced to disclose the cause of his distress. It seemed that his wealth had diminished more and more, until he and his daughters were now in a state of starvation; he was too poor even to pay the landlord what he owed him, and was threatened with imprisonment. "If that is the extent of your trouble," said Bearskin, "I have money and to spare," and he thereupon sent for the landlord, settled his account, and put a large purse of gold besides into the poor old man's pocket.

When the old man saw himself so wonderfully delivered from his trouble, he did not know how to express his gratitude. "Come home with me," he said to Bearskin. "I have three daughters, all miracles of beauty, choose one of them for your wife. When she hears what you have done for me, she will not refuse you. Your appearance is just a little peculiar, I must confess, but she will soon put all that right for you."

Bearskin was delighted with this proposal and went home with him.

At the first sight of his face, the eldest daughter was so horrified, that she screamed and rushed from the room. The second daughter did not indeed run away, but she looked at him from head to foot, then she spoke and said, "How can I marry a man who has no longer even the semblance of a human being? I would rather have the shaven bear that was on show here once, and gave himself out for a man; he had at least a good soldier's coat and a pair of white gloves. If it were only a matter of ugliness, I might grow accustomed to him." Then the youngest rose and said, "Dear father, the man who has helped you out of your trouble must be a good man, and if you have promised one of us to him as a wife, your word must not be broken." It was a pity that Bearskin's face was just then so covered with dirt and hair, or those present might have seen how the heart within him laughed for joy when he heard those words. He took a ring from his finger, broke it in two, and gave one half to the girl, and kept the other himself. Then he wrote her name in his half, and his own name in hers, begging her at the same time to keep it safely. After this he took his leave. "I must continue my travels for three more years," he said to his betrothed; "if at the end of that time I do not return, you may know that I am dead and that you are free; but pray to God for me that my life may be spared."

The poor young girl clad herself all in black, and whenever she thought of her betrothed husband, her eyes filled with tears. Her sisters treated her to nothing but scorn and derision. "Take care how you offer him your hand," the eldest would say, "for he will give you a blow with his paw." "You must be careful," said the other, "for bears are fond of sweet things, and if he finds you to his taste, he will eat you up." "You must never do anything to irritate him," the eldest would start again, "or he will begin to growl." "But the wedding will be very lively," continued the second, "bears dance so well." The youngest made no answer, and would not allow herself to be put out by these taunts.

Meanwhile Bearskin wandered about from place to place, doing all the good he could, and giving freely to the poor in order that they might pray for him. The last day of the seven years dawned at last. Bearskin went to the heath again, and sat down under the trees. Before long there came a sudden rush of wind, and the same figure stood looking at him as before, but this time it was evident that he was in a very bad humour. He threw his old coat back to Bearskin and asked for his green one.

"We have not come to that part of the business yet," said Bearskin, "you must first make me clean." And whether he liked it or not, the Devil was now obliged to fetch water and wash him, comb his hair, and cut his nails. Bearskin now looked once more like a brave soldier, and was handsomer than he had ever been before.

Having at last said good-bye to the Devil, Bearskin felt like a free man again. Joyful and light-hearted he went into the town, put on a magnificent garment of velvet, ordered a carriage and four horses, and drove to the house of his betrothed. No one of course recognized him; the father took him for some distinguished military officer, and led him into the house and introduced him to his daughters. He was invited to sit down between the two eldest, and they poured him out wine, and offered him the daintiest food, thinking all the while, that they had never before seen such a splendid-looking man. His betrothed sat opposite to him, with her eyes cast down and not speaking a word. When finally he asked the father if he would give him one of his daughters for wife, the two eldest sprang up and ran to their rooms to put on their richest attire, for each felt certain in her own mind that she was the chosen one. As soon as the stranger found himself alone with his betrothed, he drew out his half of the ring, and threw it into a goblet of wine which he then handed across to her. She took it from him and drank, but her heart gave a great throb as she saw the half ring at the bottom. She took her own half, which was hung round her neck by a ribbon, placed it against the other, and saw that the two pieces fitted exactly. Then he spoke and said, "I am your betrothed husband, whom you only saw as Bearskin, but, by the grace of God, my human form is returned to me, and I am clean once more." And saying this he went up to her, and embraced and kissed her. At this moment the sisters returned, clad in gorgeous apparel, but when they saw that it was their youngest sister whom the handsome man had chosen, and were told that he was Bearskin, they were so overcome with rage and envy that they both rushed out of the house, and one of them drowned herself in the well, the other hung herself on a tree.

THE ADVENTURES OF CHANTICLEER AND PARTLET

I

HOW THEY WENT TO THE MOUNTAINS TO EAT NUTS

"THE nuts are quite ripe now," said Chanticleer to his wife Partlet, "suppose we go together to the mountains, and eat as many as we can, before the squirrel takes them all away." "With all my heart," said Partlet, "let us go and make a holiday of it together."

So they went to the mountains; and as it was a lovely day, they stayed there till the evening. Now, whether it was that they had eaten so many nuts that they could not walk, or whether they were lazy and would not, I do not know: however, they took it into their heads that it did not become them to go home on foot. So Chanticleer began to build a little carriage of nutshells: and when it was finished, Partlet jumped into it and sat down, and bid Chanticleer harness himself to it and draw her home. "That's a good joke!" said Chanticleer; "no, that will never do; I had rather by half walk home; I'll sit on the box and be coachman, if you like, but I'll not draw." While this was passing, a duck came quacking up and cried out, "You thieving vagabonds, what business have you in my grounds? I'll give it you well for your insolence!" and upon that she fell upon Chanticleer most lustily. But Chanticleer was no coward, and returned the duck's blows with his sharp spurs so fiercely that she soon began to cry out for mercy; which was only granted her upon condition that she would draw the carriage home for them. This she agreed to do; and Chanticleer got upon the box, and drove, crying, "Now, duck, get on as fast as you can." And away they went at a pretty good pace.

After they had travelled along a little way, they met a needle and a pin walking together along the road: and the needle cried out, "Stop, stop!" and said it was so dark that they could hardly find their way, and such dirty walking they could not get on at all: he told them that he and his friend, the pin, had been at a public-house a few miles off, and had sat drinking till they had forgotten how late it was; he begged therefore that the travellers would be so kind as to give them a lift in their carriage. Chanticleer observing that they were but thin fellows, and not likely to take up much room, told them they might ride, but made them promise not to dirty the wheels of the carriage in getting in, nor to tread on Partlet's toes.

Late at night they arrived at an inn; and as it was bad travelling in the dark, and the duck seemed much tired, and waddled about a good deal from one side to the other, they made up their minds to fix their quarters there: but the landlord at first was unwilling, and said his house was full, thinking they might not be very respectable company: however, they spoke civilly to him, and gave him the egg which Partlet had laid by the way, and said they would give him the duck, who was in the habit of laying one every day: so at last he let them come in, and they bespoke a handsome supper, and spent the evening very jollily.

Early in the morning, before it was quite light, and when nobody was stirring in the inn, Chanticleer awakened his wife, and, fetching the egg, they pecked a hole in it, ate it up, and threw the shells into the fireplace: they then went to the pin and needle, who were fast asleep, and seizing them by the heads, stuck one into the landlord's easy chair and the other into his handkerchief; and, having done this, they crept away as softly as possible. However, the duck, who slept in the open air in the yard, heard them coming, and jumping into the brook which ran close by the inn, soon swam out of their reach.

An hour or two afterwards the landlord got up, and took his handkerchief to wipe his face, but the pin ran into him and pricked him: then he walked into the kitchen to light his pipe at the fire, but when he stirred it up the eggshells flew into his eyes, and almost blinded him. "Bless me!" said he, "all the world seems to have a design against my head this morning": and so saying, he threw himself sulkily into his easy chair; but, oh dear! the needle ran into him; and this time the pain was not in his head. He now flew into a very great passion, and, suspecting the company who had come in the night before, he went to look after them, but they were all off; so he swore that he never again would take in such a troop of vagabonds, who ate a great deal, paid no reckoning, and gave him nothing for his trouble but their apish tricks.

II
HOW CHANTICLEER AND PARTLET WENT TO VISIT MR. KORBES

Another day, Chanticleer and Partlet wished to ride out together; so Chanticleer built a handsome carriage with four red wheels, and harnessed six mice to it; and then he and Partlet got into the carriage, and away they drove. Soon afterwards a cat met them, and said, "Where are you going?" And Chanticleer replied,

"All on our way
A visit to pay
To Mr. Korbes, the fox, today."

Then the cat said, "Take me with you," Chanticleer said, "With all my heart: get up behind, and be sure you do not fall off."

"Take care of this handsome coach of mine,
Nor dirty my pretty red wheels so fine!
  Now, mice, be ready,
  And, wheels, run steady!
For we are going a visit to pay
To Mr. Korbes, the fox, today."

Soon after came up a millstone, an egg, a duck, and a pin; and Chanticleer gave them all leave to get into the carriage and go with them.

When they arrived at Mr. Korbes's house, he was not at home; so the mice drew the carriage into the coach-house, Chanticleer and Partlet flew upon a beam, the cat sat down in the fireplace, the duck got into the washing cistern, the pin stuck himself into the bed pillow, the millstone laid himself over the house door, and the egg rolled himself up in the towel.

When Mr. Korbes came home, he went to the fireplace to make a fire; but the cat threw all the ashes in his eyes: so he ran to the kitchen to wash himself; but there the duck splashed all the water in his face; and when he tried to wipe himself, the egg broke to pieces in the towel all over his face and eyes. Then he was very angry, and went without his supper to bed; but when he laid his head on the pillow, the pin ran into his cheek: at this he became quite furious, and, jumping up, would have run out of the house; but when he came to the door, the millstone fell down on his head, and killed him on the spot.

III
HOW PARTLET DIED AND WAS BURIED, AND HOW CHANTICLEER DIED OF GRIEF

Another day Chanticleer and Partlet agreed to go again to the mountains to eat nuts; and it was settled that all the nuts which they found should be shared equally between them. Now Partlet found a very large nut; but she said nothing about it to Chanticleer, and kept it all to herself: however, it was so big that she could not swallow it, and it stuck in her throat. Then she was in a great fright, and cried out to Chanticleer, "Pray run as fast as you can, and fetch me some water, or I shall be choked." Chanticleer ran as fast as he could to the river, and said, "River, give me some water, for Partlet lies in the mountain, and will be choked by a great nut." The river said, "Run first to the bride, and ask her for a silken cord to draw up the water." Chanticleer ran to the bride, and said, "Bride, you must give me a silken cord, for then the river will give me water, and the water I will carry to Partlet, who lies on the mountain, and will be choked by a great nut." But the bride said, "Run first, and bring me my garland that is hanging on a willow in the garden." Then Chanticleer ran to the garden, and took the garland from the bough where it hung, and brought it to the bride; and then the bride gave him the silken cord, and he took the silken cord to the river, and the river gave him water, and he carried the water to Partlet; but in the meantime she was choked by the great nut, and lay quite dead, and never moved any more.

Then Chanticleer was very sorry, and cried bitterly; and all the beasts came and wept with him over poor Partlet. And six mice built a little hearse to carry her to her grave; and when it was ready they harnessed themselves before it, and Chanticleer drove them. On the way they met the fox. "Where are you going, Chanticleer?" said he. "To bury my Partlet," said the other. "May I go with you?" said the fox. "Yes; but you must get up behind, or my horses will not be able to draw you." Then the fox got up behind; and presently the wolf, the bear, the goat, and all the beasts of the wood, came and climbed upon the hearse.

So on they went till they came to a rapid stream. "How shall we get over?" said Chanticleer. Then said a straw, "I will lay myself across, and you may pass over upon me." But as the mice were going over, the straw slipped away and fell into the water, and the six mice all fell in and were drowned. What was to be done? Then a large log of wood came and said, "I am big enough; I will lay myself across the stream, and you shall pass over upon me." So he laid himself down; but they managed so clumsily, that the log of wood fell in and was carried away by the stream. Then a stone, who saw what had happened, came up and kindly offered to help poor Chanticleer by laying himself across the stream; and this time he got safely to the other side with the hearse, and managed to get Partlet out of it; but the fox and the other mourners, who were sitting behind, were too heavy, and fell back into the water and were all carried away by the stream and drowned.

Thus Chanticleer was left alone with his dead Partlet; and having dug a grave for her, he laid her in it, and made a little hillock over her. Then he sat down by the grave, and wept and mourned, till at last he died too; and so all were dead.

OLD SULTAN

A SHEPHERD had a faithful dog, called Sultan, who was grown very old, and had lost all his teeth. And one day when the shepherd and his wife were standing together before the house the shepherd said, "I will shoot old Sultan tomorrow morning, for he is of no use now." But his wife said, "Pray let the poor faithful creature live; he has served us well a great many years, and we ought to give him a livelihood for the rest of his days." "But what can we do with him?" said the shepherd, "he has not a tooth in his head, and the thieves don't care for him at all; to be sure he has served us, but then he did it to earn his livelihood; tomorrow shall be his last day, depend upon it."

Poor Sultan, who was lying close by them, heard all that the shepherd and his wife said to one another, and was very much frightened to think tomorrow would be his last day; so in the evening he went to his good friend the wolf, who lived in the wood, and told him all his sorrows, and how his master meant to kill him in the morning. "Make yourself easy," said the wolf, "I will give you some good advice. Your master, you know, goes out every morning very early with his wife into the field; and they take their little child with them, and lay it down behind the hedge in the shade while they are at work. Now do you lie down close by the child, and pretend to be watching it, and I will come out of the wood and run away with it; you must run after me as fast as you can, and I will let it drop; then you may carry it back, and they will think you have saved their child, and will be so thankful to you that they will take care of you as long as you live." The dog liked this plan very well; and accordingly so it was managed. The wolf ran with the child a little way; the shepherd and his wife screamed out; but Sultan soon overtook him, and carried the poor little thing back to his master and mistress. Then the shepherd patted him on the head, and said, "Old Sultan has saved our child from the wolf, and therefore he shall live and be well taken care of, and have plenty to eat. Wife, go home, and give him a good dinner, and let him have my old cushion to sleep on as long as he lives." So from this time forward Sultan had all that he could wish for.

Soon afterwards the wolf came and wished him joy, and said, "Now, my good fellow, you must tell no tales, but turn your head the other way when I want to taste one of the old shepherd's fine fat sheep." "No," said the Sultan; "I will be true to my master." However, the wolf thought he was in joke, and came one night to get a dainty morsel. But Sultan had told his master what the wolf meant to do; so he laid wait for him behind the barn door, and when the wolf was busy looking out for a good fat sheep, he had a stout cudgel laid about his back, that combed his locks for him finely.

Then the wolf was very angry, and called Sultan "an old rogue," and swore he would have his revenge. So the next morning the wolf sent the boar to challenge Sultan to come into the wood to fight the matter. Now Sultan had nobody he could ask to be his second but the shepherd's old three-legged cat; so he took her with him, and as the poor thing limped along with some trouble, she stuck up her tail straight in the air.

The wolf and the wild boar were first on the ground; and when they espied their enemies coming, and saw the cat's long tail standing straight in the air, they thought she was carrying a sword for Sultan to fight with; and every time she limped, they thought she was picking up a stone to throw at them; so they said they should not like this way of fighting, and the boar lay down behind a bush, and the wolf jumped up into a tree. Sultan and the cat soon came up, and looked about and wondered that no one was there. The boar, however, had not quite hidden himself, for his ears stuck out of the bush; and when he shook one of them a little, the cat, seeing something move, and thinking it was a mouse, sprang upon it, and bit and scratched it, so that the boar jumped up and grunted, and ran away, roaring out, "Look up in the tree, there sits the one who is to blame." So they looked up, and espied the wolf sitting amongst the branches; and they called him a cowardly rascal, and would not suffer him to come down till he was heartily ashamed of himself, and had promised to be good friends again with old Sultan.

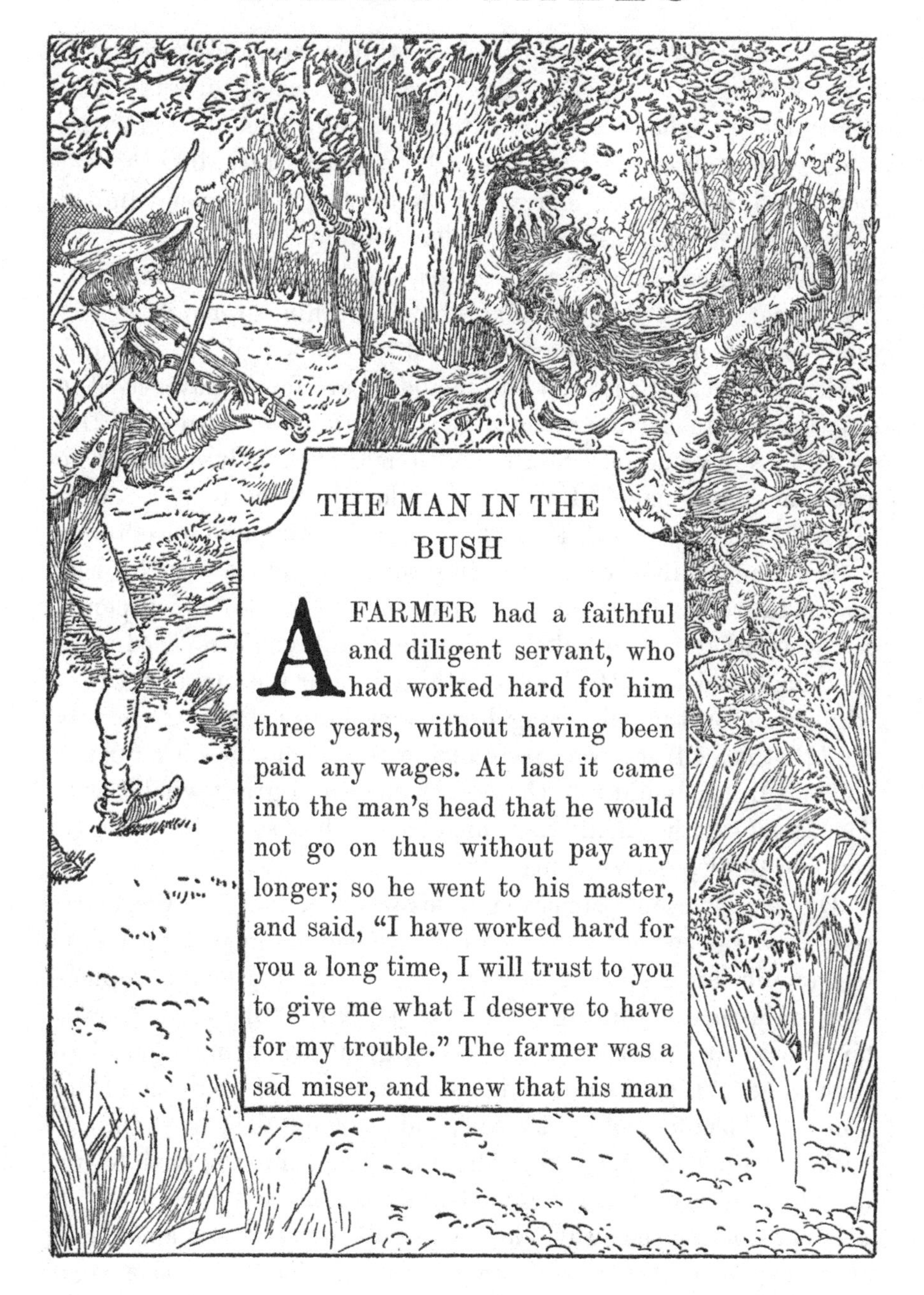

THE MAN IN THE BUSH

A FARMER had a faithful and diligent servant, who had worked hard for him three years, without having been paid any wages. At last it came into the man's head that he would not go on thus without pay any longer; so he went to his master, and said, "I have worked hard for you a long time, I will trust to you to give me what I deserve to have for my trouble." The farmer was a sad miser, and knew that his man was very simple-hearted; so he took out threepence, and gave him for every year's service a penny. The poor fellow thought it was a great deal of money to have, and said to himself, "Why should I work hard, and live here on bad fare any longer? I can now travel into the wide world, and make myself merry." With that he put his money into his purse, and set out, roaming over hill and valley.

As he jogged along over the fields, singing and dancing, a little dwarf met him, and asked him what made him so merry. "Why, what should make me down-hearted?" said he; "I am sound in health and rich in purse, what should I care for? I have saved up my three years' earnings and have it all safe in my pocket." "How much may it come to?" said the little man. "Full threepence," replied the countryman. "I wish you would give them to me," said the other; "I am very poor." Then the man pitied him, and gave him all he had; and the little dwarf said in return, "As you have such a kind honest heart, I will grant you three wishes—one for every penny; so choose whatever you like." Then the countryman rejoiced at his good luck, and said, "I like many things better than money: first, I will have a bow that will bring down everything I shoot at; secondly, a fiddle that will set everyone dancing that hears me play upon it; and thirdly, I should like that everyone should grant what I ask." The dwarf said he should have his three wishes; so he gave him the bow and fiddle, and went his way.

Our honest friend journeyed on his way too; and if he was merry before, he was now ten times more so. He had not gone far before he met an old miser: close by them stood a tree, and on the topmost twig sat a thrush singing away most joyfully. "Oh, what a pretty bird!" said the miser; "I would give a great deal of money to have such a one." "If that's all," said the countryman, "I will soon bring it down." Then he took up his bow, and down fell the thrush into the bushes at the foot of the tree. The miser crept into the bush to find it; but directly he had got into the middle, his companion took up his fiddle and played away, and the miser began to dance and spring about, capering higher and higher in the air. The thorns soon began to tear his clothes till they all hung in rags about him, and he himself was all scratched and wounded, so that the blood ran down. "Oh, for heaven's sake!" cried the miser, "Master! master! pray let the fiddle alone. What have I done to deserve this?" "Thou hast shaved many a poor soul close enough," said the other; "thou art only meeting thy reward": so he played up another tune. Then the miser began to beg and promise, and offered money for his liberty; but he did not come up to the musician's price for some time, and he danced him along brisker and brisker, and the miser bid higher and higher, till at last he offered a round hundred of florins that he had in his purse, and had just gained by cheating some poor fellow. When the countryman saw so much money, he said, "I will agree to your proposal." So he took the purse, put up his fiddle, and travelled on very pleased with his bargain.

Meanwhile the miser crept out of the bush half-naked and in a piteous plight, and began to ponder how he should take his revenge, and serve his late companion some trick. At last he went to the judge, and complained that a rascal had robbed him of his money, and beaten him into the bargain; and that the fellow who did it carried a bow at his back and a fiddle hung round his neck. Then the judge sent out his officers to bring up the accused wherever they should find him; and he was soon caught and brought up to be tried.

The miser began to tell his tale, and said he had been robbed of his money. "No, you gave it me for playing a tune to you." said the countryman; but the judge told him that was not likely, and cut the matter short by ordering him off to the gallows.

So away he was taken; but as he stood on the steps he said, "My Lord Judge, grant me one last request." "Anything but thy life," replied the other. "No," said he, "I do not ask my life; only to let me play upon my fiddle for the last time." The miser cried out, "Oh, no! no! for heaven's sake don't listen to him! don't listen to him!" But the judge said, "It is only this once, he will soon have done." The fact was, he could not refuse the request, on account of the dwarf's third gift.

Then the miser said, "Bind me fast, bind me fast, for pity's sake." But the countryman seized his fiddle, and struck up a tune, and at the first note judge, clerks, and jailer were in motion; all began capering, and no one could hold the miser. At the second note the hangman let his prisoner go, and danced also, and by the time he had played the first bar of the tune, all were dancing together—judge, court, and miser, and all the people who had followed to look on. At first the thing was merry and pleasant enough; but when it had gone on a while, and there seemed to be no end of playing or dancing, they began to cry out, and beg him to leave off; but he stopped not a whit the more for their entreaties, till the judge not only gave him his life, but promised to return him the hundred florins.

Then he called to the miser, and said, "Tell us now, you vagabond, where you got that gold, or I shall play on for your amusement only," "I stole it," said the miser in the presence of all the people; "I acknowledge that I stole it, and that you earned it fairly." Then the countryman stopped his fiddle, and left the miser to take his place at the gallows.

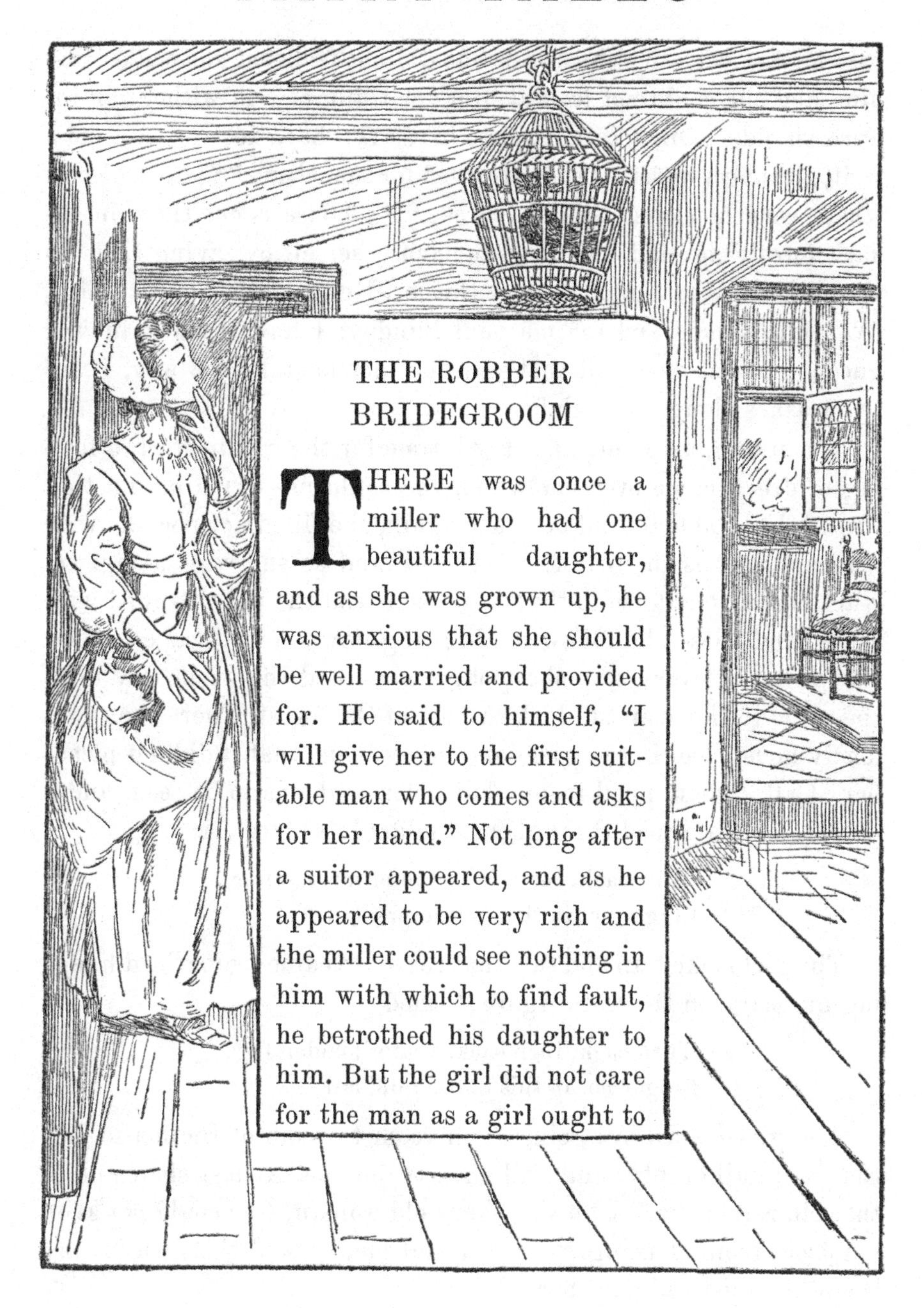

THE ROBBER BRIDEGROOM

THERE was once a miller who had one beautiful daughter, and as she was grown up, he was anxious that she should be well married and provided for. He said to himself, "I will give her to the first suitable man who comes and asks for her hand." Not long after a suitor appeared, and as he appeared to be very rich and the miller could see nothing in him with which to find fault, he betrothed his daughter to him. But the girl did not care for the man as a girl ought to care for her betrothed husband. She did not feel that she could trust him, and she could not look at him nor think of him without an inward shudder. One day he said to her, "You have not yet paid me a visit, although we have been betrothed for some time." "I do not know where your house is," she answered. "My house is out there in the dark forest," he said. She tried to excuse herself by saying that she would not be able to find the way thither. Her betrothed only replied, "You must come and see me next Sunday; I have already invited guests for that day, and that you may not mistake the way, I will strew ashes along the path."

When Sunday came, and it was time for the girl to start, a feeling of dread came over her which she could not explain, and that she might be able to find her path again, she filled her pockets with peas and lentils to sprinkle on the ground as she went along. On reaching the entrance to the forest she found the path strewed with ashes, and these she followed, throwing down some peas on either side of her at every step she took. She walked the whole day until she came to the deepest, darkest part of the forest. There she saw a lonely house, looking so grim and mysterious, that it did not please her at all. She stepped inside, but not a soul was to be seen, and a great silence reigned throughout. Suddenly a voice cried:

"Turn back, turn back, young maiden fair,
Linger not in this murderers' lair."

The girl looked up and saw that the voice came from a bird hanging in a cage on the wall. Again it cried:

"Turn back, turn back, young maiden fair,
Linger not in this murderers' lair."

The girl passed on, going from room to room of the house, but they were all empty, and still she saw no one. At last she came to the cellar, and there sat a very, very old woman, who could not keep her head from shaking. "Can you tell me," asked the girl, "if my betrothed husband lives here?"

"Ah, you poor child," answered the old woman, "what a place for you to come to! This is a murderers' den. You think yourself a promised bride, and that your marriage will soon take place, but it is with death that you will keep your marriage feast. Look, do you see that large cauldron of water which I am obliged to keep on the fire! As soon as they have you in their power they will kill you without mercy, and cook and eat you, for they are eaters of men. If I did not take pity on you and save you, you would be lost."

Thereupon the old woman led her behind a large cask, which quite hid her from view. "Keep as still as a mouse," she said; "do not move or speak, or it will be all over with you. Tonight, when the robbers are all asleep, we will flee together. I have long been waiting for an opportunity to escape."

The words were hardly out of her mouth when the godless crew returned, dragging another young girl along with them. They were all drunk, and paid no heed to her cries and lamentations. They gave her wine to drink, three glasses full, one of white wine, one of red, and one of yellow, and with that her heart gave way and she died. Then they tore off her dainty clothing, laid her on a table, and cut her beautiful body into pieces, and sprinkled salt upon it.

The poor betrothed girl crouched trembling and shuddering behind the cask, for she saw what a terrible fate had been intended for her by the robbers. One of them now noticed a gold ring still remaining on the little finger of the murdered girl, and as he could not draw it off easily, he took a hatchet and cut off the finger; but the finger sprang into the air, and fell behind the cask into the lap of the girl who was hiding there. The robber took a light and began looking for it, but he could not find it. "Have you looked behind the large cask?" said one of the others. But the old woman called out, "Come and eat your suppers, and let the thing be till tomorrow; the finger won't run away."

"The old woman is right," said the robbers, and they ceased looking for the finger and sat down.

The old woman then mixed a sleeping draught with their wine, and before long they were all lying on the floor of the cellar, fast asleep and snoring. As soon as the girl was assured of this, she came from behind the cask. She was obliged to step over the bodies of the sleepers, who were lying close together, and every moment she was filled with renewed dread lest she should awaken them. But God helped her, so that she passed safely over them, and then she and the old woman went upstairs, opened the door, and hastened as fast as they could from the murderers' den. They found the ashes scattered by the wind, but the peas and lentils had sprouted, and grown sufficiently above the ground, to guide them in the moonlight along the path. All night long they walked, and it was morning before they reached the mill. Then the girl told her father all that had happened.

The day came that had been fixed for the marriage. The bridegroom arrived and also a large company of guests, for the miller had taken care to invite all his friends and relations. As they sat at the feast, each guest in turn was asked to tell a tale; the bride sat still and did not say a word.

"And you, my love," said the bridegroom, turning to her, "is there no tale you know? Tell us something."

"I will tell you a dream, then," said the bride. "I went alone through a forest and came at last to a house; not a soul could I find within, but a bird that was hanging in a cage on the wall cried:

"Turn back, turn back, young maiden fair,
Linger not in this murderers' lair."

and again a second time it said these words."

"My darling, this is only a dream."

"I went on through the house from room to room, but they were all empty, and everything was so grim and mysterious. At last I went down to the cellar, and there sat a very, very old woman, who could not keep her head still. I asked her if my betrothed lived here, and she answered, "Ah, you poor child, you are come to a murderers' den; your betrothed does indeed live here, but he will kill you without mercy and afterwards cook and eat you.""

"My darling, this is only a dream."

"The old woman hid me behind a large cask, and scarcely had she done this when the robbers returned home, dragging a young girl along with them. They gave her three kinds of wine to drink, white, red, and yellow, and with that she died."

"My darling, this is only a dream."

"Then they tore off her dainty clothing, and cut her beautiful body into pieces and sprinkled salt upon it."

"My darling, this is only a dream."

"And one of the robbers saw that there was a gold ring still left on her finger, and as it was difficult to draw off, he took a hatchet and cut off her finger; but the finger sprang into the air and fell behind the great cask into my lap. And here is the finger with the ring." And with these words the bride drew forth the finger and shewed it to the assembled guests.

The bridegroom, who during this recital had grown deadly pale, up and tried to escape, but the guests seized him and held him fast. They delivered him up to justice, and he and all his murderous band were condemned to death for their wicked deeds.

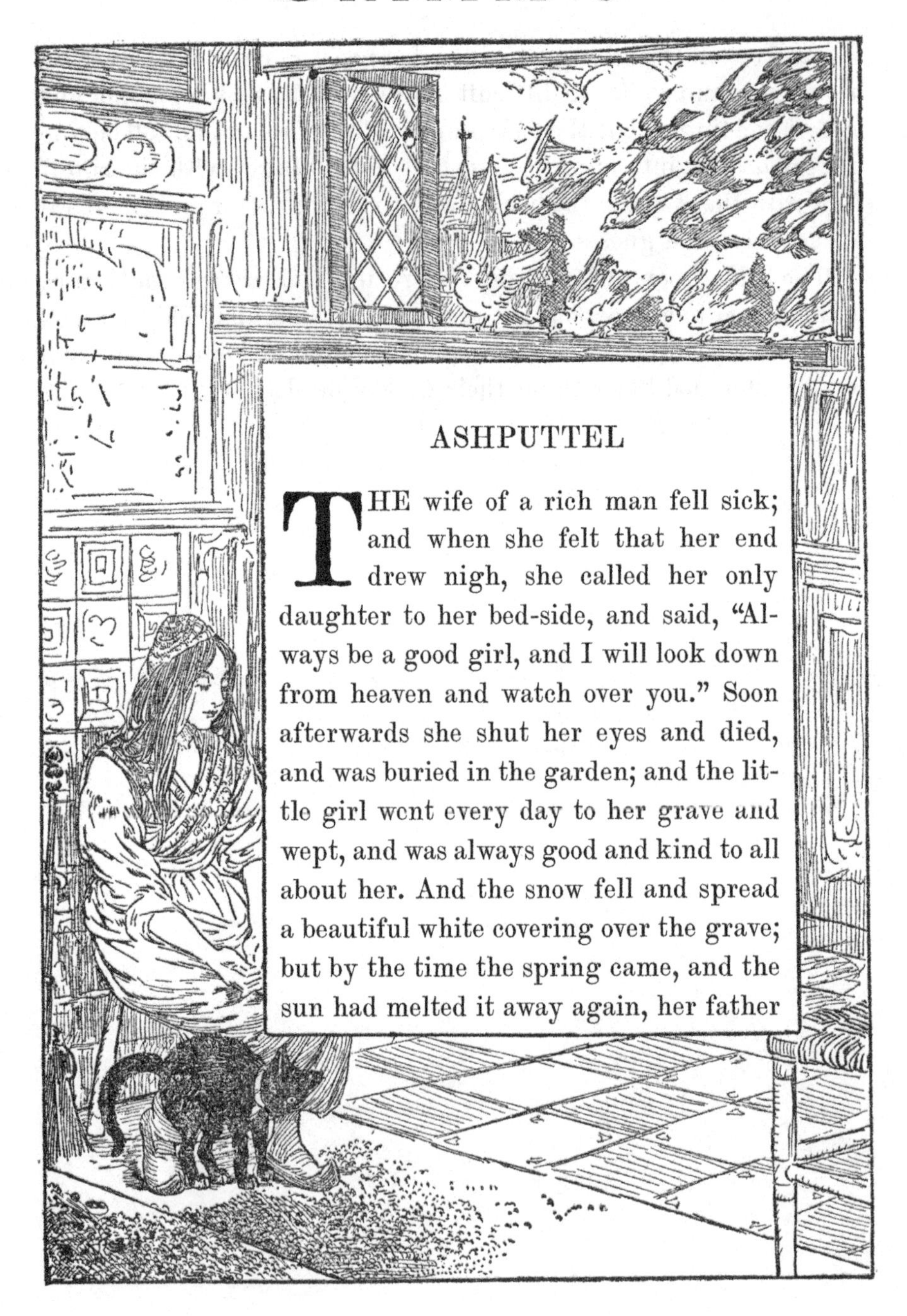

ASHPUTTEL

THE wife of a rich man fell sick; and when she felt that her end drew nigh, she called her only daughter to her bed-side, and said, "Always be a good girl, and I will look down from heaven and watch over you." Soon afterwards she shut her eyes and died, and was buried in the garden; and the little girl went every day to her grave and wept, and was always good and kind to all about her. And the snow fell and spread a beautiful white covering over the grave; but by the time the spring came, and the sun had melted it away again, her father had married another wife. This new wife had two daughters of her own, that she brought home with her; they were fair in face but foul at heart, and it was now a sorry time for the poor little girl. "What does the good-for-nothing want in the parlour?" said they; "they who would eat bread should first earn it; away with the kitchen-maid!" Then they took away her fine clothes, and gave her an old grey frock to put on, and laughed at her, and turned her into the kitchen.

There she was forced to do hard work; to rise early before daylight, to bring the water, to make the fire, to cook and to wash. Besides that, the sisters plagued her in all sorts of ways, and laughed at her. In the evening when she was tired, she had no bed to lie down on, but was made to lie by the hearth among the ashes; and as this, of course, made her always dusty and dirty, they called her Ashputtel.

It happened once that the father was going to the fair, and asked his wife's daughters what he should bring them. "Fine clothes," said the first; "Pearls and diamonds," cried the second. "Now, child," said he to his own daughter, "what will you have?" "The first twig, dear father, that brushes against your hat when you turn your face to come homewards," said she. Then he bought for the first two the fine clothes and pearls and diamonds they had asked for: and on his way home, as he rode through a green copse, a hazel twig brushed against him, and almost pushed off his hat: so he broke it off and brought it away; and when he got home he gave it to his daughter. Then she took it, and went to her mother's grave and planted it there; and cried so much that it was watered with her tears; and there it grew and became a fine tree. Three times every day she went to it and cried; and soon a little bird came and built its nest upon the tree, and talked with her, and watched over her, and brought her whatever she wished for.

Now it happened that the king of that land held a feast, which was to last three days; and out of those who came to it his son was to choose a bride for himself. Ashputtel's two sisters were asked to come; so they called her up, and said, "Now, comb our hair, brush our shoes, and tie our sashes for us, for we are going to dance at the king's feast." Then she did as she was told; but when all was done she could not help crying, for she thought to herself, she should so have liked to have gone with them to the ball; and at last she begged her mother very hard to let her go. "You, Ashputtel!" said she; "you who have nothing to wear, no clothes at all, and who cannot even dance—you want to go to the ball? And when she kept on begging, she said at last, to get rid of her, "I will throw this dishful of peas into the ash-heap, and if in two hours' time you have picked them all out, you shall go to the feast too."

Then she threw the peas down among the ashes, but the little maiden ran out at the back door into the garden, and cried out:

"Hither, hither, through the sky,
Turtle-doves and linnets, fly!
Blackbird, thrush, and chaffinch gay,
Hither, hither, haste away!
One and all come help me, quick!
Haste ye, haste ye!—pick, pick, pick!"

Then first came two white doves, flying in at the kitchen window; next came two turtle-doves; and after them came all the little birds under heaven, chirping and fluttering in: and they flew down into the ashes. And the little doves stooped their heads down and set to work, pick, pick, pick; and then the others began to pick, pick, pick: and among them all they soon picked out all the good grain, and put it into a dish but left the ashes. Long before the end of the hour the work was quite done, and all flew out again at the windows.

Then Ashputtel brought the dish to her mother, overjoyed at the thought that now she should go to the ball. But the mother said, "No, no! you slut, you have no clothes, and cannot dance; you shall not go." And when Ashputtel begged very hard to go, she said, "If you can in one hour's time pick two of those dishes of peas out of the ashes, you shall go too." And thus she thought she should at least get rid of her. So she shook two dishes of peas into the ashes.

But the little maiden went out into the garden at the back of the house, and cried out as before:

"Hither, hither, through the sky,
Turtle-doves and linnets, fly!
Blackbird, thrush, and chaffinch gay,
Hither, hither, haste away!
One and all come help me, quick!
Haste ye, haste ye!—pick, pick, pick!"

Then first came two white doves in at the kitchen window; next came two turtle-doves; and after them came all the little birds under heaven, chirping and hopping about. And they flew down into the ashes; and the little doves put their heads down and set to work, pick, pick, pick; and then the others began pick, pick, pick; and they put all the good grain into the dishes, and left all the ashes. Before half an hour's time all was done, and out they flew again. And then Ashputtel took the dishes to her mother, rejoicing to think that she should now go to the ball. But her mother said, "It is all of no use, you cannot go; you have no clothes, and cannot dance, and you would only put us to shame": and off she went with her two daughters to the ball.

Now when all were gone, and nobody left at home, Ashputtel went sorrowfully and sat down under the hazel-tree, and cried out:

"Shake, shake, hazel-tree,
Gold and silver over me!"

Then her friend the bird flew out of the tree, and brought a gold and silver dress for her, and slippers of spangled silk; and she put them on, and followed her sisters to the feast. But they did not know her, and thought it must be some strange princess, she looked so fine and beautiful in her rich clothes; and they never once thought of Ashputtel, taking it for granted that she was safe at home in the dirt.

The king's son soon came up to her, and took her by the hand and danced with her, and no one else: and he never left her hand; but when anyone else came to ask her to dance, he said, "This lady is dancing with me."

Thus they danced till a late hour of the night; and then she wanted to go home: and the king's son said, "I shall go and take care of you to your home"; for he wanted to see where the beautiful maiden lived. But she slipped away from him, unawares, and ran off towards home; and as the prince followed her, she jumped up into the pigeon-house and shut the door. Then he waited till her father came home, and told him that the unknown maiden, who had been at the feast, had hid herself in the pigeon-house. But when they had broken open the door they found no one within; and as they came back into the house, Ashputtel was lying, as she always did, in her dirty frock by the ashes, and her dim little lamp was burning in the chimney. For she had run as quickly as she could through the pigeon-house and on to the hazel-tree, and had there taken off her beautiful clothes, and put them beneath the tree, that the bird might carry them away, and had lain down again amid the ashes in her little grey frock.

The next day when the feast was again held, and her father, mother, and sisters were gone, Ashputtel went to the hazel-tree, and said:

"Shake, shake, hazel-tree,
Gold and silver over me!"

And the bird came and brought a still finer dress than the one she had worn the day before. And when she came in it to the ball, everyone wondered at her beauty: but the king's son, who was waiting for her, took her by the hand, and danced with her; and when anyone asked her to dance, he said as before, "This lady is dancing with me."

When night came she wanted to go home; and the king's son followed here as before, that he might see into what house she went: but she sprang away from him all at once into the garden behind her father's house. In this garden stood a fine large pear-tree full of ripe fruit; and Ashputtel, not knowing where to hide herself, jumped up into it without being seen. Then the king's son lost sight of her, and could not find out where she was gone, but waited till her father came home, and said to him, "The unknown lady who danced with me has slipped away, and I think she must have sprung into the pear-tree." The father thought to himself, "Can it be Ashputtel?" So he had an axe brought; and they cut down the tree, but found no one upon it. And when they came back into the kitchen, there lay Ashputtel among the ashes; for she had slipped down on the other side of the tree, and carried her beautiful clothes back to the bird at the hazel-tree, and then put on her little grey frock.

The third day, when her father and mother and sisters were gone, she went again into the garden, and said:

"Shake, shake, hazel-tree,
Gold and silver over me!"

Then her kind friend the bird brought a dress still finer than the former one, and slippers which were all of gold: so that when she

ASHPUTTEL PUT ON THE GOLDEN SLIPPER

came to the feast no one knew what to say, for wonder at her beauty: and the king's son danced with nobody but her; and when anyone else asked her to dance, he said, "This lady is *my* partner, sir."

When night came she wanted to go home; and the king's son would go with her, and said to himself, "I will not lose her this time"; but, however, she again slipped away from him, though in such a hurry that she dropped her left golden slipper upon the stairs.

The prince took the shoe, and went the next day to the king his father, and said, "I will take for my wife the lady that this golden slipper fits." Then both the sisters were overjoyed to hear it; for they had beautiful feet, and had no doubt that they could wear the golden slipper. The eldest went first into the room where the slipper was, and wanted to try it on, and the mother stood by. But her great toe could not go into it, and the shoe was altogether much too small for her. Then the mother gave her a knife, and said, "Never mind, cut it off; when you are queen you will not care about toes; you will not want to walk." So the silly girl cut off her great toe, and thus squeezed on the shoe, and went to the king's son. Then he took her for his bride, and set her beside him on his horse, and rode away with her homewards.

But on their way home they had to pass by the hazel-tree that Ashputtel had planted; and on the branch sat a little dove singing:

> "Back again! back again! look to the shoe!
> The shoe is too small, and not made for you!
> Prince! prince! look again for thy bride,
> For she's not the true one that sits by thy side."

Then the prince got down and looked at her foot; and he saw, by the blood that streamed from it, what a trick she had played him. So he turned his horse round, and brought the false bride back to her home, and said, "This is not the right bride; let the other sister try and put on the slipper." Then she went into the room and got her foot into the shoe, all but the heel, which was too large. But her mother squeezed it in till the blood came, and took her to the king's son: and he set her as his bride by his side on his horse, and rode away with her.

But when they came to the hazel-tree the little dove sat there still, and sang:

"Back again! back again! look to the shoe!
The shoe is too small, and not made for you!
Prince! prince! look again for thy bride,
For she's not the true one that sits by thy side."

Then he looked down, and saw that the blood streamed so much from the shoe, that her white stockings were quite red. So he turned his horse and brought her also back again. "This is not the true bride," said he to the father; "have you no other daughters?" "No," said he; "there is only a little dirty Ashputtel here, the child of my first wife; I am sure she cannot be the bride." The prince told him to send her. But the mother said, "No, no, she is much too dirty; she will not dare to show herself." However, the prince would have her come; and she first washed her face and hands, and then went in and curtsied to him, and he reached her the golden slipper. Then she took her clumsy shoe off her left foot, and put on the golden slipper; and it fitted her as if it had been made for her. And when he drew near and looked at her face he knew her, and said, "This is the right bride." But the mother and both the sisters were frightened, and turned pale with anger as he took Ashputtel on his horse, and rode away with her. And when they came to the hazel-tree, the white dove sang:

"Home! home! look at the shoe!
Princess! the shoe was made for you!
Prince! prince! take home thy bride,
For she is the true one that sits by thy side!"

And when the dove had done its song, it came flying, and perched upon her right shoulder, and so went home with her.

THE THREE SPINNING FAIRIES

THERE was once a girl who was lazy and would not spin, and her mother could not persuade her to it, do what she would. At last the mother became angry and out of patience, and gave her a good beating, so that she cried out loudly. At that moment the Queen was going by; as she heard the crying, she stopped; and, going into the house, she asked the mother why she was beating her daughter, so that every one outside in the street could hear her cries.

The woman was ashamed to tell of her daughter's laziness, so she said,

"I cannot stop her from spinning; she is for ever at it, and I am poor and cannot furnish her with flax enough."

Then the Queen answered,

"I like nothing better than the sound of the spinning-wheel, and always feel happy when I hear its humming; let me take your daughter with me to the castle—I have plenty of flax, she shall spin there to her heart's content."

The mother was only too glad of the offer, and the Queen took the girl with her. When they reached the castle the Queen showed her three rooms which were filled with the finest flax as full as they could hold.

"Now you can spin me this flax," said she, "and when you can show it me all done you shall have my eldest son for bridegroom; you may be poor, but I make nothing of that—your industry is dowry enough."

The girl was inwardly terrified, for she could not have spun the flax, even if she were to live to be a hundred years old, and were to sit spinning every day of her life from morning to evening. And when she found herself alone she began to weep, and sat so for three days without putting her hand to it. On the third day the Queen came, and when she saw that nothing had been done of the spinning she was much surprised; but the girl excused herself by saying that she had not been able to begin because of the distress she was in at leaving her home and her mother. The excuse contented the Queen, who said, however, as she went away,

"To-morrow you must begin to work."

When the girl found herself alone again she could not tell how to help herself or what to do, and in her perplexity she went and gazed out of the window. There she saw three women passing by, and the first of them had a broad flat foot, the second had a big under-lip that hung down over her chin, and the third had a remarkably broad thumb. They all of them stopped in front of the window, and called out to know what it was that the girl wanted. She told them all her need, and they promised her their help, and said,

"Then will you invite us to your wedding, and not be ashamed of us, and call us your cousins, and let us sit at your table; if you will promise this, we will finish off your flax-spinning in a very short time."

"With all my heart," answered the girl; "only come in now, and begin at once."

Then these same women came in, and she cleared a space in the first room for them to sit and carry on their spinning. The first one drew out the thread and moved the treddle that turned the wheel, the second moistened the thread, the third twisted it, and rapped with her finger on the table, and as often as she rapped a heap of yarn fell to the ground, and it was most beautifully spun. But the girl hid the three spinsters out of the Queen's sight, and only showed her, as often as she came, the heaps of well-spun yarn; and there was no end to the praises she received. When the first room was empty they went on to the second, and then to the third, so that at last all was finished. Then the three women took their leave, saying to the girl,

"Do not forget what you have promised, and it will be all the better for you."

So when the girl took the Queen and showed her the empty rooms, and the great heaps of yarn, the wedding was at once arranged, and the bridegroom rejoiced that he should have so clever and diligent a wife, and praised her exceedingly.

"I have three cousins," said the girl, "and as they have shown me a great deal of kindness, I would not wish to forget them in my good fortune; may I be allowed to invite them to the wedding, and to ask them to sit at the table with us?"

The Queen and the bridegroom said at once,

"There is no reason against it."

So when the feast began in came the three spinsters in strange guise, and the bride said,

"Dear cousins, you are welcome."

"Oh," said the bridegroom, "how come you to have such dreadfully ugly relations?"

And then he went up to the first spinster and said,

"How is it that you have such a broad flat foot?"

"With treading," answered she, "with treading."

Then he went up to the second and said,

"How is it that you have such a great hanging lip?"

"With licking," answered she, "with licking."

Then he asked the third,

"How is it that you have such a broad thumb?"

"With twisting thread," answered she, "with twisting thread."

Then the bridegroom said that from that time forward his beautiful bride should never touch a spinning-wheel.

And so she escaped that tiresome flax-spinning.

RUMPELSTILTSKIN

BY the side of a wood, in a country a long way off, ran a fine stream of water; and upon the stream there stood a mill. The miller's house was close by, and the miller, you must know, had a very beautiful daughter. She was, moreover, very shrewd and clever; and the miller was so proud of her, that he one day told the king of the land, who used to come and hunt in the wood, that his daughter could spin gold out of straw. Now this king was very fond of money; and when he heard the miller's boast his greediness was raised, and he sent for the girl to be brought before him. Then he led her to a chamber in his palace where there was a great heap of straw, and gave her a spinning-wheel, and said, "All this must be spun into gold before morning, as you love your life." It was in vain that the poor maiden said that it was only a silly boast of her father, for that she could do no such thing as spin straw into gold: the chamber door was locked, and she was left alone.

She sat down in one corner of the room, and began to bewail her hard fate; when on a sudden the door opened, and a droll-looking little man hobbled in, and said, "Good morrow to you, my good lass; what are you weeping for?" "Alas!" said she, "I must spin this straw into gold, and I know not how." "What will you give me," said the hobgoblin, "to do it for you?" "My necklace," replied the maiden. He took her at her word, and sat himself down to the wheel, and whistled and sang:

"Round about, round about,
Lo and behold!
Reel away, reel away,
Straw into gold!"

And round about the wheel went merrily; the work was quickly done, and the straw was all spun into gold.

When the king came and saw this, he was greatly astonished and pleased; but his heart grew still more greedy of gain, and he shut up the poor miller's daughter again with a fresh task. Then she knew not what to do, and sat down once more to weep; but the dwarf soon opened the door, and said, "What will you give me to do your task?" "The ring on my finger," said she. So her little friend took the ring, and began to work at the wheel again, and whistled and sang:

"Round about, round about,
Lo and behold!
Reel away, reel away,
Straw into gold!"

till, long before morning, all was done again.

The king was greatly delighted to see all this glittering treasure; but still he had not enough: so he took the miller's daughter to a yet larger heap, and said, "All this must be spun tonight; and if it is, you shall be my queen." As soon as she was alone that dwarf came in, and said, "What will you give me to spin gold for you this third time?" "I have nothing left," said she. "Then say you will give me," said the little man, "the first little child that you may have when you are queen." "That may never be," thought the miller's daughter: and as she knew no other way to get her task done, she said she would do what he asked. Round went the wheel again to the old song, and the manikin once more spun the heap into gold. The king came in the morning, and, finding all he wanted, was forced to keep his word; so he married the miller's daughter, and she really became queen.

At the birth of her first little child she was very glad, and forgot the dwarf, and what she had said. But one day he came into her room, where she was sitting playing with her baby, and put her in mind of it. Then she grieved sorely at her misfortune, and said she would give him all the wealth of the kingdom if he would let her off,

"WHAT WILL YOU GIVE ME TO DO IT FOR YOU!" SAID THE HOBGOBLIN

but in vain; till at last her tears softened him, and he said, "I will give you three days' grace, and if during that time you tell me my name, you shall keep your child."

Now the queen lay awake all night, thinking of all the odd names that she had ever heard; and she sent messengers all over the land to find out new ones. The next day the little man came, and she began with TIMOTHY, ICHABOD, BENJAMIN, JEREMIAH, and all the names she could remember; but to all and each of them he said, "Madam, that is not my name."

The second day she began with all the comical names she could hear of, BANDY-LEGS, HUNCHBACK, CROOK-SHANKS, and so on; but the little gentleman still said to every one of them, "Madam, that is not my name."

The third day one of the messengers came back, and said, "I have travelled two days without hearing of any other names; but yesterday, as I was climbing a high hill, among the trees of the forest where the fox and the hare bid each other good night, I saw a little hut; and before the hut burnt a fire; and round about the fire a funny little dwarf was dancing upon one leg, and singing:

"Merrily the feast I'll make.
Today I'll brew, tomorrow bake;
Merrily I'll dance and sing,
For next day will a stranger bring.
Little does my lady dream
Rumpelstiltskin is my name!"

When the queen heard this she jumped for joy, and as soon as her little friend came she sat down upon her throne, and called all her court round to enjoy the fun; and the nurse stood by her side with the baby in her arms, as if it was quite ready to be given up. Then the little man began to chuckle at the thought of having the poor child, to take home with him to his hut in the woods; and he cried out, "Now, lady, what is my name?" "Is it JOHN?" asked she. "No, madam!" "Is it TOM?" "No, madam!" "Is it JEMMY?" "It is not." "Can your name be RUMPELSTILTSKIN?" said the lady slyly. "Some witch told you that!—some witch told you that!" cried the little man, and dashed his right foot in a rage so deep into the floor, that he was forced to lay hold of it with both hands to pull it out.

Then he made the best of his way off, while the nurse laughed and the baby crowed; and all the court jeered at him for having had so much trouble for nothing, and said, "We wish you a very good morning, and a merry feast, Mr. RUMPLESTILTSKIN!"

MOTHER HOLLE

ONCE upon a time there was a widow who had two daughters; one of them was beautiful and industrious, the other ugly and lazy. The mother, however, loved the ugly and lazy one best, because she was her own daughter, and so the other, who was only her stepdaughter, was made to do all the work of the house, and was quite the Cinderella of the family. Her stepmother sent her out every day to sit by the well in the high road, there to spin until she made her fingers bleed. Now it chanced one day that some blood fell on to the spindle, and as the girl stopped over the well to wash it off, the spindle suddenly sprang out of her hand and fell into the well. She ran home crying to tell of her misfortune, but her stepmother spoke harshly to her, and after giving her a violent scolding, said unkindly, "As you have let the spindle fall into the well you may go yourself and fetch it out."

The girl went back to the well not knowing what to do, and at last in her distress she jumped into the water after the spindle.

She remembered nothing more until she awoke and found herself in a beautiful meadow, full of sunshine, and with countless flowers blooming in every direction.

She walked over the meadow, and presently she came upon a baker's oven full of bread, and the loaves cried out to her, "Take us out, take us out, or alas! we shall be burnt to a cinder; we were baked through long ago." So she took the bread-shovel and drew them all out.

She went on a little farther, till she came to a tree full of apples. "Shake me, shake me, I pray," cried the tree; "my apples, one and all, are ripe." So she shook the tree, and the apples came falling down upon her like rain; but she continued shaking until there was not a single apple left upon it. Then she carefully gathered the apples together in a heap and walked on again.

The next thing she came to was a little house, and there she saw an old woman looking out, with such large teeth, that she was terrified, and turned to run away. But the old woman called after her, "What are you afraid of, dear child? Stay with me; if you will do the work of my house properly for me, I will make you very happy. You must be very careful, however, to make my bed in the right way, for I wish you always to shake it thoroughly, so that the feathers fly about; then they say, down there in the world, that it is snowing; for I am Mother Holle." The old woman spoke so kindly, that the girl summoned up courage and agreed to enter into her service.

She took care to do everything according to the old woman's bidding and every time she made the bed she shook it with all her might, so that the feathers flew about like so many snowflakes. The old woman was as good as her word: she never spoke angrily to her, and gave her roast and boiled meats every day.

So she stayed on with Mother Holle for some time, and then she began to grow unhappy. She could not at first tell why she felt sad, but she became conscious at last of great longing to go home; then she knew she was homesick, although she was a thousand times better off with Mother Holle than with her mother and sister. After waiting awhile, she went to Mother Holle and said, "I am so homesick, that I cannot stay with you any longer, for although I am so happy here, I must return to my own people."

Then Mother Holle said, "I am pleased that you should want to go back to your own people, and as you have served me so well and faithfully, I will take you home myself."

Thereupon she led the girl by the hand up to a broad gateway. The gate was opened, and as the girl passed through, a shower of gold fell upon her, and the gold clung to her, so that she was covered with it from head to foot.

"That is a reward for your industry," said Mother Holle, and as she spoke she handed her the spindle which she had dropped into the well.

The gate was then closed, and the girl found herself back in the old world close to her mother's house. As she entered the courtyard, the cock who was perched on the well, called out:

"Cock-a-doodle-doo!
Your golden daughter's come back to you."

Then she went in to her mother and sister, and as she was so richly covered with gold, they gave her a warm welcome. She related to them all that had happened, and when the mother heard how she had come by her great riches, she thought she should like her ugly, lazy daughter to go and try her fortune. So she made the sister go and sit by the well and spin, and the girl pricked her finger and thrust her hand into a thorn-bush, so that she might drop some blood on to the spindle; then she threw it into the well, and jumped in herself.

Like her sister she awoke in the beautiful meadow, and walked over it till she came to the oven. "Take us out, take us out, or alas! we shall be burnt to a cinder; we were baked through long ago," cried the loaves as before. But the lazy girl answered, "Do you think I am going to dirty my hands for you?" and walked on.

Presently she came to the apple-tree. "Shake me, shake me, I pray; my apples, one and all, are ripe," it cried. But she only answered, "A nice thing to ask me to do, one of the apples might fall on my head," and passed on.

At last she came to Mother Holle's house, and as she had heard all about the large teeth from her sister, she was not afraid of them, and engaged herself without delay to the old woman.

The first day she was very obedient and industrious, and exerted herself to please Mother Holle, for she thought of the gold she should get in return. The next day, however, she began to dawdle over her work, and the third day she was more idle still; then she began to lie in bed in the mornings and refused to get up. Worse still, she neglected to make the old woman's bed properly, and forgot to shake it so that the feathers might fly about. So Mother Holle very soon got tired of her, and told her she might go. The lazy girl was delighted at this, and thought to herself, "The gold will soon be mine." Mother Holle led her, as she had led her sister, to the broad gateway; but as she was passing through, instead of the shower of gold, a great bucketful of pitch came pouring over her.

"That is in return for your services," said the old woman, and she shut the gate.

So the lazy girl had to go home covered with pitch, and the cock on the well called out as she saw her:

> "Cock-a-doodle-doo!
> Your dirty daughter's come back to you."

But, try what she would, she could not get the pitch off and it stuck to her as long as she lived.

THE NOSE-TREE

DID you ever hear the story of the three poor soldiers, who, after having fought hard in the wars, set out on their road home, begging their way as they went?

They had journeyed on a long way, sick at heart with their bad luck at thus being turned loose on the world in their old days; when one evening they reached a deep gloomy wood, through which lay their road. Night came fast upon them, and they found that they must, however unwillingly, sleep in this wood; so, to make all as safe as they could, it was agreed that two should lie down and sleep, while a third sat up and watched, lest wild beasts should break in and tear them to pieces. When he was tired he was to wake one of the others, and sleep in his turn; and so on with the third, so as to share the work fairly among them.

The two who were to rest first soon lay down and fell fast asleep; and the other made himself a good fire under the trees, and sat down by its side to keep watch. He had not sat long before, all on a sudden, up came a little dwarf in a red jacket. "Who is there?" said he. "A friend," said the soldier. "What sort of a friend?" "An old broken soldier," said the other, "with his two comrades, who have nothing left to live on; come, sit down and warm yourself." "Well, my worthy fellow," said the little man, "I will do what I can for you; take this and show it to your comrades in the morning." So he took out an old cloak and gave it to the soldier; telling him, that whenever he put it over his shoulders anything that he wished for would be done for him. Then the little man made him a bow and walked away.

The second soldier's turn to watch soon came, and the first laid him down to sleep; but the second man had not sat by himself long before up came the dwarf in the red jacket again. The soldier treated him in as friendly a way as his comrade had done, and the little man gave him a purse, which he told him would be always full of gold, let him draw as much as he would out of it.

Then the third soldier's turn to watch came; and he also had little Red-jacket for his guest, who gave him a wonderful horn, that drew crowds around it whenever it was played, and made every one forget his business to come and dance to its beautiful music.

In the morning each told his story, and showed the gift he had got from the elf: and as they all liked each other very much, and were old friends, they agreed to travel together to see the world, and, for a while, only to make use of the wonderful purse. And thus they spent their time very joyously; till at last they began to be tired of this roving life, and thought they should like to have a home of their own. So the first soldier put his old cloak on, and wished for a fine castle. In a moment it stood before their eyes: fine gardens and green lawns spread round it, and flocks of sheep, and goats, and herds of oxen were grazing about; and out of the gate came a grand coach with three dapple-grey horses, to meet them and bring them home.

All this was very well for a time, but they found it would not do to stay at home always; so they got together all their rich clothes, and jewels, and money, and ordered their coach with three dapple-grey horses, and set out on a journey to see a neighboring king. Now this king had an only daughter, and as he saw the three soldiers travelling in such grand style, he took them for kings' sons, and so gave them a kind welcome. One day, as the second soldier was walking with the princess, she saw that he had the wonderful purse in his hand. Then she asked him what it was, and he was foolish enough to tell her,—though, indeed, it did not much signify what he said, for she was a fairy, and knew all the wonderful things that the three soldiers brought. Now this princess was very cunning and artful; so she set to work and made a purse, so like the soldier's that no one would know one from the other; and then she asked him to come and see her, and made him drink some wine that she had got ready for him, and which soon made him fall fast asleep. Then she felt in his pocket, and took away the wonderful purse, and left the one she had made in its place.

The next morning the soldiers set out home; and soon after they reached their castle, happening to want some money, they went to their purse for it, and found something indeed in it; but to their great sorrow, when they had emptied it, none came in the place of what they took. Then the cheat was soon found out; for the second soldier knew where he had been, and how he had told the story to the princess, and he guessed that she had played him a trick. "Alas!" cried he, "poor wretches that we are, what shall we do?" "Oh!" said the first soldier, "let no grey hairs grow for this mishap: I will soon get the purse back." So he threw his cloak across his shoulders, and wished himself in the princess's chamber.

There he found her sitting alone, telling up her gold, that fell around her in a shower from the wonderful purse.

But the soldier stood looking at her too long; for she turned round, and the moment she saw him she started up and cried out with all her force, "Thieves! thieves!" so that the whole court came running in, and tried to seize on him. The poor soldier now began to be dreadfully frightened in his turn, and thought it was high time to make the best of his way off; so, without thinking of the ready way of travelling that his cloak gave him, he ran to the window, opened it, and jumped out; and unluckily, in his haste, his cloak caught and was left hanging, to the great joy of the princess, who knew its worth.

The poor soldier made the best of his way home to his comrades on foot, and in a very downcast mood; but the third soldier told him to keep up his heart, and took his horn and blew a merry tune. At the first blast a countless troop of foot and horse come rushing to their aid, and they set out to make war against their enemy. Then the king's palace was besieged, and he was told that he must give up the purse and cloak, or that not one stone should be left upon another. And the king went into his daughter's chamber and talked with her; but she said, "Let me try first if I cannot beat them some way or another." So she thought of a cunning scheme to overreach them; and dressing herself out as a poor girl, with a basket on her arm, she set out by night with her maid, and went into the enemy's camp, as if she wanted to sell trinkets.

In the morning she began to ramble about, singing ballads so beautifully that all the tents were left empty, and the soldiers ran round in crowds, and thought of nothing but hearing her sing. Amongst the rest came the soldier to whom the horn belonged, and as soon as she saw him she winked to her maid, who slipped slily through the crowd, and went into his tent where it hung, and stole it away. This done, they both got safely back to the palace, the besieging army went away, the three wonderful gifts were all left in the hands of the princess, and the three soldiers were as penniless and forlorn as when little Red-jacket found them in the wood.

Poor fellows! they began to think what was now to be done. "Comrades," at last said the second soldier, who had had the purse, "we had better part; we cannot live together, let each seek his bread as well as he can." So he turned to the right, and the other two went to the left, for they said they would rather travel together. Then on the second soldier strayed till he came to a wood (now this was the same wood where they had met with so much good luck before), and he walked on a long time till evening began to fall, when he sat down tired beneath a tree, and soon fell asleep.

Morning dawned, and he was greatly delighted, at opening his eyes, to see that the tree was laden with the most beautiful apples. He was hungry enough, so he soon plucked and ate first one, then a second, then a third apple. A strange feeling came over his nose: when he put the apple to his mouth something was in the way. He felt it—it was his nose, that grew and grew till it hung down to his breast. It did not stop there—still it grew and grew. "Heavens!" thought he, "When will it have done growing?" And well might he ask, for by this time it reached the ground as he sat on the grass,—and thus it kept creeping on, till he could not bear its weight or raise himself up; and it seemed as if it would never end, for already it stretched its enormous length all through the wood, over hill and dale.

SO THEY TRACED IT UP, TILL AT LAST THEY FOUND THEIR POOR COMRADE

Meantime his comrades were journeying on, till on a sudden one of them stumbled against something. "What can that be?" said the other. They looked, and could think of nothing that it was like but a nose. "We will follow it and find its owner, however," said they. So they traced it up, till at last they found their poor comrade, lying stretched along under the apple-tree.

What was to be done? They tried to carry him, but in vain. They caught an ass that was passing, and raised him upon its back; but it was soon tired of carrying such a load. So they sat down in despair, when before long up came their old friend the dwarf with the red jacket. "Why, how now, friend?" said he, laughing: "well, I must find a cure for you, I see." So he told them to gather a pear from another tree that grew close by, and the nose would come right again. No time was lost; and the nose was soon brought to its proper size, to the poor soldier's Joy.

"I will do something more for you yet," said the dwarf; "take some of those pears and apples with you; whoever eats one of the apples will have his nose grow like yours just now; but if you give him a pear, all will come right again. Go to the princess, and get her to eat some of your apples; her nose will grow twenty times as long as yours did: then look sharp, and you will get what you want from her."

Then they thanked their old friend very heartily for all his kindness; and it was agreed that the poor soldier, who had already tried the power of the apple, should undertake the task. So he dressed himself up as a gardener's boy, and went to the king's palace, and said he had apples to sell, so fine and so beautiful as were never seen there before. Every one that saw them was delighted, and wanted to taste; but he said they were only for the princess; and she soon sent her maid to buy his stock. They were so ripe and rosy that she soon began eating; and had not eaten above a dozen before she too began to wonder what ailed her nose, for it grew and grew down to the ground, out at the window, and over the garden, and away, nobody knows where.

Then the king made known to all his kingdom, that whoever would heal her of this dreadful disease should be richly rewarded. Many tried, but the princess got no relief. And now the old soldier dressed himself up very sprucely as a doctor, and said he could cure her. So he chopped up some of the apple, and, to punish her a little more, gave her a doze, saying he would call to-morrow and see her again. The morrow came, and, of course, instead of being better, the nose had been growing on all night as before; and the poor princess was in a dreadful fright. So the doctor then chopped up a very little of the pear and gave her, and said he was sure that would do good, and he would call again the next day. Next day came, and the nose was to be sure a little smaller, but yet it was bigger than when the doctor first began to meddle with it.

Then he thought to himself, "I must frighten this cunning princess a little more before I shall get what I want from her"; so he gave her another doze of the apple, and said he would call on the morrow. The morrow came, and the nose was ten times as bad as before. "My good lady," said the doctor, "something works against my medicine, and is too strong for it; but I know by the force of my art what it is: you have stolen goods about you, I am sure; and if you do not give them back, I can do nothing for you." But the princess denied very stoutly that she had anything of the kind. "Very well," said the doctor, "you may do as you please, but I am sure I am right, and you will die if you do not own it." Then he went to the king, and told him how the matter stood. "Daughter," said he, "send back the cloak, the purse, and the horn, that you stole from the right owners."

Then she ordered her maid to fetch all three, and gave them to the doctor, and begged him to give them back to the soldiers; and the moment he had them safe he gave her a whole pear to eat, and the nose came right. And as for the doctor, he put on the cloak, wished the king and all his court a good day, and was soon with his two brothers; who lived from that time happily at home in their palace, except when they took an airing to see the world, in their coach with the three dapple-grey horses.

THE GOOSE-GIRL

THE king of a great land died, and left his queen to take care of their only child. This child was a daughter, who was very beautiful; and her mother loved her dearly, and was very kind to her. And there was a good fairy too, who was fond of the princess, and helped her mother to watch over her. When she grew up, she was betrothed to a prince who lived a great way off; and as the time drew near for her to be married, she got ready to set off on her journey to his country. Then the queen her mother, packed up a great many costly things; jewels, and gold, and silver; trinkets, fine dresses, and in short everything that became a royal bride. And she gave her a waiting-maid to ride with her, and give her into the bridegroom's hands; and each had a horse for the journey. Now the princess's horse was the fairy's gift, and it was called Falada, and could speak.

When the time came for them to set out, the fairy went into her bed-chamber, and took a little knife, and cut off a lock of her hair, and gave it to the princess, and said, "Take care of it, dear child; for it is a charm that may be of use to you on the road." Then they all took a sorrowful leave of the princess; and she put the lock of hair into her bosom, got upon her horse, and set off on her journey to her bridegroom's kingdom.

One day, as they were riding along by a brook, the princess began to feel very thirsty: and she said to her maid, "Pray get down, and fetch me some water in my golden cup out of yonder brook, for I want to drink." "Nay," said the maid, "if you are thirsty, get off yourself, and stoop down by the water and drink; I shall not be your waiting-maid any longer." Then she was so thirsty that she got down, and knelt over the little brook, and drank; for she was frightened, and dared not bring out her golden cup; and she wept and said, "Alas! what will become of me?" And the lock answered her, and said:

"Alas! alas! if thy mother knew it,
Sadly, sadly, would she rue it."

But the princess was very gentle and meek, so she said nothing to her maid's ill behavior, but got upon her horse again.

Then all rode farther on their journey, till the day grew so warm, and the sun so scorching, that the bride began to feel very thirsty again; and at last, when they came to a river, she forgot her maid's rude speech, and said, "Pray get down, and fetch me some water to drink in my golden cup." But the maid answered her, and even spoke more haughtily than before: "Drink if you will, but I shall not be your waiting-maid." Then the princess was so thirsty that she got off her horse, and lay down, and held her head over the running stream, and cried and said, "What will become of me?" And the lock of hair answered her again:

"Alas! alas! if thy mother knew it,
Sadly, sadly, would she rue it."

And as she leaned down to drink, the lock of hair fell from her bosom, and floated away with the water. Now she was so frightened that she did not see it; but her maid saw it, and was very glad, for she knew the charm; and she saw that the poor bride would be in her power, now that she had lost the hair. So when the bride had done drinking, and would have got upon Falada again, the maid said, "I shall ride upon Falada, and you may have my horse instead"; so she was forced to give up her horse, and soon afterwards to take off her royal clothes and put on her maid's shabby ones.

At last, as they drew near the end of their journey, this treacherous servant threatened to kill her mistress if she ever told anyone what had happened. But Falada saw it all, and marked it well.

Then the waiting-maid got upon Falada, and the real bride rode upon the other horse, and they went on in this way till at last they came to the royal court. There was great joy at their coming, and the prince flew to meet them, and lifted the maid from her horse, thinking she was the one who was to be his wife; and she was led upstairs to the royal chamber; but the true princess was told to stay in the court below.

Now the old king happened just then to have nothing else to do; so he amused himself by sitting at his kitchen window, looking at what was going on; and he saw her in the courtyard. As she looked very pretty, and too delicate for a waiting-maid, he went up into the royal chamber to ask the bride who it was she had brought with her, that was thus left standing in the court below. "I brought her with me for the sake of her company on the road," said she; "pray give the girl some work to do, that she may not be idle." The old king could not for some time think of any work for her to do; but at last he said, "I have a lad who takes care of my geese; she may go and help him." Now the name of this lad, that the real bride was to help in watching the king's geese, was Curdken.

But the false bride said to the prince, "Dear husband, pray do me one piece of kindness." "That I will," said the prince. "Then tell one of your slaughterers to cut off the head of the horse I rode upon, for it was very unruly, and plagued me sadly on the road"; but the truth was, she was very much afraid lest Falada should some day or other speak, and tell all she had done to the princess. She carried her point, and the faithful Falada was killed; but when the true princess heard of it, she wept, and begged the man to nail up Falada's head against a large dark gate of the city, through which she had to pass every morning and evening, that there she might still see him sometimes. Then the slaughterer said he would do as she wished; and cut off the head, and nailed it up under the dark gate.

Early the next morning, as she and Curdken went out through the gate, she said sorrowfully:

"Falada, Falada, there thou hangest!"

and the head answered:

"Bride, bride, there thou gangest!
Alas! alas! if thy mother knew it,
Sadly, sadly, would she rue it."

Then they went out of the city, and drove the geese on. And when she came to the meadow, she sat down upon a bank there, and let down her waving locks of hair, which were all of pure silver; and when Curdken saw it glitter in the sun, he ran up, and would have pulled some of the locks out, but she cried:

"Blow, breezes, blow!
Let Curdken's hat go!
Blow, breezes, blow!
Let him after it go!
O"er hills, dales, and rocks,
  Away be it whirl'd
Till the silvery locks
  Are all comb'd and curl'd!

Then there came a wind, so strong that it blew off Curdken's hat; and away it flew over the hills: and he was forced to turn and run after it; till, by the time he came back, she had done combing and curling her hair, and had put it up again safe. Then he was very angry and sulky, and would not speak to her at all; but they watched the geese until it grew dark in the evening, and then drove them homewards.

The next morning, as they were going through the dark gate, the poor girl looked up at Falada's head, and cried:

"Falada, Falada, there thou hangest!"

and the head answered:

"Bride, bride, there thou gangest!
Alas! alas! if thy mother knew it,
Sadly, sadly, would she rue it."

Then she drove on the geese, and sat down again in the meadow, and began to comb out her hair as before; and Curdken ran up to her, and wanted to take hold of it; but she cried out quickly:

"Blow, breezes, blow!
Let Curdken's hat go!
Blow, breezes, blow!
Let him after it go!
O"er hills, dales, and rocks,
  Away be it whirl'd
Till the silvery locks
  Are all comb'd and curl'd!

THE GIRL WENT ON COMBING AND CURLING HER HAIR

Then the wind came and blew away his hat; and off it flew a great way, over the hills and far away, so that he had to run after it; and when he came back she had bound up her hair again, and all was safe. So they watched the geese till it grew dark.

In the evening, after they came home, Curdken went to the old king, and said, "I cannot have that strange girl to help me to keep the geese any longer." "Why?" said the king. "Because, instead of doing any good, she does nothing but tease me all day long." Then the king made him tell him what had happened. And Curdken said, "When we go in the morning through the dark gate with our flock of geese, she cries and talks with the head of a horse that hangs upon the wall, and says:

"Falada, Falada, there thou hangest!"

and the head answers:

"Bride, bride, there thou gangest!
Alas! alas! if thy mother knew it,
Sadly, sadly, would she rue it."

And Curdken went on telling the king what had happened upon the meadow where the geese fed; how his hat was blown away; and how he was forced to run after it, and to leave his flock of geese to themselves. But the old king told the boy to go out again the next day: and when morning came, he placed himself behind the dark gate, and heard how she spoke to Falada, and how Falada answered. Then he went into the field, and hid himself in a bush by the meadow's side; and he soon saw with his own eyes how they drove the flock of geese; and how, after a little time, she let down her hair that glittered in the sun. And then he heard her say:

"Blow, breezes, blow!
Let Curdken's hat go!
Blow, breezes, blow!
Let him after it go!
O"er hills, dales, and rocks,
Away be it whirl'd
Till the silvery locks
Are all comb'd and curl'd!

And soon came a gale of wind, and carried away Curdken's hat, and away went Curdken after it, while the girl went on combing and curling her hair. All this the old king saw: so he went home without being seen; and when the little goose-girl came back in the evening he called her aside, and asked her why she did so: but she burst into tears, and said, "That I must not tell you or any man, or I shall lose my life."

But the old king begged so hard, that she had no peace till she had told him all the tale, from beginning to end, word for word. And it was very lucky for her that she did so, for when she had done the king ordered royal clothes to be put upon her, and gazed on her with wonder, she was so beautiful. Then he called his son and told him that he had only a false bride; for that she was merely a waiting-maid, while the true bride stood by. And the young king rejoiced when he saw her beauty, and heard how meek and patient she had been; and without saying anything to the false bride, the king ordered a great feast to be got ready for all his court. The bridegroom sat at the top, with the false princess on one side, and the true one on the other; but nobody knew her again, for her beauty was quite dazzling to their eyes; and she did not seem at all like the little goose-girl, now that she had her brilliant dress on.

When they had eaten and drank, and were very merry, the old king said he would tell them a tale. So he began, and told all the story of the princess, as if it was one that he had once heard; and he asked the true waiting-maid what she thought ought to be done to anyone who would behave thus. "Nothing better," said this false bride, "than that she should be thrown into a cask stuck round with sharp nails, and that two white horses should be put to it, and should drag it from street to street till she was dead." "Thou art she!" said the old king; "and as thou has judged thyself, so shall it be done to thee." And the young king was then married to his true wife, and they reigned over the kingdom in peace and happiness all their lives; and the good fairy came to see them, and restored the faithful Falada to life again.

FAITHFUL JOHN

AN old king fell sick; and when he found his end drawing near, he said, "Let Faithful John come to me." Now Faithful John was the servant that he was fondest of, and was so called because he had been true to his master all his life long. Then when he came to the bed-side, the king said, "My faithful John, I feel that my end draws nigh, and I have now no cares save for my son, who is still young, and stands in need of good counsel. I have no friend to leave him but you; if you do not pledge yourself to teach him all he should know, and to be a father to him, I shall not shut my eyes in peace." Then John said, "I will never leave him, but will serve him faithfully, even though it should cost me my life." And the king said, "I shall now die in peace: after my death, show him the whole palace; all the rooms and vaults, and all the treasures and stores which lie there: but take care how you show him one room,—I mean the one where hangs the picture of the daughter of the king of the golden roof. If he sees it, he will fall deeply in love with her, and will then be plunged into great dangers on her account: guard him in this peril." And when Faithful John had once more pledged his word to the old king, he laid his head on his pillow, and died in peace.

Now when the old king had been carried to his grave, Faithful John told the young king what had passed upon his death-bed, and said, "I will keep my word truly, and be faithful to you as I was always to your father, though it should cost me my life." And the young king wept, and said, "Neither will I ever forget your faithfulness."

The days of mourning passed away, and then Faithful John said to his master, "It is now time that you should see your heritage; I will show you your father's palace." Then he led him about every where, up and down, and let him see all the riches and all the costly rooms; only one room, where the picture stood, he did not open. Now the picture was so placed, that the moment the door opened, you could see it; and it was so beautifully done, that one would think it breathed and had life, and that there was nothing more lovely in the whole world. When the young king saw that Faithful John always went by this door, he said, "Why do you not open that room?" "There is something inside," he answered, "which would frighten you." But the king said, "I have seen the whole palace, and I must also know what is in there;" and he went and began to force open the door: but Faithful John held him back, and said, "I gave my word to your father before his death, that I would take heed how I showed you what stands in that room, lest it should lead you and me into great trouble." "The greatest trouble to me," said the young king, "will be not to go in and see the room; I shall have no peace by day or by night until I do; so I shall not go hence until you open it."

Then Faithful John saw that with all he could do or say the young king would have his way; so, with a heavy heart and many foreboding sighs, he sought for the key out of his great bunch; and he opened the door of the room, and entered in first, so as to stand between the king and the picture, hoping he might not see it: but he raised himself upon tiptoes, and looked over John's shoulders; and as soon as he saw the likeness of the lady, so beautiful and shining with gold, he fell down upon the floor senseless. Then Faithful John lifted him up in his arms, and carried him to his bed, and was full of care, and thought to himself, "This trouble has come upon us; O Heaven! what will come of it?"

At last the king came to himself again; but the first thing that he said was, "Whose is that beautiful picture?" "It is the picture of the daughter of the king of the golden roof," said Faithful John. But the king went on, saying, "My love towards her is so great, that if all the leaves on the trees were tongues, they could not speak it; I

AS SOON AS HE SAW THE LIKENESS OF THE LADY HE FELL DOWN UPON THE FLOOR SENSELESS

care not to risk my life to win her; you are my faithful friend, you must aid me."

Then John thought for a long time what was now to be done; and at length said to the king, "All that she has about her is of gold: the tables, stools, cups, dishes, and all the things in her house are of gold; and she is always seeking new treasures. Now in your stores there is much gold; let it be worked up into every kind of vessel, and into all sorts of birds, wild beasts, and wonderful animals; then we will take it, and try our fortune." So the king ordered all the goldsmiths to be sought for; and they worked day and night, until at last the most beautiful things were made: and Faithful John had a ship loaded with them, and put on a merchant's dress, and the king did the same, that they might not be known.

When all was ready, they put out to sea, and sailed till they came to the coast of the land where the king of the golden roof reigned. Faithful John told the king to stay in the ship, and wait for him; "for perhaps," said he, "I may be able to bring away the king's daughter with me: therefore take care that everything be in order; let the golden vessels and ornaments be brought forth, and the whole ship be decked out with them." And he chose out something of each of the golden things to put into his basket, and got ashore, and went towards the king's palace. And when he came to the castle yard, there stood by the well side a beautiful maiden, who had two golden pails in her hand, drawing water. And as she drew up the water, which was glittering with gold, she turned herself round, and saw the stranger, and asked him who he was. Then he drew near, and said, "I am a merchant," and opened his basket, and let her look into it; and she cried out, "Oh! what beautiful things!" and set down her pails, and looked at one after the other. Then she said, "The king's daughter must see all these; she is so fond of such things, that she will buy all of you." So she took him by the hand, and led him in; for she was one of the waiting-maids of the daughter of the king.

When the princess saw the wares, she was greatly pleased, and said, "They are so beautiful that I will buy them all." But Faithful John said, "I am only the servant of a rich merchant; what I have here is nothing to what he has lying in yonder ship: there he has the finest and most costly things that ever were made in gold."

The princess wanted to have them all brought ashore; but he said, "That would take up many days, there are such a number; and more rooms would be wanted to place them in than there are in the greatest house." But her wish to see them grew still greater, and at last she said, "Take me to the ship, I will go myself, and look at your master's wares."

Then Faithful John led her joyfully to the ship, and the king, when he saw her, thought that his heart would leap out of his breast; and it was with the greatest trouble that he kept himself still. So she got into the ship, and the king led her down; but Faithful John staid behind with the steersman, and ordered the ship to put off: "Spread all your sail," cried he, "that she may fly over the waves like a bird through the air."

And the king showed the princess the golden wares, each one singly; the dishes, cups, basins, and the wild and wonderful beasts; so that many hours flew away, and she looked at everything with delight, and was not aware that the ship was sailing away. And after she had looked at the last, she thanked the merchant, and said she would go home; but when she came upon the deck, she saw that the ship was sailing far away from land upon the deep sea, and that it flew along at full sail. "Alas!" she cried out in her fright, "I am betrayed; I am carried off, and have fallen into the power of a roving trader; I would sooner have died." But then the king took her by the hand, and said, "I am not a merchant, I am a king, and of as noble birth as you. I have taken you away by stealth, but I did so because of the very great love I have for you; for the first time that I saw your face, I fell on the ground in a swoon." When the daughter of the king of the golden roof heard all, she was comforted, and her heart soon turned towards him, and she was willing to become his wife.

But it so happened, that whilst they were sailing on the deep sea, Faithful John, as he sat on the prow of the ship playing on his flute, saw three ravens flying in the air towards him. Then he left off playing, and listened to what they said to each other, for he understood their tongue. The first said, "There he goes! he is bearing away the daughter of the king of the golden roof; let him go!" "Nay," said the second, "there he goes, but he has not got her yet." And the third said, "There he goes; he surely has her, for she is sitting by his side in the ship." Then the first began again, and cried out, "What boots it to him? See you not that when they come to land, a horse of a foxy-red color will spring towards him; and then he will try to get upon it, and if he does, it will spring away with him into the air, so that he will never see his love again." "True! true!" said the second, "but is there no help?" "Oh! yes, yes!" said the first; "if he who sits upon the horse takes the dagger which is stuck in the saddle and strikes him dead, the young king is saved: but who knows that? and who will tell him, that he who thus saves the king's life will turn to stone from the toes of his feet to his knee?" Then the second said, "True! true! but I know more still; though the horse be dead, the king loses his bride: when they go together into the palace, there lies the bridal dress on the couch, and looks as if it were woven of gold and silver, but it is all brimstone and pitch; and if he puts it on, it will burn him, marrow and bones." "Alas! alas! is there no help?" said the third. "Oh! yes, yes!" said the second, "if some one draws near and throws it into the fire, the young king will be saved. But what boots that? who knows and will tell him, that, if he does, his body from the knee to the heart will be turned to stone?" "More! more! I know more," said the third: "were the dress burnt, still the king loses his bride. After the wedding, when the dance begins, and the young queen dances on, she will turn pale, and fall as though she were dead; and if some one does not draw near and lift her up, and take from her right breast three drops of blood, she will surely die. But if any one knew this, he would tell him, that if he does do so, his body will turn to stone, from the crown of his head to the tip of his toe."

Then the ravens flapped their wings, and flew on; but Faithful John, who had understood it all, from that time was sorrowful, and did not tell his master what he had heard; for he saw that if he told him, he must himself lay down his life to save him: at last he said to himself, "I will be faithful to my word, and save my master, if it costs me my life."

Now when they came to land, it happened just as the ravens had foretold; for there sprung out a fine foxy-red horse. "See," said the king, "he shall bear me to my palace:" and he tried to mount, but Faithful John leaped before him, and swung himself quickly upon it, drew the dagger, and smote the horse dead. Then the other servants of the king, who were jealous of Faithful John, cried out, "What a shame to kill the fine beast that was to take the king to his palace!" But the king said, "Let him alone, it is my Faithful John; who knows but he did it for some good end?"

Then they went on to the castle, and there stood a couch in one room, and a fine dress lay upon it, that shone with gold and silver; and the young king went up to it to take hold of it, but Faithful John cast it in the fire, and burnt it. And the other servants began again to grumble, and said, "See, now he is burning the wedding dress." But the king said, "Who knows what he does it for? let him alone! he is my faithful servant John."

Then the wedding feast was held, and the dance began, and the bride also came in; but Faithful John took good heed, and looked in her face; and on a sudden she turned pale, and fell as though she were dead upon the ground. But he sprung towards her quickly, lifted her up, and took her and laid her upon a couch, and drew three drops of blood from her right breast. And she breathed again, and came to herself. But the young king had seen all, and did not know why Faithful John had done it; so he was angry at his boldness, and said, "Throw him into prison."

The next morning Faithful John was led forth, and stood upon the gallows, and said, "May I speak out before I die?" and when the king answered "It shall be granted thee," he said, "I am wrongly judged, for I have always been faithful and true:" and then he told what he had heard the ravens say upon the sea, and how he meant to save his master, and had therefore done all these things.

When he had told all, the king called out, "O my most faithful John! pardon! pardon! take him down!" But Faithful John had fallen down lifeless at the last word he spoke, and lay as a stone: and the king and the queen mourned over him; and the king said, "Oh, how ill have I rewarded thy truth!" And he ordered the stone figure to be taken up, and placed in his own room near to his bed; and as often as he looked at it he wept, and said, "Oh that I could bring thee back to life again, my Faithful John!"

After a time, the queen had two little sons, who grew up, and were her great joy. One day, when she was at church, the two children staid with their father; and as they played about, he looked at the stone figure, and sighed, and cried out, "Oh that I could bring thee back to life, my Faithful John!" Then the stone began to speak, and said, "O king! thou canst bring me back to life if thou wilt give up for my sake what is dearest to thee." But the king said, "All that I have in the world would I give up for thee." "Then," said the stone, "cut off the heads of thy children, sprinkle their blood over me, and I shall live again." Then the king was greatly shocked: but he thought how Faithful John had died for his sake, and because of his great truth towards him; and rose up and drew his sword to cut off his children's heads and sprinkle the stone with their blood; but the moment he drew his sword Faithful John was alive again, and stood before his face, and said, "Your truth is rewarded." And the children sprang about and played as if nothing had happened.

Then the king was full of joy: and when he saw the queen coming, to try her, he put Faithful John and the two children in a large closet; and when she came in he said to her, "Have you been at church?" "Yes," said she, "but I could not help thinking of Faithful John, who was so true to us." "Dear wife," said the king, "we can bring him back to life again, but it will cost us both our little sons, and we must give them up for his sake." When the queen heard this, she turned pale and was frightened in her heart; but she said, "Let it be so; we owe him all, for his great faith and truth." Then he rejoiced because she thought as he had thought, and went in and opened the closet, and brought out the children and Faithful John, and said, "Heaven be praised! he is ours again, and we have our sons safe too." So he told her the whole story; and all lived happily together the rest of their lives.

THE SEVEN RAVENS

THERE was once a man who had seven sons, and last of all one daughter. Although the little girl was very pretty, she was so weak and small that they thought she could not live; but they said she should at once be christened.

So the father sent one of his sons in haste to the spring to get some water, but the other six ran with him. Each wanted to be first at drawing the water, and so they were in such a hurry that all let their pitchers fall into the well, and they stood very foolishly looking at one another, and did not know what to do, for none dared go home. In the meantime the father was uneasy, and could not tell what made the young men stay so long. "Surely," said he, "the whole seven must have forgotten themselves over some game of play"; and when he had waited still longer and they yet did not come, he flew into a rage and wished them all turned into ravens. Scarcely had he spoken these words when he heard a croaking over his head, and looked up and saw seven ravens as black as coal flying round and round. Sorry as he was to see his wish so fulfilled, he did not know how what was done could be undone, and comforted himself as well as he could for the loss of his seven sons with his dear little daughter, who soon became stronger and every day more beautiful.

For a long time she did not know that she had ever had any brothers; for her father and mother took care not to speak of them before her: but one day by chance she heard the people about her speak of them. "Yes," said they, "she is beautiful indeed, but still "tis a pity that her brothers should have been lost for her sake." Then she was much grieved, and went to her father and mother, and asked if she had any brothers, and what had become of them. So they dared no longer hide the truth from her, but said it was the will of Heaven, and that her birth was only the innocent cause of it; but the little girl mourned sadly about it every day, and thought herself bound to do all she could to bring her brothers back; and she had neither rest nor ease, till at length one day she stole away, and set out into the wide world to find her brothers, wherever they might be, and free them, whatever it might cost her.

She took nothing with her but a little ring which her father and mother had given her, a loaf of bread in case she should be hungry, a little pitcher of water in case she should be thirsty, and a little stool to rest upon when she should be weary. Thus she went on and on, and journeyed till she came to the world's end; then she came to the sun, but the sun looked much too hot and fiery; so she ran away quickly to the moon, but the moon was cold and chilly, and said, "I smell flesh and blood this way!" so she took herself away in a hurry and came to the stars, and the stars were friendly and kind to her, and each star sat upon his own little stool; but the morning star rose up and gave her a little piece of wood, and said, "If you have not this little piece of wood, you cannot unlock the castle that stands on the glass-mountain, and there your brothers live." The little girl took the piece of wood, rolled it up in a little cloth, and went on again until she came to the glass-mountain, and found the door shut. Then she felt for the little piece of wood; but when she unwrapped the cloth it was not there, and she saw she had lost the gift of the good stars. What was to be done? She wanted to save her brothers, and had no key of the castle of the glass-mountain; so this faithful little sister took a

knife out of her pocket and cut off her little finger, that was just the size of the piece of wood she had lost, and put it in the door and opened it.

As she went in, a little dwarf came up to her, and said, "What are you seeking for?" "I seek for my brothers, the seven ravens," answered she. Then the dwarf said, "My masters are not at home; but if you will wait till they come, pray step in." Now the little dwarf was getting their dinner ready, and he brought their food upon seven little plates, and their drink in seven little glasses, and set them upon the table, and out of each little plate their sister ate a small piece, and out of each little glass she drank a small drop; but she let the ring that she had brought with her fall into the last glass.

On a sudden she heard a fluttering and croaking in the air, and the dwarf said, "Here come my masters." When they came in, they wanted to eat and drink, and looked for their little plates and glasses. Then said one after the other,

"Who has eaten from my little plate? And who has been drinking out of my little glass?"

"Caw! Caw! well I ween
Mortal lips have this way been."

When the seventh came to the bottom of his glass, and found there the ring, he looked at it, and knew that it was his father's and mother's, and said, "O that our little sister would but come! then we should be free." When the little girl heard this (for she stood behind the door all the time and listened), she ran forward, and in an instant all the ravens took their right form again; and all hugged and kissed each other, and went merrily home.

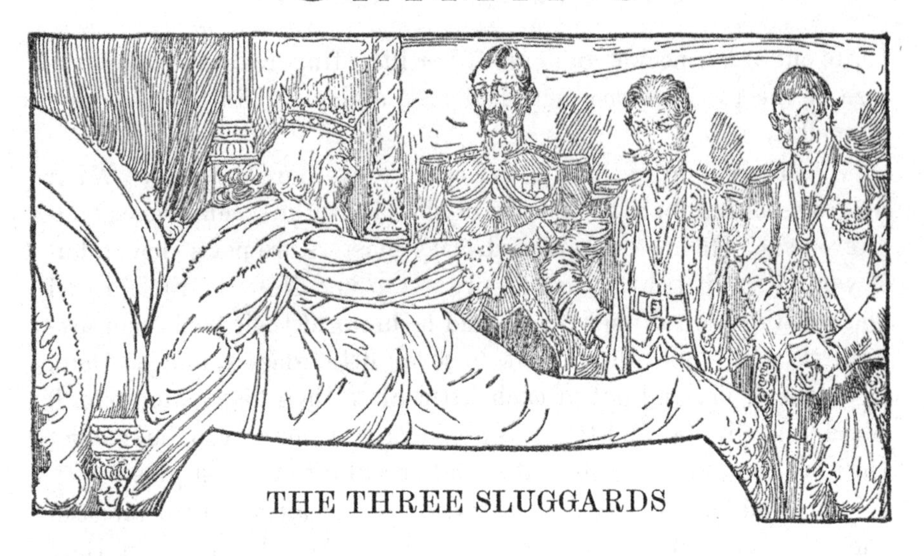

THE THREE SLUGGARDS

THE king of a country a long way off had three sons. He liked one as well as another, and did not know which to leave his kingdom to after his death: so when he was dying he called them all to him, and said, "Dear children, the laziest sluggard of the three shall be king after me." "Then," said the eldest, "the kingdom is mine; for I am so lazy that when I lie down to sleep, if anything were to fall into my eyes so that I could not shut them, I should still go on sleeping." The second said, "Father, the kingdom belongs to me; for I am so lazy that when I sit by the fire to warm myself, I would sooner have my toes burnt than take the trouble to draw my legs back." The third said, "Father, the kingdom is mine; for I am so lazy that if I were going to be hanged, with the rope round my neck, and somebody were to put a sharp knife into my hands to cut it, I had rather be hanged than raise my hand to do it." When the father heard this, he said, "You shall be the king; for you are the fittest man."

KING GRIZZLE-BEARD

A GREAT king of a land far away in the East had a daughter who was very beautiful, but so proud, and haughty, and conceited, that none of the princes who came to ask her in marriage was good enough for her, and she only made sport of them.

Once upon a time the king held a great feast, and asked thither all her suitors; and they all sat in a row, ranged according to their rank—kings, and princes, and dukes, and earls, and counts, and barons, and knights. Then the princess came in, and as she passed by them she had something spiteful to say to every one. The first was too fat: "He's as round as a tub," said she. The next was too tall: "What a maypole!" said she. The next was too short: "What a dumpling!" said she. The fourth was too pale, and she called him "Wallface." The fifth was too red, so she called him "Coxcomb." The sixth was not straight enough; so she said he was like a green stick, that had been laid to dry over a baker's oven. And thus she had some joke to crack upon every one: but she laughed more than all at a good king who was there. "Look at him," said she; "his beard is like an old mop; he shall be called Grisly-beard." So the king got the nickname of Grisly-beard.

But the old king was very angry when he saw how his daughter behaved, and how she ill-treated all his guests; and he vowed that, willing or unwilling, she should marry the first man, be he prince or beggar, that came to the door.

Two days after there came by a travelling fiddler, who began to play under the window and beg alms; and when the king heard him, he said, "Let him come in." So they brought in a dirty-looking fellow; and when he had sung before the king and the princess, he begged a boon. Then the king said, "You have sung so well, that I will give you my daughter for your wife." The princess begged and prayed; but the king said, "I have sworn to give you to the first comer, and I will keep my word." So words and tears were of no avail; the parson was sent for, and she was married to the fiddler. When this was over the king said, "Now get ready to go—you must not stay here—you must travel on with your husband."

Then the fiddler went his way, and took her with him, and they soon came to a great wood. "Pray," said she, "whose is this wood?" "It belongs to King Grisly-beard," answered he; "hadst thou taken him, all had been thine." "Ah! unlucky wretch that I am!" sighed she; "would that I had married King Grisly-beard!" Next they came to some fine meadows. "Whose are these beautiful green meadows?" said she. "They belong to King Grisly-beard, hadst thou taken him, they had all been thine." "Ah! unlucky wretch that I am!" said she; "would that I had married King Grisly-beard!"

Then they came to a great city. "Whose is this noble city?" said she. "It belongs to King Grisly-beard; hadst thou taken him, it had all been thine." "Ah! wretch that I am!" sighed she; "why did I not marry King Grisly-beard?" "That is no business of mine," said the fiddler: "why should you wish for another husband? Am not I good enough for you?"

At last they came to a small cottage. "What a paltry place!" said she; "to whom does that little dirty hole belong?" Then the fiddler said, "That is your and my house, where we are to live." "Where are your servants?" cried she. "What do we want with servants?" said he; "you must do for yourself whatever is to be done. Now make the fire, and put on water and cook my supper, for I am very tired." But the princess knew nothing of making fires and cooking, and the fiddler was forced to help her. When they had eaten a very scanty meal they went to bed; but the fiddler called her up very early in the morning to clean the house. Thus they lived for two days: and when they had eaten up all there was in the cottage, the man said, "Wife, we can't go on thus, spending money and earning nothing. You must learn to weave baskets." Then he went out and cut willows, and brought them home, and she began to weave; but it made her fingers very sore. "I see this work won't do," said he: "try and spin; perhaps you will do that better." So she sat down and tried to spin; but the threads cut her tender fingers till the blood ran. "See now," said the fiddler, "you are good for nothing; you can do no work: what a bargain I have got! However, I'll try and set up a trade in pots and pans, and you shall stand in the market and sell them." "Alas!" sighed she, "if any of my father's court should pass by and see me standing in the market, how they will laugh at me!"

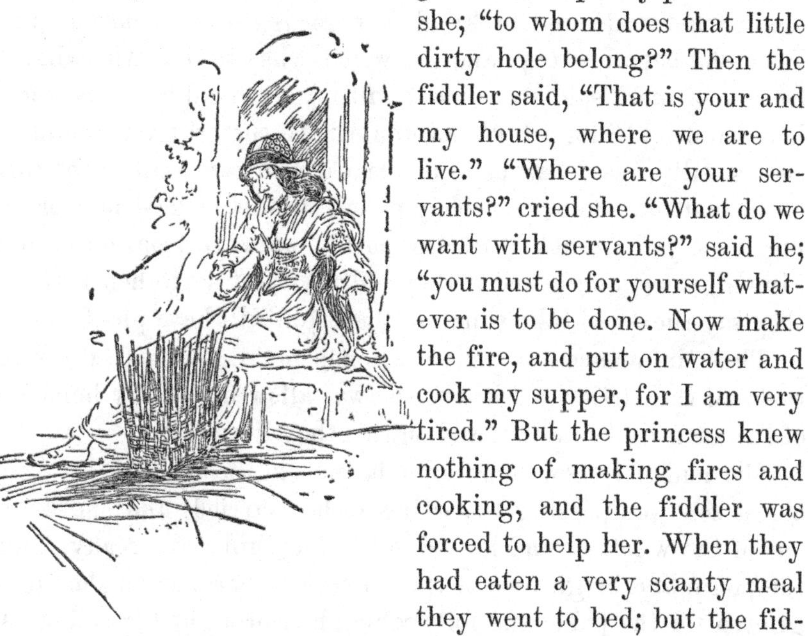

But her husband did not care for that, and said she must work, if she did not wish to die of hunger. At first the trade went well; for many people, seeing such a beautiful woman, went to buy her wares, and paid their money without thinking of taking away the goods. They lived on this as long as it lasted; and then her husband bought a fresh lot of ware, and she sat herself down with it in the corner of the market; but a drunken soldier soon came by, and rode his horse against her stall, and broke all her goods into a thousand pieces. Then she began to cry, and knew not what to do. "Ah! what will become of me?" said she; "what will my husband say?" So she ran home and told him all. "Who would have thought you would have been so silly," said he, "as to put an earthenware stall in the corner of the market, where everybody passes? but let us have no more crying; I see you are not fit for this sort of work, so I have been to the king's palace, and asked if they did not want a kitchen-maid; and they say they will take you, and there you will have plenty to eat."

Thus the princess became a kitchen-maid, and helped the cook to do all the dirtiest work; but she was allowed to carry home some of the meat that was left, and on this they lived.

She had not been there long before she heard that the king's eldest son was passing by, going to be married; and she went to one of the windows and looked out. Everything was ready, and all the pomp and brightness of the court was there. Then she bitterly grieved for the pride and folly which had brought her so low. And the servants gave her some of the rich meats, which she put into her basket to take home.

All on a sudden, as she was going out, in came the king's son in golden clothes; and when he saw a beautiful woman at the door, he took her by the hand, and said she should be his partner in the dance; but she trembled for fear, for she saw that it was King Grisly-beard, who was making sport of her. However, he kept fast hold, and led her in; and the cover of the basket came off, so that the meats in it fell about. Then everybody laughed and jeered at her; and she was so abashed, that she wished herself a thousand feet deep in the earth. She sprang to the door to run away; but on the steps King Grisly-beard overtook her, and brought her back and said, "Fear me not! I am the fiddler who has lived with you in the hut. I brought you there because I really loved you. I am also the soldier that overset your stall. I have done all this only to cure you of your silly pride, and to show you the folly of your ill-treatment of me. Now all is over: you have learnt wisdom, and it is time to hold our marriage feast."

Then the chamberlains came and brought her the most beautiful robes; and her father and his whole court were there already, and welcomed her home on her marriage. Joy was in every face and every heart. The feast was grand; they danced and sang; all were merry; and I only wish that you and I had been of the party.

THE TOM-TIT AND THE BEAR

ONE summer day, as the wolf and the bear were walking together in a wood, they heard a bird singing most delightfully. "Brother," said the bear, "what can that bird be that is singing so sweetly?" "O!" said the wolf, "that is his majesty the king of the birds, we must take care to show him all possible respect." (Now I should tell you that this bird was after all no other than the tom-tit.) "If that is the case," said the bear, "I should like to see the royal palace; so pray come along and show it to me." "Gently, my friend," said the wolf, "we cannot see it just yet, we must wait till the queen comes home."

Soon afterwards the queen came with food in her beak, and she and the king began to feed their young ones. "Now for it!" said the bear; and was about to follow them, to see what was to be seen. "Stop a little, master Bruin," said the wolf, "we must wait now till their majesties are gone again." So they marked the hole where they had seen the nest, and went away. But the bear, being very eager to see the royal palace, soon came back again, and peeping into the nest, saw five or six young birds lying at the bottom of it. "What nonsense!" said Bruin, "this is not a royal palace: I never saw such a filthy place in my life; and you are no royal children, you little base-born brats!" As soon as the young tom-tits heard this they were very angry, and screamed out "We are not base-born, you stupid bear! our father and mother are honest good sort of people: and depend upon it you shall suffer for your insolence!" At this the wolf and the bear grew frightened, and ran away to their dens. But the young tom-tits kept crying and screaming; and when their father and mother came home and offered them food, they all said, "We will not touch a bit; no, not the leg of a fly, though we should die of hunger, till that rascal Bruin has been punished for calling us base-born brats." "Make yourselves easy, my darlings," said the old king, "you may be sure he shall meet with his deserts."

So he went out and stood before the bear's den, and cried out with a loud voice, "Bruin the bear! thou hast shamefully insulted our lawful children: we therefore hereby declare bloody and cruel war against thee and thine, which shall never cease until thou hast been punished as thou so richly deservest." Now when the bear heard this, he called together the ox, the ass, the stag, and all the beasts of the earth, in order to consult about the means of his defence. And the tom-tit also enlisted on his side all the birds of the air, both great and small, and a very large army of hornets, gnats, bees, and flies, and other insects.

As the time approached when the war was to begin, the tom-tit sent out spies to see who was the commander-in-chief of the enemy's forces; and the gnat, who was by far the cleverest spy of them all, flew backwards and forwards in the wood where the enemy's troops were, and at last hid himself under a leaf on a tree, close by which the orders of the day were given out. And the bear, who was standing so near the tree that the gnat could hear all he said, called to the fox and said, "Reynard, you are the cleverest of all the beasts;

therefore you shall be our general and lead us to battle: but we must first agree upon some signal, by which we may know what you want us to do." "Behold," said the fox, "I have a fine, long, bushy tail, which is very like a plume of red feathers, and gives me a very warlike air: now remember, when you see me raise up my tail, you may be sure that the battle is won, and you have then nothing to do but to rush down upon the enemy with all your force. On the other hand, if I drop my tail, the day is lost, and you must run away as fast as you can." Now when the gnat had heard all this, she flew back to the tom-tit and told him everything that had passed.

At length the day came when the battle was to be fought; and as soon as it was light, behold! the army of beasts came rushing forward with such a fearful sound that the earth shook. And his majesty the tom-tit, with his troops, came flying along in warlike array, flapping and fluttering, and beating the air, so that it was quite frightful to hear; and both armies set themselves in order of battle upon the field. Now the tom-tit gave orders to a troop of hornets that at the first onset they should march straight towards Captain Reynard, and fixing themselves about his tail, should sting him with all their might and main. The hornets did as they were told: and when Reynard felt the first sting, he started aside and shook one of his legs, but still held up his tail with wonderful bravery; at the second sting he was forced to drop his tail for a moment; but when the third hornet had fixed itself, he could bear it no longer, but clapped his tail between his legs and scampered away as fast as he could. As soon as the beasts saw this, they thought of course all was lost, and scoured across the country in the greatest dismay, leaving the birds masters of the field.

And now the king and queen flew back in triumph to their children, and said, "Now, children, eat, drink, and be merry, for the victory is ours!" But the young birds said, "No: not till Bruin has humbly begged our pardon for calling us base-born." So the king flew back to the bear's den, and cried out, "Thou villain bear! come forthwith to my abode, and humbly beseech my children to forgive thee the insult thou hast offered them; for, if thou wilt not do this, every bone in thy wretched body shall be broken to pieces." So the bear was forced to crawl out of his den very sulkily, and do what the king bade him: and after that the young birds sat down together, and ate and drank and made merry till midnight.

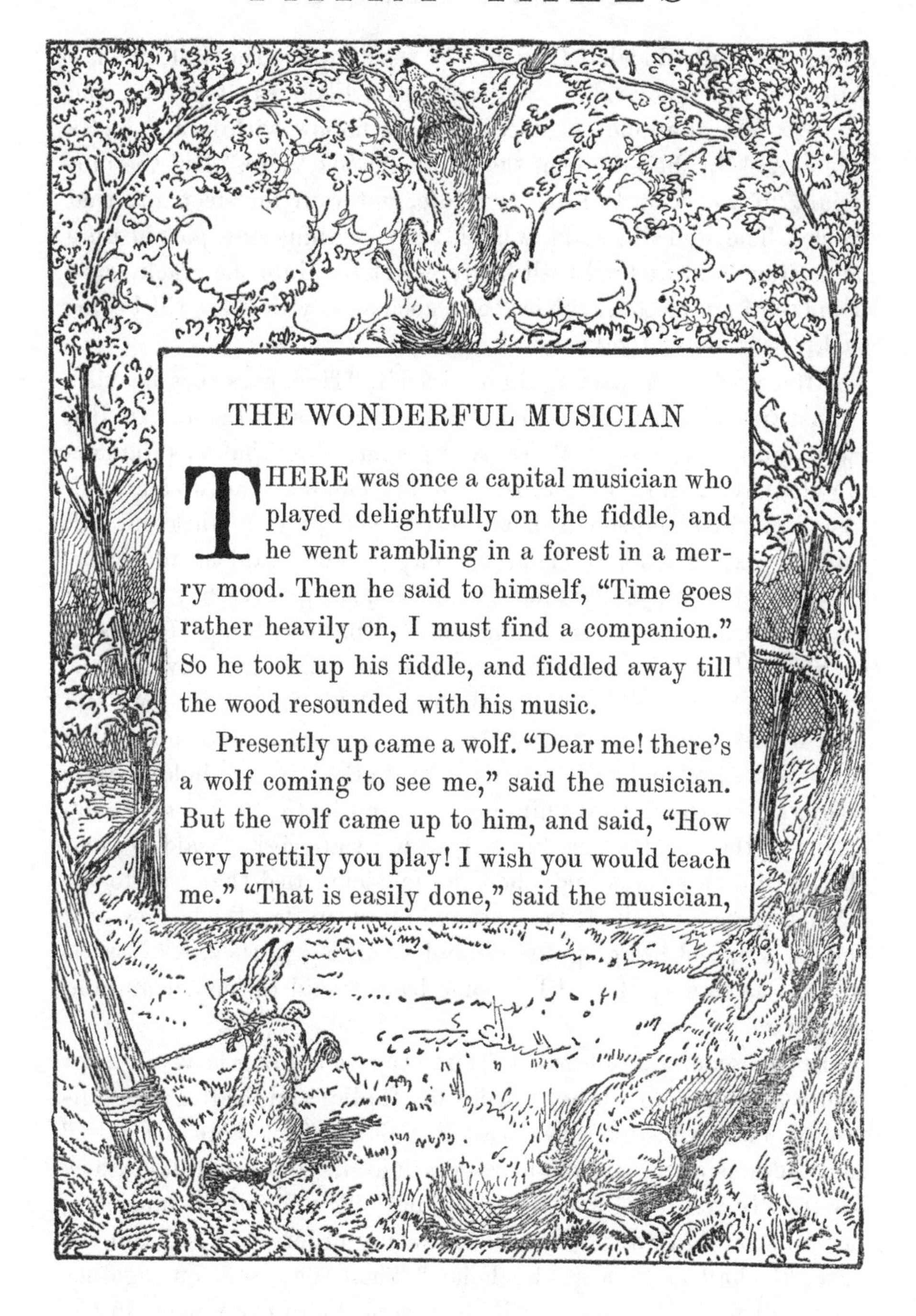

THE WONDERFUL MUSICIAN

THERE was once a capital musician who played delightfully on the fiddle, and he went rambling in a forest in a merry mood. Then he said to himself, "Time goes rather heavily on, I must find a companion." So he took up his fiddle, and fiddled away till the wood resounded with his music.

Presently up came a wolf. "Dear me! there's a wolf coming to see me," said the musician. But the wolf came up to him, and said, "How very prettily you play! I wish you would teach me." "That is easily done," said the musician, "if you will only do what I bid you." "Yes," replied the wolf, "I shall be a very apt scholar." So they went on a little way together, and came at last to an old oak tree that was hollow within, and had a large crack in the middle of the trunk. "Look there," said the musician, "if you wish to learn to fiddle, put your fore-feet into that crack." The wolf did as he was bid: but the musician picked up a large stone and wedged both his fore-feet fast into the crack, so as to make him a prisoner. "Now be so good as to wait there till I come back," said he, and jogged on.

After a while, he said again to himself, "Time goes very heavily, I must find another companion." So he took his fiddle, and fiddled away again in the wood. Presently up came a fox that was wandering close by. "Ah! there is a fox," said he. The fox came up and said, "You delightful musician, how prettily you play! I must and will learn to play as you do." "That you may soon do," said the musician, "if you do as I tell you." "That I will," said the fox. So they travelled on together till they came to a narrow footpath with high bushes on each side. Then the musician bent a stout hazel stem down to the ground from one side of the path, and set his foot on the top, and held it fast; and bent another from the other side, and said to the fox, "Now, pretty fox, if you want to fiddle, give me hold of your left paw." So the fox gave him his paw; and he tied it fast to the top of one of the hazel stems. "Now give me your right," said he; and the fox did as he was told: then the musician tied that paw to the other hazel; and took off his foot, and away up flew the bushes, and the fox too, and hung sprawling and swinging in the air. "Now be so kind as to stay there till I come back," said the musician, and jogged on.

But he soon said to himself, "Time begins to hang heavy, I must find a companion." So he took up his fiddle, and fiddled away divinely. Then up came a hare running along. "Ah! there is a hare," said the musician. And the hare said to him, "You fine fiddler, how beautifully you play! will you teach me?" "Yes," said the musician, "I will soon do that, if you will follow my orders." "Yes," said the hare, "I shall make a good scholar." Then they went on together very well for a long while, till they came to an open space in the wood. The musician tied a string round the hare's neck, and fastened the other end to the tree. "Now," said he, "pretty hare, quick, jump about, run round the tree twenty times." So the silly hare did as she was bid: and when she had run twenty times round the tree, she had twisted the string twenty times round the trunk, and was fast prisoner; and she might pull and pull away as long as she pleased, and only pulled the string faster about her neck. "Now wait there till I come back," said the musician.

But the wolf had pulled and bitten and scratched at the stone a long while, till at last he had got his feet out and was at liberty. Then he said in a great passion, "I will run after that rascally musician and tear him in pieces." As the fox saw him run by, he said, "Ah, brother wolf, pray let me down, the musician has played tricks with me." So the wolf set to work at the bottom of the hazel stem, and bit it in two; and away went both together to find the musician: and as they came to the hare, she cried out too for help. So they went and set her free, and all followed the enemy together.

Meantime the musician had been fiddling away, and found another companion; for a poor woodcutter had been pleased with the music, and could not help following him with his axe under his arm. The musician was pleased to get a man for his companion, and behaved very civilly to him, and played him no tricks, but stopped and played his prettiest tunes till his heart overflowed for joy. While the woodcutter was standing listening, he saw the wolf, the fox, and the hare coming, and knew by their faces that they were in a great rage, and coming to do some mischief. So he stood before the musician with his great axe, as much as to say, No one shall hurt him as long as I have this axe. And when the beasts saw this, they were so frightened that they ran back into the wood. Then the musician played the woodcutter one of his best tunes for his pains, and went on with his journey.

THE QUEEN BEE

THE kings' sons once upon a time went into the world to seek their fortunes; but they soon fell into a wasteful foolish way of living, so that they could not return home again. Then their brother, who was a little insignificant dwarf, went out to seek for his brothers: but when he had found them they only laughed at him, to think that he, who was so young and simple, should try to travel through the world, when they, who were so much wiser, had been unable to get on. However, they all set out on their journey together, and came at last to an ant-hill. The two elder brothers would have pulled it down, in order to see how the poor ants in their fright would run about and carry off their eggs. But the little dwarf said, "Let the poor things enjoy themselves, I will not suffer you to trouble them."

So on they went, and came to a lake where many many ducks were swimming about. The two brothers wanted to catch two, and roast them. But the dwarf said, "Let the poor things enjoy themselves, you shall not kill them." Next they came to a bees"-nest in a hollow tree, and there was so much honey that it ran down the trunk; and the two brothers wanted to light a fire under the tree and kill the bees, so as to get their honey. But the dwarf held them back, and said, "Let the pretty insects enjoy themselves, I cannot let you burn them."

At length the three brothers came to a castle: and as they passed by the stables they saw fine horses standing there, but all were of marble, and no man was to be seen. Then they went through all the rooms, till they came to a door on which were three locks: but in the middle of the door was a wicket, so that they could look into the next room. There they saw a little grey old man sitting at a table; and they called to him once or twice, but he did not hear: however, they called a third time, and then he rose and came out to them.

He said nothing, but took hold of them and led them to a beautiful table covered with all sorts of good things: and when they had eaten and drunk, he showed each of them to a bed-chamber.

The next morning he came to the eldest and took him to a marble table, where there were three tablets, containing an account of the means by which the castle might be disenchanted. The first tablet said: "In the wood, under the moss, lie the thousand pearls belonging to the king's daughter; they must all be found: and if one be missing by set of sun, he who seeks them will be turned into marble."

The eldest brother set out, and sought for the pearls the whole day: but the evening came, and he had not found the first hundred: so he was turned into stone as the tablet had foretold.

The next day the second brother undertook the task; but he succeeded no better than the first; for he could only find the second hundred of the pearls; and therefore he too was turned into stone.

At last came the little dwarf's turn; and he looked in the moss; but it was so hard to find the pearls, and the job was so tiresome!—so he sat down upon a stone and cried. And as he sat there, the king of the ants (whose life he had saved) came to help him, with five thousand ants; and it was not long before they had found all the pearls and laid them in a heap.

The second tablet said: "The key of the princess's bed-chamber must be fished up out of the lake." And as the dwarf came to the brink of it, he saw the two ducks whose lives he had saved swimming about; and they dived down and soon brought in the key from the bottom.

The third task was the hardest. It was to choose out the youngest and the best of the king's three daughters. Now they were all beautiful, and all exactly alike: but he was told that the eldest had eaten a piece of sugar, the next some sweet syrup, and the youngest a spoonful of honey; so he was to guess which it was that had eaten the honey.

Then came the queen of the bees, who had been saved by the little dwarf from the fire, and she tried the lips of all three; but at last she sat upon the lips of the one that had eaten the honey: and so the dwarf knew which was the youngest. Thus the spell was broken, and all who had been turned into stones awoke, and took their proper forms. And the dwarf married the youngest and the best of the princesses, and was king after her father's death; but his two brothers married the other two sisters.

THE DOG AND THE SPARROW

A SHEPHERD'S dog had a master who took no care of him, but often let him suffer the greatest hunger. At last he could bear it no longer; so he took to his heels, and off he ran in a very sad and sorrowful mood. On the road he met a sparrow that said to him, "Why are you so sad, my friend?" "Because," said the dog, "I am very very hungry, and have nothing to eat." "If that be all," answered the sparrow, "come with me into the next town, and I will soon find you plenty of food." So on they went together into the town: and as they passed by a butcher's shop, the sparrow said to the dog, "Stand there a little while till I peck you down a piece of meat."

So the sparrow perched upon the shelf: and having first looked carefully about her to see if anyone was watching her, she pecked and scratched at a steak that lay upon the edge of the shelf, till at last down it fell. Then the dog snapped it up, and scrambled away with it into a corner, where he soon ate it all up. "Well," said the sparrow, "you shall have some more if you will; so come with me to the next shop, and I will peck you down another steak." When the dog had eaten this too, the sparrow said to him, "Well, my good friend, have you had enough now?" "I have had plenty of meat," answered he, "but I should like to have a piece of bread to eat after it." "Come with me then," said the sparrow, "and you shall soon have that too." So she took him to a baker's shop, and pecked at two rolls that lay in the window, till they fell down: and as the dog still wished for more, she took him to another shop and pecked down some more for him. When that was eaten, the sparrow asked him whether he had had enough now. "Yes," said he; "and now let us take a walk a little way out of the town." So they both went out upon the high road; but as the weather was warm, they had not gone far before the dog said, "I am very much tired—I should like to take a nap." "Very well," answered the sparrow, "do so, and in the meantime I will perch upon that bush." So the dog stretched himself out on the road, and fell fast asleep. Whilst he slept, there came by a carter with a cart drawn by three horses, and loaded with two casks of wine. The sparrow, seeing that the carter did not turn out of the way, but would go on in the track in which the dog lay, so as to drive over him, called out, "Stop! stop! Mr Carter, or it shall be the worse for you." But the carter, grumbling to himself, "You make it the worse for me, indeed! what can you do?" cracked his whip, and drove his cart over the poor dog, so that the wheels crushed him to death. "There," cried the sparrow, "thou cruel villain, thou hast killed my friend the dog. Now mind what I say. This deed of thine shall cost thee all thou art worth." "Do your worst, and welcome," said the brute, "what harm can you do me?" and passed on. But the sparrow crept under the tilt of the cart, and pecked at the bung of one of the casks till she loosened it; and then all the wine ran out, without the carter seeing it. At last he looked round, and saw that the cart was dripping, and the cask quite empty. "What an unlucky wretch I am!" cried he. "Not wretch enough yet!" said the sparrow, as she alighted upon the head of one of the horses, and pecked at him till he reared up and kicked. When the carter saw this, he drew out his hatchet and aimed a blow at the sparrow, meaning to kill her; but she flew away, and the blow fell upon the poor horse's head with such force, that he fell down dead. "Unlucky wretch that I am!" cried he. "Not wretch enough yet!" said the sparrow. And as the carter went on with the other two horses, she again crept under the tilt of the cart, and pecked out the bung of the second cask, so that all the wine ran out. When the carter saw this, he again cried out, "Miserable wretch that I am!" But the sparrow answered, "Not wretch enough yet!" and perched on the head of the second horse, and pecked at him too. The carter ran up and struck at her again with his hatchet; but away she flew, and the blow fell upon the second horse and killed him on the spot. "Unlucky wretch that I am!" said he. "Not wretch enough yet!" said the sparrow; and perching upon the third horse, she began to peck him too. The carter was mad with fury; and without looking about him, or caring what he was about, struck again at the sparrow; but killed his third horse as he done the other two. "Alas! miserable wretch that I am!" cried he. "Not wretch enough yet!" answered the sparrow as she flew away; "now will I plague and punish thee at thy own house." The carter was forced at last to leave his cart behind him, and to go home overflowing with rage and vexation. "Alas!" said he to his wife, "what ill luck has befallen me!—my wine is all spilt, and my horses all three dead." "Alas! husband," replied she, "and a wicked bird has come into the house, and has brought with her all the birds in the world, I am sure, and they have fallen upon our corn in the loft, and are eating it up at such a rate!" Away ran the husband upstairs, and saw thousands of birds sitting upon the floor eating up his corn, with the sparrow in the midst of them. "Unlucky wretch that I am!" cried the carter; for he saw that the corn was almost all gone. "Not wretch enough yet!" said the sparrow; "thy cruelty shall cost thee thy life yet!" and away she flew.

The carter, seeing that he had thus lost all that he had, went down into his kitchen; and was still not sorry for what he had done, but sat himself angrily and sulkily in the chimney corner. But the sparrow sat on the outside of the window, and cried "Carter! thy cruelty shall cost thee thy life!" With that he jumped up in a rage, seized his hatchet, and threw it at the sparrow; but it missed her, and only broke the window. The sparrow now hopped in, perched upon the window-seat, and cried, "Carter! it shall cost thee thy life!" Then he became mad and blind with rage, and struck the window-seat with such force that he cleft it in two: and as the sparrow flew from place to place, the carter and his wife were so furious, that they broke all their furniture, glasses, chairs, benches, the table, and at last the walls, without touching the bird at all. In the end, however, they caught her: and the wife said, "Shall I kill her at once?" "No," cried he, "that is letting her off too easily: she shall die a much more cruel death; I will eat her." But the sparrow began to flutter about, and stretch out her neck and cried, "Carter! it shall cost thee thy life yet!" With that he could wait no longer: so he gave his wife the hatchet, and cried, "Wife, strike at the bird and kill her in my hand." And the wife struck; but she missed her aim, and hit her husband on the head so that he fell down dead, and the sparrow flew quietly home to her nest.

THE MAN IN THE BAG

THERE were two brothers, who were both soldiers, the one had grown rich, but the other had had no luck, and was very poor. The poor man thought he would try to better himself; so pulling off his red coat, he became a gardener, and dug his ground well, and sowed turnips.

When the crop came up, there was one plant bigger than all the rest; and it kept getting larger and larger, and seemed as if it would never cease growing; so that it might have been called the prince of turnips, for there never was such a one seen before and never will again. At last it was so big that it filled a cart, and two oxen could hardly draw it; but the gardener did not know what in the world to do with it, nor whether it would be a blessing or a curse to him. One day he said to himself, "What shall I do with it? if I sell it, it will bring me no more than another would; and as for eating, the little turnips I am sure are better than this great one: the best thing perhaps that I can do will be to give it to the king, as a mark of my respect."

Then he yoked his oxen, and drew the turnip to the court, and gave it to the king. "What a wonderful thing!" said the king. "I have seen many strange things in my life, but such a monster as this I never saw before. Where did you get the seed, or is it only your good luck? If so, you are a true child of fortune."

"Ah, no!" answered the gardener, "I am no child of fortune; I am a poor soldier, who never yet could get enough to live upon: so I set to work, tilling the ground. I have a brother who is rich, and your majesty knows him well, and all the world knows him; but as I am poor, everybody forgets me."

Then the king took pity on him, and said, "You shall be poor no longer. I will give you so much, that you shall be even richer than your brother." So he gave him money, and lands, and flocks, and herds; and made him so rich, that his brother's wealth could not at all be compared with his.

When the brother heard of all this, and how a turnip had made the gardener so rich, he envied him sorely; and bethought himself how he could please the king and get the same good luck for himself. However, he thought he would manage more cleverly than his brother; so he got together a rich gift of jewels and fine horses for the king, thinking that he must have a much larger gift in return: for if his brother had so much given him for a turnip, what must his gift be worth?

The king took the gift very graciously, and said he knew not what he could give in return more costly and wonderful than the great turnip; so the soldier was forced to put it into a cart, and drag it home with him. When he reached home, he knew not upon whom to vent his rage and envy; and at length wicked thoughts came into his head, and he sought to kill his brother.

So he hired some villains to murder him; and having shown them where to lie in ambush, he went to his brother, and said, "Dear brother, I have found a hidden treasure; let us go and dig it up, and share it between us." The other had no thought or fear of his brother's roguery: so they went out together; and as they were travelling along, the murderers rushed out upon him, bound him, and were going to hang him on a tree.

But whilst they were getting all ready, they heard the trampling of a horse afar off, which so frightened them that they pushed their prisoner neck and shoulders together into a sack, and swung him up by a cord to the tree; where they left him dangling, and ran away, meaning to come back and despatch him in the evening.

Meantime, however, he worked and worked away, till he had made a hole large enough to put out his head. When the horseman came up, he proved to be a student, a merry fellow, who was journeying along on his nag, and singing as he went. As soon as the man in the bag saw him passing under the tree, he cried out, "Good morning! good morning to thee, my friend!" The student looked about, and seeing no one, and not knowing where the voice came from, cried out, "Who calls me?"

Then the man in the bag cried out, "Lift up thine eyes, for behold here I sit in the sack of wisdom! Here have I, in a short time, learned great and wondrous things. Compared to what is taught in this seat, all the learning of the schools is as empty air. A little longer and I shall know all that man can know, and shall come forth wiser than the wisest of mankind. Here I discern the signs and motions of the heavens and the stars; the laws that control the winds; the number of the sands on the sea-shore; the healing of the sick; the virtues of all simples, of birds, and of precious stones. Wert thou but once here, my friend, thou wouldst soon feel the power of knowledge."

The student listened to all this, and wondered much. At last he said, "Blessed be the day and hour when I found you! cannot you let me into the sack for a little while?" Then the other answered, as if very unwillingly, "A little space I may allow thee to sit here, if thou wilt reward me well and treat me kindly: but thou must tarry yet an hour below, till I have learnt some little matters that are yet unknown to me."

So the student sat himself down and waited awhile; but the time hung heavy upon him, and he begged hard that he might ascend forthwith, for his thirst of knowledge was very great. Then the other began to give way, and said, "Thou must let the bag of wisdom descend, by untying yonder cord, and then thou shalt enter." So the student let him down, opened the bag, and set him free. "Now then," cried he, "let me mount quickly!" As he began to put himself into the sack heels first, "Wait a while!" said the gardener, "that is not the way." Then he pushed him in head first, tied up the bag's mouth, and soon swung up the searcher after wisdom, dangling in the air. "How is it with thee, friend?" said he; "dost thou not feel that wisdom cometh unto thee? Rest there in peace, till thou art a wiser man than thou wert."

So saying, he borrowed the student's nag to ride home upon, and trotted off as fast as he could, for fear the villains should return; and he left the poor student to gather wisdom, till somebody should come and let him down, when he had found out in which posture he was wisest,—on his head or his heels.

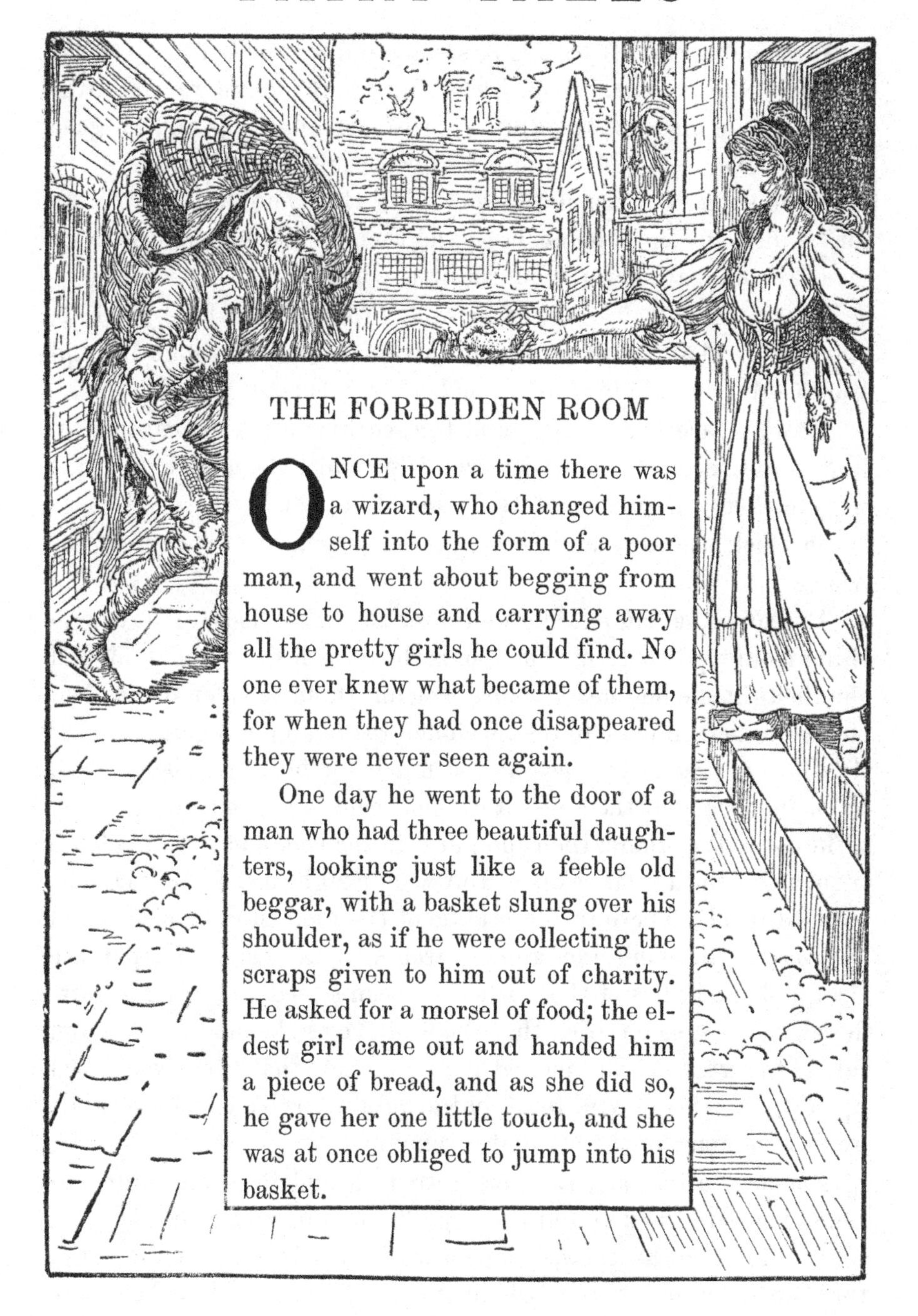

THE FORBIDDEN ROOM

ONCE upon a time there was a wizard, who changed himself into the form of a poor man, and went about begging from house to house and carrying away all the pretty girls he could find. No one ever knew what became of them, for when they had once disappeared they were never seen again.

One day he went to the door of a man who had three beautiful daughters, looking just like a feeble old beggar, with a basket slung over his shoulder, as if he were collecting the scraps given to him out of charity. He asked for a morsel of food; the eldest girl came out and handed him a piece of bread, and as she did so, he gave her one little touch, and she was at once obliged to jump into his basket.

He then hurried off with long strides and carried her to his house in the middle of a dark wood. Everything in the house was magnificent, and she had but to express a wish for anything and he gave it her at once. "You are happy here with me, dearest one, are you not?" he said; "for you have everything that your heart can wish for." This went on for some days, and then he told her that he must go away and leave her alone for a little while.

"Here are the house-keys," he said. "You can go where you like, and look at what you like; there is only one room into which I forbid you to enter on pain of death; this little key belongs to it."

He also gave her an egg, and begged her to take great care of it. "Always carry it about with you, if possible," he added, "for if it were to be lost, a great misfortune would happen."

She took the keys and the egg, and promised to carry out his wishes.

As soon as he had left she went over the house, looking at everything from top to bottom. The rooms shone with silver and gold, and she thought she had never before seen anything so splendid. At last she found herself close to the forbidden room, and was going to pass it, when her curiosity became too much for her, and she paused. First she looked at the key—it did not seem to her to be in any way different to the others; then she put it in the lock and gave it a little turn, and—the door flew open. But what a sight met her eyes as she stepped inside! There in the middle of the room stood a block, and on it lay a glittering axe, and all around there was blood upon the floor and the bodies of those who had been seized and cruelly murdered. She was so terrified that she let the egg she held in her hand fall to the ground. She picked it up and saw that there was blood upon it; she tried to wipe it off, but in vain, for rub and scrape as she would, the mark of the blood still remained.

Not long after this, the man returned, and the first things he asked for were the key and the egg. Trembling with fear, she gave them to him, but he knew at once when he saw the mark on the egg, that she had been into the forbidden room. "Since you have been into that room," he cried, "against my will, you shall now go there again against your own. Your life is ended." With these words he threw her to the ground, and dragging her by her hair to where the block stood, he cut off her head and her limbs, so that her blood flowed over the floor, and there he left her with the bodies of his other victims.

"I will now go and fetch the second one," he said; and once again he went to the same house, begging like a poor old man. The second daughter brought him a piece of bread, and he caught her and carried her away as he had the eldest one.

She did not meet with any better fate than her sister; for she was also overcome by her curiosity and looked into the forbidden room, and had to pay for it with her life on the man's return.

He next went and carried away the third sister. Now this sister was wiser and more cunning than the others, and after the wizard had given her the keys and the egg, and had left her, the first thing she did was to put the egg safely away. Then she looked over the house, and, finally, went into the forbidden room. Alas! what did she see! her two dear sisters lying murdered and cut to pieces. But she took the head and the body, and the arms and the legs, of each, and put them carefully together, and she had no sooner done this than the limbs began to move, and the different parts became joined to one another, and both sisters opened their eyes and were alive again. Then they kissed and embraced each other in their great joy.

As soon as the wizard returned he asked for the key and the egg, and when he saw that there was no trace of blood upon this, he said, "You have stood the test, you shall be my wife."

He had now lost all power over her, and was obliged in his turn to do whatever she wished.

"Very well," she answered, "but you must first take a basketful of gold to my father and mother, and carry it to them yourself; meanwhile I will prepare for our marriage."

Then she ran to the little room where she had hidden her sisters, and cried, "The moment has come for me to save you; the villain shall carry you home himself; but be sure you send someone to help me as soon as you get there." She put them both in a basket and covered them with gold, so that nothing of them could be seen. Then she called the wizard, and said to him, "Now carry away this basket, and mind you do not stop on the way to rest, for I shall be watching you from my little window." The wizard slung the basket over his shoulder and went off, but he found it such a weight to carry that the perspiration ran down his face, and he felt ready to die of exhaustion. He longed so to rest, that he stopped and sat down, but immediately a voice called out from the basket, "I am watching from my little window; I can see you stopping to rest; will you please to go on!" He thought it was his bride calling after him, so he got up and went on. Presently he sat down again, but the same voice called out, "I am watching you from my little window; I can see you stopping to rest; will you please to go on at once!" And as often as he stopped to rest, he heard

the same voice, so that he was obliged to go on till, gasping for breath, he had carried the girls and the gold into the parents' house.

At home, meanwhile, the bride was preparing for the wedding festivities. She took one of his victims' heads, put a smart headdress and wreath of flowers upon it, and placed it looking out of the garret window. She then invited all the wedding-guests, and when that was done, she got into a barrel of honey, and then cut open a bed and rolled herself in the feathers, so that she looked like some wonderful bird, and no one would have known who she was. Then she left the house, and as she went along she met some of the wedding guests, who said—

"Fitcher's bird, whence come you I pray?
I come from Fitcher's house to-day,
And what is the young bride doing now?
She has swept the house, all round and about,
And sits at her window looking out."

By and by she met the bridegroom returning, and he also said—

> "Fitcher's bird, whence come you I pray?
> I come from Fitcher's house to-day,
> And what is the young bride doing now?
> She has swept the house, all round and about,
> And sits at her window looking out."

The bridegroom looked up and saw the head at the window, and thinking it was his bride, he nodded and smiled at it. But no sooner were he and his guests assembled in the house, than the friends arrived who had been sent by the sisters. They locked all the doors, so that no one might escape, and then set fire to the house, and the wizard and all his companions were burnt to death.

KARL KATZ

In the midst of the Hartz forests there is a high mountain, of which the neighbors tell all sorts of stories: how the goblins and fairies dance on it by night; and how the old Emperor Redbeard holds his court there, and sits on his marble throne, with his long beard sweeping on the ground.

A great many years ago there lived in a village at the foot of this mountain, one Karl Katz. Now Karl was a goatherd, and every morning he drove his flock to feed upon the green spots that are here and there found on the mountain's side. In the evening he sometimes thought it too late to drive his charge home; so he used in such cases to shut it up in a spot amongst the woods, where the old ruined walls of some castle that had long ago been deserted were left standing, and were high enough to form a fold, in which he could count his goats, and let them rest for the night. One evening he found that the prettiest goat of his flock had vanished, soon after they were driven into this fold. He searched everywhere for it in vain; but, to his surprise and delight, when he counted his flock in the morning, what should he see, the first of the flock, but his lost goat! Again and again the same strange thing happened. At last he thought he would watch still more narrowly; and, having looked carefully over the old walls, he found a narrow doorway, through which it seemed that his favorite made her way. Karl followed, and found a path leading downwards through a cleft in the rocks. On he went, scrambling as well as he could, down the side of the rock, and at last came to the mouth of a cave, where he lost sight of his goat. Just then he saw that his faithful dog was not with him. He whistled, but no dog was there; and he was therefore forced to go into the cave and try to find his goat by himself

He groped his way for a while, and at last came to a place where a little light found its way in; and there he wondered not a little to find his goat, employing itself very much at its ease in the cavern, in eating corn, which kept dropping from some place over its head. He went up and looked about him, to see where all this corn, that rattled about his ears like a hail-storm, could come from: but all overhead was dark, and he could find no clue to this strange business.

At last, as he stood listening, he thought he heard the neighing and stamping of horses. He listened again; it was plainly so; and after a while he was sure that horses were feeding above him, and that the corn fell from their mangers. What could these horses be, which were thus kept in the clefts of rocks, where none but the goat's foot ever trod? There must be people of some sort or other living here; and who could they be? and was it safe to trust himself in such company? Karl pondered awhile; but his wonder only grew greater and greater, when on a sudden he heard his own name, "Karl Katz!" echo through the cavern. He turned round, but could see nothing. "Karl Katz!" again sounded sharply in his ears; and soon out came a little dwarfish page, with a high-peaked hat and a scarlet cloak, from a dark corner at one end of the cave.

The dwarf nodded, and beckoned him to follow. Karl thought he should first like to know a little about who it was that thus sought his company. He asked: but the dwarf shook his head, answering not a word, and again beckoned him to follow. He did so; and winding his way through ruins, he soon heard rolling overhead what sounded like peals of thunder, echoing among the rocks: the noise grew louder and louder as he went on, and at last he came to a courtyard surrounded by old ivy-grown walls. The spot seemed to be the bosom of a little valley; above rose on every hand high masses of rock; wide-branching trees threw their arms overhead, so that nothing but a glimmering twilight made its way through; and here, on the cool smooth-shaven turf, Karl saw twelve strange old figures amusing themselves very sedately with a game of nine-pins.

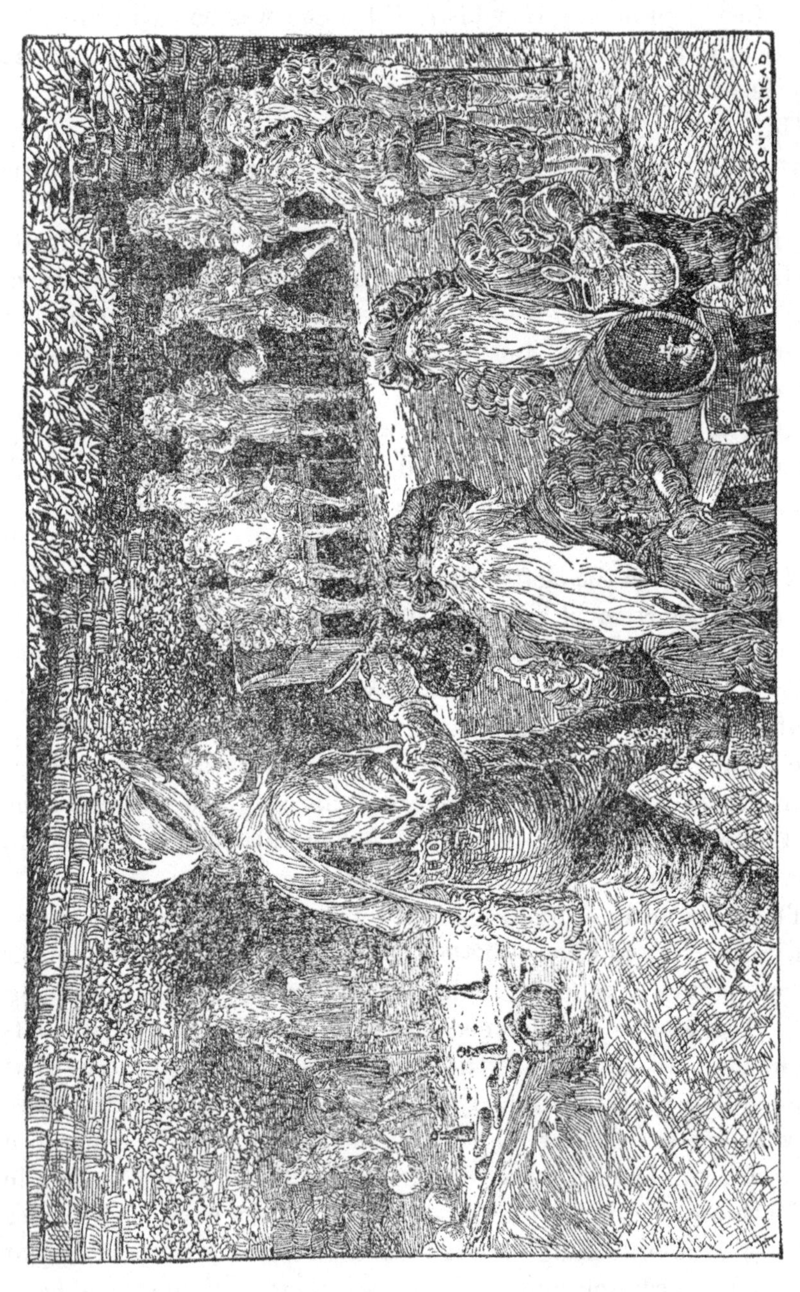

KARL THOUGHT HE NEVER TASTED ANYTHING HALF SO GOOD BEFORE

Their dress did not seem altogether strange to Karl, for in the church of the town whither he went every week to market there was an old monument, with figures of queer old knights upon it, dressed in the very same fashion. Not a word fell from any of their lips. They moved about soberly and gravely, each taking his turn at the game; but the oldest of them ordered Karl Katz, by dumb signs, to busy himself in setting up the pins as they knocked them down. At first his knees trembled, as he hardly dared snatch a stolen sidelong glance at the long beards and old-fashioned dresses of the worthy knights; but he soon saw that as each knight played out his game he went to his seat, and there took a hearty draught at a flagon, which the dwarf kept filled, and which sent up the smell of the richest old wine.

Little by little Karl got bolder; and at last he plucked up his heart so far as to beg the dwarf, by signs, to let him, too, take his turn at the flagon. The dwarf gave it him with a grave bow, and Karl thought he never tasted anything half so good before. This gave him new strength for his work; and as often as he flagged at all, he turned to the same kind friend for help in his need.

Which was tired first, he or the knights, Karl never could tell; or whether the wine got the better of his head: but what he knew was, that sleep at last over-powered him, and that when he awoke he found himself stretched out upon the old spot within the walls where he had folded his flock, and saw that the bright sun was high up in the heavens. The same green turf was spread beneath, and the same tottering ivy-clad walls surrounded him. He rubbed his eyes and called his dog; but neither dog nor goat was to be seen; and when he looked about him again, the grass seemed to be longer under his feet than it was yesterday; and trees hung over his head, which he had either never seen before, or had quite forgotten. Shaking his head, and hardly knowing whether he was in his right mind, he got up and stretched himself: somehow or other his joints felt stiffer than they were. "It serves me right," said he; "this comes of sleeping out of one's own bed." Little by little he recollected his evening's sport, and licked his lips as he thought of the charming wine he had taken so much of. "But who," thought he, "can those people be, that come to this odd place to play at nine-pins?"

His first step was to look for the doorway through which he had followed his goat; but to his astonishment, not the least trace of an opening of any sort was to be seen. There stood the wall, without chink or crack big enough for a rat to pass through. Again he paused and scratched his head. His hat was full of holes: "Why, it was new last Shrove-tide!" said he. By chance his eye fell next on his shoes, which were almost new when he last left home; but now they looked so old, that they were likely to fall to pieces before he could get home. All his clothes seemed in the same sad plight. The more he looked, the more he pondered, the more he was at a loss to know what could have happened to him.

At length he turned round, and left the old walls to look for his flock. Slow and out of heart he wound his way among the mountain steeps, through paths where his flocks were wont to wander: still not a goat was to be seen. Again he whistled and called his dog, but no dog came. Below him in the plain lay the village where his home was; so at length he took the downward path, and set out with a heavy heart and a faltering step in search of his flock.

"Surely," said he, "I shall soon meet some neighbor, who can tell me where my goats are?" But the people who met him, as he drew near to the village, were all unknown to him. They were not even dressed as his neighbors were, and they seemed as if they hardly spoke the same tongue. When he eagerly asked each, as he came up, after his goats, they only stared at him and stroked their chins. At last he did the same too; and what was his wonder to find that his beard was grown at least a foot long! "The world," said he to himself, "is surely turned upside down, or if not, I must be bewitched": and yet he knew the mountain, as he turned round again, and looked back on its woody heights; and he knew the houses and cottages also, with their little gardens, as he entered the village. All were in the places he had always known them in; and he heard some children, too (as a traveller that passed by was asking his way), call the village by the very same name he had always known it to bear.

Again he shook his head, and went straight through the village to his own cottage. Alas! it looked sadly out of repair; the windows were broken, the door off its hinges, and in the courtyard lay an unknown child, in a ragged dress, playing with a rough, toothless old dog, whom he thought he ought to know, but who snarled and barked in his face when he called to him. He went in at the open doorway; but he found all so dreary and empty, that he staggered out again like a drunken man, and called his wife and children loudly by their names: but no one heard, at least no one answered him.

A crowd of women and children soon flocked around the strange-looking man with the long grey beard; and all broke upon him at once with the questions, "Who are you?" "Who is it that you want?" It seemed to him so odd to ask other people, at his own door, after his wife and children, that, in order to get rid of the crowd, he named the first man that came into his head. "Hans the blacksmith?" said he. Most held their tongues and stared; but at last an old woman said, "He went these seven years ago to a place that you will not reach to-day." "Fritz the tailor, then?" "Heaven rest his soul!" said an old beldam upon crutches; "he has lain these ten years in a house that he'll never leave."

Karl Katz looked at the old woman again, and shuddered, as he knew her to be one of his old gossips; but saw she had a strangely altered face. All wish to ask further questions was gone; but at last a young woman made her way through the gaping throng, with a baby in her arms, and a little girl of about three years old clinging to her other hand. All three looked the very image of his own wife. "What is thy name? " asked he, wildly. "Liese!" said she. "And your father's?" "Karl Katz! Heaven bless him!" said she: "but, poor man! he is lost and gone. It is now full twenty years since we sought for him day and night on the mountain. His dog and his flock came back, but he never was heard of any more. I was then seven years old."

Poor Karl could hold no longer: "I am Karl Katz, and no other!" said he, as he took the child from his daughter's arms and kissed it over and over again.

All stood gaping, and hardly knowing what to say or think, when old Stropken the schoolmaster hobbled by, and took a long and close look at him. "Karl Katz! Karl Katz!" said he slowly: "why it is Karl Katz, sure enough! There is my own mark upon him; there is the scar over his right eye, that I gave him myself one day with my oak stick." Then several others also cried out, "Yes it is! it is Karl Katz! Welcome neighbor, welcome home!" "But where," said or thought all, "can an honest steady fellow like you have been these twenty years?"

And now the whole village had flocked around; the children laughed, the dogs barked, and all were glad to see neighbor Karl home alive and well. As to where he had been for the twenty years, that was a part of the story at which Karl shrugged up his shoulders; for he never could very well explain it, and seemed to think the less that was said about it the better. But it was plain enough that what dwelt most on his memory was the noble wine that had tickled his mouth while the knights played their game of nine-pins.

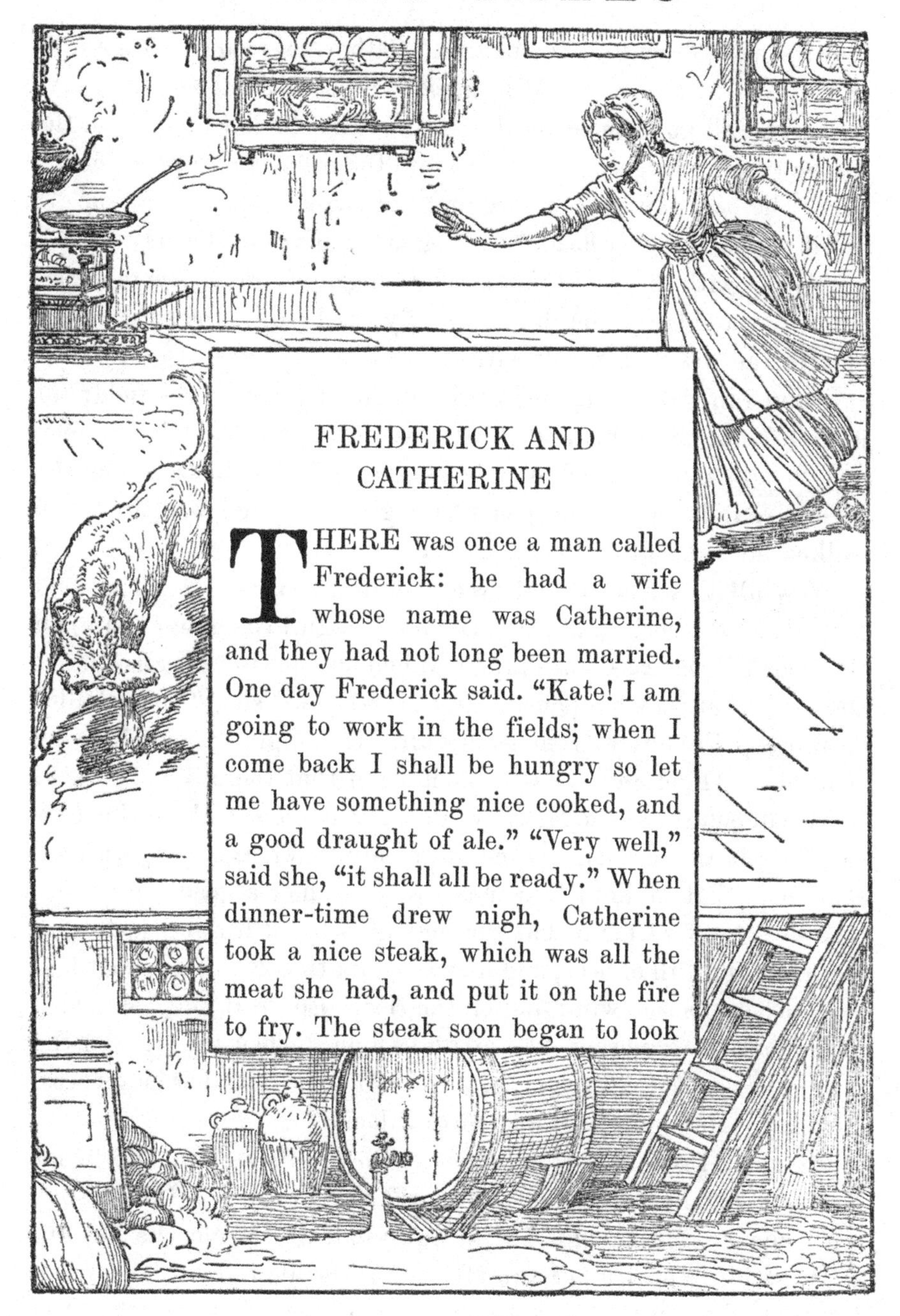

FREDERICK AND CATHERINE

THERE was once a man called Frederick: he had a wife whose name was Catherine, and they had not long been married. One day Frederick said. "Kate! I am going to work in the fields; when I come back I shall be hungry so let me have something nice cooked, and a good draught of ale." "Very well," said she, "it shall all be ready." When dinner-time drew nigh, Catherine took a nice steak, which was all the meat she had, and put it on the fire to fry. The steak soon began to look brown, and to crackle in the pan; and Catherine stood by with a fork and turned it: then she said to herself, "The steak is almost ready, I may as well go to the cellar for the ale." So she left the pan on the fire and took a large jug and went into the cellar and tapped the ale cask. The beer ran into the jug and Catherine stood looking on. At last it popped into her head, "The dog is not shut up—he may be running away with the steak; that's well thought of." So up she ran from the cellar; and sure enough the rascally cur had got the steak in his mouth, and was making off with it.

Away ran Catherine, and away ran the dog across the field: but he ran faster than she, and stuck close to the steak. "It's all gone, and "what can't be cured must be endured"," said Catherine. So she turned round; and as she had run a good way and was tired, she walked home leisurely to cool herself.

Now all this time the ale was running too, for Catherine had not turned the cock; and when the jug was full the liquor ran upon the floor till the cask was empty. When she got to the cellar stairs she saw what had happened. "My stars!" said she, "what shall I do to keep Frederick from seeing all this slopping about?" So she thought a while; and at last remembered that there was a sack of fine meal bought at the last fair, and that if she sprinkled this over the floor it would suck up the ale nicely. "What a lucky thing," said she, "that we kept that meal! we have now a good use for it." So away she went for it: but she managed to set it down just upon the great jug full of beer, and upset it; and thus all the ale that had been saved was set swimming on the floor also. "Ah! well," said she, "when one goes another may as well follow." Then she strewed the meal all about the cellar, and was quite pleased with her cleverness, and said, "How very neat and clean it looks!"

At noon Frederick came home. "Now, wife," cried he, "what have you for dinner?" "O Frederick!" answered she, "I was cooking you a steak; but while I went down to draw the ale, the dog ran away with it; and while I ran after him, the ale ran out; and when I went to dry up the ale with the sack of meal that we got at the fair, I upset the jug: but the cellar is now quite dry, and looks so clean!" "Kate, Kate," said he, "how could you do all this?" Why did you leave the steak to fry, and the ale to run, and then spoil all the meal?" "Why, Frederick," said she, "I did not know I was doing wrong; you should have told me before."

The husband thought to himself, "If my wife manages matters thus, I must look sharp myself." Now he had a good deal of gold in the house: so he said to Catherine, "What pretty yellow buttons these are! I shall put them into a box and bury them in the garden; but take care that you never go near or meddle with them." "No, Frederick," said she, "that I never will." As soon as he was gone, there came by some pedlars with earthenware plates and dishes, and they asked her whether she would buy. "Oh dear me, I should like to buy very much, but I have no money: if you had any use for yellow buttons, I might deal with you." "Yellow buttons!" said they: "let us have a look at them." "Go into the garden and dig where I tell you, and you will find the yellow buttons: I dare not go myself." So the rogues went: and when they found what these yellow buttons were, they took them all away, and left her plenty of plates and dishes. Then she set them all about the house for a show: and when Frederick came back, he cried out, "Kate, what have you been doing?" "See," said she, "I have bought all these with your yellow buttons: but I did not touch them myself; the pedlars went themselves and dug them up." "Wife, wife," said Frederick, "what a pretty piece of work you have made! those yellow buttons were all my money: how came you to do such a thing?" "Why," answered she, "I did not know there was any harm in it; you should have told me."

Catherine stood musing for a while, and at last said to her husband, "Hark ye, Frederick, we will soon get the gold back: let us run after the thieves." "Well, we will try," answered he; "but take some butter and cheese with you, that we may have something to eat by the way." "Very well," said she; and they set out: and as Frederick walked the fastest, he left his wife some way behind. "It does not matter," thought she: "when we turn back, I shall be so much nearer home than he."

Presently she came to the top of a hill, down the side of which there was a road so narrow that the cart wheels always chafed the trees on each side as they passed. "Ah, see now," said she, "how they have bruised and wounded those poor trees; they will never get well." So she took pity on them, and made use of the butter to grease them all, so that the wheels might not hurt them so much.

While she was doing this kind office one of her cheeses fell out of the basket, and rolled down the hill. Catherine looked, but could not see where it had gone; so she said, "Well, I suppose the other will go the same way and find you; he has younger legs than I have." Then she rolled the other cheese after it; and away it went, nobody knows where, down the hill. But she said she supposed that they knew the road, and would follow her, and she could not stay there all day waiting for them.

At last she overtook Frederick, who desired her to give him something to eat. Then she gave him the dry bread. "Where are the butter and cheese?" said he. "Oh!" answered she, "I used the butter to grease those poor trees that the wheels chafed so: and one of the cheeses ran away so I sent the other after it to find it, and I suppose they are both on the road together somewhere." "What a goose you are to do such silly things!" said the husband. "How can you say so?" said she; "I am sure you never told me not."

They ate the dry bread together; and Frederick said, "Kate, I hope you locked the door safe when you came away." "No," answered she, "you did not tell me." "Then go home, and do it now before we go any farther," said Frederick, "and bring with you something to eat."

Catherine did as he told her, and thought to herself by the way, "Frederick wants something to eat; but I don't think he is very fond of butter and cheese: I'll bring him a bag of fine nuts, and the vinegar, for I have often seen him take some."

When she reached home, she bolted the back door, but the front door she took off the hinges, and said, "Frederick told me to lock the door, but surely it can nowhere be so safe if I take it with me." So she took her time by the way; and when she overtook her husband she cried out, "There, Frederick, there is the door itself, you may watch it as carefully as you please." "Alas! alas!" said he, "what a clever wife I have! I sent you to make the house fast, and you take the door away, so that everybody may go in and out as they please—however, as you have brought the door, you shall carry it about with you for your pains." "Very well," answered she, "I'll carry the door; but I'll not carry the nuts and vinegar bottle also—that would be too much of a load; so if you please, I'll fasten them to the door."

Frederick of course made no objection to that plan, and they set off into the wood to look for the thieves; but they could not find them: and when it grew dark, they climbed up into a tree to spend the night there. Scarcely were they up, than who should come by but the very rogues they were looking for. They were in truth great rascals, and belonged to that class of people who find things before they are lost; they were tired; so they sat down and made a fire under the very tree where Frederick and Catherine were. Frederick slipped down on the other side, and picked up some stones. Then he climbed up again, and tried to hit the thieves on the head with them: but they only said, "It must be near morning, for the wind shakes the fir-apples down."

Catherine, who had the door on her shoulder, began to be very tired; but she thought it was the nuts upon it that were so heavy: so she said softly, "Frederick, I must let the nuts go." "No," answered he, "not now, they will discover us." "I can't help that: they must go." "Well, then, make haste and throw them down, if you will." Then away rattled the nuts down among the boughs and one of the thieves cried, "Bless me, it is hailing."

A little while after, Catherine thought the door was still very heavy: so she whispered to Frederick, "I must throw the vinegar down." "Pray don't," answered he, "it will discover us." "I can't help that," said she, "go it must." So she poured all the vinegar down; and the thieves said, "What a heavy dew there is!"

At last it popped into Catherine's head that it was the door itself that was so heavy all the time: so she whispered, "Frederick, I must throw the door down soon." But he begged and prayed her not to do so, for he was sure it would betray them. "Here goes, however," said she: and down went the door with such a clatter upon the thieves, that they cried out "Murder!" and not knowing what was coming, ran away as fast as they could, and left all the gold. So when Frederick and Catherine came down, there they found all their money safe and sound.

THE THREE CHILDREN OF FORTUNE

ONCE upon a time a father sent for his three sons, and gave to the eldest a cock, to the second a scythe, and to the third a cat. "I am now old," said he, "my end is approaching, and I would fain provide for you before I die. Money I have none, and what I now give you seems of but little worth; yet it rests with yourselves alone to turn my gifts to good account. Only seek out for a land where what you have is as yet unknown, and your fortune is made."

After the death of the father, the eldest set out with his cock: but wherever he went, in every town he saw from afar off a cock sitting upon the church steeple, and turning round with the wind. In the villages he always heard plenty of them crowing, and his bird was therefore nothing new; so there did not seem much chance of his making his fortune. At length it happened that he came to an island where the people who lived there had never heard of a cock, and knew not even how to reckon the time. They knew, indeed, if it were morning or evening; but at night, if they lay awake, they had no means of knowing how time went. "Behold," said he to them, "what a noble animal this is! how like a knight he is! he carries a bright red crest upon his head, and spurs upon his heels; he crows three times every night, at stated hours, and at the third time the sun is about to rise. But this is not all; sometimes he screams in broad day-light, and then you must take warning, for the weather is surely about to change." This pleased the natives mightily; they kept awake one whole night, and heard, to their great joy, how gloriously the cock called the hour, at two, four, and six o'clock. Then they asked him whether the bird was to be sold, and how much he would sell it for. "About as much gold as an ass can carry," said he. "A very fair price for such an animal," cried they with one voice; and agreed to give him what he asked.

When he returned home with his wealth, his brothers wondered greatly; and the second said, "I will now set forth likewise, and see if I can turn my scythe to as good an account." There did not seem, however, much likelihood of this; for go where he would, he was met by peasants who had as good a scythe on their shoulders as he had. But at last, as good luck would have it, he came to an island where the people had never heard of a scythe: there, as soon as the corn was ripe, they went into the fields and pulled it up; but this was very hard work, and a great deal of it was lost. The man then set to work with his scythe; and mowed down their whole crop so quickly, that the people stood staring open-mouthed with wonder. They were willing to give him what he asked for such a marvellous thing: but he only took a horse laden with as much gold as it could carry.

Now the third brother had a great longing to go and see what he could make of his cat. So he set out: and at first it happened to him as it had to the others, so long as he kept upon the mainland, he met with no success; there were plenty of cats everywhere, indeed too many, so that the young ones were for the most part, as soon as they came into the world, drowned in the water. At last he passed over to an island, where, as it chanced most luckily for him, nobody had ever seen a cat; and they were overrun with mice to such a degree, that the little wretches danced upon the tables and chairs, whether the master of the house were at home or not. The people complained loudly of this grievance; the king himself knew not how to rid himself of them in his palace; in every corner mice were squeaking, and they gnawed everything that their teeth could lay hold of. Here was a fine field for Puss—she soon began her chase, and had cleared two rooms in the twinkling of an eye; when the people besought their king to buy the wonderful animal, for the good of the public, at any price. The king willingly gave what was asked,—a mule laden with gold and jewels; and thus the third brother returned home with a richer prize than either of the others.

Meantime the cat feasted away upon the mice in the royal palace, and devoured so many that they were no longer in any great numbers. At length, quite spent and tired with her work, she became extremely thirsty; so she stood still, drew up her head, and cried, "Miau, Miau!" The king gathered together all his subjects when they heard this strange cry, and many ran shrieking in a great fright out of the palace. But the king held a council below as to what was best to be done; and it was at length fixed to send a herald to the cat, to warn her to leave the castle forthwith, or that force would be used to remove her. "For," said the counsellors, "we would far more willingly put up with the mice (since we are used to that evil), than get rid of them at the risk of our lives." A page accordingly went, and asked the cat whether she were willing to quit the castle. But Puss, whose thirst became every moment more and more pressing, answered nothing but "Miau! Miau!" which the page interpreted to mean "No! No!" and therefore carried this answer to the king. "Well," said the counsellors, "then we must try what force will do." So the guns were planted, and the palace was fired upon from all sides. When the fire reached the room where the cat was, she sprang out of the window and ran away; but the besiegers did not see her, and went on firing until the whole palace was burnt to the ground.

MRS. FOX

THERE was once a sly old fox with nine tails, who was very curious to know whether his wife was true to him: so he stretched himself out under a bench, and pretended to be dead as a mouse.

Then Mrs. Fox went up into her own room and locked the door: but her maid, the cat, sat at the kitchen fire cooking; and soon after it became known that the old fox was dead, some one knocked at the door, saying,

"Miss Pussy! Miss Pussy! how fare you to-day?
Are you sleeping or watching the time away?"

Then the cat went and opened the door, and there stood a young fox; so she said to him,

"No, no, Master Fox, I don't sleep in the day,

I'm making some capital white wine whey.

Will your honor be pleased to dinner to stay?"

"No, I thank you," said the fox; "but how is poor Mrs. Fox?" Then the cat answered,

> "She sits all alone in her chamber up stairs,
> And bewails her misfortune with floods of tears:
> She weeps till her beautiful eyes are red;
> For, alas! alas! Mr. Fox is dead."

"Go to her," said the other, "and say that there is a young fox come, who wishes to marry her."

> Then up went the cat,—trippety trap,
> And knocked at the door,—tippety tap;
> "Is good Mrs. Fox within?" said she.
> "Alas! my dear, what want you with me?"
> "There waits a suitor below at the gate."

Then said Mrs. Fox,

> "How looks he, my dear! is he tall and straight?
> Has he nine good tails? There must be nine,
> Or he never shall be a suitor of mine."

"Ah!" said the cat, "he has but one." "Then I will never have him," answered Mrs. Fox.

So the cat went down, and sent this suitor about his business. Soon after, some one else knocked at the door; it was another fox that had two tails, but he was not better welcomed than the first. After this came several others, till at last one came that had really nine tails just like the old fox.

When the widow heard this, she jumped up and said,

> "Now, Pussy, my dear, open windows and doors,
> And bid all our friends at our wedding to meet;
> And as for that nasty old master of ours,
> Throw him out of the window, Puss, into the street."

But when the wedding feast was all ready, up sprang the old gentleman on a sudden, and taking a club drove the whole company, together with Mrs. Fox, out of doors.

After some time, however, the old fox really died; and soon afterwards a wolf came to pay his respects, and knocked at the door.

> *Wolf.* Good day, Mrs. Cat, with your whiskers so trim;
> How comes it you're sitting alone so prim?
> What's that you are cooking so nicely, I pray?

Cat. O, that's bread and milk for my dinner to-day.
Will your worship be pleased to stay and dine,
Or shall I fetch you a glass of wine?

"No, I thank you: Mrs. Fox is not at home, I suppose?"

Cat. She sits all alone,
Her griefs to bemoan;
For, alas! alas! Mr. Fox is gone.

Wolf. Ah! dear Mrs. Puss! that's a loss indeed;
D'ye think she'd take me for a husband instead?

Cat. "Indeed, Mr. Wolf, I don't know but she may,
If you'll sit down a moment, I'll step up and see."

So she gave him a chair, and shaking her ears,
She very obligingly tripped it up stairs.
She knocked at the door with the rings on her toes,
And said, "Mrs. Fox, you're within, I suppose?"
"O yes," said the widow, "pray come in, my dear,
And tell me whose voice in the kitchen I hear."
"It's a wolf," said the cat, "with a nice smooth skin,
Who was passing this way, and just stepped in
To see (as old Mr. Fox is dead)
If you like to take him for a husband instead."

"But," said Mrs. Fox, "has he red feet and a sharp snout?" "No," said the cat. "Then he won't do for me." Soon after the wolf was sent about his business, there came a dog, then a goat, and after that a bear, a lion, and all the beasts, one after another. But they all wanted something that old Mr. Fox had, and the cat was ordered to send them all away. At last came a young Fox, and Mrs. Fox said "Has he four red feet and a sharp snout?" "Yes," said the cat.

"Then, Puss, make the parlour look clean and neat,
And throw the old gentleman into the street;
A stupid old rascal! I'm glad that he's dead,
Now I've got such a charming young fox instead."
So the wedding was held, and the merry bells rung,
And the friends and relations they danced and they sung,
And feasted and drank, I can't tell how long.

THE CHANGELING

A MOTHER once had her child stolen from her by the elves. They took it out of the cradle and placed in its stead a changeling with a large head and staring eyes, that would do nothing but eat and drink. In her distress, she went to one of her neighbors and asked her advice. The neighbor told her to carry the changeling into the kitchen and seat it on the hearth, then to light a fire and boil some water in two egg-shells. That, she said, would make the changeling laugh, and if he once laughed, it would be all over with him. The mother went back and followed out all these directions. As she put the egg-shells with water in them on the fire, the little gnome-child said—

> "I am old as the woods,
> But from ages of yore,
> I never saw shells
> Used for boiling before."

and with that he began to laugh. While he was laughing a company of elves came crowding into the kitchen, bringing with them the woman's own child, which they laid down on the hearth. Then they took up the changeling and disappeared with him.

HANS IN LUCK

SOME men are born to good luck: all they do or try to do comes right—all that falls to them is so much gain—all their geese are swans—all their cards are trumps—toss them which way you will, they will always, like poor puss, alight upon their legs, and only move on so much the faster. The world may very likely not always think of them as they think of themselves, but what care they for the world? what can it know about the matter?

One of these lucky beings was neighbour Hans. Seven long years he had worked hard for his master. At last he said, "Master, my time is up; I must go home and see my poor mother once more: so pray pay me my wages and let me go." And the master said, "You have been a faithful and good servant, Hans, so your pay shall be handsome." Then he gave him a lump of silver as big as his head.

Hans took out his pocket-handkerchief, put the piece of silver into it, threw it over his shoulder, and jogged off on his road homewards. As he went lazily on, dragging one foot after another, a man came in sight, trotting gaily along on a capital horse. "Ah!" said Hans aloud, "what a fine thing it is to ride on horseback! There he sits as easy and happy as if he was at home, in the chair by his fireside; he trips against no stones, saves shoe-leather, and gets on he hardly knows how." Hans did not speak so softly but the horseman heard it all, and said, "Well, friend, why do you go on foot then?" "Ah!" said he, "I have this load to carry: to be sure it is silver, but it is so heavy that I can't hold up my head, and you must know it hurts my shoulder sadly." "What do you say of making an exchange?" said the horseman. "I will give you my horse, and you shall give me the silver; which will save you a great deal of trouble in carrying such a heavy load about with you." "With all my heart," said Hans: "but as you are so kind to me, I must tell you one thing—you will have a weary task to draw that silver about with you." However, the horseman got off, took the silver, helped Hans up, gave him the bridle into one hand and the whip into the other, and said, "When you want to go very fast, smack your lips loudly together, and cry 'Jip!'"

Hans was delighted as he sat on the horse, drew himself up, squared his elbows, turned out his toes, cracked his whip, and rode merrily off, one minute whistling a merry tune, and another singing,

"No care and no sorrow,
A fig for the morrow!
We'll laugh and be merry,
Sing neigh down derry!"

After a time he thought he should like to go a little faster, so he smacked his lips and cried "Jip!" Away went the horse full gallop; and before Hans knew what he was about, he was thrown off, and lay on his back by the road-side. His horse would have ran off, if a shepherd who was coming by, driving a cow, had not stopped it. Hans soon came to himself, and got upon his legs again, sadly vexed, and said to the shepherd, "This riding is no joke, when a man has the luck to get upon a beast like this that stumbles and flings him off as if it would break his neck. However, I'm off now once for all: I like your cow now a great deal better than this smart beast that played me this trick, and has spoiled my best coat, you see, in this puddle; which, by the by, smells not very like a nosegay. One can walk along at one's leisure behind that cow—keep good company, and have milk, butter, and cheese, every day, into the bargain. What would I give to have such a prize!" "Well," said the shepherd, "if you are so fond of her, I will change my cow for your horse; I like to do good to my neighbors, even though I lose by it myself." "Done!" said Hans, merrily. "What a noble heart that good man has!" thought he. Then the shepherd jumped upon the horse, wished Hans and the cow good morning, and away he rode.

Hans brushed his coat, wiped his face and hands, rested a while, and then drove off his cow quietly, and thought his bargain a very lucky one. "If I have only a piece of bread (and I certainly shall always be able to get that), I can, whenever I like, eat my butter and cheese with it; and when I am thirsty I can milk my cow and drink the milk: and what can I wish for more?" When he came to an inn, he halted, ate up all his bread, and gave away his last penny for a glass of beer. When he had rested himself he set off again, driving his cow towards his mother's village. But the heat grew greater as soon as noon came on, till at last, as he found himself on a wide heath that would take him more than an hour to cross, he began to be so hot and parched that his tongue clave to the roof of his mouth. "I can find a cure for this," thought he; "now I will milk my cow and quench my thirst": so he tied her to the stump of a tree, and held his leathern cap to milk into; but not a drop was to be had. Who would have thought that this cow, which was to bring him milk and butter and cheese, was all that time utterly dry? Hans had not thought of looking to that.

While he was trying his luck in milking, and managing the matter very clumsily, the uneasy beast began to think him very troublesome; and at last gave him such a kick on the head as knocked him down; and there he lay a long while senseless. Luckily a butcher soon came by, driving a pig in a wheelbarrow. "What is the matter with you, my man?" said the butcher, as he helped him up. Hans told him what had happened, how he was dry, and wanted to milk his cow, but found the cow was dry too. Then the butcher gave him a flask of ale, saying, "There, drink and refresh yourself; your cow will give you no milk: don't you see she is an old beast, good for nothing but the slaughter-house?" "Alas, alas!" said Hans, "who would have thought it? What a shame to take my horse, and give me only a dry cow! If I kill her, what will she be good for? I hate cow-beef; it is not tender enough for me. If it were a pig now—like that fat gentleman you are driving along at his ease—one could do something with it; it would at any rate make sausages." "Well," said the butcher, "I don't like to say no, when one is asked to do a kind, neighborly thing. To please you I will change, and give you my fine fat pig for the cow." "Heaven reward you for your kindness and self-denial!" said Hans, as he gave the butcher the cow; and taking the pig off the wheel-barrow, drove it away, holding it by the string that was tied to its leg.

So on he jogged, and all seemed now to go right with him: he had met with some misfortunes, to be sure; but he was now well repaid for all. How could it be otherwise with such a travelling companion as he had at last got?

The next man he met was a countryman carrying a fine white goose. The countryman stopped to ask what was o'clock; this led to further chat; and Hans told him all his luck, how he had so many good bargains, and how all the world went gay and smiling with him. The countryman then began to tell his tale, and said he was going to take the goose to a christening. "Feel," said he, "how heavy it is, and yet it is only eight weeks old. Whoever roasts and eats it will find plenty of fat upon it, it has lived so well!" "You're right," said Hans, as he weighed it in his hand; "but if you talk of fat, my pig is no trifle." Meantime the countryman began to look grave, and shook his head. "Hark ye!" said he, "my worthy friend, you seem a good sort of fellow, so I can't help doing you a kind turn. Your pig may get you into a scrape. In the village I just came from, the squire has had a pig stolen out of his sty. I was dreadfully afraid when I saw you that you had got the squire's pig. If you have, and they catch you, it will be a bad job for you. The least they will do will be to throw you into the horse-pond. Can you swim?"

"HARK YE! MY WORTHY FRIEND. YOUR PIG MAY GET YOU INTO A SCRAPE."

Poor Hans was sadly frightened. "Good man," cried he, "pray get me out of this scrape. I know nothing of where the pig was either bred or born; but he may have been the squire's for aught I can tell: you know this country better than I do, take my pig and give me the goose." "I ought to have something into the bargain," said the countryman; "give a fat goose for a pig, indeed! 'Tis not everyone would do so much for you as that. However, I will not be hard upon you, as you are in trouble." Then he took the string in his hand, and drove off the pig by a side path; while Hans went on the way homewards free from care. "After all," thought he, "that chap is pretty well taken in. I don't care whose pig it is, but wherever it came from it has been a very good friend to me. I have much the best of the bargain. First there will be a capital roast; then the fat will find me in goose-grease for six months; and then there are all the beautiful white feathers. I will put them into my pillow, and then I am sure I shall sleep soundly without rocking. How happy my mother will be! Talk of a pig, indeed! Give me a fine fat goose."

As he came to the next village, he saw a scissor-grinder with his wheel, working and singing,

"O'er hill and o'er dale
So happy I roam,
Work light and live well,
All the world is my home;
Then who so blythe, so merry as I?"

Hans stood looking on for a while, and at last said, "You must be well off, master grinder! you seem so happy at your work." "Yes," said the other, "mine is a golden trade; a good grinder never puts his hand into his pocket without finding money in it—but where did you get that beautiful goose?" "I did not buy it, I gave a pig for it." "And where did you get the pig?" "I gave a cow for it." "And the cow?" "I gave a horse for it." "And the horse?" "I gave a lump of silver as big as my head for it." "And the silver?" "Oh! I worked hard for that seven long years." "You have thriven well in the world hitherto," said the grinder, "now if you could find money in your pocket whenever you put your hand in it, your fortune would be made." "Very true: but how is that to be managed?" "How? Why, you must turn grinder like myself," said the other; "you only want a grindstone; the rest will come of itself. Here is one that is but little the worse for wear: I would not ask more than the value of your goose for it—will you buy?" "How can you ask?" said Hans; "I should be the happiest man in the world, if I could have money whenever I put my hand in my pocket: what could I want more? there's the goose." "Now," said the grinder, as he gave him a common rough stone that lay by his side, "this is a most capital stone; do but work it well enough, and you can make an old nail cut with it."

Hans took the stone, and went his way with a light heart: his eyes sparkled for joy, and he said to himself, "Surely I must have been born in a lucky hour; everything I could want or wish for comes of itself. People are so kind; they seem really to think I do them a favor in letting them make me rich, and giving me good bargains."

Meantime he began to be tired, and hungry too, for he had given away his last penny in his joy at getting the cow.

At last he could go no farther, for the stone tired him sadly: and he dragged himself to the side of a river, that he might take a drink of water, and rest a while. So he laid the stone carefully by his side on the bank: but, as he stooped down to drink, he forgot it, pushed it a little, and down it rolled, plump into the stream.

For a while he watched it sinking in the deep clear water; then sprang up and danced for joy, and again fell upon his knees and thanked Heaven, with tears in his eyes, for its kindness in taking away his only plague, the ugly heavy stone.

"How happy am I!" cried he; "nobody was ever so lucky as I." Then up he got with a light heart, free from all his troubles, and walked on till he reached his mother's house, and told her how very easy the road to good luck was.

THE BEAR AND THE SKRATTEL

ONE Christmas Day, the King of Norway sat in the great hall of his palace, holding a feast. "Here's a health," said he, "to our brother the King of Denmark! What present shall we send our royal brother, as a pledge of our good-will, this Christmas time?" "Send him, please your majesty," said the Norseman Gunter, who was the king's chief huntsman, "one of our fine white bears, that his liegemen may show their little ones what sort of kittens we play with." "Well said, Gunter!" cried the king; "but how shall we find a bear that will travel so long a journey willingly, and will know how to behave himself to our worthy brother when he reaches him?" "Please your majesty," said Gunter, "I have a glorious fellow, as white as snow, that I caught when he was a cub; he will follow me wherever I go, play with my children, stand on his hind legs, and behave himself as well as any gentleman ought to do. He is at your service, and I will myself take him wherever you choose."

So the king was well pleased, and ordered Gunter to set off at once with master Bruin: "Start with the morning's dawn," said he, "and make the best of your way."

The Norseman went home to his house in the forest; and early next morning he waked master Bruin, put the king's collar round his neck, and away they went over rocks and valleys, lakes and seas, the nearest road to the court of the King of Denmark. When they arrived there, the king was away on a journey, and Gunter and his fellow-traveller set out to follow. It was bright weather, the sun shone, and the birds sang, as they journeyed merrily on, day after day, over hill and over dale, till they came within a day's journey of where the king was.

All that afternoon they travelled through a gloomy dark forest; but towards evening the wind began to whistle through the trees, and the clouds began to gather and threaten a stormy night. The road, too, was very rough, and it was not easy to tell which was most tired, Bruin or his master. What made the matter worse was, that they had found no inn that day by the roadside, and their provisions had fallen short, so that they had no very pleasant prospect before them for the night. "A pretty affair this!" said Gunter, "I am likely to be charmingly off here in the woods, with an empty stomach, a damp bed, and a bear for my bedfellow."

While the Norseman was turning this over in his mind, the wind blew harder and harder, and the clouds grew darker and darker: the bear shook his ears, and his master looked at his wits' end, when to his great joy a woodman came whistling along out of the woods, by the side of his horse dragging a load of fagots. As soon as he came up, Gunter stopped him, and begged hard for a night's lodging for himself and his countryman.

The woodman seemed hearty and good-natured enough, and was quite ready to find shelter for the huntsman; but as to the bear, he had never seen such a beast before in his life, and would have nothing to do with him on any terms. The huntsman begged hard for his friend, and told how he was bringing him as a present to the King of Denmark; and how he was the most good-natured, best-behaved animal in the world, though he must allow that he was by no means one of the handsomest.

The woodman, however, was not to be moved. His wife, he was sure, would not like such a guest, and who could say what he might take into his head to do? Besides, he should lose his dog and his cat, his ducks and his geese; for they would all run away for fright, whether the bear was disposed to be friends with them or not.

"Good-night, master huntsman!" said he; "if you and old shaggy-back there cannot part, I am afraid you must e'en stay where you are, though you will have a sad night of it, no doubt." Then he cracked his whip, whistled up his horse, and set off once more on his way homewards.

The huntsman grumbled, and Bruin grunted, as they followed slowly after; when to their great joy they saw the woodman, before he had gone many yards, pull up his horse once more and turn round. "Stay, stay!" said he; "I think I can tell you of a plan better than sleeping in a ditch. I know where you may find shelter, if you will run the risk of a little trouble from an unlucky imp, that has taken up its abode in my old house down the hill yonder. You must know, friend, that till last winter I lived in yon snug little house that you will see at the foot of the hill if you come this way. Everything went smoothly on with us till one unlucky night, when the storm blew as it seems likely to do to-night, some spiteful guest took it into his head to pay us a visit; and there have ever since been such noises, clattering, and scampering up stairs and down, from midnight till the cock crows in the morning, that at last we were fairly driven out of house and home. What he is like no one knows; for we never saw him or anything belonging to him, except a little crooked high-heeled shoe, that he left one night in the pantry. But though we have not seen him, we know he has a hand or a paw as heavy as lead; for when it pleases him to lay it upon any one, down he goes as if the blacksmith's hammer had hit him. There is no end of his monkey tricks. If the linen is hung out to dry, he cuts the line. If he wants a cup of ale, he leaves the tap running. If the fowls are shut up, he lets them loose. He puts the pig into the garden, rides upon the cows, and turns the horses into the hay-yard; and several times he nearly burnt the house down, by leaving a candle alight among the fagots. And then he is sometimes so nimble and active, that when he is once in motion, nothing stands still around him. Dishes and plates—pots and pans—dance about, clattering, making the most horrible music, and breaking each other to pieces: and sometimes, when the whim takes him, the chairs and tables seem as if they were alive, and dancing a hornpipe, or playing battledore and shuttlecock together. Even the stones and beams of the house seem rattling against one another; and it is of no use putting things in order, for the first freak the imp took would turn everything upside down again.

"My wife and I bore such a lodger as long as we could, but at length we were fairly beaten; and as he seemed to have taken up his abode in the house, we thought it best to give up to him what he wanted: and the little rascal knew what we were about when we were moving, and seemed afraid we should not go soon enough. So he helped us off: for on the morning we were to start, as we were going to put our goods upon the waggon, there it stood before the door ready loaded: and when we started we heard a loud laugh; and a little sharp voice cried out of the window, 'Good-bye, neighbors!" So now he has our old house all to himself to play his gambols in, whenever he likes to sleep within doors; and we have built ourselves a snug cottage on the other side of the hill, where we live as well as we can, though we have no great room to make merry in. Now if you, and your ugly friend there, like to run the hazard of taking up your quarters in the elf's house, pray do! Yonder is the road. He may not be at home to-night."

"We will try our luck," said Gunter; "anything is better to my mind than sleeping out of doors such a night as this. Your troublesome neighbor will perhaps think so too, and we may have to fight for our lodging: but never mind, Bruin is rather an awkward hand to quarrel with; and the goblin may perhaps find a worse welcome from him than your house-dog could give him. He will at anyrate let him know what a bear's hug is; for I dare say he has not been far enough north to know much about it yet."

Then the woodman gave Gunter a fagot to make his fire with, and wished him a good-night. He and the bear soon found their way to the deserted house; and no one being at home they walked into the kitchen and made a capital fire.

"Lack-a-day!" said the Norseman; "I forgot one thing—I ought to have asked that good man for some supper; I have nothing left but some dry bread. However, this is better than sleeping in the woods: we must make the most of what we have, keep ourselves warm, and get to bed as soon as we can." So after eating up all their crusts, and drinking some water from the well close by, the huntsman wrapt himself up close in his cloak, and lay down in the snuggest corner he could find. Bruin rolled himself up in the corner of the wide fireplace; and both were fast asleep, the fire out, and everything quiet within doors, long before midnight.

Just as the clock struck twelve the storm began to get louder—the wind blew—a slight noise within the room wakened the huntsman, and all on a sudden in popped a little ugly skrattel, scarce three spans high; with a hump on his back, a face like a dried pippin, a nose like a ripe mulberry, and an eye that had lost its neighbor. He had high-heeled shoes, and a pointed red cap; and came dragging after him a nice fat kid, ready skinned, and fit for roasting. "A rough night this," grumbled the goblin to himself; "but, thanks to that booby woodman, I've a house to myself: and now for a hot supper and a glass of good ale till the cock crows."

No sooner said than done: the skrattel busied himself about, here and there; presently the fire blazed up, the kid was put on the spit and turned merrily round. A keg of ale made its appearance from a closet: the cloth was laid, and the kid was soon dished up for eating. Then the little imp, in the joy of his heart, rubbed his hands, tossed up his red cap, danced before the hearth, and sang his song—

"Oh! 'tis weary enough abroad to bide,
In the shivery midnight blast;
And 'tis dreary enough alone to ride,
Hungry and cold,
On the wintry mold,
Where the drifting snow falls fast.

But 'tis cheery enough to revel by night,
In the crackling fagot's light:
'Tis merry enough to have and to hold
The savory roast,
And the nut-brown toast,
With jolly good ale and old."

The huntsman lay snug all this time; sometimes quaking, in dread of getting into trouble, and sometimes licking his lips at the savory supper before him, and half in the mind to fight for it with the imp. However, he kept himself quiet in his corner; till all of a sudden the little man's eye wandered from his cheering ale-cup to Bruin's carcase, as he lay rolled up like a ball, fast asleep in the chimney-corner.

The imp turned round sharp in an instant, and crept softly nearer and nearer to where Bruin lay, looking at him very closely, and not able to make out what in the world he was. "One of the family, I suppose!" said he to himself. But just then Bruin gave his ears a shake, and showed a little of his shaggy muzzle. "Oh ho!" said the imp, "that's all, is it? But what a large one! Where could he come from? and how came he here? What shall I do? Shall I let him alone or drive him out? Perhaps he may do me some mischief, and I am not afraid of mice or rats. So here goes! I have driven all the rest of the live stock out of the house, and why should I be afraid of sending this brute after them?"

With that the elf walked softly to the corner of the room, and taking up the spit, stole back on tip-toe till he got quite close to the bear; then raising up his weapon, down came a rattling thump across Bruin's mazard, that sounded as hollow as a drum. The bear raised himself slowly up, snorted, shook his head, then scratched it,—opened first one eye, then the other, took a turn across the room, and grinned at his enemy; who, somewhat alarmed, ran back a few paces, and stood with the spit in his hand, foreseeing a rough attack. And it soon came; for the bear, rearing himself up, walked leisurely forward, and putting out one of his paws caught hold of the spit, jerked it out of the goblin's hand, and sent it spinning to the other end of the kitchen.

And now began a fierce battle. This way and that way flew tables and chairs, pots and pans. The elf was one moment on the bear's back, lugging his ears and pommelling him with blows that might have felled an ox. In the next, the bear would throw him up in the air, and treat him as he came down with a hug that would make the little imp squall. Then up he would jump upon one of the beams out of Bruin's reach; and soon, watching his chance, would be down astride upon his back.

Meantime Gunter had become sadly frightened, and seeing the oven door open, crept in for shelter from the fray, and lay there quaking for fear. The struggle went on thus a long time, without its seeming at all clear who would get the better—biting, scratching, hugging, clawing, roaring, and growling, till the whole house rang. The elf, however, seemed to grow weaker and weaker: the rivals stood for a moment as if to get breath, and the bear was getting ready for a fierce attack, when, all in a moment, the skrattel dashed his red cap right in his eye, and while Bruin was smarting with the blow and trying to recover his sight, darted to the door, and was out of sight in a moment, though the wind blew, the rain pattered, and the storm raged, in a merciless manner.

THE BEAR GRINNED AT HIS ENEMY, WHO, SOME-
WHAT ALARMED, RAN BACK A FEW PACES

"Well done! Bravo, Bruin!" cried the huntsman, as he crawled out of the oven, and ran and bolted the door: "thou hast combed his locks rarely; and as for thine own ears, they are rather the worse for pulling. But come, let us make the best of the good cheer our friend has left us!" So saying, they fell to and ate a hearty supper. The huntsman, wishing the skrattel a good night and pleasant dreams in a cup of his sparkling ale, laid himself down and slept till morning; and Bruin tried to do the same, as well as his aching bones would let him.

In the morning the huntsman made ready to set out on his way: and had not got far from the door before he met the woodman, who was eager to hear how he had passed the night. Then Gunter told him how he had been awakened, what sort of creature the elf was, and how he and Bruin had fought it out. "Let us hope," said he, "you will now be well rid of the gentleman: I suspect he will not come where he is likely to get any more of Bruin's hugs; and thus you will be well paid for your entertainment of us, which, to tell the truth, was none of the best: for if your ugly little tenant had not brought his supper with him, we should have had but empty stomachs this morning."

The huntsman and his fellow-traveller journeyed on: and let us hope they reached the King of Denmark safe and sound: but, to tell the truth, I know nothing more of that part of the story.

The woodman, meantime, went to his work; and did not fail to watch at night to see whether the skrattel came, or whether he was thoroughly frightened out of his old haunt by the bear, or whatever he might take the beast to be that had handled him as he never was handled before. But three nights passed over, and no traces being seen or heard of him, the woodman began to think of moving back to his old house.

On the fourth day he was out at his work in the forest; and as he was taking shelter under a tree from a cold storm of sleet and rain that passed over, he heard a little cracked voice singing, or rather croaking in a mournful tone. So he crept along quietly, and peeped over some bushes, and there sat the very same figure that the huntsman had described to him. The goblin was sitting without any hat or cap on his head, with a woe-begone face, and with his jacket torn into shreds, and his leg scratched and smeared with blood, as if he had been creeping through a bramble-bush. The woodman listened quietly to his song, and it ran as before—

"Oh! 'tis weary enough abroad to bide,
In the shivery midnight blast;
And 'tis dreary enough alone to ride
Hungry and cold,
On the wintry mold,
Where the drifting snow falls fast."

"Sing us the other verse, man!" cried the woodman; for he could not help cracking a joke on his old enemy, who he saw was sadly in the dumps at the loss of his good cheer and the shelter against the bad weather. But the instant his voice was heard the little imp jumped up, stamped with rage, and was out of sight in the twinkling of an eye.

The woodman finished his work and was going home in the evening, whistling by his horse's side, when, all of a sudden, he saw, standing on a high bank by the way-side, the very same little imp, looking as grim and sulky as before. "Hark ye, bumpkin!" cried the skrattel; "canst thou hear, fellow? Is thy great cat alive, and at home still?" "My cat?" said the woodman. "Thy great white cat, man!" thundered out the little imp. "Oh, my cat!" said the woodman, at last recollecting himself. "Oh, yes to be sure! alive and well, I thank you: very happy, I'm sure, to see you and all friends, whenever you will do us the favor to call. And hark ye, friend! as you seem to be so fond of my great cat, you may like to know that she had five kittens last night." "Five kittens?" muttered the elf. "Yes," replied the woodman, "five of the most beautiful white kits you ever saw,—so like the old cat, it would do your heart good to see the whole family—such soft, gentle paws—such delicate whiskers—such pretty little mouths!" "Five kittens?" muttered or rather shrieked out the imp again. "Yes, to be sure!" said the woodman; "five kittens! Do look in to-night, about twelve o'clock—the time, you know, that you used to come and see us. The old cat will be so glad to show them to you, and we shall be so happy to see you once more. But where can you have been all this time?"

"I come? not I, indeed!" shrieked the skrattel. "What do I want with the little wretches? Did not I see the mother once? Keep your kittens to yourself: I must be off,—this is no place for me. Five kittens! So there are six of them now! Good-bye to you, you'll see me no more; so bad luck to your ugly cat and your beggarly house!" "And bad luck to you, Mr Crookback!" cried the woodman, as he threw him the red cap he had left behind in his battle with Bruin. "Keep clear of my cat, and let us hear no more of your pranks, and be hanged to you!"

So, now that he knew his troublesome guest had taken his leave, the woodman soon moved back all his goods, and his wife and children, into their snug old house. And there they lived happily, for the elf never came to see them any more; and the woodman every day after dinner drank, "Long life to the King of Norway," for sending the cat that cleared his house of vermin.

FAIRY TALES

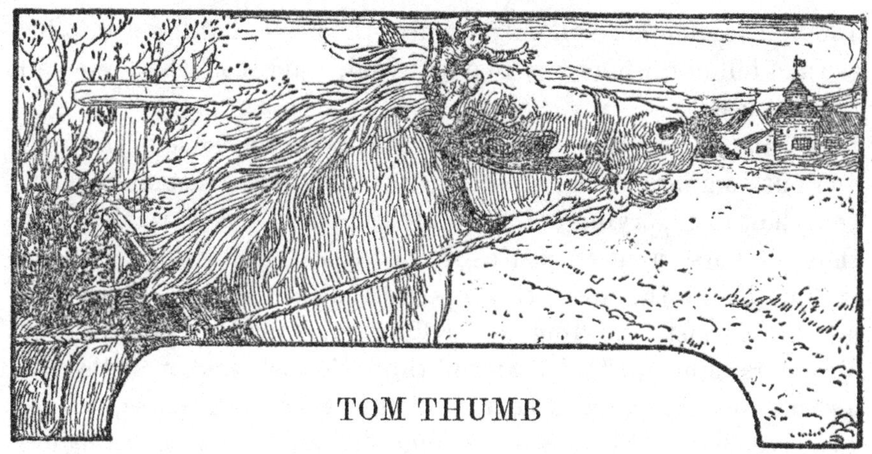

TOM THUMB

A POOR woodman sat in his cottage one night, smoking his pipe by the fireside, while his wife sat by his side spinning. "How lonely it is, wife," said he, as he puffed out a long curl of smoke, "for you and me to sit here by ourselves, without any children to play about and amuse us while other people seem so happy and merry with their children!" "What you say is very true," said the wife, sighing, and turning round her wheel; "how happy should I be if I had but one child! If it were ever so small—nay, if it were no bigger than my thumb—I should be very happy, and love it dearly." Now—odd as you may think it—it came to pass that this good woman's wish was fulfilled, just in the very way she had wished it; for, not long afterwards, she had a little boy, who was quite healthy and strong, but was not much bigger than my thumb. So they said, "Well, we cannot say we have not got what we wished for, and, little as he is, we will love him dearly." And they called him Thomas Thumb.

They gave him plenty of food, yet for all they could do he never grew bigger, but kept just the same size as he had been when he was born. Still, his eyes were sharp and sparkling, and he soon showed himself to be a clever little fellow, who always knew well what he was about.

One day, as the woodman was getting ready to go into the wood to cut fuel, he said, "I wish I had someone to bring the cart after me, for I want to make haste." "Oh, father," cried Tom, "I will take care of that; the cart shall be in the wood by the time you want it." Then the woodman laughed, and said, "How can that be? you cannot reach up to the horse's bridle." "Never mind that, father," said

Tom; "if my mother will only harness the horse, I will get into his ear and tell him which way to go." "Well," said the father, "we will try for once."

When the time came the mother harnessed the horse to the cart, and put Tom into his ear; and as he sat there the little man told the beast how to go, crying out, "Go on!" and "Stop!" as he wanted: and thus the horse went on just as well as if the woodman had driven it himself into the wood. It happened that as the horse was going a little too fast, and Tom was calling out, "Gently! gently!" two strangers came up. "What an odd thing that is!" said one: "there is a cart going along, and I hear a carter talking to the horse, but yet I can see no one." "That is queer, indeed," said the other; "let us follow the cart, and see where it goes." So they went on into the wood, till at last they came to the place where the woodman was. Then Tom Thumb, seeing his father, cried out, "See, father, here I am with the cart, all right and safe! now take me down!" So his father took hold of the horse with one hand, and with the other took his son out of the horse's ear, and put him down upon a straw, where he sat as merry as you please.

The two strangers were all this time looking on, and did not know what to say for wonder. At last one took the other aside, and said, "That little urchin will make our fortune, if we can get him, and carry him about from town to town as a show; we must buy him." So they went up to the woodman, and asked him what he would take for the little man. "He will be better off," said they, "with us than with you." "I won't sell him at all," said the father; "my own flesh and blood is dearer to me than all the silver and gold in the world." But Tom, hearing of the bargain they wanted to make, crept up his father's coat to his shoulder and whispered in his ear, "Take the money, father, and let them have me; I'll soon come back to you."

So the woodman at last said he would sell Tom to the strangers for a large piece of gold, and they paid the price. "Where would you like to sit?" said one of them. "Oh, put me on the rim of your hat; that will be a nice gallery for me; I can walk about there and see the country as we go along." So they did as he wished; and when Tom had taken leave of his father they took him away with them.

THE COOK GOT UP EARLY, BEFORE DAYBREAK, TO FEED THE COWS

They journeyed on till it began to be dusky, and then the little man said, "Let me get down, I'm tired." So the man took off his hat, and put him down on a clod of earth, in a ploughed field by the side of the road. But Tom ran about amongst the furrows, and at last slipped into an old mouse-hole. "Good night, my masters!" said he, "I'm off! mind and look sharp after me the next time." Then they ran at once to the place, and poked the ends of their sticks into the mouse-hole, but all in vain; Tom only crawled farther and farther in; and at last it became quite dark, so that they were forced to go their way without their prize, as sulky as could be.

When Tom found they were gone, he came out of his hiding-place. "What dangerous walking it is," said he, "in this ploughed field! If I were to fall from one of these great clods, I should undoubtedly break my neck." At last, by good luck, he found a large empty snail-shell. "This is lucky," said he, "I can sleep here very well"; and in he crept.

Just as he was falling asleep, he heard two men passing by, chatting together; and one said to the other, "How can we rob that rich parson's house of his silver and gold?" "I'll tell you!" cried Tom. "What noise was that?" said the thief, frightened; "I'm sure I heard someone speak." They stood still listening, and Tom said, "Take me with you, and I'll soon show you how to get the parson's money." "But where are you?" said they. "Look about on the ground," answered he, "and listen where the sound comes from." At last the thieves found him out, and lifted him up in their hands. "You little urchin!" they said, "what can you do for us?" "Why, I can get between the iron window-bars of the parson's house, and throw you out whatever you want." "That's a good thought," said the thieves; "come along, we shall see what you can do."

When they came to the parson's house, Tom slipped through the window-bars into the room, and then called out as loud as he could bawl, "Will you have all that is here?" At this the thieves were frightened, and said, "Softly, softly! Speak low, that you may not awaken anybody." But Tom seemed as if he did not understand them, and bawled out again, "How much will you have? Shall I throw it all out?" Now the cook lay in the next room; and hearing a noise she raised herself up in her bed and listened. Meantime the thieves were frightened, and ran off a little way; but at last they plucked up their hearts, and said, "The little urchin is only trying to make fools of us." So they came back and whispered softly to him, saying, "Now let us have no more of your roguish jokes; but throw us out some of the money." Then Tom called out as loud as he could, "Very well! hold your hands! here it comes."

The cook heard this quite plain, so she sprang out of bed, and ran to open the door. The thieves ran off as if a wolf was at their tails: and the maid, having groped about and found nothing, went away for a light. By the time she came back, Tom had slipped off into the barn; and when she had looked about and searched every hole and corner, and found nobody, she went to bed, thinking she must have been dreaming with her eyes open.

The little man crawled about in the hay-loft, and at last found a snug place to finish his night's rest in; so he laid himself down, meaning to sleep till daylight, and then find his way home to his father and mother. But alas! how woefully he was undone! what crosses and sorrows happen to us all in this world! The cook got up early, before daybreak, to feed the cows; and going straight to the hay-loft, carried away a large bundle of hay, with the little man in the middle of it, fast asleep. He still, however, slept on, and did not awake till he found himself in the mouth of the cow; for the cook had put the hay into the cow's rick, and the cow had taken Tom up in a mouthful of it. "Good lack-a-day!" said he, "how came I to tumble into the mill?" But he soon found out where he really was; and was forced to have all his wits about him, that he might not get between the cow's teeth, and so be crushed to death. At last down he went into her stomach. "It is rather dark," said he; "they forgot to build windows in this room to let the sun in; a candle would be no bad thing."

Though he made the best of his bad luck, he did not like his quarters at all; and the worst of it was, that more and more hay was always coming down, and the space left for him became smaller and smaller. At last he cried out as loud as he could, "Don't bring me any more hay! Don't bring me any more hay!"

The maid happened to be just then milking the cow; and hearing someone speak, but seeing nobody, and yet being quite sure it was the same voice that she had heard in the night, she was so frightened that she fell off her stool, and overset the milk-pail. As soon as she could pick herself up out of the dirt, she ran off as fast as she could to her master the parson, and said, "Sir, sir, the cow is talking!" But the parson said, "Woman, thou art surely mad!" However, he went with her into the cow-house, to try and see what was the matter.

Scarcely had they set foot on the threshold, when Tom called out, "Don't bring me any more hay!" Then the parson himself was frightened; and thinking the cow was surely bewitched, told his man to kill her on the spot. So the cow was killed, and cut up; and the stomach, in which Tom lay, was thrown out upon a dunghill.

Tom soon set himself to work to get out, which was not a very easy task; but at last, just as he had made room to get his head out, fresh ill-luck befell him. A hungry wolf sprang out, and swallowed up the whole stomach, with Tom in it, at one gulp, and ran away.

Tom, however, was still not disheartened; and thinking the wolf would not dislike having some chat with him as he was going along, he called out, "My good friend, I can show you a famous treat." "Where's that?" said the wolf. "In such and such a house," said Tom, describing his own father's house. "You can crawl through the drain into the kitchen and then into the pantry, and there you will find cakes, ham, beef, cold chicken, roast pig, apple-dumplings, and everything that your heart can wish."

The wolf did not want to be asked twice; so that very night he went to the house and crawled through the drain into the kitchen, and then into the pantry, and ate and drank there to his heart's content. As soon as he had had enough he wanted to get away; but he had eaten so much that he could not go out by the same way he came in.

This was just what Tom had reckoned upon; and now he began to set up a great shout, making all the noise he could. "Will you be easy?" said the wolf; "you'll awaken everybody in the house if you make such a clatter." "What's that to me?" said the little man; "you have had your frolic, now I've a mind to be merry myself"; and he began, singing and shouting as loud as he could.

The woodman and his wife, being awakened by the noise, peeped through a crack in the door; but when they saw a wolf was there, you may well suppose that they were sadly frightened; and the woodman ran for his axe, and gave his wife a scythe. "Do you stay behind," said the woodman, "and when I have knocked him on the head you must rip him up with the scythe." Tom heard all this, and cried out, "Father, father! I am here, the wolf has swallowed me." And his father said, "Heaven be praised! we have found our dear child again"; and he told his wife not to use the scythe for fear she should hurt him. Then he aimed a great blow, and struck the wolf on the head, and killed him on the spot! and when he was dead they cut open his body, and set Tommy free. "Ah!" said the father, "what fears we have had for you!" "Yes, father," answered he; "I have travelled all over the world, I think, in one way or other, since we parted; and now I am very glad to come home and get fresh air again." "Why, where have you been?" said his father. "I have been in a mouse-hole—and in a snail-shell—and down a cow's throat—and in the wolf's belly; and yet here I am again, safe and sound."

"Well," said they, "you are come back, and we will not sell you again for all the riches in the world."

Then they hugged and kissed their dear little son, and gave him plenty to eat and drink, for he was very hungry; and then they fetched new clothes for him, for his old ones had been quite spoiled on his journey. So Master Thumb stayed at home with his father and mother, in peace; for though he had been so great a traveller, and had done and seen so many fine things, and was fond enough of telling the whole story, he always agreed that, after all, there's no place like HOME!

SNOW-WHITE

ONCE upon a time, in the middle of winter, when the flakes of snow were falling like feathers from the sky, a Queen sat at a window sewing, and the frame of the window was made of black ebony.

And whilst she was sewing and looking out of the window at the snow, she pricked her finger with the needle, and three drops of blood fell upon the snow. And the red looked pretty upon the white snow, and she thought to herself, "Would that I had a child as white as snow, as red as blood, and as black as the wood of the window-frame."

Soon after that she had a little daughter, who was as white as snow, and as red as blood, and her hair was as black as ebony. She was therefore called little Snow-White. And when the child was born, the Queen died.

After a year had passed the King took to himself another wife. She was a beautiful woman, but proud and haughty, and she could not bear that any one else should surpass her in beauty. She had a wonderful looking-glass, and when she stood in front of it and looked at herself in it, and said:

"Looking-Glass, Looking-Glass, on the wall,
Who in this land is the fairest of all?"

the Looking-Glass answered:

"Thou, O Queen, art the fairest of all!"

Then she was satisfied, for she knew that the Looking-Glass spoke the truth.

But little Snow-White was growing up, and grew more and more beautiful. When she was seven years old she was as beautiful as the day, and more beautiful than the Queen herself. And once when the Queen asked her Looking-Glass:

> "Looking-Glass, Looking-Glass, on the wall,
> Who in this land is the fairest of all?"

it answered:

> "Thou art fairer than all who are here, Lady Queen.
> But more beautiful still is Snow-White, I ween."

Then the Queen was shocked, and turned yellow and green with envy. From that hour, whenever she looked at little Snow-White, her heart heaved in her breast, she hated the maiden so much.

And envy and pride grew higher and higher in her heart like a weed, so that she had no peace day or night. She called a huntsman, and said, "Take the child away into the forest. I will no longer have her in my sight. Kill her."

The huntsman obeyed, and took her away. But when he had drawn his knife, and was about to pierce little Snow-White's innocent heart, she began to weep, and said, "Ah, dear Huntsman, leave me my life! I will run away into the wild forest, and never come home again."

And as she was so beautiful, the huntsman had pity on her and said, "Run away, then, you poor child." "The wild beasts will soon have devoured you," thought he, and yet it seemed as if a stone had been rolled from his heart since it was no longer needful for him to kill her.

But now, the poor child was all alone in the great forest, and so terrified that she looked at every leaf of every tree, and did not know what to do. Then she began to run, and ran over sharp stones and through thorns, and the wild beasts ran past her, but did her no harm.

She ran as long as her feet would go, until it was almost evening. Then she saw a little cottage and went into it to rest herself. Everything in the cottage was small, but neater and cleaner than can be told. There was a table on which was a white cover, and seven little plates, and on each plate a little spoon. Moreover, there were seven little knives and forks, and seven little mugs. Against the wall stood seven little beds side by side, and covered with snow-white counterpanes.

THE SEVEN DWARFS FIND SNOW-WHITE IN THEIR LITTLE BED

Little Snow-White was so hungry and thirsty, that she ate some vegetables and bread from each plate and drank a drop of wine out of each mug, for she did not wish to take all from one only. Then, as she was so tired, she laid herself down on one of the little beds, but none of them suited her. One was too long, another too short, but at last she found that the seventh one was right, so she remained in it, said a prayer and went to sleep.

When it was quite dark the owners of the cottage came back. They were seven Dwarfs who dug and delved in the mountains for ore. They lit their seven candles, and, as it was now light within the cottage, they saw that some one had been there, for everything was not in the same order in which they had left it.

The first said, "Who has been sitting on my chair?"

The second, "Who has been eating off my plate?"

The third, "Who has been taking some of my bread?"

The fourth, "Who has been eating my vegetables?"

The fifth, "Who has been using my fork?"

The sixth, "Who has been cutting with my knife?"

The seventh, "Who has been drinking out of my mug?"

Then the first looked round and saw that there was a little hole on his bed, and he said, "Who has been getting into my bed?"

The others came up and each called out, "Somebody has been lying in my bed too."

But the seventh when he looked at his bed saw little Snow-White, who was lying fast asleep therein. And he called the others, who came running up, and they cried out with astonishment, and brought their seven little candles and let the light fall on little Snow-White.

"Oh, oh!" cried they, "what a lovely child!" and they were so glad that they did not wake her up, but let her sleep on in the bed. And the seventh Dwarf slept with his companions, one hour with each, and so got through the night.

The next morning, little Snow-White awoke, and was frightened when she saw the seven Dwarfs. But they were friendly and asked her what her name was.

"My name is little Snow-White," she answered.

"How have you come to our house?" said the Dwarfs.

Then she told them that the wicked Queen had wished to have her killed, but that the huntsman had spared her life, and that she had run for the whole day, until at last she had found their dwelling.

The Dwarfs said, "If you will take care of our house, cook, make the beds, wash, sew, and knit, and if you will keep everything neat and clean, you may stay with us and you shall want for nothing."

"Yes," said little Snow-White, "with all my heart," and she stayed with them.

She kept the house in order for them. In the mornings they went to the mountains and looked for copper and gold, in the evenings they came back, and then their supper had to be ready.

The maiden was alone the whole day, so the good Dwarfs warned her and said, "Beware of the Queen, she will soon know that you are here. Be sure to let no one come in."

But the Queen, believing that little Snow-White was dead, could not but think that she herself was again the first and most beautiful of all. She went to her Looking-Glass, and said:

> "Looking-Glass, Looking-Glass, on the wall,
> Who in this land is the fairest of all?"

and the Glass answered:

> "Oh, Queen, thou art fairest of all I see,
> But over the hills, where the Seven Dwarfs dwell,
> Little Snow-White is alive and well,
> And none is so fair as she."

Then she was astounded, for she knew that the Looking-Glass never spoke falsely, and she knew that the huntsman had betrayed her, for that little Snow-White was still alive.

And so she thought and thought again how she might kill her, for so long as she herself was not the fairest in the whole land, envy let her have no rest. And when she had at last thought of something to do, she painted her face, and dressed herself like an old peddler-woman, and no one could have known her.

In this disguise she went over the Seven Mountains to the Seven Dwarfs, and knocked at the door and cried, "Pretty things to sell, very cheap, very cheap!"

Little Snow-White looked out at the window, and called, "Good-day, my dear woman, what have you to sell?"

"Good things, pretty things," she answered; "stay-laces of all colors," and she pulled out one which was woven of bright-colored silk.

"I may let the worthy old woman in," thought little Snow-White, and she unbolted the door and bought the pretty laces.

"Child," said the old woman, "what a fright you look. Come, I will lace you properly for once."

Little Snow-White had no suspicion, but stood before her, and let herself be laced with the new laces. But the old woman laced so quickly and laced so tightly that little Snow-White lost her breath and fell down as if dead.

"Now I am the most beautiful," said the Queen to herself, and ran away.

Not long afterward, in the evening, the Seven Dwarfs came home. But how shocked they were when they saw their dear little Snow-White lying on the ground, and that she neither stirred nor moved, and seemed to be dead. They lifted her up, and, as they saw that she was laced too tightly, they cut the laces. Than she began to breathe a little, and after a while came to life again.

When the Dwarfs heard what had happened, they said, "The old peddler-woman was no one else than the wicked Queen. Take care and let no one come in when we are not with you."

But the wicked woman, when she had reached home, went in front of the Glass and asked:

> "Looking-Glass, Looking-Glass, on the wall,
> Who in this land is the fairest of all?"

and it answered as before:

> "Oh, Queen, thou art fairest of all I see,
> But over the hills, where the Seven Dwarfs dwell,
> Little Snow-White is alive and well,
> And none is so fair as she."

When she heard that, all her blood rushed to her heart with fear, for she saw plainly that little Snow-White was again alive. "But now," she said, "I will think of something that shall put an end to you," and by the help of witchcraft, which she understood, she made a poisonous comb.

Then she disguised herself, and took the shape of another old woman. So she went over the Seven Mountains to the Seven Dwarfs, knocked at the door, and cried, "Good things to sell, cheap, cheap!"

Little Snow-White looked out, and said, "Go away. I cannot let any one come in."

"I suppose you may look," said the old woman, and pulled the poisonous comb out and held it up.

It pleased the maiden so well that she let herself be beguiled, and opened the door. When they had made a bargain, the old woman said, "Now I will comb you properly for once."

Poor little Snow-White had no suspicion, and let the Old Woman do as she pleased. But hardly had she put the comb in her hair, then the poison in it took effect, and the maiden fell down senseless.

"You paragon of beauty," said the wicked woman, "you are done for now!" and she went away.

But fortunately it was almost evening, and the Seven Dwarfs came home. When they saw little Snow-White lying as if dead upon the ground, they at once suspected the Queen. They looked and found the poisoned comb. Scarcely had they taken it out, when little Snow-White came to herself, and told them what had happened. Then they warned her once more to be upon her guard, and to open the door to no one.

The Queen, at home, went in front of the Glass and said:

> "Looking-Glass, Looking-Glass, on the wall,
> Who in this land is the fairest of all?"

then it answered as before:

> "Oh, Queen, thou art fairest of all I see,
> But over the hills, where the Seven Dwarfs dwell,
> Little Snow-White is alive and well,
> And none is so fair as she."

When she heard the Glass speak thus, she trembled and shook with rage. "Little Snow-White shall die," she cried, "even if it costs me my life!"

Thereupon she went into a secret, lonely room, where no one ever came, and there she made a very poisonous apple. Outside it looked pretty, white with a red cheek, so that every one who saw it longed for it. But whoever ate a piece of it must surely die.

When the apple was ready, she painted her face, and dressed herself as a countrywoman, and so she went over the Seven Mountains to the Seven Dwarfs. She knocked at the door. Little Snow-

White put her head out of the window and said, "I cannot let any one in. The Seven Dwarfs have forbidden me."

"It is all the same to me," answered the woman, "I shall soon get rid of my apples. There, I will give you one."

"No," said little Snow-White, "I dare not take anything."

"Are you afraid of poison?" said the old woman. "Look, I will cut the apple in two pieces. You eat the red cheek, and I will eat the white."

The apple was so cunningly made that only the red cheek was poisoned. Little Snow-White longed for the fine apple, and when she saw that the woman ate part of it, she could resist no longer, and stretched out her hand and took the poisonous half. But hardly had she a bit of it in her mouth, than she fell down dead.

Then the Queen looked at her with a dreadful look, and laughed aloud, and said, "White as snow, red as blood, black as ebony-wood! This time the Dwarfs cannot wake you up again!"

And when she asked of the Looking-Glass at home:

> "Looking-Glass, Looking-Glass, on the wall,
> Who in this land is the fairest of all?"

it answered at last:

> "Oh, Queen, in this land thou art fairest of all."

Then her envious heart had rest, so far as an envious heart can have rest.

The Dwarfs, when they came home in the evening, found little Snow-White lying upon the ground. She breathed no longer and was dead. They lifted her up, looked to see whether they could find anything poisonous, unlaced her, combed her hair, washed her with water and wine, but it was all of no use. The poor child was dead, and remained dead. They laid her upon a bier, and all seven of them sat round it and wept for her, and wept three days long.

Then they were going to bury her, but she still looked as if she was living, and still had her pretty red cheeks. They said, "We could not bury her in the dark ground," and they had a transparent coffin of glass made, so that she might be seen from all sides. They laid her in it, and wrote her name upon it in golden letters, and that she was a King's Daughter.

Then they put the coffin out upon the mountain, and one of them always stayed by it to watch it. And birds came too, and wept for little Snow-White; first an owl, then a raven, and last a dove.

And now little Snow-White lay a long, long time in the coffin. She did not change, but looked as if she were asleep; for she was as white as snow, as red as blood, and her hair was as black as ebony.

It happened, however, that a King's Son came into the forest, and went to the Dwarfs' house to spend the night. He saw the coffin on the mountain, and the beautiful little Snow-White within it, and read what was written upon it in golden letters.

Then he said to the Dwarfs, "Let me have the coffin. I will give you whatever you want for it."

But the Dwarfs answered, "We will not part with it for all the gold in the world."

Then he said, "Let me have it as a gift, for I cannot live without seeing little Snow-White. I will honor and prize her as my dearest possession," As he spoke in this way the good Dwarfs took pity upon him, and gave him the coffin.

And now the King's Son had it carried away by his servants on their shoulders. And it happened, that they stumbled over a tree-stump, and with the shock the poisonous piece of apple, which little Snow-White had bitten off, came out of her throat. And before long she opened her eyes, lifted up the lid of the coffin, sat up, and was once more alive.

"Oh, where am I?" she cried.

The King's Son, full of joy, said, "You are with me," and told her what had happened, and said, "I love you more than everything in the world. Come with me to my father's palace, you shall be my wife."

And little Snow-White was willing, and went with him, and their wedding was held with great show and splendor. But the wicked Queen was also bidden to the feast. When she had arrayed herself in beautiful clothes, she went before the Looking-Glass, and said:

"Looking-Glass, Looking-Glass, on the wall,
Who in this land is the fairest of all?"

the Glass answered:

"Oh, Queen, of all here the fairest art thou,
But the young Queen is fairer by far, I trow!"

Then the wicked woman uttered a curse, and was so wretched, so utterly wretched, that she knew not what to do. At first she would not go to the wedding at all, but she had no peace, and must go to see the young Queen.

And when she went in she knew little Snow-White. And she stood still with rage and fear, and could not stir. But iron slippers had already been put upon the fire, and they were brought in with tongs, and set before her. Then she was forced to put on the red-hot shoes, and dance until she dropped down dead.

THE FOUR CRAFTSMEN.

DEAR children," said a poor man to his four sons, "I have nothing to give you; you must go out into the wide world and try your luck. Begin by learning some craft or another, and see how you can get on." So the four brothers took their walking-sticks in their hands, and their little bundles on their shoulders, and after bidding their father good-bye, went all out at the gate together. When they had got on some way they came to four cross-ways, each leading to a different country. Then the eldest said, "Here we must part; but this day four years we will come back to this spot, and in the meantime each must try what he can do for himself."

So each brother went his way; and as the eldest was hastening on a man met him, and asked him where he was going, and what he wanted. "I am going to try my luck in the world, and should like to begin by learning some art or trade," answered he. "Then," said the man, "go with me, and I will teach you how to become the cunningest thief that ever was." "No," said the other, "that is not an honest calling, and what can one look to earn by it in the end but the gallows?" "Oh!" said the man, "you need not fear the gallows; for I will only teach you to steal what will be fair game: I meddle with nothing but what no one else can get or care anything about, and where no one can find you out." So the young man agreed to follow his trade, and he soon showed himself so clever, that nothing could escape him that he had once set his mind upon.

The second brother also met a man, who, when he found out what he was setting out upon, asked him what craft he meant to follow. "I do not know yet," said he. "Then come with me, and be a star-gazer. It is a noble art, for nothing can be hidden from you, when once you understand the stars." The plan pleased him much, and he soon became such a skilful star-gazer, that when he had served out his time, and wanted to leave his master, he gave him a glass, and said, "With this you can see all that is passing in the sky and on earth, and nothing can be hidden from you."

The third brother met a huntsman, who took him with him, and taught him so well all that belonged to hunting, that he became very clever in the craft of the woods; and when he left his master he gave him a bow, and said, "Whatever you shoot at with this bow you will be sure to hit."

The youngest brother likewise met a man who asked him what he wished to do. "Would not you like," said he, "to be a tailor?" "Oh, no!" said the young man; "sitting cross-legged from morning to night, working backwards and forwards with a needle and goose, will never suit me." "Oh!" answered the man, "that is not my sort of tailoring; come with me, and you will learn quite another kind of craft from that." Not knowing what better to do, he came into the plan, and learnt tailoring from the beginning; and when he left his master, he gave him a needle, and said, "you can sew anything with this, be it as soft as an egg or as hard as steel; and the joint will be so fine that no seam will be seen."

After the space of four years, at the time agreed upon, the four brothers met at the four cross-roads; and having welcomed each other, set off towards their father's home, where they told him all that had happened to them, and how each had learned some craft.

Then, one day, as they were sitting before the house under a very high tree, the father said, "I should like to try what each of you can do in this way." So he looked up, and said to the second son, "At the top of this tree there is a chaffinch's nest; tell me how many eggs there are in it." The star-gazer took his glass, looked up, and said, "Five." "Now," said the father to the eldest son, "take away the eggs without letting the bird that is sitting upon them and hatching them know anything of what you are doing." So the cunning thief climbed up the tree, and brought away to his father the five eggs from under the bird; and it never saw or felt what he was doing, but kept sitting on at its ease. Then the father took the eggs, and put one on each corner of the table, and the fifth in the middle; and said to the huntsman, "Cut all the eggs in two pieces at one shot." The huntsman took up his bow, and at one shot struck all the
Princess and the Dragon

five eggs as his father wished. "Now comes your turn," said he to the young tailor; "sew the eggs and the young birds in them together again, so neatly that the shot shall have done them no harm." Then the tailor took his needle, and sewed the eggs as he was told; and when he had done, the thief was sent to take them back to the nest, and put them under the bird without its knowing it. Then she went on sitting, and hatched them: and in a few days they crawled out, and had only a little red streak across their necks, where the tailor had sewn them together.

"Well done, sons!" said the old man: "you have made good use of your time, and learnt something worth the knowing; but I am sure I do not know which ought to have the prize. Oh! that a time might soon come for you to turn your skill to some account!"

Not long after this there was a great bustle in the country; for the king's daughter had been carried off by a mighty dragon, and the king mourned over his loss day and night, and made it known that whoever brought her back to him should have her for a wife. Then the four brothers said to each other, "Here is a chance for us;

let us try what we can do." And they agreed to see whether they could not set the princess free. "I will soon find out where she is, however," said the star-gazer, as he looked through his glass: and he soon cried out, "I see her afar off, sitting upon a rock in the sea; and I can spy the dragon close by, guarding her." Then he went to the king, and asked for a ship for himself and his brothers; and they sailed together over the sea, till they came to the right place. There they found the princess sitting, as the star-gazer had said, on the rock; and the dragon was lying asleep, with his head upon her lap. "I dare not shoot at him," said the huntsman, "for I should kill the beautiful young lady also." "Then I will try my skill," said the thief; and went and stole her away from under the dragon, so quietly and gently that the beast did not know it, but went on snoring.

Then away they hastened with her full of joy in their boat towards the ship; but soon came the dragon roaring behind them through the air; for he awoke and missed the princess. But when he got over the boat, and wanted to pounce upon them and carry off the princess, the huntsman took up his bow and shot him straight through the heart, so that he fell down dead. They were still not safe; for he was such a great beast that in his fall he overset the boat, and they had to swim in the open sea upon a few planks. So the tailor took his needle, and with a few large stitches put some of the planks together; and he sat down upon these, and sailed about and gathered up all the pieces of the boat; and then tacked them together so quickly that the boat was soon ready, and they then reached the ship and got home safe.

When they had brought home the princess to her father, there was great rejoicing; and he said to the four brothers, "One of you shall marry her, but you must settle amongst yourselves which it is to be." Then there arose a quarrel between them; and the star-gazer said, "If I had not found the princess out, all your skill would have been of no use; therefore she ought to be mine." "Your seeing her would have been of no use," said the thief, "if I had not taken her away from the dragon; therefore she ought to be mine." "No, she is mine," said the huntsman; "for if I had not killed the dragon, he would, after all, have torn you and the princess into pieces." "And if I had not sewn the boat together again," said the tailor, "you would all have been drowned; therefore she is mine." Then the king put in a word, and said, "Each of you is right; and as all cannot have the young lady, the best way is for neither of you to have her: for the truth is, there is somebody she likes a great deal better. But to make up for your loss, I will give each of you, as a reward for his skill, half a kingdom." So the brothers agreed that this plan would be much better than either quarrelling or marrying a lady who had no mind to have them. And the king then gave to each half a kingdom, as he had said; and they lived very happily the rest of their days, and took good care of their father; and somebody took better care of the young lady, than to let either the dragon or one of the Crafts-men have her again.

CAT-SKIN

THERE was once a king, whose queen had hair of the purest gold, and was so beautiful that her match was not to be met with on the whole face of the earth. But this beautiful queen fell ill, and when she felt that her end drew near she called the king to her and said, "Promise me that you will never marry again, unless you meet with a wife who is as beautiful as I am, and who has golden hair like mine." Then when the king in his grief promised all she asked, she shut her eyes and died. But the king was not to be comforted, and for a long time never thought of taking another wife. At last, however, his wise men said, "this will not do; the king must marry again, that we may have a queen." So messengers were sent far and wide, to seek for a bride as beautiful as the late queen. But there was no princess in the world so beautiful; and if there had been, still there was not one to be found who had golden hair. So the messengers came home, and had had all their trouble for nothing.

Now the king had a daughter, who was just as beautiful as her mother, and had the same golden hair. And when she was grown up, the king looked at her and saw that she was just like this late queen: then he said to his courtiers, "May I not marry my daughter? She is the very image of my dead wife: unless I have her, I shall not find any bride upon the whole earth, and you say there must be a queen." When the courtiers heard this they were shocked, and said, "Heaven forbid that a father should marry his daughter! Out of so great a sin no good can come." And his daughter was also shocked, but hoped the king would soon give up such thoughts; so she said to him, "Before I marry anyone I must have three dresses: one must be of gold, like the sun; another must be of shining silver, like the moon; and a third must be dazzling as the stars: besides this, I want a mantle of a thousand different kinds of fur put together, to which every beast in the kingdom must give a part of his skin." And thus she thought he would think of the matter no more. But the king made the most skilful workmen in his kingdom weave the three dresses: one golden, like the sun; another silvery, like the moon; and a third sparkling, like the stars: and his hunters were told to hunt out all the beasts in his kingdom, and to take the finest fur out of their skins: and thus a mantle of a thousand furs was made.

When all were ready, the king sent them to her; but she got up in the night when all were asleep, and took three of her trinkets, a golden ring, a golden necklace, and a golden brooch, and packed the three dresses—of the sun, the moon, and the stars—up in a nutshell, and wrapped herself up in the mantle made of all sorts of fur, and besmeared her face and hands with soot. Then she threw herself upon Heaven for help in her need, and went away, and journeyed on the whole night, till at last she came to a large wood. As she was very tired, she sat herself down in the hollow of a tree and soon fell asleep: and there she slept on till it was midday.

Now as the king to whom the wood belonged was hunting in it, his dogs came to the tree, and began to snuff about, and run round and round, and bark. “Look sharp!” said the king to the huntsmen, “and see what sort of game lies there.” And the huntsmen went up to the tree, and when they came back again said, “In the hollow tree there lies a most wonderful beast, such as we never saw before; its skin seems to be of a thousand kinds of fur, but there it lies fast asleep.” “See,” said the king, “if you can catch it alive, and we will take it with us.” So the huntsmen took it up, and the maiden awoke and was greatly frightened, and said, “I am a poor child that has neither father nor mother left; have pity on me and take me with you.” Then they said, “Yes, Miss Cat-skin, you will do for the kitchen; you can sweep up the ashes, and do things of that sort.” So they put her into the coach, and took her home to the king’s palace. Then they showed her a little corner under the staircase, where no light of day ever peeped in, and said, “Cat-skin, you may lie and sleep there.” And she was sent into the kitchen, and made to fetch wood and water, to blow the fire, pluck the poultry, pick the herbs, sift the ashes, and do all the dirty work.

Thus Cat-skin lived for a long time very sorrowfully. “Ah! pretty princess!” thought she, “what will now become of thee?” But it happened one day that a feast was to be held in the king’s castle, so she said to the cook, “May I go up a little while and see what is going on? I will take care and stand behind the door.” And the cook said, “Yes, you may go, but be back again in half an hour’s time, to rake out the ashes.” Then she took her little lamp, and went into her cabin, and took off the fur skin, and washed the soot from off her face and hands, so that her beauty shone forth like the sun from behind the clouds. She next opened her nutshell, and brought out of it the dress that shone like the sun, and so went to the feast. Everyone made way for her, for nobody knew her, and they thought she could be no less than a king’s daughter. But the king came up to her, and held out his hand and danced with her; and he thought in his heart, “I never saw any one half so beautiful.”

When the dance was at an end she curtsied; and when the king looked round for her, she was gone, no one knew wither. The guards that stood at the castle gate were called in: but they had seen no one. The truth was, that she had run into her little cabin, pulled off her dress, blackened her face and hands, put on the fur-skin cloak, and was Cat-skin again. When she went into the kitchen to her work, and began to rake the ashes, the cook said, "Let that alone till the morning, and heat the king's soup; I should like to run up now and give a peep: but take care you don't let a hair fall into it, or you will run a chance of never eating again."

As soon as the cook went away, Cat-skin heated the king's soup, and toasted a slice of bread first, as nicely as ever she could; and when it was ready, she went and looked in the cabin for her little golden ring, and put it into the dish in which the soup was. When the dance was over, the king ordered his soup to be brought in; and it pleased him so well, that he thought he had never tasted any so good before. At the bottom he saw a gold ring lying; and as he could not make out how it had got there, he ordered the cook to be sent for. The cook was frightened when he heard the order, and said to Cat-skin, "You must have let a hair fall into the soup; if it be so, you will have a good beating." Then he went before the king, and he asked him who had cooked the soup. "I did," answered the cook. But the king said, "That is not true; it was better done than you could do it." Then he answered, "To tell the truth I did not cook it, but Cat-skin did." "Then let Cat-skin come up," said the king: and when she came he said to her, "Who are you?" "I am a poor child," said she, "that has lost both father and mother." "How came you in my palace?" asked he. "I am good for nothing," said she, "but to be scullion-girl, and to have boots and shoes thrown at my head." "But how did you get the ring that was in the soup?" asked the king. Then she would not own that she knew anything about the ring; so the king sent her away again about her business.

After a time there was another feast, and Cat-skin asked the cook to let her go up and see it as before. "Yes," said he, "but come again in half an hour, and cook the king the soup that he likes so much." Then she ran to her little cabin, washed herself quickly, and took her dress out which was silvery as the moon, and put it on; and when she went in, looking like a king's daughter, the king went up to her, and rejoiced at seeing her again, and when the dance began he danced with her. After the dance was at an end she managed to slip out, so slyly that the king did not see where she was gone; but she sprang into her little cabin, and made herself into Cat-skin again, and went into the kitchen to cook the soup. Whilst the cook was above stairs, she got the golden necklace and dropped it into the soup; then it was brought to the king, who ate it, and it pleased him as well as before; so he sent for the cook, who was again forced to tell him that Cat-skin had cooked it. Cat-skin was brought again before the king, but she still told him that she was only fit to have boots and shoes thrown at her head.

But when the king had ordered a feast to be got ready for the third time, it happened just the same as before. "You must be a witch, Cat-skin," said the cook; "for you always put something into your soup, so that it pleases the king better than mine." However, he let her go up as before. Then she put on her dress which sparkled like the stars, and went into the ball-room in it; and the king danced with her again, and thought she had never looked so beautiful as she did then. So whilst he was dancing with her, he put a gold ring on her finger without her seeing it, and ordered that the dance should be kept up a long time. When it was at an end, he would have held her fast by the hand, but she slipped away, and sprang so quickly through the crowd that he lost sight of her: and she ran as fast as she could into her little cabin under the stairs. But this time she kept away too long, and stayed beyond the half-hour; so she had not time to take off her fine dress, and threw her fur mantle over it, and in her haste did not blacken herself all over with soot, but left one of her fingers white.

Then she ran into the kitchen, and cooked the king's soup; and as soon as the cook was gone, she put the golden brooch into the dish. When the king got to the bottom, he ordered Cat-skin to be called once more, and soon saw the white finger, and the ring that he had put on it whilst they were dancing: so he seized her hand, and kept fast hold of it, and when she wanted to loose herself and spring away, the fur cloak fell off a little on one side, and the starry dress sparkled underneath it.

Then he got hold of the fur and tore it off, and her golden hair and beautiful form were seen, and she could no longer hide herself: so she washed the soot and ashes from her face, and showed herself to be the most beautiful princess upon the face of the earth. But the king said, "You are my beloved bride, and we will never more be parted from each other." And the wedding feast was held, and a merry day it was, as ever was heard of or seen in that country, or indeed in any other.

JORINDA AND JORINDEL

THERE was once an old castle, that stood in the middle of a deep gloomy wood, and in the castle lived an old fairy. Now this fairy could take any shape she pleased. All the day long she flew about in the form of an owl, or crept about the country like a cat; but at night she always became an old woman again. When any young man came within a hundred paces of her castle, he became quite fixed, and could not move a step till she came and set him free; which she would not do till he had given her his word never to come there again: but when any pretty maiden came within that space she was changed into a bird, and the fairy put her into a cage, and hung her up in a chamber in the castle. There were seven hundred of these cages hanging in the castle, and all with beautiful birds in them.

Now there was once a maiden whose name was Jorinda. She was prettier than all the pretty girls that ever were seen before, and a shepherd lad, whose name was Jorindel, was very fond of her, and they were soon to be married. One day they went to walk in the wood, that they might be alone; and Jorindel said, "We must take care that we don't go too near to the fairy's castle." It was a beautiful evening; the last rays of the setting sun shone bright through the long stems of the trees upon the green underwood beneath, and the turtle-doves sang from the tall birches.

Jorinda sat down to gaze upon the sun; Jorindel sat by her side; and both felt sad, they knew not why; but it seemed as if they were to be parted from one another for ever. They had wandered a long way; and when they looked to see which way they should go home, they found themselves at a loss to know what path to take.

The sun was setting fast, and already half of its circle had sunk behind the hill: Jorindel on a sudden looked behind him, and saw through the bushes that they had, without knowing it, sat down close under the old walls of the castle. Then he shrank for fear, turned pale, and trembled. Jorinda was just singing,

"The ring-dove sang from the willow spray,
Well-a-day! Well-a-day!
He mourn'd for the fate of his darling mate,
Well-a-day!"

when her song stopped suddenly. Jorindel turned to see the reason, and beheld his Jorinda changed into a nightingale, so that her song ended with a mournful *jug, jug*. An owl with fiery eyes flew three times round them, and three times screamed:

"Tu whu! Tu whu! Tu whu!"

Jorindel could not move; he stood fixed as a stone, and could neither weep, nor speak, nor stir hand or foot. And now the sun went quite down; the gloomy night came; the owl flew into a bush; and a moment after the old fairy came forth pale and meagre, with staring eyes, and a nose and chin that almost met one another.

She mumbled something to herself, seized the nightingale, and went away with it in her hand. Poor Jorindel saw the nightingale was gone—but what could he do? He could not speak, he could not move from the spot where he stood. At last the fairy came back and sang with a hoarse voice:

"Till the prisoner is fast,
And her doom is cast,
There stay! Oh, stay!
When the charm is around her,
And the spell has bound her,
Hie away! away!"

On a sudden Jorindel found himself free. Then he fell on his knees before the fairy, and prayed her to give him back his dear Jorinda: but she laughed at him, and said he should never see her again; then she went her way.

He prayed, he wept, he sorrowed, but all in vain. "Alas!" he said, "what will become of me?" He could not go back to his own home, so he went to a strange village, and employed himself in keeping sheep. Many a time did he walk round and round as near to the hated castle as he dared go, but all in vain; he heard or saw nothing of Jorinda.

At last he dreamt one night that he found a beautiful purple flower, and that in the middle of it lay a costly pearl; and he dreamt that he plucked the flower, and went with it in his hand into the castle, and that everything he touched with it was disenchanted, and that there he found his Jorinda again.

In the morning when he awoke, he began to search over hill and dale for this pretty flower; and eight long days he sought for it in vain: but on the ninth day, early in the morning, he found the beautiful purple flower; and in the middle of it was a large dewdrop, as big as a costly pearl. Then he plucked the flower, and set out and travelled day and night, till he came again to the castle.

He walked nearer than a hundred paces to it, and yet he did not become fixed as before, but found that he could go quite close up to the door. Jorindel was very glad indeed to see this. Then he touched the door with the flower, and it sprang open; so that he went in through the court, and listened when he heard so many birds singing. At last he came to the chamber where the fairy sat, with the seven hundred birds singing in the seven hundred cages. When she saw Jorindel she was very angry, and screamed with rage; but she could not come within two yards of him, for the flower he held in his hand was his safeguard. He looked around at the birds, but alas! there were many, many nightingales, and how then should he find out which was his Jorinda? While he was thinking what to do, he saw the fairy had taken down one of the cages, and was making the best of her way off through the door. He ran or flew after her, touched the cage with the flower, and Jorinda stood before him, and threw her arms round his neck looking as beautiful as ever, as beautiful as when they walked together in the wood.

Then he touched all the other birds with the flower, so that they all took their old forms again; and he took Jorinda home, where they were married, and lived happily together many years: and so did a good many other lads, whose maidens had been forced to sing in the old fairy's cages by themselves, much longer than they liked.

THUMBLING THE DWARF AND THUMBLING THE GIANT

AN honest husbandman had once upon a time a son born to him who was no bigger than my thumb, and who for many years did not grow one hair's breadth taller. One day, as the father was going to plough in his field, the little fellow said, "Father, let me go too." "No," said his father, "stay where you are; you can do no good out of doors, and if you go perhaps I may lose you." Then little Thumbling fell a-crying: and his father, to quiet him, at last said he might go. So he put him in his pocket, and when he was in the field pulled him out, and set him upon the top of a newly-made furrow, that he might be able to look about him.

While he was sitting there, a great giant came striding over the hill. "Do you see that tall steeple-man?" said the father; "if you don't take care he will run away with you." Now he only said this to frighten the little boy and keep him from straying away. But the giant had long legs, and with two or three strides he really came close to the furrow, and picked up Master Thumbling, to look at him as he would at a beetle or a cockchafer. Then he let him run about his broad hand, and taking a liking to the little chap went off with him. The father stood by all the time, but could not say a word for fright; for he thought his child was really lost, and that he should never see him again.

But the giant took care of him at his house in the woods, and laid him in his bosom, and fed him with the same food that he lived upon himself. So Thumbling, instead of being a little dwarf, became like the giant—tall, and stout, and strong:—so that at the end of two years, when the old giant took him into the woods to try him, and said, "Pull up that birch-tree for yourself to walk with," the lad was so strong that he tore it up by the root. The giant thought he would make him a still stronger man than this: so after taking care of him two years more he took him into the wood to try his strength again. This time he took hold of one of the thickest oaks, and pulled it up as if it were mere sport to him. Then the old giant said, "Well done, my man! you will do now." So he carried him back to the field where he first found him.

His father happened to be just then ploughing his field again, as he was when he lost his son. The young giant went up to him and said, "Look here, father, see who I am:—don't you know your own son?" But the husbandman was frightened, and cried out, "No, no, you are not my son; begone about your business." "Indeed, I am your son; let me plough a little, I can plough as well as you." "No, go your ways," said the father; but as he was afraid of the tall man, he at last let go the plough, and sat down on the ground beside it. Then the youth laid hold of the plowshare, and though he only pushed with one hand, he drove it deep into the earth. The plowman cried out, "If you must plough, pray do not push so hard; you are doing more harm than good": but his son took off the horses, and said, "Father, go home, and tell my mother to get ready a good dinner; I'll go round the field meanwhile." So he went on driving the plough without any horses, till he had done two mornings' work by himself. Then he harrowed it; and when all was over, took up plough, harrow, horses and all, and carried them home like a bundle of straw.

When he reached the house he sat himself down on the bench, saying, "Now, mother, is dinner ready?" "Yes," said she, for she dared not deny him anything, so she brought two large dishes full, enough to have lasted herself and her husband eight days; however, he soon ate it all up, and said that was but a taste. "I see very well, father, that I shall not get enough to eat at your house; so if you will give me an iron walking-stick, so strong that I cannot break it against my knees, I will go away again." The husbandman very gladly put his two horses to the cart, and drove them to the forge;

THE GIANT PICKED UP MASTER THUMBLING, TO LOOK AT HIM AS HE WOULD AT A BEETLE OR A COCKCHAFER

and brought back a bar of iron, as long and as thick as his two horses could draw: but the lad laid it against his knee, and snap it went, like a beanstalk. "I see, father," said he, "you can get no stick that will do for me, so I'll go and try my luck by myself."

Then away he went, and turned blacksmith, and travelled till he came to a village where lived a miserly smith, who earned a good deal of money, but kept all he got to himself, and gave nothing away to anybody. The first thing he did was to step into the smithy, and ask if the smith did not want a journeyman. "Ay," said the cunning fellow, as he looked at him and thought what a stout chap he was, and how lustily he would work and earn his bread,—"What wages do you ask?" "I want no pay," said he; "but every fortnight, when the other workmen are paid, you shall let me give you two strokes over the shoulders, just to amuse myself." The old smith thought to himself he could bear this very well, and reckoned on saving a great deal of money, so the bargain was soon struck.

The next morning the new workman was about to begin to work, but at the first stroke that he hit, when his master brought him the iron red hot, he shivered it in pieces, and the anvil sunk so deep into the earth that he could not get it out again. This made the old fellow very angry: "Holla!" cried he, "I can't have you for a workman, you are too clumsy; we must put an end to our bargain." "Very well," said the other, "but you must pay for what I have done; so let me give you only one little stroke, and then the bargain is all over." So saying, he gave him a thump that tossed him over a load of hay that stood near. Then he took the thickest bar of iron in the forge for a walking-stick, and went on his way.

When he had journeyed some way he came to a farmhouse, and asked the farmer if he wanted a foreman. The farmer said, "Yes," and the same wages were agreed for as before with the blacksmith. The next morning the workmen were all to go into the wood; but the giant was found to be fast asleep in his bed when the rest were all up and ready to start, "Come, get up," said one of them to him;" it is high time to be stirring: you must go with us." "Go your way," muttered he, sulkily; "I shall have done my work and get home long before you." So he lay in bed two hours longer, and at last got up and cooked and ate his breakfast, and then at his leisure harnessed his horses to go to the wood.

Just before the wood was a hollow way, through which all must pass; so he drove the cart on first, and built up behind him such a mound of fagots and briers that no horse could pass. This done, he drove on, and as he was going into the wood met the others coming out on their road home. "Drive away," said he, "I shall be home before you still." However, he only went a very little way into the wood, and tearing up one of the largest timber trees, put it into his cart, and turned about homewards. When he came to the pile of fagots, he found all the others standing there, not being able to pass by. "So," said he, "you see if you had staid with me, you would have been home just as soon, and might have slept an hour or two longer." Then he took his tree on one shoulder, and his cart on the other, and pushed through as easily as though he were laden with feathers; and when he reached the yard he showed the tree to the farmer, and asked if it was not a famous walking-stick. "Wife," said the farmer, "this man is worth something; if he sleeps longer, still he works better than the rest."

Time rolled on, and he had worked for the farmer his whole year; so when his fellow-labourers were paid, he said he also had a right to take his wages. But great dread came upon the farmer, at the thought of the blows he was to have, so he begged him to give up the old bargain, and take his whole farm and stock instead. "Not I," said he. "I will be no farmer; I am foreman, and so I mean to keep, and to be paid as we agreed." Finding he could do nothing with him, the farmer only begged one fortnight's respite, and called together all his friends, to ask their advice in the matter. They bethought themselves for a long time, and at last agreed that the shortest way was to kill this troublesome foreman. The next thing was to settle how it was to be done; and it was agreed that he should be ordered to carry into the yard some great mill-stones, and to put them on the edge of the well; that then he should be sent down to clean it out, and when he was at the bottom, the mill-stones should be pushed down upon his head.

Everything went right, and when the foreman was safe in the well, the stones were rolled in. As they struck the bottom, the water splashed to the very top. Of course they thought his head must be crushed to pieces; but he only cried out, "Drive away the chickens from the well; they are scratching about in the sand above, and they throw it into my eyes, so that I cannot see." When his job was done, up he sprang from the well, saying, "Look here! see what a fine neckcloth I have!" as he pointed to one of the mill-stones that had fallen over his head and hung about his neck.

The farmer was again overcome with fear, and begged another fortnight to think of it. So his friends were called together again, and at last gave this advice; that the foreman should be sent and made to grind corn by night at the haunted mill, whence no man had ever yet come out in the morning alive. That very evening he was told to carry eight bushels of corn to the mill, and grind them in the night. Away he went to the loft, put two bushels into his right pocket, two into his left, and four into a long sack slung over his shoulders, and then set off to the mill. The miller told him he might grind there in the day time, but not by night; for the mill was bewitched, and whoever went in at night had been found dead in the morning. "Never mind, miller, I shall come out safe," said he; "only make haste and get out of the way, and look out for me in the morning."

So he went into the mill, and put the corn into the hopper, and about twelve o'clock sat himself down on the bench in the miller's room. After a little time the door all at once opened of itself, and in came a large table. On the table stood wine and meat, and many good things besides. All seemed placed there by themselves; at any rate there was no one to be seen. The chairs next moved themselves round it, but still neither guests nor servants came; till all at once he saw ringers handling the knives and forks, and putting food on the plates, but still nothing else was to be seen. Now our friend felt somewhat hungry as he looked at the dishes, so he sat himself down at the table and ate whatever he liked best. "A little wine would be well after this cheer," said he; "but the good folks of this house seem to take but little of it." Just as he spoke, however, a flagon of the best moved on, and our guest filled a bumper, smacked his lips, and drank "Health and long life to all the company, and success to our next merry meeting!"

When they had had enough, and the plates and dishes, bottles and glasses, were all empty, on a sudden he heard something blow out the lights. "Never mind!" thought he; "one wants no candle to show one light to go to sleep by." But now that it was pitch dark he felt a huge blow fall upon his head. "Foul play!" cried he; "if I get such another box on the ear I shall just give it back again": and this he really did when the next blow came. Thus the game went on all night; and he never let fear get the better of him, but kept dealing his blows round, till at daybreak all was still. "Well, miller," said he in the morning, "I have had some little slaps on the face, but I've given as good, I warrant you; and meantime I have eaten just as much as I liked." The miller was glad to find the charm was broken, and would have given him a great deal of money. "I want no money, I have quite enough," said he, as he took his meal on his back, and went home to his master to claim his wages.

But the farmer was in great trouble, knowing there was now no help for him; and he paced the room up and down, while the drops of sweat ran down his forehead. Then he opened the window for a little fresh air, and before he was aware his foreman gave him the first blow, and such a blow, that off he flew over the hills and far away. The next blow sent his wife after him, and, for aught I know, they may not have reached the ground yet; but, without waiting to know, the young giant took up his iron walking-stick and walked off.

THE JUNIPER-TREE

LONG, long ago, some two thousand years or so, there lived a rich man with a good and beautiful wife. They loved each other dearly, but sorrowed much that they had no children. So greatly did they desire to have one, that the wife prayed for it day and night, but still they remained childless.

In front of the house there was a court, in which grew a juniper-tree. One winter's day the wife stood under the tree to peel some apples, and as she was peeling them, she cut her finger, and the blood fell on the snow. "Ah," sighed the woman heavily, "if I had but a child, as red as blood and as white as snow," and as she spoke the words, her heart grew light within her, and it seemed to her that her wish was granted, and she returned to the house feeling glad and comforted. A month passed, and the snow had all disappeared; then another month went by, and all the earth was green. So the months followed one another, and first the trees budded in the woods, and soon the green branches grew thickly intertwined, and then the blossoms began to fall. Once again the wife stood under the juniper-tree, and it was so full of sweet scent that her heart leaped for joy, and she was so overcome with her happiness, that she fell on her knees. Presently the fruit became round and firm, and she was glad and at peace; but when they were fully ripe she picked the berries and ate eagerly of them, and then she grew sad and ill. A little while later she called her husband, and said to him, weeping. "If I die, bury me under the juniper-tree." Then she felt comforted and happy again, and before another month had passed she had a little child, and when she saw that it was as white as snow and as red as blood, her joy was so great that she died.

Her husband buried her under the juniper-tree, and wept bitterly for her. By degrees, however, his sorrow grew less, and although at times he still grieved over his loss, he was able to go about as usual, and later on he married again.

He now had a little daughter born to him; the child of his first wife was a boy, who was as red as blood and as white as snow. The mother loved her daughter very much, and when she looked at her and then looked at the boy, it pierced her heart to think that he would always stand in the way of her own child, and she was continually thinking how she could get the whole of the property for her. This evil thought took possession of her more and more, and made her behave very unkindly to the boy. She drove him from place to place with cuffings and buffetings, so that the poor child went about in fear, and had no peace from the time he left school to the time he went back.

One day the little daughter came running to her mother in the store-room, and said, "Mother, give me an apple." "Yes, my child," said the wife, and she gave her a beautiful apple out of the chest; the chest had a very heavy lid and a large iron lock.

"Mother," said the little daughter again, "may not brother have one too?" The mother was angry at this, but she answered, "Yes, when he comes out of school."

Just then she looked out of the window and saw him coming, and it seemed as if an evil spirit entered into her, for she snatched the apple out of her little daughter's hand, and said, "You shall not have one before your brother." She threw the apple into the chest and shut it to. The little boy now came in, and the evil spirit in the wife made her say kindly to him, "My son, will you have an apple?" but she gave him a wicked look. "Mother," said the boy, "how dreadful you look! Yes, give me an apple." The thought came to her that she would kill him. "Come with me," she said, and she lifted up the lid of the chest; "take one out for yourself." And as he bent over to do so, the evil spirit urged her, and crash! down went the lid, and off went the little boy's head. Then she was overwhelmed with fear at the thought of what she had done. "If only I can prevent anyone knowing that I did it," she thought. So she went upstairs to her room, and took a white handkerchief out of her top drawer; then she set the boy's head again on his shoulders, and bound it with the handkerchief so that nothing could be seen, and placed him on a chair by the door with an apple in his hand.

Soon after this, little Marleen came up to her mother who was stirring a pot of boiling water over the fire, and said, "Mother, brother is sitting by the door with an apple in his hand, and he looks so pale; and when I asked him to give me the apple, he did not answer, and that frightened me."

"Go to him again," said her mother, "and if he does not answer, give him a box on the ear." So little Marleen went, and said, "Brother, give me that apple," but he did not say a word; then she gave him a box on the ear, and his head rolled off. She was so terrified at this, that she ran crying and screaming to her mother. "Oh!" she said, "I have knocked off brother's head," and then she wept and wept, and nothing would stop her.

"What have you done!" said her mother, "but no one must know about it, so you must keep silence; what is done can't be undone; we will make him into puddings." And she took the little boy and cut him up, made him into puddings, and put him in the pot. But Marleen stood looking on, and wept and wept, and her tears fell into the pot, so that there was no need of salt.

Presently the father came home and sat down to his dinner; he asked, "Where is my son?" The mother said nothing, but gave him a large dish of black pudding, and Marleen still wept without ceasing.

The father again asked, "Where is my son?"

"Oh," answered the wife, "he is gone into the country to his mother's great uncle; he is going to stay there some time."

"What has he gone there for, and he never even said goodbye to me!"

"Well, he likes being there, and he told me he should be away quite six weeks; he is well looked after there."

"I feel very unhappy about it," said the husband, "in case it should not be all right, and he ought to have said goodbye to me."

With this he went on with his dinner, and said, "Little Marleen, why do you weep? Brother will soon be back." Then he asked his wife for more pudding, and as he ate, he threw the bones under the table.

THEN SHE LAID THEM IN THE GREEN GRASS UNDER THE JUNIPER TREE

Little Marleen went upstairs and took her best silk handkerchief out of her bottom drawer, and in it she wrapped all the bones from under the table and carried them outside, and all the time she did nothing but weep. Then she laid them in the green grass under the juniper-tree, and she had no sooner done so, then all her sadness seemed to leave her, and she wept no more. And now the juniper-tree began to move, and the branches waved backwards and forwards, first away from one another, and then together again, as it might be someone clapping their hands for joy. After this a mist came round the tree, and in the midst of it there was a burning as of fire, and out of the fire there flew a beautiful bird, that rose high into the air, singing magnificently, and when it could no more be seen, the juniper-tree stood there as before, and the silk handkerchief and the bones were gone.

Little Marleen now felt as lighthearted and happy as if her brother were still alive, and she went back to the house and sat down cheerfully to the table and ate.

The bird flew away and alighted on the house of a goldsmith and began to sing:

"My mother killed her little son;
My father grieved when I was gone;
My sister loved me best of all;
She laid her kerchief over me,
And took my bones that they might lie
Underneath the juniper-tree
Kywitt, Kywitt, what a beautiful bird am I!"

The goldsmith was in his workshop making a gold chain, when he heard the song of the bird on his roof. He thought it so beautiful that he got up and ran out, and as he crossed the threshold he lost one of his slippers. But he ran on into the middle of the street, with a slipper on one foot and a sock on the other; he still had on his apron, and still held the gold chain and the pincers in his hands, and so he stood gazing up at the bird, while the sun came shining brightly down on the street.

"Bird," he said, "how beautifully you sing! Sing me that song again."

"Nay," said the bird, "I do not sing twice for nothing. Give that gold chain, and I will sing it you again."

"Here is the chain, take it," said the goldsmith. "Only sing me that again."

The bird flew down and took the gold chain in his right claw, and then he alighted again in front of the goldsmith and sang:

"My mother killed her little son;
My father grieved when I was gone;
My sister loved me best of all;
She laid her kerchief over me,
And took my bones that they might lie
Underneath the juniper-tree
Kywitt, Kywitt, what a beautiful bird am I!"

Then he flew away, and settled on the roof of a shoemaker's house and sang:

"My mother killed her little son;
My father grieved when I was gone;
My sister loved me best of all;
She laid her kerchief over me,
And took my bones that they might lie
Underneath the juniper-tree
Kywitt, Kywitt, what a beautiful bird am I!"

The shoemaker heard him, and he jumped up and ran out in his shirt-sleeves, and stood looking up at the bird on the roof with his hand over his eyes to keep himself from being blinded by the sun.

"Bird," he said, "how beautifully you sing!" Then he called through the door to his wife: "Wife, come out; here is a bird, come and look at it and hear how beautifully it sings." Then he called his daughter and the children, then the apprentices, girls and boys, and they all ran up the street to look at the bird, and saw how splendid it was with its red and green feathers, and its neck like burnished gold, and eyes like two bright stars in its head.

"Bird," said the shoemaker, "sing me that song again."

"Nay," answered the bird, "I do not sing twice for nothing; you must give me something."

"Wife," said the man, "go into the garret; on the upper shelf you will see a pair of red shoes; bring them to me." The wife went in and fetched the shoes.

"There, bird," said the shoemaker, "now sing me that song again."

The bird flew down and took the red shoes in his left claw, and then he went back to the roof and sang:

> "My mother killed her little son;
> My father grieved when I was gone;
> My sister loved me best of all;
> She laid her kerchief over me,
> And took my bones that they might lie
> Underneath the juniper-tree
> Kywitt, Kywitt, what a beautiful bird am I!"

When he had finished, he flew away. He had the chain in his right claw and the shoes in his left, and he flew right away to a mill, and the mill went "Click clack, click clack, click clack." Inside the mill were twenty of the miller's men hewing a stone, and as they went "Hick hack, hick hack, hick hack," the mill went "Click clack, click clack, click clack."

The bird settled on a lime-tree in front of the mill and sang:

> "My mother killed her little son;

then one of the men left off,

> My father grieved when I was gone;

two more men left off and listened,

> My sister loved me best of all;

then four more left off,

> She laid her kerchief over me,
> And took my bones that they might lie

now there were only eight at work,

> Underneath

And now only five,

> the juniper-tree.

And now only one,

> Kywitt, Kywitt, what a beautiful bird am I!"

then he looked up and the last one had left off work.

"Bird," he said, "what a beautiful song that is you sing! Let me hear it too; sing it again."

"Nay," answered the bird, "I do not sing twice for nothing; give me that millstone, and I will sing it again."

"If it belonged to me alone," said the man, "you should have it."

"Yes, yes," said the others: "if he will sing again, he can have it."

The bird came down, and all the twenty millers set to and lifted up the stone with a beam; then the bird put his head through the hole and took the stone round his neck like a collar, and flew back with it to the tree and sang—

"My mother killed her little son;
My father grieved when I was gone;
My sister loved me best of all;
She laid her kerchief over me,
And took my bones that they might lie
Underneath the juniper-tree
Kywitt, Kywitt, what a beautiful bird am I!"

And when he had finished his song, he spread his wings, and with the chain in his right claw, the shoes in his left, and the millstone round his neck, he flew right away to his father's house.

The father, the mother, and little Marleen were having their dinner.

"How lighthearted I feel," said the father, "so pleased and cheerful."

"And I," said the mother, "I feel so uneasy, as if a heavy thunderstorm were coming."

But little Marleen sat and wept and wept.

Then the bird came flying towards the house and settled on the roof.

"I do feel so happy," said the father, "and how beautifully the sun shines; I feel just as if I were going to see an old friend again."

"Ah!" said the wife, "and I am so full of distress and uneasiness that my teeth chatter, and I feel as if there were a fire in my veins," and she tore open her dress; and all the while little Marleen sat in the corner and wept, and the plate on her knees was wet with her tears.

The bird now flew to the juniper-tree and began singing:

"My mother killed her little son;

the mother shut her eyes and her ears, that she might see and hear nothing, but there was a roaring sound in her ears like that of a violent storm, and in her eyes a burning and flashing like lightning:

My father grieved when I was gone;

"Look, mother," said the man, "at the beautiful bird that is singing so magnificently; and how warm and bright the sun is, and what a delicious scent of spice in the air!"

My sister loved me best of all;

then little Marleen laid her head down on her knees and sobbed.

"I must go outside and see the bird nearer," said the man.

"Ah, do not go!" cried the wife. "I feel as if the whole house were in flames!"

But the man went out and looked at the bird.

She laid her kerchief over me,
And took my bones that they might lie
Underneath the juniper-tree
Kywitt, Kywitt, what a beautiful bird am I!"

With that the bird let fall the gold chain, and it fell just round the man's neck, so that it fitted him exactly.

He went inside, and said, "See, what a splendid bird that is; he has given me this beautiful gold chain, and looks so beautiful himself."

But the wife was in such fear and trouble, that she fell on the floor, and her cap fell from her head.

Then the bird began again:

"My mother killed her little son;

"Ah me!" cried the wife, "if I were but a thousand feet beneath the earth, that I might not hear that song."

My father grieved when I was gone;

then the woman fell down again as if dead.

My sister loved me best of all;

"Well," said little Marleen, "I will go out too and see if the bird will give me anything."

So she went out.

She laid her kerchief over me,
And took my bones that they might lie

and he threw down the shoes to her,

Underneath the juniper-tree
Kywitt, Kywitt, what a beautiful bird am I!"

And she now felt quite happy and lighthearted; she put on the shoes and danced and jumped about in them. "I was so miserable," she said, "when I came out, but that has all passed away; that is indeed a splendid bird, and he has given me a pair of red shoes."

The wife sprang up, with her hair standing out from her head like flames of fire. "Then I will go out too," she said, "and see if it will lighten my misery, for I feel as if the world were coming to an end."

But as she crossed the threshold, crash! the bird threw the mill-stone down on her head, and she was crushed to death.

The father and little Marleen heard the sound and ran out, but they only saw mist and flame and fire rising from the spot, and when these had passed, there stood the little brother, and he took the father and little Marleen by the hand; then they all three re-joiced, and went inside together and sat down to their dinners and ate.

THE WATER OF LIFE

LONG before you or I were born, there reigned, in a country a great way off, a king who had three sons. This king once fell very ill—so ill that nobody thought he could live. His sons were very much grieved at their father's sickness; and as they were walking together very mournfully in the garden of the palace, a little old man met them and asked what was the matter. They told him that their father was very ill, and that they were afraid nothing could save him. "I know what would," said the little old man; "it is the Water of Life. If he could have a draught of it he would be well again; but it is very hard to get." Then the eldest son said, "I will soon find it": and he went to the sick king, and begged that he might go in search of the Water of Life, as it was the only thing that could save him. "No," said the king. "I had rather die than place you in such great danger as you must meet with in your journey." But he begged so hard that the king let him go; and the prince thought to himself, "If I bring my father this water, he will make me sole heir to his kingdom."

Then he set out: and when he had gone on his way some time he came to a deep valley, overhung with rocks and woods; and as he looked around, he saw standing above him on one of the rocks a little ugly dwarf, with a sugarloaf cap and a scarlet cloak; and the dwarf called to him and said, "Prince, whither so fast?" "What is that to thee, you ugly imp?" said the prince haughtily, and rode on.

But the dwarf was enraged at his behavior, and laid a fairy spell of ill-luck upon him; so that as he rode on the mountain pass became narrower and narrower, and at last the way was so straitened that he could not go to step forward: and when he thought to have turned his horse round and go back the way he came, he heard a loud laugh ringing round him, and found that the path was closed behind him, so that he was shut in all round. He next tried to get off his horse and make his way on foot, but again the laugh rang in his ears, and he found himself unable to move a step, and thus he was forced to abide spellbound.

Meantime the old king was lingering on in daily hope of his son's return, till at last the second son said, "Father, I will go in search of the Water of Life." For he thought to himself, "My brother is surely dead, and the kingdom will fall to me if I find the water." The king was at first very unwilling to let him go, but at last yielded to his wish. So he set out and followed the same road which his brother had done, and met with the same elf, who stopped him at the same spot in the mountains, saying, as before, "Prince, prince, whither so fast?" "Mind your own affairs, busybody!" said the prince scornfully, and rode on.

But the dwarf put the same spell upon him as he put on his elder brother, and he, too, was at last obliged to take up his abode in the heart of the mountains. Thus it is with proud silly people, who think themselves above everyone else, and are too proud to ask or take advice.

When the second prince had thus been gone a long time, the youngest son said he would go and search for the Water of Life, and trusted he should soon be able to make his father well again. So he set out, and the dwarf met him too at the same spot in the valley, among the mountains, and said, "Prince, whither so fast?" And the prince said, "I am going in search of the Water of Life, because my father is ill, and like to die: can you help me? Pray be kind, and aid me if you can!" "Do you know where it is to be found?" asked the dwarf. "No," said the prince, "I do not. Pray tell me if you know." "Then as you have spoken to me kindly, and are wise enough to seek for advice, I will tell you how and where to go. The water you seek springs from a well in an enchanted castle; and, that you may be able to reach it in safety, I will give you an iron wand and two little loaves of bread; strike the iron door of the castle three times with the wand, and it will open: two hungry lions will be lying down inside gaping for their prey, but if you throw them the bread they will let you pass; then hasten on to the well, and take some of the Water of Life before the clock strikes twelve; for if you tarry longer the door will shut upon you for ever."

Then the prince thanked his little friend with the scarlet cloak for his friendly aid, and took the wand and the bread, and went travelling on and on, over sea and over land, till he came to his journey's end, and found everything to be as the dwarf had told him. The door flew open at the third stroke of the wand, and when the lions were quieted he went on through the castle and came at length to a beautiful hall. Around it he saw several knights sitting in a trance; then he pulled off their rings and put them on his own fingers. In another room he saw on a table a sword and a loaf of bread, which he also took. Further on he came to a room where a beautiful young lady sat upon a couch; and she welcomed him joyfully, and said, if he would set her free from the spell that bound her, the kingdom should be his, if he would come back in a year and marry her. Then she told him that the well that held the Water of Life was in the palace gardens; and bade him make haste, and draw what he wanted before the clock struck twelve.

He walked on; and as he walked through beautiful gardens he came to a delightful shady spot in which stood a couch; and he thought to himself, as he felt tired, that he would rest himself for a while, and gaze on the lovely scenes around him. So he laid himself down, and sleep fell upon him unawares, so that he did not wake up till the clock was striking a quarter to twelve. Then he sprang from the couch dreadfully frightened, ran to the well, filled a cup that was standing by him full of water, and hastened to get away in time. Just as he was going out of the iron door it struck twelve, and the door fell so quickly upon him that it snapped off a piece of his heel.

When he found himself safe, he was overjoyed to think that he had got the Water of Life; and as he was going on his way homewards, he passed by the little dwarf, who, when he saw the sword and the loaf, said, "You have made a noble prize; with the sword you can at a blow slay whole armies, and the bread will never fail you." Then the prince thought to himself, "I cannot go home to my father

E. LOUIS RHEAD

without my brothers"; so he said, "My dear friend, cannot you tell me where my two brothers are, who set out in search of the Water of Life before me, and never came back?" "I have shut them up by a charm between two mountains," said the dwarf, "because they were proud and ill-behaved, and scorned to ask advice." The prince begged so hard for his brothers, that the dwarf at last set them free, though unwillingly, saying, "Beware of them, for they have bad hearts." Their brother, however, was greatly rejoiced to see them, and told them all that had happened to him; how he had found the Water of Life, and had taken a cup full of it; and how he had set a beautiful princess free from a spell that bound her; and how she had engaged to wait a whole year, and then to marry him, and to give him the kingdom.

Then they all three rode on together, and on their way home came to a country that was laid waste by war and a dreadful famine, so that it was feared all must die for want. But the prince gave the king of the land the bread, and all his kingdom ate of it. And he lent the king the wonderful sword, and he slew the enemy's army with it; and thus the kingdom was once more in peace and plenty. In the same manner he befriended two other countries through which they passed on their way.

When they came to the sea, they got into a ship and during their voyage the two eldest said to themselves, "Our brother has got the water which we could not find, therefore our father will forsake us and give him the kingdom, which is our right"; so they were full of envy and revenge, and agreed together how they could ruin him. Then they waited till he was fast asleep, and poured the Water of Life out of the cup, and took it for themselves, giving him bitter sea-water instead.

When they came to their journey's end, the youngest son brought his cup to the sick king, that he might drink and be healed. Scarcely, however, had he tasted the bitter sea-water when he became worse even than he was before; and then both the elder sons came in, and blamed the youngest for what they had done; and said that he wanted to poison their father, but that they had found the Water of Life, and had brought it with them. He no sooner began to drink of what they brought him, than he felt his sickness leave him, and was as strong and well as in his younger days. Then they went to their brother, and laughed at him, and said, "Well, brother, you found the Water of Life, did you? You have had the trouble and we shall have the reward. Pray, with all your cleverness, why did not you manage to keep your eyes open? Next year one of us will take away your beautiful princess, if you do not take care. You had better say nothing about this to our father, for he does not believe a word you say; and if you tell tales, you shall lose your life into the bargain: but be quiet, and we will let you off."

The old king was still very angry with his youngest son, and thought that he really meant to have taken away his life; so he called his court together, and asked what should be done, and all agreed that he ought to be put to death. The prince knew nothing of what was going on, till one day, when the king's chief huntsmen went a-hunting with him, and they were alone in the wood together, the huntsman looked so sorrowful that the prince said, "My friend, what is the matter with you?" "I cannot and dare not tell you," said he. But the prince begged very hard, and said, "Only tell me what it is, and do not think I shall be angry, for I will forgive you." "Alas!" said the huntsman; "the king has ordered me to shoot you." The prince started at this, and said, "Let me live, and I will change dresses with you; you shall take my royal coat to show to my father, and do you give me your shabby one." "With all my heart," said the huntsman; "I am sure I shall be glad to save you, for I could not have shot you." Then he took the prince's coat, and gave him the shabby one, and went away through the wood.

Some time after, three grand embassies came to the old king's court, with rich gifts of gold and precious stones for his youngest son; now all these were sent from the three kings to whom he had lent his sword and loaf of bread, in order to rid them of their enemy and feed their people. This touched the old king's heart, and he thought his son might still be guiltless, and said to his court, "O that my son were still alive! how it grieves me that I had him killed!" "He is still alive," said the huntsman; "and I am glad that I had pity on him, but let him go in peace, and brought home his royal coat." At this the king was overwhelmed with joy, and made it known throughout all his kingdom, that if his son would come back to his court he would forgive him.

Meanwhile the princess was eagerly waiting till her deliverer should come back; and had a road made leading up to her palace all of shining gold; and told her courtiers that whoever came on horseback, and rode straight up to the gate upon it, was her true lover; and that they must let him in: but whoever rode on one side of it, they must be sure was not the right one; and that they must send him away at once.

The time soon came, when the eldest brother thought that he would make haste to go to the princess, and say that he was the one who had set her free, and that he should have her for his wife, and the kingdom with her. As he came before the palace and saw the golden road, he stopped to look at it, and he thought to himself, "It is a pity to ride upon this beautiful road"; so he turned aside and rode on the right-hand side of it. But when he came to the gate, the guards, who had seen the road he took, said to him, he could not be what he said he was, and must go about his business.

The second prince set out soon afterwards on the same errand; and when he came to the golden road, and his horse had set one foot upon it, he stopped to look at it, and thought it very beautiful, and said to himself, "What a pity it is that anything should tread here!" Then he too turned aside and rode on the left side of it. But when he came to the gate the guards said he was not the true prince, and that he too must go away about his business; and away he went.

Now when the full year was come round, the third brother left the forest in which he had lain hid for fear of his father's anger, and set out in search of his betrothed bride. So he journeyed on, thinking of her all the way, and rode so quickly that he did not even see what the road was made of, but went with his horse straight over it; and as he came to the gate it flew open, and the princess welcomed him with joy, and said he was her deliverer, and should now be her husband and lord of the kingdom. When the first joy at their meeting was over, the princess told him she had heard of his father having forgiven him, and of his wish to have him home again: so, before his wedding with the princess, he went to visit his father, taking her with him. Then he told him everything; how his brothers had cheated and robbed him, and yet that he had borne all those wrongs for the love of his father. And the old king was very angry, and wanted to punish his wicked sons; but they made their escape, and got into a ship and sailed away over the wide sea, and where they went to nobody knew and nobody cared.

And now the old king gathered together his court, and asked all his kingdom to come and celebrate the wedding of his son and the princess. And young and old, noble and squire, gentle and simple, came at once on the summons; and among the rest came the friendly dwarf, with the sugarloaf hat, and a new scarlet cloak.

> And the wedding was held, and the merry bells run.
> And all the good people they danced and they sung,
> And feasted and frolick'd I can't tell how long.

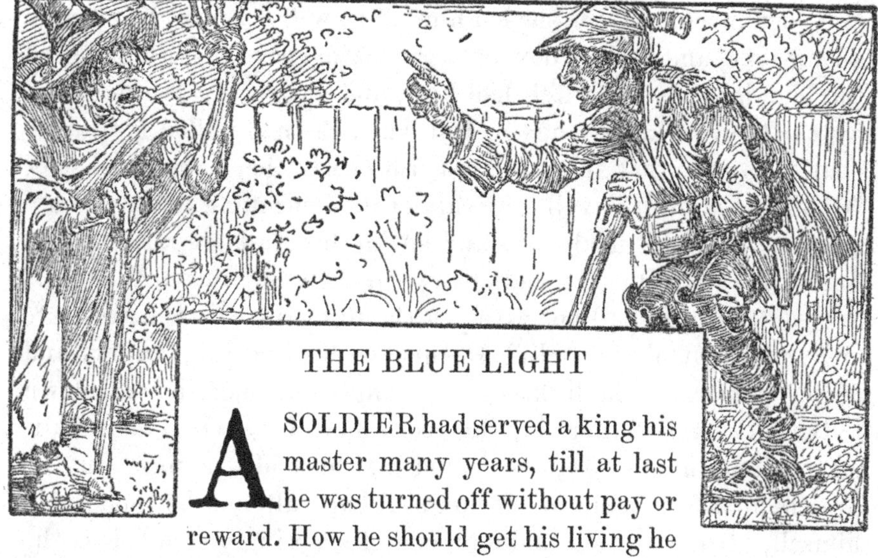

THE BLUE LIGHT

A SOLDIER had served a king his master many years, till at last he was turned off without pay or reward. How he should get his living he did not know: so he set out and journeyed homeward all day in a very downcast mood, until in the evening he came to the edge of a deep wood. The road leading that way, he pushed forward, but had not gone far before he saw a light glimmering through the trees, towards which he bent his weary steps; and soon came to a hut where no one lived but an old witch. The poor fellow begged for a night's lodging and something to eat and drink; but she would listen to nothing: however, he was not easily got rid of; and at last she said, "I think I will take pity on you this once; but if I do, you must dig over all my garden for me in the morning." The soldier agreed very willingly to anything she asked, and he became her guest.

The next day he kept his word and dug the garden very neatly. The job lasted all day; and in the evening, when his mistress would have sent him away, he said, "I am so tired with my work that I must beg you to let me stay over the night." The old lady vowed at first she would not do any such thing; but after a great deal of talk he carried his point, agreeing to chop up a whole cart-load of wood for her the next day.

This task too was duly ended; but not till towards night; and then he found himself so tired, that he begged a third night's rest: and this too was given, but only on his pledging his word that he next day would fetch the witch the blue light that burnt at the bottom of the well.

When morning came she led him to the well's mouth, tied him to a long rope, and let him down. At the bottom sure enough he found the blue light as the witch had said, and at once made the signal for her to draw him up again. But when she had pulled him up so near to the top that she could reach him with her hands, she said, "Give me the light, I will take care of it,"—meaning to play him a trick, by taking it for herself and letting him fall again to the bottom of the well. But the soldier saw through her wicked thoughts, and said, "No, I shall not give you the light till I find myself safe and sound out of the well." At this she became very angry, and dashed him, with the light she had longed for many a year, down to the bottom. And there lay the poor soldier for a while in despair, on the damp mud below, and feared that his end was nigh. But his pipe happened to be in his pocket still half full, and he thought to himself, "I may as well make an end of smoking you out; it is the last pleasure I shall have in this world." So he lit it at the blue light, and began to smoke.

Up rose a cloud of smoke, and on a sudden a little black dwarf was seen making his way through the midst of it, "What do you want with me, soldier?" said he. "I have no business with you," answered he. But the dwarf said, "I am bound to serve you in everything, as lord and master of the blue light." "Then first of all be so good as to help me out of this well." No sooner said than done: the dwarf took him by the hand and drew him up, and the blue light of course with him. "Now do me another piece of kindness," said the soldier; "pray let that old lady take my place in the well." When the dwarf had done this, and lodged the witch safely at the bottom, they began to ransack her treasures; and the soldier made bold to carry off as much of her gold and silver as he well could. Then the dwarf said, "if you should chance at any time to want me, you have nothing to do but to light your pipe at the blue light, and I will soon be with you."

The soldier was not a little pleased at his good luck, and went to the best inn in the first town he came to, and ordered some fine clothes to be made, and a handsome room to be got ready for him. When all was ready, he called his little man to him, and said, "The king sent me away penniless, and left me to hunger and want: I have a mind to show him that it is my turn to be master now; so

A LITTLE BLACK DWARF WAS SEEN MAKING HIS WAY THROUGH THE MIDST OF THE BLUE LIGHT

bring me his daughter here this evening, that she may wait upon me, and do what I bid her." "That is rather a dangerous task," said the dwarf. But away he went, took the princess out of her bed, fast asleep as she was, and brought her to the soldier.

Very early in the morning he carried her back: and as soon as she saw her father, she said, "I had a strange dream last night: I thought I was carried away through the air to a soldier's house, and there I waited upon him as his servant." Then the king wondered greatly at such a story; but told her to make a hole in her pocket and fill it with peas, so that if it were really as she said, and the whole was not a dream, the peas might fall out in the streets as she passed through, and leave a clue to tell whither she had been taken. She did so; but the dwarf had heard the king's plot; and when evening came, and the soldier said he must bring him the princess again, he strewed peas over several of the streets, so that the few that fell from her pocket were not known from the others; and the people amused themselves all the next day picking up peas, and wondering where so many came from.

When the princess told her father what had happened to her the second time, he said, "Take one of your shoes with you, and hide it in the room you are taken to." The dwarf heard this also; and when the soldier told him to bring the king's daughter again, he said, "I cannot save you this time; it will be an unlucky thing for you if you are found out—as I think you will." But the soldier would have his own way. "Then you must take care and make the best of your way out of the city gate very early in the morning," said the dwarf. The princess kept one shoe on as her father bid her, and hid it in the soldier's room: and when she got back to her father, he ordered it to be sought for all over the town; and at last it was found where she had hid it. The soldier had run away, it is true; but he had been too slow, and was soon caught and thrown into a strong prison, and loaded with chains:—what was worse, in the hurry of his flight, he had left behind him his great treasure the blue light and all his gold, and had nothing left in his pocket but one poor ducat.

As he was standing very sorrowful at the prison grating, he saw one of his comrades, and calling out to him said, "If you will bring me a little bundle I left in the inn, I will give you a ducat." His comrade thought this very good pay for such a job: so he went away, and soon came back bringing the blue light and the gold. Then the prisoner soon lit his pipe: up rose the smoke, and with it came his old friend the little dwarf. "Do not fear, master," said he: "keep up your heart at your trial, and leave everything to take its course;—only mind to take the blue light with you." The trial soon came on; the matter was sifted to the bottom; the prisoner found guilty, and his doom passed:—he was ordered to be hung forthwith on the gallows-tree.

But as he was led out, he said he had one favor to beg of the king. "What is it?" said his majesty. "That you will deign to let me smoke one pipe on the road." "Two, if you like," said the king. Then he lit his pipe at the blue light, and the black dwarf was before him in a moment. "Be so good as to kill, slay, or put to flight all these people," said the soldier: "and as for the king, you may cut him into three pieces." Then the dwarf began to lay about him, and soon got rid of the crowd around: but the king begged hard for mercy; and, to save his life, agreed to let the soldier have the princess for his wife, and to leave the kingdom to him when he died.

THE WATER FAIRY

ONCE upon a time there was a miller and his wife, who together led a life of contentment and ease. They possessed both money and lands, and their prosperity steadily increased from year to year. But fortune is fickle, and misfortune comes upon us unawares; and even so it happened, that as their riches had increased, so gradually, year by year, they disappeared. This went on until the miller could scarcely call the mill he lived in his own. He was now full of trouble, and even after his day's work was done, he was unable to rest, for he tossed from side to side on his bed, his anxiety keeping him awake.

One morning he got up before daybreak, and went out; he thought the heaviness of his heart might perhaps be lightened in the open air. Just as he crossed the mill-dam, the first beam of the morning sun shot forth, and at the same moment he heard the sound of something disturbing the waters of the mill-pond. He turned, and saw the figure of a beautiful woman slowly rising above the surface. Her long hair, which she held back over her shoulders with her fair slender hands, fell around her like a bright garment. The miller knew that this must be the fairy of the water, and in his fear, was uncertain whether to go or stay. Then he heard her soft voice calling him by name, and asking him the reason of his sadness. At first he was struck dumb, but her kind tones revived his courage, and he then told her how he had formerly lived in happiness and luxury, but that now he was so poor that he did not know which way to turn.

"Be at peace," answered the fairy, "I will make you richer and happier than you were before, only you must in return promise to give me what has just been born in your house."

LOUIS RHEAD

"That can be none other than a puppy or a kitten," thought the miller, and he gave his promise to her as she desired. The fairy then vanished beneath the waters, and he hurried joyfully back to his home, greatly comforted at heart. He was but a little way from the house, when a maid-servant ran out calling to him to rejoice, for a little son had been born to him. The miller stood still as if thunder-struck, for it flashed across him in an instant that the fairy had known of this, and had beguiled him.

With drooping head he went in to his wife, and when she asked, "Why do you show no sign of joy at the sight of your beautiful boy?" he related to her what had happened and told her of the promise he had made the fairy. "And of what use or pleasure to me are good fortune and riches," he continued, "if I must lose my son! But what am I to do?" And not one among the relations who had come in to wish them joy knew how to help or advise.

In the meantime prosperity returned to the miller's house. He was successful in all his undertakings and it seemed as if his chests and coffers filled of their own accord, and as if the money he put away multiplied itself during the night. In a little while his wealth was greater than it had been before, but he could not enjoy it in perfect peace, for the remembrance of the promise he had made to the fairy continually tormented him. He never went near the mill-pond without a dread at his heart that she would rise out of the water and remind him of what he owed her. He would not let the boy himself approach it: "Beware," he said to him, "if you but touch the water, a hand will come up out of it, seize you, and drag you down."

Year after year, however, passed, and the fairy never showed herself again, so that at last the miller's fears began to be allayed.

The boy grew towards manhood; he was placed under a huntsman to be trained, and when he had himself become an accomplished huntsman, he was taken into the service of the Lord of the village.

There lived in the village a beautiful and true-hearted girl, with whom the young huntsman fell in love. When his master knew of this he made him a present of a little house, and the two were married, and lived happily and peacefully together.

One day the huntsman was chasing a roe. The animal turned from the wood into the open and he followed it and finally shot it.

He did not notice that he was now in the neighborhood of the dangerous mill-pond, and so, after touching the animal, he went to the water to wash the blood off his hands. He had scarcely dipped them in, when the fairy rose, flung her wet arms around him laughing, and dragged him down so quickly, that in a moment the waters had closed over him and all was again still.

When the evening came on and the huntsman did not return, his wife became alarmed. She went out to look for him, and as he had so often spoken to her of his fear of going near the mill-pond lest the fairy should by her wiles get possession of him, she suspected what had happened. She hastened to the waters, and her worst suspicions were confirmed when she saw her husband's hunting-pouch lying on the bank. Wailing and wringing her hands, she called her beloved one by name, but in vain; she ran to the further side of the pond, and again called him; she poured angry abuse on the fairy, but still no answer came. The surface of the pond remained unstirred by a single ripple, and only the reflection of the half moon looked calmly up at her from the water.

The poor wife would not leave the pond; she walked round and round it without rest or pause, sometimes in silence, sometimes uttering a loud cry of distress, sometimes crying softly to herself. But her strength failed her at last; she sank to the ground and fell into a deep sleep. Ere long a dream took possession of her.

She was climbing painfully up between large masses of rock; her feet were caught by the thorns and briars, the rain beat in her face, and her long hair was blown about by the wind. When, however, she reached the summit, the whole scene changed. The sky was now blue, a soft air was blowing, and the ground sloped gently away to a pretty cottage, which stood in a green meadow, studded with many colored flowers. She went up to it and opened the door, and there sat an old woman with white hair, who gave her a friendly nod. At this moment the poor wife awoke. Day had already dawned, and she resolved at once to follow the guidance of her dream. She climbed up the mountain with difficulty, and everything was exactly as she had seen it in the night. The old woman gave her a kindly welcome, and pointed to a chair, telling her to sit down. "Some great trouble must have befallen you," she said, "to bring you in search of my lonely cottage." The wife told her, amidst her tears, what had happened.

"Be comforted," said the old woman, "I will help you. Here is a golden comb; wait till the moon is at its full, then go and comb your long black hair as you sit beside the mill-pond; when you have finished, lay the comb by the water's edge, and you will see what will happen."

The woman returned home, but the time seemed long to her before the full moon appeared. At last its luminous disc was seen shining in the heavens, and then she went to the mill-pond and sat down and combed her long black hair. When she had done this, she laid the comb down beside the water. She had not long to wait, before the depths became troubled and stormy, and a great wave rose and rolled towards the shore, bearing the comb away with it as it retired. After no longer space of time than was required for the comb to reach the bottom, the surface of the water parted, and the head of the huntsman rose above it. He did not speak, but he looked mournfully towards his wife. In the same instant, a second wave came rushing up and swept over the man's head, and again everything had disappeared. The waters of the pond were as tranquil as before, and only the face of the full moon lay shining upon them. Full of sorrow and disappointment, the woman turned away, but again that night a dream showed her the old woman's cottage. The following morning she once more made her way to the wise woman and poured out her grief to her. This time the old woman gave her a golden flute, and said, "Wait till the full moon comes again, then take the flute and play a beautiful air upon it as you sit by the mill-pond; afterwards lay it on the sand; you will see what will happen."

The wife did as the old woman told her. She had hardly laid the flute down on the sand, when the depths of the water were troubled as before, a great wave rose and rolled towards the shore, and bore away the flute. Again the water divided, and this time not only the head, but half the body of the huntsman appeared. He stretched out his arms towards his wife with a longing gesture, but a second wave rose and overwhelmed him, and drew him down again beneath the water.

"Alas!" exclaimed the unhappy wife, "of what comfort is it to me to see my beloved one, only to lose him again!"

Grief overflowed her heart, but a third time a dream took her to the cottage of the old woman. So she went again to her and the wise woman gave her a golden spinning-wheel, and spoke cheeringly to her, saying, "Everything has not yet been fully accomplished; wait till there is again a full moon, then take the spinning-wheel, and sit down by the shore and spin the spindle full; when that is done, place the wheel near the water, and you will see what will happen."

The wife followed out all these directions with care. As soon as the full moon appeared, she carried the spinning-wheel to the side of the mill-pond, and there sat down and span industriously until she had used up all the flax and had filled the spindle. She had but just placed the wheel near the water, when its depths were stirred even more violently than before, and then an enormous wave rolled rapidly towards the shore and carried away the wheel. In the same moment a column of water rose into the air, and with it the head and the whole body of her husband. He quickly leaped on to the bank, seized his wife by the hand and fled. But they had gone but a little distance, when, with a tremendous roar, the whole mill-pond rose, and with a gigantic force sent its waters rushing over the surrounding country. The fugitives saw themselves face to face with death; in her terror the wife called upon the old woman for help, and she and her husband were instantly changed, she into a toad and he into a frog. The flood as it reached them, could not now kill them, but it tore them away from one another and carried them far in opposite directions.

When the waters had subsided and they again found themselves on dry land, they were changed back again into their human form. But neither knew what had become of the other; they were both among strangers who knew nothing of their native land. High mountains and deep valleys lay between them. In order to support themselves, they were both obliged to tend sheep, and for many long years they led their flocks over the plains and through the forests, full of sorrow and longing.

Once more the spring had broken forth over the earth, when, as fate would have it, they met one another one day while out with their flocks. The husband saw a flock of sheep on a distant hill-side and drove his own towards them, and in a valley on the way he came upon his wife. They did not recognise each other, but both of them were glad to think that they would no longer be so lonely as heretofore. From this time forth they tended their flocks side by side; they did not speak much, but they felt comforted.

One evening, when the full moon was shining in the heavens above them, and the sheep were already lying down for the night, the shepherd drew his flute out of his pocket and played on it a beautiful but melancholy air. When he had finished, he saw that the shepherdess was weeping bitterly. "Why do you weep?" he asked. "Alas, she answered, "even as now the full moon was shining, when I played that tune for the last time upon the flute, and saw my beloved one's head rise above the waters." He looked at her, and it seemed to him as if a veil fell from before his eyes, and he recognized his dearest wife. And she looked up and saw the moonlight shining on her husband's face, and she also knew him again.

They kissed and embraced one another, and there is no need to ask if they were happy.

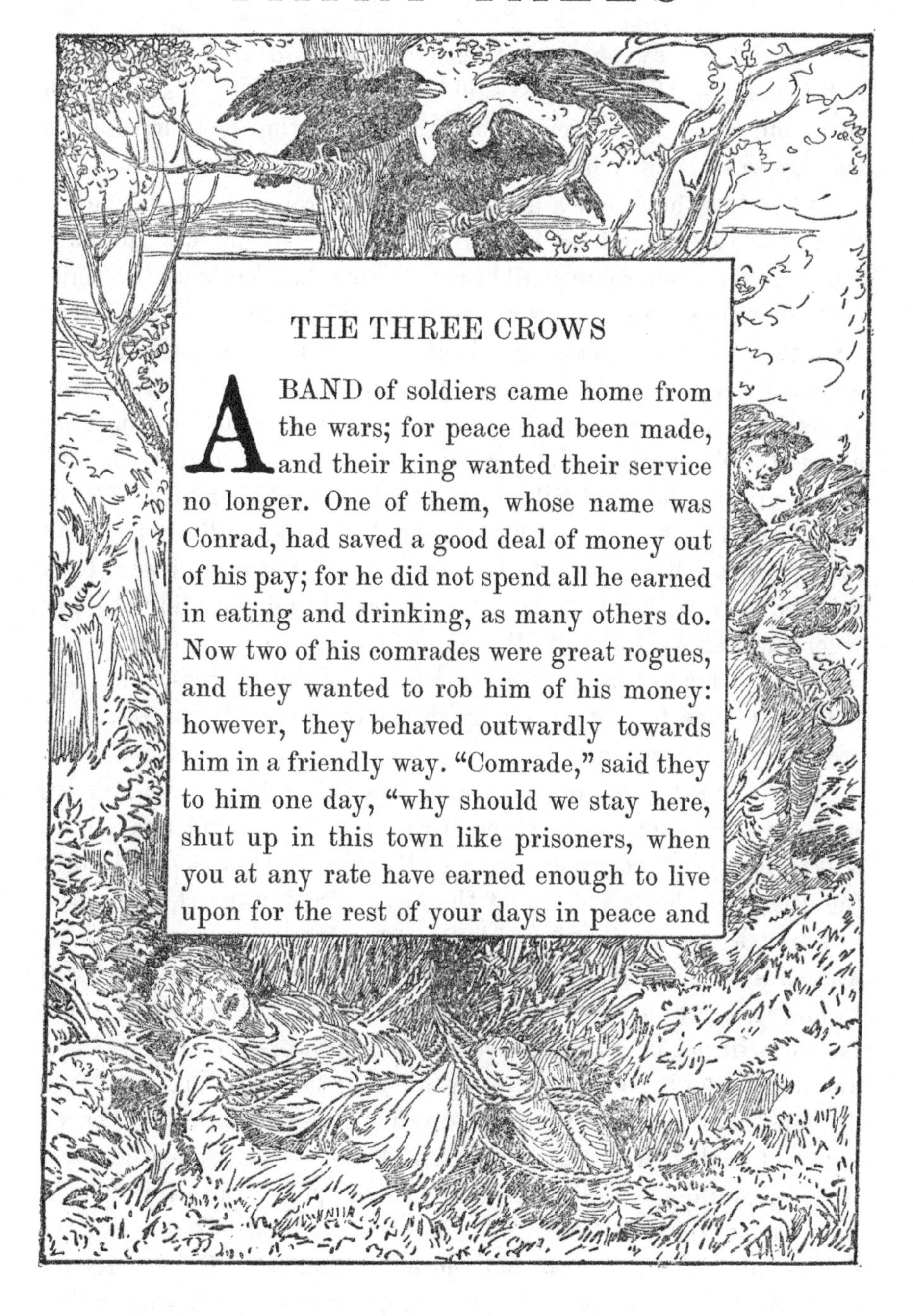

THE THREE CROWS

A BAND of soldiers came home from the wars; for peace had been made, and their king wanted their service no longer. One of them, whose name was Conrad, had saved a good deal of money out of his pay; for he did not spend all he earned in eating and drinking, as many others do. Now two of his comrades were great rogues, and they wanted to rob him of his money: however, they behaved outwardly towards him in a friendly way. "Comrade," said they to him one day, "why should we stay here, shut up in this town like prisoners, when you at any rate have earned enough to live upon for the rest of your days in peace and plenty, at home by your own fireside?" They talked so often to him in this manner, that he at last said he would go and try his luck with them; but they all the time thought of nothing but how they should manage to steal away his money from him.

When they had gone a little way, the two rogues said, "We must go by the right-hand road, for that will take us quickest into another country, where we shall be safe." Now they knew all the while that what they were saying was untrue; and as soon as Conrad said, "No, that will take us straight back into the town we came from—we must keep on the left hand," they picked a quarrel with him, and said, "What do you give yourself airs for? you know nothing about it." Then they fell upon him and knocked him down, and beat him over the head till he was blind. And having taken all the money out of his pockets, they dragged him to a gallows-tree that stood hard by, bound him fast down at the foot of it, and went back into the town with the money. But the poor blind man did not know where he was; and he felt all around him, and finding that he was bound to a large beam of wood, thought it was a cross, and said, "After all, they have done kindly in leaving me under a cross; now Heaven will guard me."

When night came on, he heard something fluttering over his head. It turned out to be three crows that flew round and round, and at last perched upon the tree. By and by they began to talk together, and he heard one of them say, "Sister, what is the best news with you to-day?" "Oh! if men did but know all that we know!" said the other. "The princess is ill, and the king has vowed to marry her to any one who will cure her: but this none can do, for she will not be well until yonder blue flower is burned to ashes and swallowed by her." "Oh, indeed," said the other crow, "if men did but know what we know! To-night there will fall from heaven a dew of such power, that even a blind man, if he washed his eyes with it, would see again." And the third spoke, and said, "Oh! if men knew what we know! The flower is wanted but for one, the dew is wanted but for few; but there is a great dearth of water for all in the town. All the wells are dried up; and no one knows that they must take away the large square stone by the fountain in the market-place, and dig underneath it, and that then the finest water will spring up."

Conrad lay all this time quite quiet; and when the three crows had done talking, he heard them fluttering round again, and at last away they flew. Greatly wondering at what he had heard, and overjoyed at the thoughts of getting his sight, he tried with all his strength to break loose. At last he found himself free, and plucked some of the grass that grew beneath him, and washed his eyes with the dew that had fallen upon it. At once his eye-sight came to him again, and he saw, by the light of the moon and the stars, that he was beneath the gallows-tree, and not beneath a cross, as he had thought. Then he gathered together in a bottle as much of the dew as he could, to take away with him; and looked around till he saw the blue flower that grew close by; and when he had burned it he gathered up the ashes, and set out on his way towards the king's court.

When he reached the palace, he told the king he was come to cure the princess; and when he had given her the ashes and made her well, he claimed her for his wife, as the reward that was to be given. But the princess, looking upon him and seeing that his clothes were so shabby, had no mind to be his wife; and the king would not keep his word, but thought to get rid of him by saying, "Whoever wants to have the princess for his wife, must find enough water for the use of the town, where there is this summer a great dearth." Then the soldier went out, and told the people to take up the square stone by the fountain in the market-place, and to dig for water underneath; and when they had done so, there came up a fine spring, that gave enough water for the whole town. So the king could no longer get off giving him his daughter; and as the princess began to think better of him, they were married, and lived very happily together after all.

Soon after, as he was walking one day through a field, he met his two wicked comrades who had treated him so basely. Though they did not know him, he knew them at once, and went up to them and said, "Look at me! I am your old comrade whom you beat and robbed and left blind; Heaven has defeated your wicked wishes, and turned all the mischief which you brought upon me into good luck." When they heard this they fell at his feet, and begged for pardon; and as he had a very kind and good heart he forgave them, and took them to his palace, and gave them food and clothes. And he told them all that had happened to him, and how he had reached these honours. After they had heard the whole story they said to themselves, "Why should not we go and sit some night under the gallows? we may hear something that will bring us good luck, too."

Next night they stole away; and when they had sat under the tree a little while, they heard a fluttering noise over their heads; and the three crows came and perched upon it. "Sisters," said one of them, "some one must have overheard us, for all the world is talking of the wonderful things that have happened;—the princess is well; the flower has been plucked and burned; a blind man has found his sight; and they have found the spring that gives water to the whole town. Let us look round, perhaps we may find some one skulking about; if we do, he shall rue the day."

Then they began fluttering about, and soon spied out the two men below, and flew at them in a rage, beating and pecking them in the face with their wings and beaks till they were quite blind, and lay half dead upon the ground, under the gallows-tree.

The next day passed over, and they did not return to the palace; so Conrad began to wonder where they were, and went out the following morning in search of them, and at last he found them where they lay, dreadfully repaid for all their folly and baseness.

THE FROG PRINCE

ONE fine evening a young princess went into a wood, and sat down by the side of a cool spring of water. She had a golden ball in her hand, which was her favorite play-thing, and she amused herself with tossing it into the air and catching it again as it fell. After a time she threw it up so high that when she stretched out her hand to catch it, the ball bounded away and rolled along upon the ground, till at last it fell into the spring. The princess looked into the spring after her ball; but it was very deep, so deep that she could not see the bottom of it. Then she began to lament her loss, and said, "Alas! if I could only get my ball again, I would give all my fine clothes and jewels, and everything that I have in the world." Whilst she was speaking a frog put its head out of the water, and said, "Princess, why do you weep so bitterly?" "Alas!" said she, "what can you do for me, you nasty frog? My golden ball has fallen into the spring." The frog said, "I want not your pearls and jewels and fine clothes; but if you will love me and let me live with you, and eat from your little golden plate, and sleep upon your little bed, I will bring you your ball again." "What nonsense," thought the princess, "this silly frog is talking! He can never get out of the well: however, he may be able to get my ball for me; and therefore I will promise him what he asks." So she said to the frog, "Well, if you will bring me my ball, I promise to do all you require." Then the frog put his

THE FROG DIVED DEEP AND CAME UP AGAIN WITH THE BALL IN HIS MOUTH

head down, and dived deep under the water; and after a little while he came up again with the ball in his mouth, and threw it on the ground. As soon as the young princess saw her ball, she ran to pick it up, and was so overjoyed to have it in her hand again, that she never thought of the frog, but ran home with it as fast as she could. The frog called after her, "Stay, princess, and take me with you as you promised;" but she did not stop to hear a word.

The next day, just as the princess had sat down to dinner, she heard a strange noise, tap-tap, as if somebody was coming up the marble-staircase; and soon afterwards something knocked gently at the door, and said,

"Open the door, my princess dear,
Open the door to thy true love here!
And mind the words that thou and I said
By the fountain cool in the greenwood shade."

Then the princess ran to the door and opened it, and there she saw the frog, whom she had quite forgotten; she was terribly frightened, and shutting the door as fast as she could, came back to her seat. The king her father asked her what had frightened her. "There is a nasty frog," said she, "at the door, who lifted my ball out of the spring this morning: I promised him that he should live with me here, thinking that he could never get out of the spring; but there he is at the door and wants to come in!" While she was speaking the frog knocked again at the door, and said,

"Open the door, my princess dear,
Open the door to thy true love here!
And mind the words that thou and I said
By the fountain cool in the greenwood shade."

The king said to the young princess, "As you have made a promise, you must keep it; so go and let him in." She did so, and the frog hopped into the room, and came up close to the table. "Pray lift me upon a chair," said he to the princess, "and let me sit next to you." As soon as she had done this, the frog said, "Put your plate closer to me that I may eat out of it." This she did, and when he had eaten as much as he could, he said, "Now I am tired; carry me upstairs and put me into your little bed." And the princess took him up in her hand and put him upon the pillow of her own little bed, where he slept all night long. As soon as it was light he jumped up, hopped downstairs, and went out of the house. "Now," thought the princess, "he is gone, and I shall be troubled with him no more."

But she was mistaken; for when night came again, she heard the same tapping at the door, and when she opened it, the frog came in and slept upon her pillow as before till the morning broke: and the third night he did the same; but when the princess awoke on the following morning, she was astonished to see, instead of the frog, a handsome prince gazing on her with the most beautiful eyes that ever were seen, and standing at the head of her bed.

He told her that he had been enchanted by a malicious fairy, who had changed him into the form of a frog, in which he was fated to remain till some princess should take him out of the spring and let him sleep upon her bed for three nights. "You," said the prince, "have broken this cruel charm, and now I have nothing to wish for but that you should go with me into my father's kingdom, where I will marry you, and love you as long as you live."

The young princess, you may be sure, was not long in giving her consent; and as they spoke a splendid carriage drove up with eight beautiful horses decked with plumes of feathers and golden harness, and behind rode the prince's servant, the faithful Henry, who had bewailed the misfortune of his dear master so long and bitterly that his heart had well nigh burst. Then all set out full of joy for the prince's kingdom; where they arrived safely, and lived happily a great many years.

THE ELVES AND THE COBBLER

THERE was once a cobbler, who worked very hard and was very honest: but still he could not earn enough to live upon; and at last all he had in the world was gone, save just leather enough to make one pair of shoes.

Then he cut his leather out, all ready to make up the next day, meaning to rise early in the morning to his work. His conscience was clear and his heart light amidst all his troubles; so he went peaceably to bed, left all his cares to Heaven, and soon fell asleep. In the morning after he had said his prayers, he sat himself down to his work; when, to his great wonder, there stood the shoes all ready made, upon the table. The good man knew not what to say or think at such an odd thing happening. He looked at the workmanship; there was not one false stitch in the whole job; all was so neat and true, that it was quite a masterpiece.

The same day a customer came in, and the shoes suited him so well that he willingly paid a price higher than usual for them; and the poor shoemaker, with the money, bought leather enough to make two pair more. In the evening he cut out the work, and went to bed early, that he might get up and begin betimes next day; but he was saved all the trouble, for when he got up in the morning the work was done ready to his hand. Soon in came buyers, who paid him handsomely for his goods, so that he bought leather enough for four pair more. He cut out the work again over-night and found it done in the morning, as before; and so it went on for some time: what was got ready in the evening was always done by daybreak, and the good man soon became thriving and well off again.

THE SHOEMAKER AND HIS WIFE WATCHED FROM BEHIND THE CURTAIN

One evening, about Christmas time, as he and his wife were sitting over the fire chatting together, he said to her, "I should like to sit up and watch to-night, that we may see who it is that comes and does my work for me." The wife liked the thought; so they left a light burning, and hid themselves in a corner of the room, behind a curtain that was hung up there, and watched what should happen.

As soon as it was midnight, there came in two little naked dwarfs; and they sat themselves upon the shoemaker's bench, took up all the work that was cut out, and began to ply with their little fingers, stitching and rapping and tapping away at such a rate, that the shoemaker was all wonder, and could not take his eyes off them. And on they went, till the job was quite done, and the shoes stood ready for use upon the table. This was long before daybreak; and then they bustled away as quick as lightning.

The next day the wife said to the shoemaker, "These little wights have made us rich, and we ought to be thankful to them, and do them a good turn if we can. I am quite sorry to see them run about as they do; and indeed it is not very decent, for they have nothing upon their backs to keep off the cold. I'll tell you what, I will make each of them a shirt, and a coat and waistcoat, and a pair of pantaloons into the bargain; and do you make each of them a little pair of shoes."

The thought pleased the good cobbler very much; and one evening, when all the things were ready, they laid them on the table, instead of the work that they used to cut out, and then went and hid themselves, to watch what the little elves would do.

About midnight in they came, dancing and skipping, hopped round the room, and then went to sit down to their work as usual; but when they saw the clothes lying for them, they laughed and chuckled, and seemed mightily delighted.

Then they dressed themselves in the twinkling of an eye, and danced and capered and sprang about, as merry as could be; till at last they danced out at the door, and away over the green.

The good couple saw them no more; but every thing went well with them from that time forward, as long as they lived

THE FROG-BRIDE

THERE was once a king who had three sons. Not far from his kingdom lived an old woman, who had an only daughter called Cherry. The king sent his sons out to see the world, that they might learn the ways of other lands, and get wisdom and skill in ruling the kingdom, which they were one day to have for their own. But the old woman lived at peace at home with her daughter, who was called Cherry, because she liked cherries better than any other kind of food, and would eat scarcely anything else.

Now her poor old mother had no garden, and no money to buy cherries every day for her daughter. And at last she was tempted by the sight of some in a neighboring garden to go in and beg a few of the gardener. But, as ill-luck would have it, the mistress of the garden was as fond of the fruit as Cherry was, and she soon found out that all the best were gone, and was not a little angry at their loss. Now she was a fairy too, though Cherry's mother did not know it, and could tell in a moment who she had to thank for the loss of her dessert. So she vowed to be even with Cherry one of these days.

The princes, while wandering on, came one day to the town where Cherry and her mother lived; and as they passed along the street, saw the fair maiden standing at the window, combing her long and beautiful locks of hair.

Then each of the three fell deeply in love with her, and began to say how much he longed to have her for his wife! Scarcely had the wish been spoken, than each broke out into a great rage with the others, for wanting to have poor Cherry, who could only be wife to one of them. At last all drew their swords, and a dreadful battle began. The fight lasted long, and their rage grew hotter and hotter, when at length the old fairy, to whom the garden belonged, hearing the uproar, came to her gate to know what was the matter. Finding that it was all about her fair neighbor, her old spite for the loss of the cherries broke forth at once, worse than ever. "Now then," said she, "I will have my revenge"; and in her rage she wished Cherry turned into an ugly frog, and sitting in the water, under the bridge at the world's end. No sooner said than done; and poor Cherry became a frog, and vanished out of their sight. The princes now had nothing to fight for; so, sheathing their swords again, they shook hands as brothers, and went on towards their father's home.

The old king meanwhile found that he grew weak, and ill-fitted for the business of reigning; so he thought of giving up his kingdom: but to whom should it be? This was a point that his fatherly heart could not settle; for he loved all his sons alike. "My dear children," said he, "I grow old and weak, and should like to give up my kingdom; but I cannot make up my mind which of you to choose for my heir, for I love you all three; and besides, I should wish to give my people the cleverest and best of you for their king. However, I will give you three trials, and the one who wins the prize shall have the kingdom. The first is to seek me out one hundred ells of cloth, so fine that I can draw it through my golden ring." The sons said they would do their best, and set out on the search.

The two elder brothers took with them many followers, and coaches and horses of all sorts, to bring home all the beautiful cloths which they should find; but the youngest went alone by himself. They soon came to where the roads branched off into several ways: two ran through smiling meadows, with smooth paths and shady groves, but the third looked dreary and dirty, and went over barren wastes. The two eldest chose the pleasant ways; but the youngest took his leave, and whistled along over the dreary road. Whenever fine linen was to be seen, the two elder brothers bought it, and bought so much that their coaches and horses bent under their burthen.

The youngest, on the other hand, journeyed on many a weary day, and could find no place where he could buy even one piece of cloth, that was at all fine and good. His heart sank beneath him, and every mile he grew more and more heavy and sorrowful.

At last he came to the bridge at the world's end; and there he sat himself down to rest and sigh over his bad luck, when an ugly-looking frog popped its head out of the water, and asked, with a voice that had not at all a harsh sound to his ears, what was the matter. The prince said in a pet, "Silly frog! thou canst not help me." "Who told you so?" said the frog; "tell me what ails you." The prince still sat down moping and sighing, but after a while he began to tell the whole story, and why his father had sent him out. "I will help you," said the frog; so it jumped into the stream again, and soon came back, dragging a small piece of linen not bigger than one's hand, and by no means the cleanest in the world in its look. However, there it was, and the frog told the prince to take it away with him. He had no great liking for such a dirty rag; but still there was something in the frog's speech that pleased him much, and he thought to himself, "It can do no harm, it is better than nothing;" so he picked it up, put it in his pocket, and thanked the frog, who dived down again, panting and quite tired, as it seemed, with its work. The further he went the heavier he found the pocket grow, and so he turned himself homewards, trusting greatly in his good luck.

He reached home nearly about the same time that his brothers came up, with their horses and coaches all heavily laden. Then the old king was very glad to see his children again, and pulled the ring off his finger to try who had done the best; but in all the stock that the two eldest had brought there was not one piece, a tenth part of which would go through the ring. At this they were greatly abashed; for they had made a laughingstock of their brother, who came home, as they thought, empty-handed. But how great was their anger when they saw him pull from his pocket a piece, that for softness, beauty, and whiteness, was a thousand times better than anything that was ever before seen! It was so fine that it passed with ease through the ring; indeed, two such pieces would readily have gone in together. The father embraced the lucky youth, told his servants to throw the coarse linen into the sea, and said to his children, "Now you must set about the second task which I am to set you;—bring me home a little dog so small that it will lie in a nut-shell."

His sons were not a little frightened at such a task, but they all longed for the crown, and made up their minds to go and try their hands; and so after a few days they set out once more on their travels. At the cross-ways they parted as before; and the youngest chose his old dreary rugged road, with all the bright hopes that his former good luck gave him. Scarcely had he sat himself down again at the bridge foot when his old friend the frog jumped out, set itself beside him, and as before opened its big wide mouth, and croaked out, "What is the matter?" The prince had this time no doubt of the frog's power, and therefore told what he wanted. "It shall be done for you," said the frog; and springing into the stream it soon brought up a hazelnut, laid it at his feet, and told him to take it home to his father, and crack it gently, and then see what would happen. The prince went his way very well pleased, and the frog, tired with its task, jumped back into the water.

His brothers had reached home first, and brought with them a great many very pretty little dogs. There were Wag-tails, Cur-tails, and Bob-tails, Crops and Brushes, Spitzes and Sprightlies, Fans and Frisks, Diamonds and Dashes, enough to stock the bowers of all the fair ladies in the land. The old king, willing to help them all he could, sent for a large walnut-shell, and tried it with every one of the little dogs. But one stuck fast with the hind-foot out, another with the head out, and a third with the fore-foot, a fourth with its tail out—in short, some one way and some another; but none were at all likely to sit easily in this new kind of kennel. When all had been tried, the youngest made his father a dutiful bow, and gave him the hazel-nut, begging him to crack it very carefully. The moment this was done out ran a beautiful little white dog upon the king's hand; and it wagged its tail, bowed to and fondled its new master; and soon turned about and barked at the other little beasts in the most graceful manner, to the delight of the whole court; and then went back and lay down in its kennel without a bit of either tail, ear, or foot peeping out. The joy of every one was great; the old king again embraced his lucky son, told his people to drown all the other dogs in the sea, and said to his children, "Dear sons, your weightiest tasks are now over, listen to my last wish: whoever brings home the fairest lady shall be at once the heir to my crown."

The prize was so tempting, and the chance so fair for all, that none made any doubts about setting to work, each in his own way, to try and be the winner. The youngest was not in such good spirits as he was the last time; he thought to himself, "The old frog has been able to do a great deal for me, but all its power must be nothing to me now: for where should it find me a fair maiden, and a fairer maiden too than was ever seen at my father's court? The swamps where it lives have no living things in them but toads, snakes, and such vermin." Meantime he went on, and sighed as he sat down again with a heavy heart by the bridge. "Ah, frog!" said he, "this time thou canst do me no good." "Never mind," croaked the frog, "only tell me what is the matter now." Then the prince told his old friend what trouble had now come upon him. "Go thy ways home!" said the frog; "the fair maiden will follow hard after: but take care, and do not laugh at whatever may happen!" This said, it sprang as before into the water, and was soon out of sight.

The prince still sighed on, for he trusted very little this time to the frog's word; but he had not set many steps towards home before he heard a noise behind him, and looking round saw six large water-rats dragging along, at full trot, a large pumpkin cut out into the shape of a coach. On the box sat an old fat toad, as coachman; and behind stood two little frogs, as footmen; and two fine mice, with stately whiskers, ran on before, as outriders. Within sat his old friend the frog, rather misshapen and unseemly to be sure, but still with somewhat of a graceful air, as it bowed, and kissed its hand to him in passing.

The prince was much too deeply wrapt up in thought as to his chance of finding the fair lady whom he was seeking, to take any heed of the strange scene before him. He scarcely looked at it, and had still less mind to laugh. The coach passed on a little way, and soon turned a corner that hid it from his sight; but how astonished was he, on turning the corner himself, to find a handsome coach and six black horses standing there, with a coachman in gay livery, and with the most beautiful lady he had ever seen sitting inside! And who should this lady be but the long-lost Cherry, for whom his heart had so long ago panted, and whom he knew again the moment he saw her! As he came up, one of the footmen made him a low bow, as he let down the steps and opened the coach door; and he was allowed to get in, and seat himself by the beautiful lady's side.

They soon came to his father's city, where his brothers also came, with trains of fair ladies; but as soon as Cherry was seen, all the court, with one voice, gave the prize to her, as the most beautiful.

The delighted father embraced his son, and named him the heir to his crown; and ordered all the other ladies to be sent to keep company with the little dogs. Then the prince married Cherry, and lived long and happily with her; and indeed lives with her still—if he be not dead.

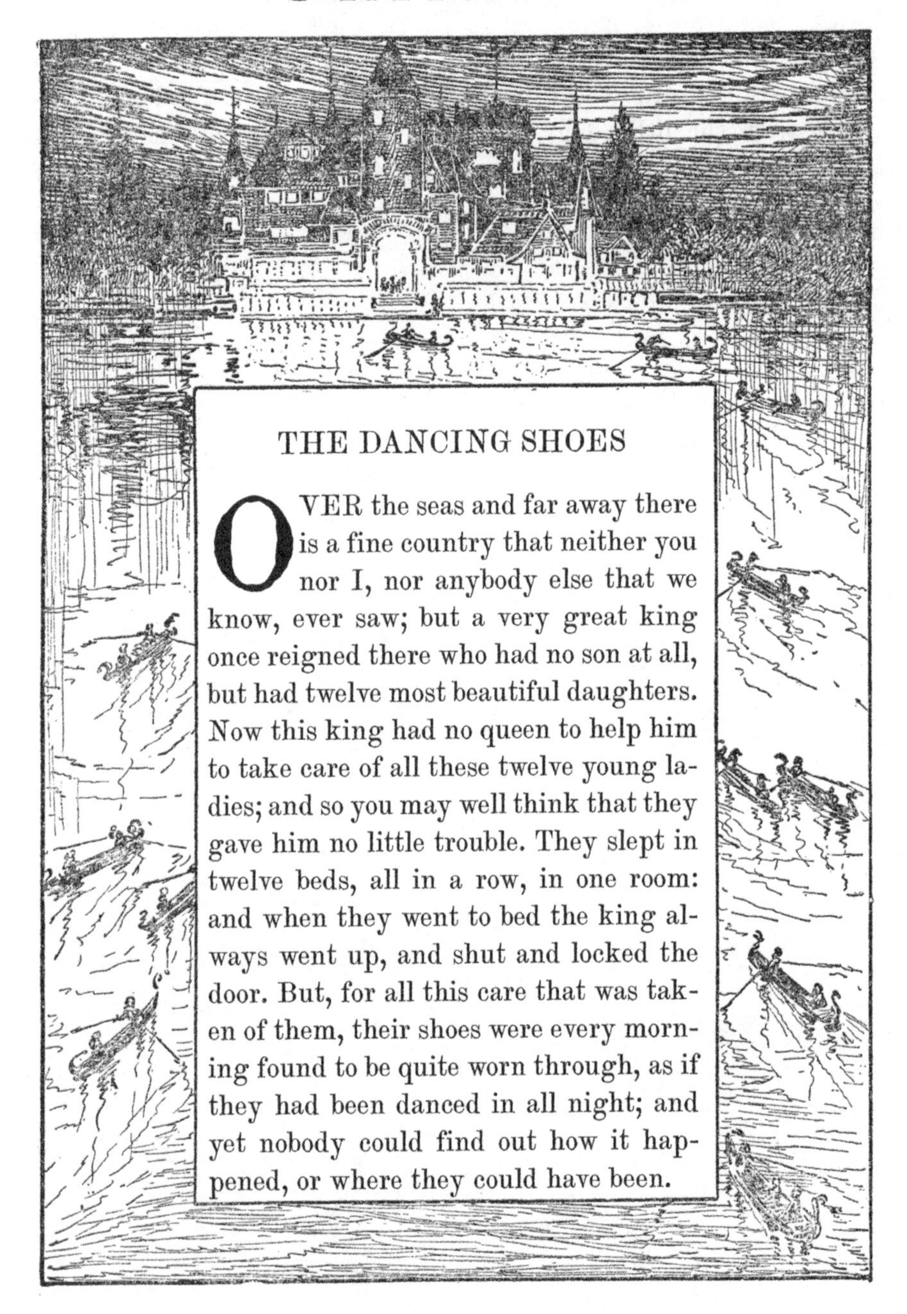

THE DANCING SHOES

OVER the seas and far away there is a fine country that neither you nor I, nor anybody else that we know, ever saw; but a very great king once reigned there who had no son at all, but had twelve most beautiful daughters. Now this king had no queen to help him to take care of all these twelve young ladies; and so you may well think that they gave him no little trouble. They slept in twelve beds, all in a row, in one room: and when they went to bed the king always went up, and shut and locked the door. But, for all this care that was taken of them, their shoes were every morning found to be quite worn through, as if they had been danced in all night; and yet nobody could find out how it happened, or where they could have been.

Then the king, you may be sure, was very angry at having to buy so many new shoes; and he made it known to all the land, that if anybody could find out where it was that the princesses danced in the night, he should have the one he liked best of the whole twelve for his wife, and should be king after his death; but that whoever tried, and could not, after three days and nights, make out the truth, should be put to death.

A king's son soon came. He was well lodged and fed, and in the evening was taken to the chamber next to the one where the princesses lay in their twelve beds. There he was to sit and watch where they went to dance; and in order that nothing might pass without his hearing it, the door of his chamber was left open. But the prince soon fell asleep; and when he awoke in the morning, he found that the princesses had all been dancing, for the soles of their shoes were full of holes. The same thing happened the second and third nights: so the king soon had this young gentleman's head cut off.

After him came many others; but they had all the same luck, and lost their lives in the same way.

Now it chanced that an old soldier, who had been wounded in battle, and could fight no longer, passed through this country; and as he was travelling through a wood, he met a little old woman, who asked him where he was going. "I hardly know where I am going, or what I had better do," said the soldier; "but I think I should like very well to find out where it is that these princesses dance, about whom people talk so much; and then I might have a wife, and in time I might be a king, which would be a mighty pleasant sort of a thing for me in my old days." "Well, well," said the old dame, nodding her head, "that is no very hard task: only take care not to drink the wine that one of the princesses will bring to you in the evening; and as soon as she leaves you, you must seem to fall fast asleep."

Then she gave him a cloak, and said, "As soon as you put that on you will become invisible; and you will then be able to follow the princesses wherever they go, without their being at all aware of it." When the soldier heard this he thought he would try his luck: so he went to the king, and said he was willing to undertake the task.

He was as well lodged as the others had been, and the king ordered fine royal robes to be given him; and when the evening came, he was led to the outer chamber. Just as he was going to lie down, the eldest of the princesses brought him a cup of wine; but the soldier slily threw it all away, taking care not to drink a drop. Then he laid himself down on his bed, and in a little while began to snore very loud, as if he was fast asleep. When the twelve princesses heard this they all laughed heartily; and the eldest said, "This fellow, too, might have done a wiser thing than lose his life in this way!" Then they rose up and opened their drawers and boxes, and took out all their fine clothes, and dressed themselves at the glass; and put on the twelve pair of new shoes that the king had just bought them, and skipped about as if they were eager to begin dancing. But the youngest said, "I don't know how it is, but though you are so happy, I feel very uneasy; I am sure some mischance will befall us." "You simpleton!" said the eldest, "you are always afraid; have you forgotten how many kings' sons have already watched us in vain? As for this soldier, he had one eye shut already, when he came into the room; and even if I had not given him his sleeping draught he would have slept soundly enough."

When they were all ready, they went and looked at the soldier; but he snored on, and did not stir hand or foot: so they thought they were quite safe; and the eldest went up to her own bed, and clapped her hands, and the bed sank into the floor, and a trap door flew open. The soldier saw them going down through the trap-door, one after another, the eldest leading the way; and thinking he had no time to lose, he jumped up, put on the cloak which the old fairy had given him, and followed them. In the middle of the stairs he trod on the gown of the youngest, and she cried out, "All is not right; some one took hold of my gown." "You silly thing!" said the eldest; "it was nothing but a nail in the wall."

Then down they all went, and then ran along a dark walk, till they came to a door; and there they found themselves in a most delightful grove of trees; and the leaves were all of silver, and glittered and sparkled beautifully. The soldier wished to take away some token of the place; so he broke off a little branch, and there came a loud noise from the tree. Then the youngest daughter said again, "I am sure all is not right: did not you hear that noise? That never happened before." But the eldest said, "It is only the princes, who are shouting for joy at our approach."

They soon came to another grove of trees, where all the leaves were of gold; and afterwards to a third, where the leaves were all glittering diamonds. And the soldier broke a branch from each; and every time there came a loud noise, that made the youngest sister shiver with fear: but the eldest still said, it was only the princes, who were shouting for joy. So they went on till they came to a great lake; and at the side of the lake there lay twelve little boats, with twelve handsome princes in them, waiting for the princesses.

One of the princesses went into each boat, and as the boats were very small the soldier hardly knew what to do. "My company will not be very agreeable to any of them," said he; "but, however, I must not be left behind": so he stepped into the same boat with the youngest. As they were rowing over the lake, the prince who was in the boat with the youngest princess and the soldier said, "I do not know how it is, but, though I am rowing with all my might, we get on very slowly, and I am quite tired: the boat seems very heavy to-day, especially at one end." "It is only the heat of the weather," said the princess; "I feel it very warm, too."

On the other side of the lake stood a fine illuminated castle, from which came the merry music of horns and trumpets. There they all landed, and went into the castle, and each prince danced with his princess; and the soldier, who was all the time invisible, danced with them too; and when any of the princesses had a cup of wine set by her, he drank it all up, so that when she put the cup to her mouth it was empty. At this, too, the youngest sister was sadly frightened; but the eldest always stopped her mouth. They danced on till three o'clock in the morning, and then all their shoes were worn out, so that they were forced to leave off. The princes rowed them back again over the lake; but this time the soldier sat himself in the boat by the eldest princess, and her friend too found it very hard work to row that night. On the other shore they all took leave, saying they would come again the next night.

When they came to the stairs, the soldier ran on before the princesses, and laid himself down; and as they came up slowly, panting for breath and very much tired, they heard him snoring in his bed, and said, "Now all is quite safe." Then they undressed themselves, put away their fine clothes, pulled off their shoes, and went to bed, and to sleep.

In the morning the soldier said nothing about what had happened, for he wished to see more of this sport. So he went again the second and third nights, and every thing happened just as before, the princesses dancing each time till their shoes were worn to pieces, and then going home tired; but the third night the soldier carried away one of the golden cups, as a token of where he had been.

On the morning of the fourth day he was ordered to appear before the king; so he took with him the three branches and the golden cup. The twelve princesses stood listening behind the door, to hear what he would say, laughing within themselves to think how cleverly they had taken him in, as well as all the rest who had watched them. Then the king asked him, "Where do my twelve daughters dance at night?" and the soldier said, "With twelve princes in a castle under ground." So he told the king all that had happened, and showed him the three branches and the golden cup, that he had brought with him. On this the king called for the princesses, and asked them whether what the soldier said was true or not; and when they saw they were found out, and that it was of no use to deny what had happened, they said it was all true.

Then the king asked the soldier which of them he would choose for his wife: and he said, "I am not very young, so I think I had better take the eldest." And they were married that very day, and the soldier in due time was heir to the kingdom, after the king his father-in-law died; but what became of the other eleven princesses, or of the twelve princes, I never heard.

THE VALIANT TAILOR

IT was a fine summer morning when Master Snip the tailor, who was a very little man, bound his girdle round his body, cocked his hat, took up his walking-stick, and looked about his house, to see if there was anything good that he could take with him on his journey into the wide world. He could only find a cheese; but that was better than nothing, so he took it off the shelf; and as he went out the old hen met him at the door, so he packed her too into his wallet with the cheese.

Then off he set, and as he climbed a high hill he saw a giant sitting on the top, who looked down upon him with a friendly smile. "Good day, comrade," said Snip; "there you sit at your ease like a gentleman, looking the wide world over; I have a mind to go and try my luck in that same world. What do you say to going with me?" Then the giant looked down, turned up his nose at him, and said, "You are a poor trumpery little knave!" "That may be," said the tailor; "but we shall see by and by who is the best man of the two."

The giant, rinding the little man so bold, began to be somewhat more respectful, and said, "Very well, we shall soon see who is to be master." So he took up a large stone into his hand, and squeezed it till water dropped from it. "Do that," said he, "if you have a mind to be thought a strong man." "Is that all?" said the tailor; "I will soon do as much": so he put his hand into his wallet, pulled out of it the cheese (which was rather new), and squeezed it till the whey ran out. "What do you say now, Mr Giant? my squeeze was a better one than yours." Then the giant, not seeing that it was only a cheese, did not know what to say for himself, though he could hardly believe his eyes. At last he took up a stone, and threw it up so high that it went almost out of sight. "Now then, little pigmy, do that if you can." "Very good," said the other; "your throw was not a very bad one, but after all your stone fell to the ground: I will throw something that shall not fall at all." "That you can't do," said the giant. But the tailor took his old hen out of the wallet, and threw her up in the air; and she, pleased enough to be set free, flew away out of sight. "Now, comrade," said he, "what do you say to that?" "I say you are a clever hand," said the giant; "but we will now try how you can work."

Then he led him into the wood, where a fine oak-tree lay felled. "Come, let us drag it out of the wood together." "Oh, very well," said Snip: "do you take hold of the trunk, and I will carry all the top and the branches, which are much the largest and heaviest." So the giant took the trunk and laid it on his shoulder; but the cunning little rogue, instead of carrying any thing, sprang up and sat himself at his ease among the branches, and so let the giant carry stem, branches, and tailor into the bargain. All the way they went he made merry, and whistled and sang his song, as if carrying the tree were mere sport; while the giant, after he had borne it a good way, could carry it no longer, and said, "I must let it fall." Then the tailor sprang down, and held the tree as if he were carrying it, saying, "What a shame that such a big lout as you cannot carry a tree like this!"

On they went together, till they came to a tall cherry-tree; the giant took hold of the top stem, and bent it down, to pluck the ripest fruit, and when he had done gave it over to his friend, that he too might eat. But the little man was so weak that he could not hold the tree down, and up he went with it, dangling in the air like a scarecrow. "Holla!" said the giant, "what now? can't you hold that twig?" "To be sure I could," said the other; "but don't you see that sportsman, who is going to shoot into the bush where we stood? I took a jump over the tree to be out of his way: you had better do the same." The giant tried to follow, but the tree was far too high to jump over, and he only stuck fast in the branches, for the tailor to laugh at him. "Well, you are a fine fellow after all," said the giant; "so come home and sleep with me and a friend of mine in the mountains to-night, we will give you a hot supper and a good bed."

The tailor had no business upon his hands, so he did as he was bid, and the giant gave him a good supper and a bed to sleep upon; but the tailor was too cunning to lie down upon the bed, and crept slily into a corner, and there slept soundly. When midnight came, the giant stepped softly in with his iron walking-stick, and gave such a stroke upon the bed, where he thought his guest was lying, that he said to himself, "It's all up now with that grasshopper; I shall have no more of his tricks."

In the morning the giants went off into the woods, and quite forgot Snip, till all on a sudden they met him trudging along, whistling a merry tune; and so frightened were they at the sight, that they both ran away as fast as they could.

Then on went the little tailor, following his spuddy nose, till at last he reached the king's court; and then he began to brag very loud of his mighty deeds, saying he was come to serve the king. To try him, they told him that the two giants, who lived in a part of the kingdom a long way off, were become the dread of the whole land; for they had begun to rob, plunder, and ravage all about them, and that if he was so great a man as he said, he should have a hundred soldiers, and should set out to fight these giants; and that if he beat them he should have half the kingdom. "With all my heart!" said he; "but as for your hundred soldiers, I believe I shall do as well without them."

However they set off together, till they came to a wood. "Wait here, my friends," said he to the soldiers. "I will soon give a good account of these giants": and on he went, casting his sharp little eyes, here, there, and everywhere around him. After a while he spied them both lying under a tree, and snoring away, till the very boughs whistled with the breeze. "The game's won, for a ducat!" said the little man, as he filled his wallet with stones, and climbed up into the tree under which they lay.

As soon as he was safely up, he threw one stone after another at the nearest giant, till at last he woke up in a rage, and shook his companion, crying out, "What did you strike me for?" "Nonsense, you are dreaming," said the other, "I did not strike you." Then both lay down to sleep again, and the tailor threw a stone at the second giant, that hit him on the tip of his nose. Up he sprang, and cried, "What are you about? you struck me." "I did not," said the other; and on they wrangled for a while, till, as both were tired, they made up the matter and fell asleep again. But then the tailor began his game once more, and flung the largest stone he had in his wallet with all his force, and hit the first giant on the eye. "That is too bad," cried he, roaring as if he was mad, "I will not bear it." So he struck the other a mighty blow. He, of course, was not pleased with this, and gave him just such another box on the ear, and at last a bloody battle began; up flew the trees by the roots, the rocks and stones were sent bang at one another's head, and in the end both lay dead upon the spot. "It is a good thing," said the tailor, "that they let my tree stand, or I must have made a fine jump."

Then down he ran, and took his sword and gave each of them two or three very deep wounds on the breast, and set off to look for the soldiers. "There lie the giants," said he, "I have killed them: but it was no small job, for they even tore trees up in their struggle." "Have you any wounds?" asked they. "Wounds! that is a likely matter, truly," said he; "they could not touch a hair of my head." But the soldiers would not believe him till they rode into the wood, and found the giants weltering in their blood, and the trees lying around torn up by the roots.

The king, after he had got rid of his enemies, was not much pleased at the thoughts of giving up half his kingdom to a tailor. So he said, "You have not done yet; there is a unicorn running wild about the neighboring woods and doing a great deal of damage, and before I give you my daughter, you must go after it and catch it, and bring it to me here alive."

"After the two giants, I shall not have much to fear from a unicorn," said the tailor, and he started off, carrying with him an axe and a rope.

On reaching the wood he bade his followers wait on the outskirts while he went in by himself. It was not long before the unicorn came in sight and forthwith made a rush for the tailor, as if to run him through without more ado.

"Not quite so fast, not quite so fast," cried the little man, "gently does it," and he stood still until the animal was nearly upon him, and then sprang nimbly behind a tree. The unicorn now made a fierce leap towards the tree, and drove his horn into the trunk with such violence that he had not the strength to pull it out again, and so he remained caught.

"I have him safely now," said the tailor, and coming forward from behind the tree, he put the rope round the animal's neck, cut off the horn with his axe, and led him captive before the king.

After this further brave deed, the king could no longer help keeping his word; and thus a little man became a great one.

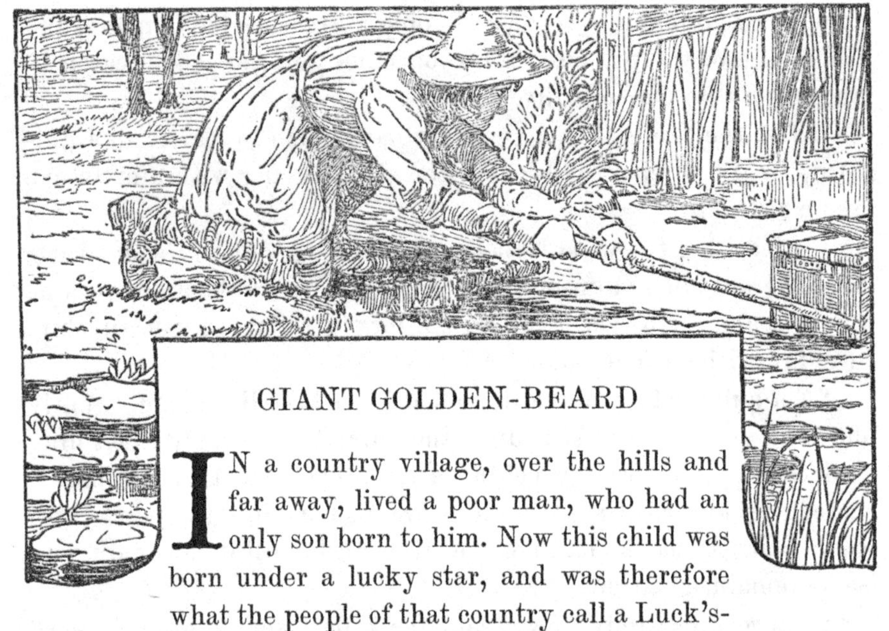

GIANT GOLDEN-BEARD

IN a country village, over the hills and far away, lived a poor man, who had an only son born to him. Now this child was born under a lucky star, and was therefore what the people of that country call a Luck's-child; and those who told his fortune said, that in his fourteenth year he would marry no less a lady than the king's own daughter.

It so happened that the king of that land, soon after the child's birth, passed through the village in disguise, and stopping at the blacksmith's shop, asked what news was stirring. "Great news!" said the people. "Master Brock, down that lane, has just had a child born to him that they say is a Luck's-child; and we are told that, when he is fourteen years old, he is fated to marry our noble king's daughter." This did not please the king; so he went to the poor child's parents, and asked them whether they would sell him their son? "No," said they. But the stranger begged very hard, and said he would give a great deal of money: so as they had scarcely bread to eat, they at last agreed, saying to themselves, "He is a Luck's-child; all, therefore, is no doubt for the best—he can come to no harm."

The king took the child, put it into a box, and rode away; but when he came to a deep stream he threw it into the current, and said to himself, "That young gentleman will never be my daughter's husband." The box, however, floated down the stream. Some kind fairy watched over it, so that no water reached the child; and at last, about two miles from the king's chief city, it stopped at the dam of a mill. The miller soon saw it, and took a long pole and drew it towards the shore, and finding it heavy, thought there was gold inside; but when he opened it he found a pretty little boy that smiled upon him merrily. Now the miller and his wife had no children, and they therefore rejoiced to see their prize, saying, "Heaven has sent it to us"; so they treated it very kindly, and brought it up with such care that everyone liked and loved it.

About thirteen years passed over their heads, when the same king came by chance to the mill, and seeing the boy, asked the miller if that was his son. "No," said he, "I found him, when a babe, floating down the river in a box into the mill-dam." "How long ago?" asked the king. "Some thirteen years," said the miller. "He is a fine fellow," said the king; "can you spare him to carry a letter to the queen? It will please me very much, and I will give him two pieces of gold for his trouble." "As your majesty pleases," said the miller.

Now the king had guessed at once that this must be the child he had tried to drown, so he wrote a letter by him to the queen, saying, "As soon as the bearer of this reaches you, let him be killed and buried, so that all may be over before I come back."

The young man set out with this letter but missed his way, and came in the evening to a dark wood. Through the gloom he saw a light afar off, to which he bent his steps, and found that it came from a little cottage. There was no one within except an old woman, who was frightened at seeing him, and said, "Why do you come hither, and whither are you going?" "I am going to the queen, to whom I was to have given a letter; but I have lost my way, and shall be glad if you will give me a night's rest." "You are very unlucky," said she, "for this is a robbers' hut; and if the band come back while you are here it may be worse for you." "I am so tired, however," replied he, "that I must take my chance, for I can go no further"; so he laid the letter on the table, stretched himself out upon a bench, and fell asleep.

When the robbers came home and saw him, they asked the old woman who the strange lad was. "I have given him shelter for charity," said she; "he had a letter to carry to the queen, and lost his way." The robbers took up the letter, broke it open, and read the orders which were in it to murder the bearer. Then their leader was very angry at the king's trick; so he tore his letter, and wrote a fresh one, begging the queen, as soon as the young man reached her, to marry him to the princess. Meantime they let him sleep on till morning broke, and then showed him the right way to the queen's palace; where, as soon as she had read the letter, she made all ready for the wedding: and as the young man was very handsome, the princess was very dutiful, and took him then and there for a husband.

After a while the king came back; and when he saw that this Luck's-child was married to the princess, notwithstanding all the art and cunning he had used to thwart his luck, he asked eagerly how all this had happened, and what were the orders which he had given. "Dear husband," said the queen, "here is your own letter—read it for yourself." The king took it, and seeing that an exchange had been made, asked his son-in-law what he had done with the letter he gave him to carry. "I know nothing of it," said he; "if it is not the one you gave me, it must have been taken away in the night, when I slept." Then the king was very wroth, and said, "No man shall have my daughter who does not go down into the wonderful cave and bring me three golden hairs from the beard of the giant king who reigns there; do this, and you shall have my free leave to be my daughter's husband." "I will soon do that," said the youth; so he took leave of his wife, and set out on his journey.

At the first city that he came to, the guard at the gate stopped him, and asked what trade he followed, and what he knew. "I know everything," said he. "If that be so," said they, "you are just the man we want; be so good as to find out why our fountain in the market-place is dry, and will give no water. Tell us the cause of that, and we will give you two asses loaded with gold." "With all my heart," said he, "when I come back."

Then he journeyed on, and came to another city, and there the guard also asked him what trade he followed, and what he understood. "I know everything," answered he. "Then pray do us a good turn," said they; "tell us why a tree, which always before bore us golden apples, does not even bear a leaf this year." "Most willingly," said he, "as I come back."

At last his way led him to the side of a great lake of water, over which he must pass. The ferryman soon began to ask, as the others

LOUIS RHEAD

had done, what was his trade, and what he knew. "Everything," said he. "Then," said the other, "pray tell me why I am forced for ever to ferry over this water, and have never been able to get my freedom; I will reward you handsomely." "Ferry me over," said the young man, "and I will tell you all about it as I come home."

When he had passed the water, he came to the wonderful cave. It looked very black and gloomy; but the wizard king was not at home, and his grandmother sat at the door in her easy chair. "What do you want?" said she. "Three golden hairs from the giant's beard," answered he. "You will run a great risk," said she, "when he comes home; yet I will try what I can do for you." Then she changed him into an ant, and told him to hide himself in the folds of her cloak. "Very well," said he: "but I want also to know why the city fountain is dry; why the tree that bore golden apples is now leafless; and what it is that binds the ferryman to his post." "You seem fond of asking puzzling things," said the old dame; "but lie still, and listen to what the giant says when I pull the golden hairs, and perhaps you may learn what you want." Soon night set in, and the old gentleman came home. As soon as he entered he began to snuff up the air, and cried, "All is not right here: I smell man's flesh." Then he searched all round in vain, and the old dame scolded, and said, "Why should you turn everything topsy-turvy? I have just set all straight." Upon this he laid his head in her lap, and soon fell asleep. As soon as he began to snore, she seized one of the golden hairs of his beard and pulled it out. "Mercy!" cried he, starting up: "what are you about?" "I had a dream that roused me," said she, "and in my trouble I seized hold of your hair. I dreamt that the fountain in the market-place of the city was become dry, and would give no water; what can be the cause?" "Ah! if they could find that out they would be glad," said the giant: "under a stone in the fountain sits a toad; when they kill him, it will flow again."

This said, he fell asleep, and the old lady pulled out another hair. "What would you be at?" cried he in a rage. "Don't be angry," said she, "I did it in my sleep; I dreamt that I was in a great kingdom a long way off, and that there was a beautiful tree there, that used to bear golden apples, but that now has not even a leaf upon it; what is the meaning of that?" "Aha!" said the giant, "they would like very well to know that. At the root of the tree a mouse is gnawing; if they were to kill him, the tree would bear golden apples again: if not, it will soon die. Now do let me sleep in peace; if you wake me again, you shall rue it."

Then he fell once more asleep; and when she heard him snore she pulled out the third golden hair, and the giant jumped up and threatened her sorely; but she soothed him, and said, "It was a very strange dream I had this time: methought I saw a ferryman, who was bound to ply backwards and forwards over a great lake, and could never find out how to set himself free; what is the charm that binds him?" "A silly fool!" said the giant: "if he were to give the rudder into the hand of any passenger that came, he would find himself free, and the other would be forced to take his place. Now pray let me sleep."

In the morning the giant arose and went out; and the old woman gave the young man the three golden hairs, reminded him of the three answers, and sent him on his way.

He soon came to the ferryman, who knew him again, and asked for the answer which he had said he would give him. "Ferry me over first," said he, "and then I will tell you." When the boat reached the other side, he told him to give the rudder to the first passenger that came, and then he might run away as soon as he pleased. The next place that he came to was the city where the barren tree stood: "Kill the mouse," said he, "that is gnawing the tree's root, and you will have golden apples again." They gave him a rich gift for this news, and he journeyed on to the city where the fountain had dried up; and the guard asked him how to make the water flow. So he told them how to cure that mischief, and they thanked him, and gave him the two asses laden with gold.

And now at last this Luck's-child reached home, and his wife was very glad to see him, and to hear how well everything had gone with him. Then he gave the three golden hairs to the king, who could no longer deny him, though he was at heart quite as spiteful against his son-in-law as ever. The gold, however, astonished him, and when he saw all the treasure he cried out with joy, "My dear son, where did you find all this gold?" "By the side of a lake," said the youth, "where there is plenty more to be had." "Pray tell me where it lies," said the king, "that I may go and get some too." "As much as you please," replied the other. "You must set out and travel on and on, till you come to the shore of a great lake: there you will see a ferryman; let him carry you across, and when once you are over, you will see gold as plentiful as sand upon the shore."

Away went the greedy king; and when he came to the lake he beckoned to the ferryman, who gladly took him into his boat; and as soon as he was there gave the rudder into his hand and sprang ashore, leaving the old king to ferry away, as a reward for his craftiness and treachery.

"And is his majesty plying there to this day?" You may be sure of that, for nobody will trouble himself to take the rudder out of his hands.

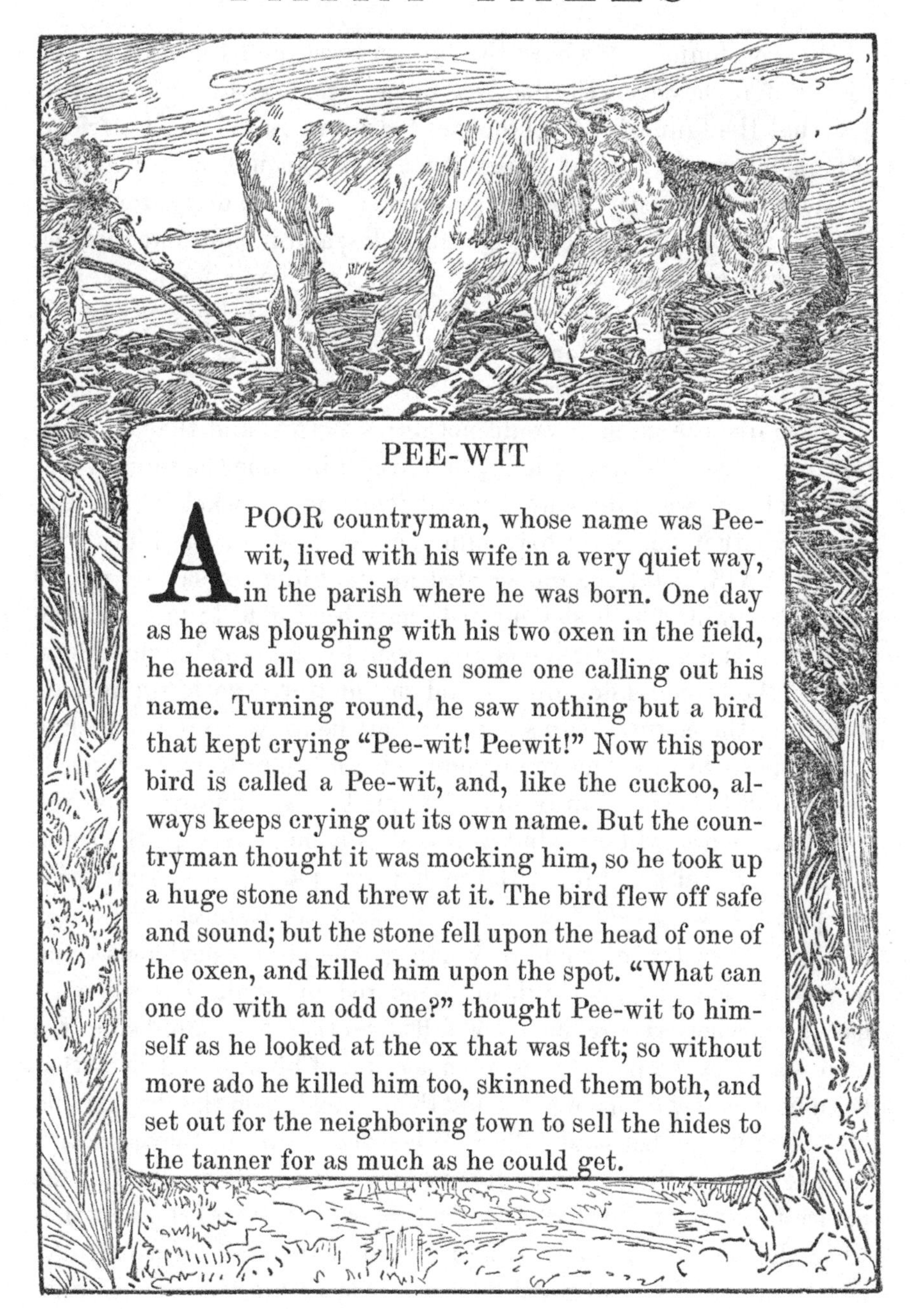

PEE-WIT

A POOR countryman, whose name was Pee-wit, lived with his wife in a very quiet way, in the parish where he was born. One day as he was ploughing with his two oxen in the field, he heard all on a sudden some one calling out his name. Turning round, he saw nothing but a bird that kept crying "Pee-wit! Peewit!" Now this poor bird is called a Pee-wit, and, like the cuckoo, always keeps crying out its own name. But the countryman thought it was mocking him, so he took up a huge stone and threw at it. The bird flew off safe and sound; but the stone fell upon the head of one of the oxen, and killed him upon the spot. "What can one do with an odd one?" thought Pee-wit to himself as he looked at the ox that was left; so without more ado he killed him too, skinned them both, and set out for the neighboring town to sell the hides to the tanner for as much as he could get.

He soon found out where the tanner lived, and knocked at the door. Before, however, the door was opened, he saw through the window that the tanner's daughter was hiding in an old chest a friend of hers, whom she seemed to wish that no one should see. By and by the door was opened. "What do you want?" said the daughter. Then Pee-wit told her he wanted to sell his hides; and it came out that the tanner was not at home, and that no one there ever made bargains but himself. The countryman said he would sell cheap, and did not mind giving his hides for the old chest in the corner; meaning the one he had seen the young woman's friend get into.

Of course the maiden would not agree to this; and they went on talking the matter over so long, that at last in came the tanner, and asked what it was all about. Pee-wit told him the whole story, and asked whether he would give him the old chest for the hides. "To be sure I will," said he; and scolded his daughter for saying nay to such a bargain, which she ought to have been glad to make, if the countryman was willing. Then up he took the chest on his shoulders, and all the tanner's daughter could say mattered nothing; away it went into the countryman's cart, and off he drove. But when they had gone some way, the young man within began to make himself heard, and to beg and pray to be let out. Pee-wit, however, was not so soon to be brought over; but at last after a long parley, a thousand dollars were bid and taken; the money was paid, and at that price the poor fellow was set free, and went about his business.

Then Pee-wit went home very happy, and built a new house, and seemed so rich that his neighbors wondered and said, "Pee-wit must have been where the golden snow falls." So they took him before the next justice of the peace, to give an account of himself and show that he came honestly by his wealth; and then he told them that he had sold his hides for one thousand dollars. When they heard it, they all killed their oxen, that they might sell the hides to the same tanner; but the justice said, "My maid shall have the first chance"; so off she went: but when she came to the tanner, he laughed at them all for a parcel of noodles, and said he had given their neighbor nothing but an old chest.

At this they were all very angry, and laid their heads together to work him some mischief, which they thought they could do while he was digging in his garden. All this, however, came to the ears of the countryman, who was plagued with a sad scold for his wife; and he thought to himself, "If any one is to come into trouble, I don't see why it should not be my wife rather than Pee-wit"; so he told her that he wished she would humour him in a whim he had taken into his head, and would put on his clothes and dig the garden in his stead.

The wife did what was asked, and next morning began digging. But soon came some of the neighbors, and, thinking it was Pee-wit, threw a stone at her,—harder, perhaps, than they meant,—and killed her at once. Poor Pee-wit was rather sorry at this; but still he thought that he had had a lucky escape for himself, and that perhaps he might, after all, turn the death of his wife to some account: so he dressed her in her own clothes, put a basket with fine fruit (which was now scarce, it being winter) into her hand, and set her by the road-side, on a broad bench. After a while came by a fine coach with six horses, servants, and outriders, and within sat a noble lord, who lived not far off. When his lordship saw the beautiful fruit, he sent one of the servants to the woman, to ask what was the price of her goods. The man went and asked, "What is the price of this fruit?" No answer. He asked again. No answer. And when this had happened three times, he became angry, and, thinking she was asleep, gave her a box on the ear, when down she fell backwards into the pond that was behind the seat. Then up ran Pee-wit, and cried out and sorrowed, because they had drowned his poor dear wife; and threatened to have the lord and his servants tried for what they had done. His lordship begged him to be easy, and offered to give him the coach and horses, servants and all; so the countryman, after a long time, let himself be appeased a little, took what they gave, got into the coach, and set off towards his own home again.

As he came near, the neighbors wondered much at the beautiful coach and horses, and still more when they stopped and Pee-wit got out at his own door. Then he told them the whole story, which only vexed them still more; so they took him and fastened him up in a tub, and were going to throw him into the lake that was hard by. But whilst they were rolling the tub on before them towards the water they passed by an alehouse, and stopped to refresh themselves a little before they put an end to Pee-wit. Meantime they tied the tub fast to a tree, and there left it while they were enjoying themselves within doors.

Pee-wit no sooner found himself alone, than he began to turn over in his mind how he could get free. He listened, and soon heard,

Ba, ba! from a flock of sheep and lambs that were coming by. Then he lifted up his voice, and shouted out, "I will not be burgomaster, I say; I will not be made burgomaster." The shepherd hearing this went up and said, "What is all this noise about?" "Oh!" said Pee-wit, "my neighbors will make me burgomaster against my will; and when I told them I would not agree, they put me into this cask, and are going to throw me into the lake." "I should like very well to be burgomaster, if I were you," said the shepherd. "Open the cask, then," said the other, "and let me out, and get in yourself, and they will make you burgomaster instead of me." No sooner said than done; the shepherd was in, Pee-wit was out: and as there was nobody to take care of the shepherd's flock, Pee-wit drove it off merrily towards his own house.

When the neighbors came out of the alehouse they rolled the cask on, and the shepherd began to cry out, "I will be burgomaster now; I will be burgomaster now." "I dare say you will, but you shall take a swim first," said a neighbor, as he gave the cask the last push over into the lake. This done, away they went home merrily, leaving the shepherd to get out as well as he could.

But as they came in at one side of the village, who should they meet coming in by the other way but Pee-wit, driving a fine flock of sheep and lambs before him! "How came you here?" cried all with one voice. "Oh! the lake is enchanted," said he; "when you threw me in I sunk deep and deep into the water, till at last I came to the bottom; there I knocked out the bottom of the cask, and then I found myself in a beautiful meadow, with fine flocks grazing upon it; so I chose a few for myself, and here I am." "Cannot we have some too?" said they. "Why not? there are hundreds and thousands left; you have nothing to do but to jump in, and fetch them out."

So they all agreed they would dive for sheep; the justice first, then his clerk, then the constables, and then the rest of the parish one after the other. When they came to the side of the lake, the blue sky was covered over with little white clouds, like flocks of sheep, and all were reflected in the clear water: so they called out, "There they are! there they are already!" and fearing lest the justice should get everything, they jumped in all at once; but Pee-wit jogged home, and made himself happy with what he had got, leaving his neighbors to find flocks for themselves as well as they could.

FAIRY TALES

HANSEL AND GRETHEL

NEAR a great forest there lived a poor woodcutter and his wife, and his two children; the boy's name was Hansel and the girl's Grethel. They had very little to bite or to sup, and once, when there was great dearth in the land, the man could not even gain the daily bread. As he lay in bed one night thinking of this, and turning and tossing, he sighed heavily, and said to his wife,

"What will become of us? we cannot even feed our children; there is nothing left for ourselves."

"I will tell you what, husband," answered the wife; "we will take the children early in the morning into the forest, where it is thickest; we will make them a fire, and we will give each of them a piece of bread, then we will go to our work and leave them alone; they will never find the way home again, and we shall be quit of them."

"No, wife," said the man, "I cannot do that; I cannot find in my heart to take my children into the forest and to leave them there alone; the wild animals would soon come and devour them."

"O you fool," said she, "then we will all four starve; you had better get the coffins ready,"—and she left him no peace until he consented.

"But I really pity the poor children," said the man.

The two children had not been able to sleep for hunger, and had heard what their step-mother had said to their father. Grethel wept bitterly, and said to Hansel,

"It is all over with us."

"Do be quiet, Grethel," said Hansel, "and do not fret; I will manage something." And when the parents had gone to sleep he got up, put on his little coat, opened the back door, and slipped out. The moon was shining brightly, and the white flints that lay in front of the house glistened like pieces of silver. Hansel stooped and filled the little pocket of his coat as full as it would hold. Then he went back again, and said to Grethel,

"Be easy, dear little sister, and go to sleep quietly; God will not forsake us," and laid himself down again in his bed.

When the day was breaking, and before the sun had risen, the wife came and awakened the two children, saying,

"Get up, you lazy bones; we are going into the forest to cut wood."

Then she gave each of them a piece of bread, and said,

"That is for dinner, and you must not eat it before then, for you will get no more."

Grethel carried the bread under her apron, for Hansel had his pockets full of the flints. Then they set off all together on their way to the forest. When they had gone a little way Hansel stood still and looked back towards the house, and this he did again and again, till his father said to him,

"Hansel, what are you looking at? take care not to forget your legs."

"O father," said Hansel, "I am looking at my little white kitten, who is sitting up on the roof to bid me good-bye."

"You young fool," said the woman, "that is not your kitten, but the sunshine on the chimney-pot."

Of course Hansel had not been looking at his kitten, but had been taking every now and then a flint from his pocket and dropping it on the road.

When they reached the middle of the forest the father told the children to collect wood to make a fire to keep them warm; and Hansel and Grethel gathered brushwood enough for a little mountain; and it was set on fire, and when the flame was burning quite high the wife said,

"Now lie down by the fire and rest yourselves, you children, and we will go and cut wood; and when we are ready we will come and fetch you."

So Hansel and Grethel sat by the fire, and at noon they each ate their pieces of bread. They thought their father was in the wood all the time, as they seemed to hear the strokes of the axe: but really it was only a dry branch hanging to a withered tree that the wind moved to and fro. So when they had stayed there a long time their eyelids closed with weariness, and they fell fast asleep. When at last they woke it was night, and Grethel began to cry, and said,

"How shall we ever get out of this wood?" But Hansel comforted her, saying,

"Wait a little while longer, until the moon rises, and then we can easily find the way home."

And when the full moon got up Hansel took his little sister by the hand, and followed the way where the flint stones shone like silver, and showed them the road. They walked on the whole night through, and at the break of day they came to their father's house. They knocked at the door, and when the wife opened it and saw that it was Hansel and Grethel she said,

"You naughty children, why did you sleep so long in the wood? we thought you were never coming home again!"

But the father was glad, for it had gone to his heart to leave them both in the woods alone.

Not very long after that there was again great scarcity in those parts, and the children heard their mother say at night in bed to their father,

"Everything is finished up; we have only half a loaf, and after that the tale comes to an end. The children must be off; we will take them farther into the wood this time, so that they shall not be able to find the way back again; there is no other way to manage."

The man felt sad at heart, and he thought,

"It would better to share one's last morsel with one's children."

But the wife would listen to nothing that he said, but scolded and reproached him. He who says A must say B too, and when a man has given in once he has to do it a second time.

But the children were not asleep, and had heard all the talk. When the parents had gone to sleep Hansel got up to go out and get more flint stones, as he did before, but the wife had locked the door, and Hansel could not get out; but he comforted his little sister, and said,

"Don't cry, Grethel, and go to sleep quietly, and God will help us."

Early the next morning the wife came and pulled the children out of bed. She gave them each a little piece of bread—less than before; and on the way to the wood Hansel crumbled the bread in his pocket, and often stopped to throw a crumb on the ground.

"Hansel, what are you stopping behind and staring for?" said the father.

"I am looking at my little pigeon sitting on the roof, to say good-bye to me," answered Hansel.

"You fool," said the wife, "that is no pigeon, but the morning sun shining on the chimney pots."

Hansel went on as before, and strewed bread crumbs all along the road.

The woman led the children far into the wood, where they had never been before in all their lives. And again there was a large fire made, and the mother said,

"Sit still there, you children, and when you are tired you can go to sleep; we are going into the forest to cut wood, and in the evening, when we are ready to go home we will come and fetch you."

So when noon came Grethel shared her bread with Hansel, who had strewed his along the road. Then they went to sleep, and the evening passed, and no one came for the poor children. When they awoke it was dark night, and Hansel comforted his little sister, and said,

"Wait a little, Grethel, until the moon gets up, then we shall be able to see the way home by the crumbs of bread that I have scattered along it."

So when the moon rose they got up, but they could find no crumbs of bread, for the birds of the woods and of the fields had come and picked them up. Hansel thought they might find the way all the same, but they could not. They went on all that night, and the next day from the morning until the evening, but they could not find the way out of the wood, and they were very hungry, for they had nothing to eat but the few berries they could pick up. And when they were so tired that they could no longer drag themselves along, they lay down under a tree and fell asleep.

It was now the third morning since they had left their father's house. They were always trying to get back to it, but instead of that they only found themselves farther in the wood, and if help had not soon come they would have been starved. About noon they saw a pretty snow-white bird sitting on a bough, and singing so sweetly that they stopped to listen. And when he had finished the bird spread his wings and flew before them, and they followed after him until they came to a little house, and the bird perched on the roof, and when they came nearer they saw that the house was built of bread, and roofed with cakes; and the window was of transparent sugar.

"We will have some of this," said Hansel, "and make a fine meal. I will eat a piece of the roof, Grethel, and you can have some of the window—that will taste sweet."

So Hansel reached up and broke off a bit of the roof, just to see how it tasted, and Grethel stood by the window and gnawed at it. Then they heard a thin voice call out from inside,

"Nibble, nibble, like a mouse,
Who is nibbling at my house?"

And the children answered,

"Never mind,
It is the wind."

And they went on eating, never disturbing themselves. Hansel, who found that the roof tasted very nice, took down a great piece of it, and Grethel pulled out a large round window-pane, and sat her down and began upon it. Then the door opened, and an aged woman came out, leaning upon a crutch. Hansel and Grethel felt very frightened, and let fall what they had in their hands. The old woman, however, nodded her head, and said,

"Ah, my dear children, how come you here? you must come indoors and stay with me, you will be no trouble."

So she took them each by the hand, and led them into her little house. And there they found a good meal laid out, of milk and pancakes, with sugar, apples, and nuts. After that she showed them two little white beds, and Hansel and Grethel laid themselves down on them, and thought they were in heaven.

The old woman, although her behavior was so kind, was a wicked witch, who lay in wait for children, and had built the little house on purpose to entice them. When they were once inside she used to kill them, cook them, and eat them, and then it was a feast-day with her. The witch's eyes were red, and she could not see very far, but she had a keen scent, like the beasts, and knew very well when human creatures were near. When she knew that Hansel and Grethel were coming, she gave a spiteful laugh, and said triumphantly,

"I have them, and they shall not escape me!"

Early in the morning, before the children were awake, she got up to look at them, and as they lay sleeping so peacefully with round rosy cheeks, she said to herself,

"What a fine feast I shall have!"

Then she grasped Hansel with her withered hand, and led him into a little stable, and shut him up behind a grating; and call and scream as he might, it was no good. Then she went back to Grethel and shook her, crying,

"Get up, lazy bones; fetch water, and cook something nice for your brother; he is outside in the stable, and must be fattened up. And when he is fat enough I will eat him."

Grethel began to weep bitterly, but it was of no use, she had to do what the wicked witch bade her.

And so the best kind of victuals was cooked for poor Hansel, while Grethel got nothing but crab-shells. Each morning the old woman visited the little stable, and cried,

"Hansel, stretch out your finger, that I may tell if you will soon be fat enough."

Hansel, however, used to hold out a little bone, and the old woman, who had weak eyes, could not see what it was, and supposing it to be Hansel's finger, wondered very much that it was not getting fatter. When four weeks had passed and Hansel seemed to remain so thin, she lost patience and could wait no longer.

"Now then, Grethel," cried she to the little girl; "be quick and draw water; be Hansel fat or be he lean, to-morrow I must kill and cook him."

"CREEP IN," SAID THE WITCH, "AND SEE IF IT IS PROPERLY HOT"

Oh what a grief for the poor little sister to have to fetch water, and how the tears flowed down over her cheeks!

"Dear God, pray help us!" cried she; "if we had been devoured by wild beasts in the wood at least we should have died together."

"Spare me your lamentations," said the old woman; "they are of no avail."

Early next morning Grethel had to get up, make the fire, and fill the kettle.

"First we will do the baking," said the old woman; "I have heated the oven already, and kneaded the dough."

She pushed poor Grethel towards the oven, out of which the flames were already shining.

"Creep in," said the witch, "and see if it is properly hot, so that the bread may be baked."

And Grethel once in, she meant to shut the door upon her and let her be baked, and then she would have eaten her. But Grethel perceived her intention, and said,

"I don't know how to do it: how shall I get in?"

"Stupid goose," said the old woman, "the opening is big enough, do you see? I could get in myself!" and she stooped down and put her head in the oven's mouth. Then Grethel gave her a push, so that she went in farther, and she shut the iron door upon her, and put up the bar. Oh how frightfully she howled! but Grethel ran away, and left the wicked witch to burn miserably. Grethel went straight to Hansel, opened the stable-door, and cried,

"Hansel, we are free! the old witch is dead!"

Then out flew Hansel like a bird from its cage as soon as the door is opened. How rejoiced they both were! how they fell each on the other's neck! and danced about, and kissed each other! And as they had nothing more to fear they went over all the old witch's house, and in every corner there stood chests of pearls and precious stones.

"This is something better than flint stones," said Hansel, as he filled his pockets, and Grethel, thinking she also would like to carry something home with her, filled her apron full.

"Now, away we go," said Hansel;—"if we only can get out of the witch's wood."

When they had journeyed a few hours they came to a great piece of water.

"We can never get across this," said Hansel, "I see no stepping-stones and no bridge."

"And there is no boat either," said Grethel; "but here comes a white duck; if I ask her she will help us over." So she cried,

> "Duck, duck, here we stand,
> Hansel and Grethel, on the land,
> Stepping-stones and bridge we lack,
> Carry us over on your nice white back."

And the duck came accordingly, and Hansel got upon her and told his sister to come too.

"No," answered Grethel, "that would be too hard upon the duck; we can go separately, one after the other."

And that was how it was managed, and after that they went on happily, until they came to the wood, and the way grew more and more familiar, till at last they saw in the distance their father's house. Then they ran till they came up to it, rushed in at the door, and fell on their father's neck. The man had not had a quiet hour since he left his children in the wood; but the wife was dead. And when Grethel opened her apron the pearls and precious stones were scattered all over the room, and Hansel took one handful after another out of his pocket. Then was all care at an end, and they lived in great joy together.

> Sing every one,
> My story is done.
> And look! round the house
> There runs a little mouse.
> He that can catch her before she scampers in,
> May make himself a very very large fur cap out of her skin.

LILY AND THE LION

A MERCHANT, who had three daughters, was once setting out upon a journey; but before he went he asked each daughter what gift he should bring back for her. The eldest wished for pearls; the second for jewels; but the third, who was called Lily, said, "Dear father, bring me a rose." Now it was no easy task to find a rose, for it was the middle of winter; yet as she was his prettiest daughter, and was very fond of flowers, her father said he would try what he could do. So he kissed all three, and bid them goodbye.

And when the time came for him to go home, he had bought pearls and jewels for the two eldest, but he had sought everywhere in vain for the rose; and when he went into any garden and asked for such a thing, the people laughed at him, and asked him whether he thought roses grew in snow. This grieved him very much, for Lily was his dearest child; and as he was journeying home, thinking what he should bring her, he came to a fine castle; and around the castle was a garden, in one half of which it seemed to be summer-time and in the other half winter. On one side the finest flowers were in full bloom, and on the other everything looked dreary and buried in the snow. "A lucky hit!" said he, as he called to his servant, and told him to go to a beautiful bed of roses that was there, and bring him away one of the finest flowers.

This done, they were riding away well pleased, when up sprang a fierce lion, and roared out, "Whoever has stolen my roses shall be eaten up alive!" Then the man said, "I knew not that the garden belonged to you; can nothing save my life?" "No!" said the lion, "nothing, unless you undertake to give me whatever meets you on your return home; if you agree to this, I will give you your life, and the rose too for your daughter." But the man was unwilling to do so and said, "It may be my youngest daughter, who loves me most, and always runs to meet me when I go home." Then the servant was greatly frightened, and said, "It may perhaps be only a cat or a dog." And at last the man yielded with a heavy heart, and took the rose; and said he would give the lion whatever should meet him first on his return.

And as he came near home, it was Lily, his youngest and dearest daughter, that met him; she came running, and kissed him, and welcomed him home; and when she saw that he had brought her the rose, she was still more glad. But her father began to be very sorrowful, and to weep, saying, "Alas, my dearest child! I have bought this flower at a high price, for I have said I would give you to a wild lion; and when he has you, he will tear you in pieces, and eat you." Then he told her all that had happened, and said she should not go, let what would happen.

But she comforted him, and said, "Dear father, the word you have given must be kept; I will go to the lion, and soothe him: perhaps he will let me come safe home again."

The next morning she asked the way she was to go, and took leave of her father, and went forth with a bold heart into the wood. But the lion was an enchanted prince. By day he and all his court were lions, but in the evening they took their right forms again.

And when Lily came to the castle, he welcomed her so courteously that she agreed to marry him. The wedding-feast was held, and they lived happily together a long time. The prince was only to be seen as soon as evening came, and then he held his court; but every morning he left his bride, and went away by himself, she knew not whither, till the night came again.

After some time he said to her, "Tomorrow there will be a great feast in your father's house, for your eldest sister is to be married; and if you wish to go and visit her my lions shall lead you thither." Then she rejoiced much at the thoughts of seeing her father once more, and set out with the lions; and everyone was overjoyed to see her, for they had thought her dead long since. But she told them how happy she was, and stayed till the feast was over, and then went back to the wood.

Her second sister was soon after married, and when Lily was asked to go to the wedding, she said to the prince, "I will not go alone this time—you must go with me." But he would not, and said that it would be a very hazardous thing; for if the least ray of the torch-light should fall upon him his enchantment would become still worse, for he should be changed into a dove, and be forced to wander about the world for seven long years. However, she gave him no rest, and said she would take care no light should fall upon him. So at last they set out together, and took with them their little child; and she chose a large hall with thick walls for him to sit in while the wedding-torches were lighted; but, unluckily, no one saw that there was a crack in the door. Then the wedding was held with great pomp, but as the train came from the church, and passed with the torches before the hall, a very small ray of light fell upon the prince. In a moment he disappeared, and when his wife came in and looked for him, she found only a white dove; and it said to her, "Seven years must I fly up and down over the face of the earth, but every now and then I will let fall a white feather, that will show you the way I am going; follow it, and at last you may overtake and set me free."

This said, he flew out at the door, and poor Lily followed; and every now and then a white feather fell, and showed her the way she was to journey. Thus she went roving on through the wide world, and looked neither to the right hand nor to the left, nor took any rest, for seven years. Then she began to be glad, and thought to herself that the time was fast coming when all her troubles should end; yet repose was still far off, for one day as she was travelling on she missed the white feather, and when she lifted up her eyes she could nowhere see the dove. "Now," thought she to herself, "no aid of man can be of use to me." So she went to the sun and said, "Thou shinest everywhere, on the hill's top and the valley's depth—hast thou anywhere seen my white dove?" "No," said the sun, "I have not seen it; but I will give thee a casket—open it when thy hour of need comes."

So she thanked the sun, and went on her way till eventide; and when the moon arose, she cried unto it, and said, "Thou shinest through the night, over field and grove—hast thou nowhere seen my white dove?" "No," said the moon, "I cannot help thee but I will give thee an egg—break it when need comes."

Then she thanked the moon, and went on till the night-wind blew; and she raised up her voice to it, and said, "Thou blowest through every tree and under every leaf—hast thou not seen my white dove?" "No," said the night-wind, "but I will ask three other winds; perhaps they have seen it." Then the east wind and the west wind came, and said they too had not seen it, but the south wind said, "I have seen the white dove—he has fled to the Red Sea, and is changed once more into a lion, for the seven years are passed away, and there he is fighting with a dragon; and the dragon is an enchanted princess, who seeks to separate him from you." Then the night-wind said, "I will give thee counsel. Go to the Red Sea; on the right shore stand many rods—count them, and when thou comest to the eleventh, break it off, and smite the dragon with it; and so the lion will have the victory, and both of them will appear to you in their own forms. Then look round and thou wilt see a griffin, winged like bird, sitting by the Red Sea; jump on to his back with thy beloved one as quickly as possible, and he will carry you over the waters to your home. I will also give thee this nut," continued the night-wind. "When you are half-way over, throw it down, and out of the waters will immediately spring up a high nut-tree on which the griffin will be able to rest, otherwise he would not have the strength to bear you the whole way; if, therefore, thou dost forget to throw down the nut, he will let you both fall into the sea."

So our poor wanderer went forth, and found all as the night-wind had said; and she plucked the eleventh rod, and smote the dragon, and the lion forthwith became a prince, and the dragon a princess again. But no sooner was the princess released from the spell, than she seized the prince by the arm and sprang on to the griffin's back, and went off carrying the prince away with her.

Thus the unhappy traveller was again forsaken and forlorn; but she took heart and said, "As far as the wind blows, and so long as the cock crows, I will journey on, till I find him once again." She went on for a long, long way, till at length she came to the castle whither the princess had carried the prince; and there was a feast got ready, and she heard that the wedding was about to be held. "Heaven aid me now!" said she; and she took the casket that the sun had given her, and found that within it lay a dress as dazzling as the sun itself. So she put it on, and went into the palace, and all the people gazed upon her; and the dress pleased the bride so much that she asked whether it was to be sold. "Not for gold and silver." said she, "but for flesh and blood." The princess asked what she meant, and she said, "Let me speak with the bridegroom this night in his chamber, and I will give thee the dress." At last the princess agreed, but she told her chamberlain to give the prince a sleeping draught, that he might not hear or see her. When evening came, and the prince had fallen asleep, she was led into his chamber, and she sat herself down at his feet, and said: "I have followed thee seven years. I have been to the sun, the moon, and the night-wind, to seek thee, and at last I have helped thee to overcome the dragon. Wilt thou then forget me quite?" But the prince all the time slept so soundly, that her voice only passed over him, and seemed like the whistling of the wind among the fir-trees.

Then poor Lily was led away, and forced to give up the golden dress; and when she saw that there was no help for her, she went out into a meadow, and sat herself down and wept. But as she sat she bethought herself of the egg that the moon had given her; and when she broke it, there ran out a hen and twelve chickens of pure gold, that played about, and then nestled under the old one's wings, so as to form the most beautiful sight in the world. And she rose up and drove them before her, till the bride saw them from her window, and was so pleased that she came forth and asked her if she would sell the brood. "Not for gold or silver, but for flesh and blood: let me again this evening speak with the bridegroom in his chamber, and I will give thee the whole brood."

Then the princess thought to betray her as before, and agreed to what she asked: but when the prince went to his chamber he asked the chamberlain why the wind had whistled so in the night. And the chamberlain told him all—how he had given him a sleeping draught, and how a poor maiden had come and spoken to him in his chamber, and was to come again that night. Then the prince took care to throw away the sleeping draught; and when Lily came and began again to tell him what woes had befallen her, and how faithful and true to him she had been, he knew his beloved wife's voice, and sprang up, and said, "You have awakened me as from a dream, for the strange princess had thrown a spell around me, so that I had altogether forgotten you; but Heaven hath sent you to me in a lucky hour."

And they stole away out of the palace by night unawares, and seated themselves on the griffin, who flew back with them over the Red Sea. When they were half-way across Lily let the nut fall into the water, and immediately a large nut-tree arose from the sea, whereon the griffin rested for a while, and then carried them safely home. There they found their child, now grown up to be comely and fair; and after all their troubles they lived happily together to the end of their days.

RAPUNZEL

THERE once lived a man and his wife, who had long wished for a child, but in vain. Now there was at the back of their house a little window which overlooked a beautiful garden full of the finest vegetables and flowers; but there was a high wall all round it, and no one ventured into it, for it belonged to a witch of great might, and of whom all the world was afraid. One day that the wife was standing at the window, and looking into the garden, she saw a bed filled with the finest rampion; and it looked so fresh and green that she began to wish for some; and at length she longed for it greatly. This went on for days, and as she knew she could not get the rampion, she pined away, and grew pale and miserable. Then the man was uneasy, and asked, "What is the matter, dear wife?"

"Oh," answered she, "I shall die unless I can have some of that rampion to eat that grows in the garden at the back of our house." The man, who loved her very much, thought to himself,

"Rather than lose my wife I will get some rampion, cost what it will."

So in the twilight he climbed over the wall into the witch's garden, plucked hastily a handful of rampion and brought it to his wife. She made a salad of it at once, and ate of it to her heart's content. But she liked it so much, and it tasted so good, that the next day she longed for it thrice as much as she had done before; if she was to have any rest the man must climb over the wall once more. So he went in the twilight again; and as he was climbing back, he saw, all at once, the witch standing before him, and was terribly frightened, as she cried, with angry eyes,

"How dare you climb over into my garden like a thief, and steal my rampion! it shall be the worse for you!"

"Oh," answered he, "be merciful rather than just, I have only done it through necessity; for my wife saw your rampion out of the window, and became possessed with so great a longing that she would have died if she could not have had some to eat." Then the witch said,

"If it is all as you say you may have as much rampion as you like, on one condition—the child that will come into the world must be given to me. It shall go well with the child, and I will care for it like a mother."

In his distress of mind the man promised everything; and when the time came when the child was born the witch appeared, and, giving the child the name of Rapunzel (which is the same as rampion), she took it away with her.

Rapunzel was the most beautiful child in the world. When she was twelve years old the witch shut her up in a tower in the midst of a wood, and it had neither steps nor door, only a small window above. When the witch wished to be let in, she would stand below and would cry,

"Rapunzel, Rapunzel! let down your hair!"

Rapunzel had beautiful long hair that shone like gold. When she heard the voice of the witch she would undo the fastening of the upper window, unbind the plaits of her hair, and let it down twenty ells below, and the witch would climb up by it.

After they had lived thus a few years it happened that as the King's son was riding through the wood, he came to the tower; and as he drew near he heard a voice singing so sweetly that he stood still and listened. It was Rapunzel in her loneliness trying to pass away the time with sweet songs. The King's son wished to go in to her, and sought to find a door in the tower, but there was none. So he rode home, but the song had entered into his heart, and every day he went into the wood and listened to it. Once, as he was standing there under a tree, he saw the witch come up, and listened while she called out,

AND SHE LET DOWN HER HAIR AND THE KING'S SON CLIMBED UP BY IT

"O Rapunzel, Rapunzel! let down your hair."

Then he saw how Rapunzel let down her long tresses, and how the witch climbed up by it and went in to her, and he said to himself,

"Since that is the ladder I will climb it, and seek my fortune." And the next day, as soon as it began to grow dusk, he went to the tower and cried,

"O Rapunzel, Rapunzel! let down your hair."

And she let down her hair, and the King's son climbed up by it.

Rapunzel was greatly terrified when she saw that a man had come in to her, for she had never seen one before; but the King's son began speaking so kindly to her, and told how her singing had entered into his heart, so that he could have no peace until he had seen her herself. Then Rapunzel forgot her terror, and when he asked her to take him for her husband, and she saw that he was young and beautiful, she thought to herself,

"I certainly like him much better than old mother Gothel," and she put her hand into his hand, saying,

"I would willingly go with thee, but I do not know how I shall get out. When thou comest, bring each time a silken rope, and I will make a ladder, and when it is quite ready I will get down by it out of the tower, and thou shalt take me away on thy horse." They agreed that he should come to her every evening, as the old woman came in the day-time. So the witch knew nothing of all this until once Rapunzel said to her unwittingly,

"Mother Gothel, how is it that you climb up here so slowly, and the King's son is with me in a moment?"

"O wicked child," cried the witch, "what is this I hear! I thought I had hidden thee from all the world, and thou hast betrayed me!"

In her anger she seized Rapunzel by her beautiful hair, struck her several times with her left hand, and then grasping a pair of shears in her right—snip, snap—the beautiful locks lay on the ground. And she was so hard-hearted that she took Rapunzel and put her in a waste and desert place, where she lived in great woe and misery.

The same day on which she took Rapunzel away she went back to the tower in the evening and made fast the severed locks of hair to the window-hasp, and the King's son came and cried,

"Rapunzel, Rapunzel! let down your hair."

Then she let the hair down, and the King's son climbed up, but instead of his dearest Rapunzel he found the witch looking at him with wicked glittering eyes.

"Aha!" cried she, mocking him, "you came for your darling, but the sweet bird sits no longer in the nest, and sings no more; the cat has got her, and will scratch out your eyes as well! Rapunzel is lost to you; you will see her no more."

The King's son was beside himself with grief, and in his agony he sprang from the tower: he escaped with life, but the thorns on which he fell put out his eyes. Then he wandered blind through the wood, eating nothing but roots and berries, and doing nothing but lament and weep for the loss of his dearest wife.

So he wandered several years in misery until at last he came to the desert place where Rapunzel lived with her twin-children that she had borne, a boy and a girl. At first he heard a voice that he thought he knew, and when he reached the place from which it seemed to come Rapunzel knew him, and fell on his neck and wept. And when her tears touched his eyes they became clear again, and he could see with them as well as ever.

Then he took her to his kingdom, where he was received with great joy, and there they lived long and happily.

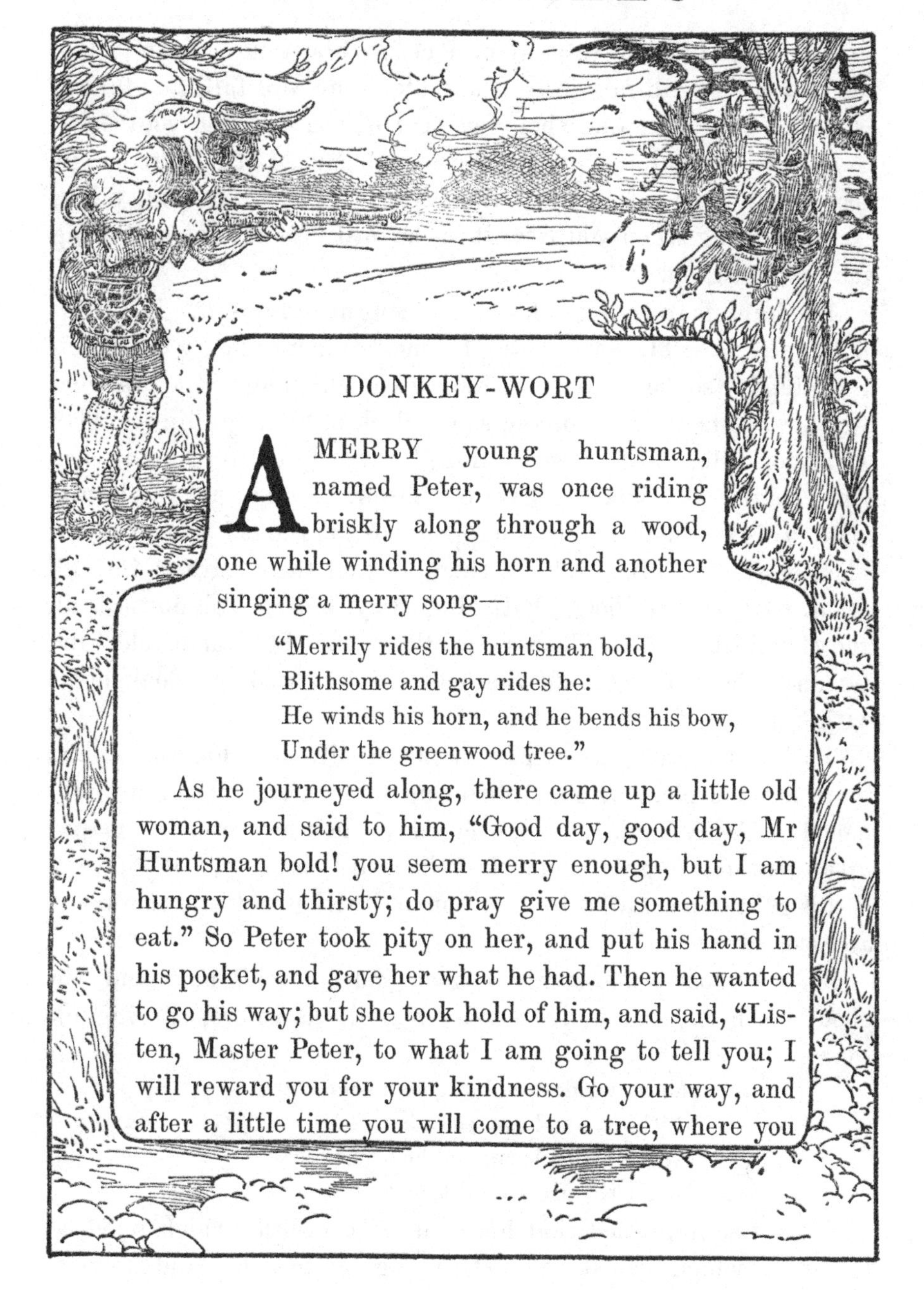

DONKEY-WORT

A MERRY young huntsman, named Peter, was once riding briskly along through a wood, one while winding his horn and another singing a merry song—

> "Merrily rides the huntsman bold,
> Blithsome and gay rides he:
> He winds his horn, and he bends his bow,
> Under the greenwood tree."

As he journeyed along, there came up a little old woman, and said to him, "Good day, good day, Mr Huntsman bold! you seem merry enough, but I am hungry and thirsty; do pray give me something to eat." So Peter took pity on her, and put his hand in his pocket, and gave her what he had. Then he wanted to go his way; but she took hold of him, and said, "Listen, Master Peter, to what I am going to tell you; I will reward you for your kindness. Go your way, and after a little time you will come to a tree, where you will see nine birds sitting upon a cloak. Shoot into the midst of them, and one will fall down dead. The cloak will fall, too; take it as a wishing-cloak, and when you wear it, you will find yourself at any place you may wish to be. Cut open the dead bird, take out its heart and keep it, and you will find a piece of gold under your pillow every morning when you rise. It is the bird's heart that will bring you this good luck."

The huntsman thanked her, and thought to himself, "If all this do happen, it will be a fine thing for me." When he had gone a hundred steps or so, he heard a screaming and chirping in the branches over him; so he looked up, and saw a flock of birds, pulling a cloak with their bills and feet; screaming, fighting, and tugging at each other, as if each wished to have it himself. "Well," said the huntsman, "this is wonderful; this happens just as the old woman said." Then he shot into the midst of them, so that their feathers flew all about. Off went the flock chattering away; but one fell down dead, and the cloak with it. Then Peter did as the old woman told him, cut open the bird, took out the heart, and carried the cloak home with him.

The next morning, when he awoke, he lifted up his pillow, and there lay the piece of gold glittering underneath; the same happened next day, and, indeed, every day when he arose. He heaped up a great deal of gold, and at last thought to himself, "Of what use is this gold to me whilst I am at home? I will go out into the world, and look about me."

Then he took leave of his friends, and hung his horn and bow about his neck, and went his way merrily as before, singing his song—

"Merrily rides the huntsman bold,
Blithsome and gay rides he:
He winds his horn, and he bends his bow,
Under the greenwood tree."

Now it so happened that his road led through a thick wood, at the end of which was a large castle in a green meadow; and at one of the windows stood an old woman, with a very beautiful young lady by her side, looking about them. The old woman was a fairy, and she said to the young lady, whose name was Meta, "There comes a young man out of the wood, with a wonderful prize; we must get it away from him, my dear child, for it is more fit for us than for him. He has a bird's heart that brings a piece of gold under his pillow every morning." Meantime the huntsman came nearer, and looked at the lady, and said to himself, "I have been travelling so long, that I should like to go into this castle and rest myself, for I have money enough to pay for anything I want"; but the real reason was, that he wanted to see more of the beautiful lady. Then he went into the house, and was welcomed kindly; and it was not long before he was so much in love, that he thought of nothing else but looking at Meta's eyes, and doing everything that she wished. Then the old woman said, "Now is the time for getting the bird's heart." So Meta stole it away, and he never found any more gold under his pillow; for it lay now under Meta's, and the old woman took it away every morning: but he was so much in love that he never missed his prize.

"Well," said the old fairy, "we have got the bird's heart, but not the wishing-cloak yet, and that we must also get." "Let us leave him that," said Meta; "he has

already lost all his wealth." Then the fairy was very angry, and said, "Such a cloak is a very rare and wonderful thing, and I must and will have it." So Meta did as the old woman told her, and sat herself at the window, and looked about the country, and seemed very sorrowful. Then the huntsman said, "What makes you so sad?" "Alas, dear sir," said she, "yonder lies the granite rock, where all the costly diamonds grow, and I want so much to go there, that, whenever I think of it, I cannot help being sorrowful; for who can reach it? only the birds and the flies,—man cannot." "If that's all your grief," said huntsman Peter, "I'll take you there with all my heart." So he drew her under his cloak, and the moment he wished to be on the granite mountain, they were both there.

The diamonds glittered so on all sides, that they were delighted with the sight, and picked up the finest. But the old fairy made a deep drowsiness come upon him; and he said to the young lady, "Let us sit down and rest ourselves a little, I am so tired that I cannot stand any longer." So they sat down, and he laid his head in her lap and fell asleep; and whilst he was sleeping on, the false Meta took the cloak from his shoulders, hung it on her own, picked up the diamonds, and wished herself at her own home again.

When poor Peter awoke, and found that his faithless Meta had tricked him, and left him alone on the wild rock, he said, "Alas! what roguery there is in the world!" And there he sat in great grief and fear upon the mountain, not knowing what in the world he should do.

Now this rock belonged to fierce giants, who lived upon it; and as he saw three of them striding about, he thought to himself, "I can only save myself by feigning to be asleep"; so he laid himself down, as if he were in a sound sleep. When the giants came up to him, the first kicked him with his foot, and said, "What worm is this that lies here curled up?" "Tread upon him and kill him," said the second. "It's not worth the trouble," said the third; "let him live: he will go climbing higher up the mountain, and some cloud will come rolling and carry him away." Then they passed on. But the huntsman had heard all they said, and as soon as they were gone he climbed to the top of the mountain; and when he had sat there a short time, a cloud came rolling around him, and caught him in a whirlwind, and bore him along for some time, till it settled in a garden, and he fell quite gently to the ground, amongst the greens and cabbages.

Then Master Peter got up and scratched his head, and looked around him, and said, "I wish I had something to eat; if I have not I shall be worse off than before: for here I see neither apples nor pears, nor any kind of fruits; nothing but vegetables." At last he thought to himself, "I can eat salad, it will refresh and strengthen me." So he picked out a fine head of some plant that he took for a salad, and ate of it; but scarcely had he swallowed two bites, when he felt himself quite changed, and saw with horror that he was turned into an ass. However, he still felt very hungry, and the green herbs tasted very nice; so he ate on till he came to another plant, which looked very like the first: but it really was quite different, for he had scarcely tasted it when he felt another change come over him, and soon saw that he was lucky enough to have found his old shape, and to have become Peter again.

Then he laid himself down and slept off a little of his weariness; and when he awoke the next morning he brake off a head of each sort of salad, and thought to himself, "This will help me to my fortune again, and enable me to punish some folks for their treachery." So he set about trying to find the castle of his old friends;

and, after wandering about a few days, he luckily found it. Then he stained his face all over brown, so that even his mother would not have known him, and went into the castle and asked for a lodging; "I am so tired," said he, "that I can go no further." "Countryman," said the fairy, "who are you? and what is your business?" "I am," said he, "a messenger sent by the king to find the finest salad that grows under the sun. I have been lucky enough to find it, and have brought it with me; but the heat of the sun is so scorching that it begins to wither, and I don't know that I can carry it any further."

When the fairy and the young lady heard of this beautiful salad, they longed to taste it, and said, "Dear countryman, let us just taste it!" "To be sure!" answered he; "I have two heads of it with me, and I will give you one"; so he opened his bag and gave them the bad sort. Then the fairy herself took it into the kitchen to be dressed; and when it was ready she could not wait till it was carried up, but took a few leaves immediately, and put them in her mouth: but scarcely were they swallowed when she lost her own form, and ran braying down into the court in the form of an ass. Now the servant-maid came into the kitchen, and seeing the salad ready was going to carry it up; but on the way she, too, felt a wish to taste it, as the old woman had done, and ate some leaves: so she also was turned into an ass, and ran after the other, letting the dish with the salad fall on the ground.

Peter had been sitting all this time chatting with the fair Meta, and as nobody came with the salad, and she longed to taste it, she said, "I don't know where the salad can be." Then he thought something must have happened, and said, "I will go into the kitchen and see." And as he went he saw two asses in the court running about, and the salad lying on the ground. "All right!" said he, "those two have had their share." Then he took up the rest of the leaves, laid them on the dish, and brought them to the young lady, saying, "I bring you the dish myself, that you may not wait any longer." So she ate of it, and, like the others, ran off into the court braying away.

Then Peter the huntsman washed his face and went into the court, that they might know him. "Now you shall be paid for your roguery," said he, and tied them all three to a rope, and took them along with him, till he came to a mill, and knocked at the window.

"What's the matter?" said the miller. "I have three tiresome beasts here," said the other; "if you will take them, give them food and room, and treat them as I tell you, I will pay you whatever you ask." "With all my heart," said the miller; "but how shall I treat them?" Then the huntsman said, "Give the old one stripes three times a-day and hay once; give the next (who was the servant-maid) stripes once a-day and hay three times; and give the youngest (who was the pretty Meta) hay three times a-day and no stripes": for he could not find it in his heart to have her beaten. After this he went back to the castle, where he found everything he wanted.

Some days after the miller came to him and told him the old ass was dead. "The other two," said he, "are alive and eat; but they are so sorrowful that they cannot last long." Then Peter pitied them, and told the miller to drive them back to him; and when they came, he gave them some of the good salad to eat.

The moment they had eaten, they were both changed into their right forms, and poor Meta fell on her knees before the huntsman and said, "Forgive me all the ill I have done thee; my mother forced me to it, and it was sorely against my will, for I always loved you well. Your wishing-cloak hangs up in the closet; and as for the bird's heart, I will give you that too." But Peter said, "Keep it; it will be just the same thing in the end, for I mean to make you my wife."

So Meta was very glad to come off so easily; and they were married, and lived together very happily till they died.

THE KING OF THE GOLDEN MOUNTAIN

THERE was once a merchant who had only one child, a son, that was very young, and barely able to run alone. He had two richly laden ships then making a voyage upon the seas, in which he had embarked all his wealth, in the hope of making great gains, when the news came that both were lost. Thus from being a rich man he became all at once so very poor that nothing was left to him but one small plot of land; and there he often went in an evening to take his walk, and ease his mind of a little of his trouble.

One day, as he was roaming along in a brown study, thinking with no great comfort on what he had been and what he now was, and was like to be, all on a sudden there stood before him a little, rough-looking, black dwarf. "Prithee, friend, why so sorrowful?" said he to the merchant; "what is it you take so deeply to heart?" "If you would do me any good I would willingly tell you," said the merchant. "Who knows but I may?" said the little man: "tell me what ails you, and perhaps you will find I may be of some use." Then the merchant told him how all his wealth was gone to the bottom of the sea, and how he had nothing left but that little plot of land. "Oh, trouble not yourself about that," said the dwarf; "only undertake to bring me here, twelve years hence, whatever meets you first on your going home, and I will give you as much as you please." The merchant thought this was no great thing to ask; that it would most likely be his dog or his cat, or something of that sort, but forgot his little boy Heinel; so he agreed to the bargain, and signed and sealed the bond to do what was asked of him.

But as he drew near home, his little boy was so glad to see him that he crept behind him, and laid fast hold of his legs, and looked up in his face and laughed. Then the father started, trembling with fear and horror, and saw what it was that he had bound himself to do; but as no gold was come, he made himself easy by thinking that it was only a joke that the dwarf was playing him, and that, at any rate, when the money came, he should see the bearer, and would not take it in.

About a month afterwards he went upstairs into a lumber-room to look for some old iron, that he might sell it and raise a little money; and there, instead of his iron, he saw a large pile of gold lying on the floor. At the sight of this he was overjoyed, and forgetting all about his son, went into trade again, and became a richer merchant than before.

Meantime little Heinel grew up, and as the end of the twelve years drew near the merchant began to call to mind his bond, and became very sad and thoughtful; so that care and sorrow were written upon his face. The boy one day asked what was the matter, but his father would not tell for some time; at last, however, he said that he had, without knowing it, sold him for gold to a little, ugly-looking, black dwarf, and that the twelve years were coming round when he must keep his word. Then Heinel said, "Father, give yourself very little trouble about that; I shall be too much for the little man."

When the time came, the father and son went out together to the place agreed upon: and the son drew a circle on the ground, and set himself and his father in the middle of it. The little black dwarf soon came, and walked round and round about the circle, but could not find any way to get into it, and he either could not, or dared not, jump over it. At last the boy said to him. "Have you anything to say to us, my friend, or what do you want?" Now Heinel had found a friend in a good fairy, that was fond of him, and had told him what to do; for this fairy knew what good luck was in store for him. "Have you brought me what you said you would?" said the dwarf to the merchant. The old man held his tongue, but Heinel said again, "What do you want here?" The dwarf said, "I come to talk with your father, not with you." "You have cheated and taken in my father," said the son; "pray give him up his bond at once." "Fair and softly," said the little old man; "right is right; I have paid my money, and your father has had it, and spent it; so be so good as to let me have what I paid it for." "You must have my consent to that first," said Heinel, "so please to step in here, and let us talk it over." The old man grinned, and showed his teeth, as if he should have been very glad to get into the circle if he could. Then at last, after a long talk, they came to terms. Heinel agreed that his father must give him up, and that so far the dwarf should have his way: but, on the other hand, the fairy had told Heinel what fortune was in store for him, if he followed his own course; and he did not choose to be given up to his hump-backed friend, who seemed so anxious for his company.

So, to make a sort of drawn battle of the matter, it was settled that Heinel should be put into an open boat, that lay on the sea-shore hard by; that the father should push him off with his own hand, and that he should thus be set adrift, and left to the bad or good luck of wind and weather. Then he took leave of his father, and set himself in the boat, but before it got far off a wave struck it, and it fell with one side low in the water, so the merchant thought that poor Heinel was lost, and went home very sorrowful, while the dwarf went his way, thinking that at any rate he had had his revenge.

The boat, however, did not sink, for the good fairy took care of her friend, and soon raised the boat up again, and it went safely on. The young man sat safe within, till at length it ran ashore upon an unknown land. As he jumped upon the shore he saw before him a beautiful castle but empty and dreary within, for it was enchanted. "Here," said he to himself, "must I find the prize the good fairy told me of." So he once more searched the whole palace through, till at last he found a white snake, lying coiled up on a cushion in one of the chambers.

Now the white snake was an enchanted princess; and she was very glad to see him, and said, "Are you at last come to set me free? Twelve long years have I waited here for the fairy to bring you hither as she promised, for you alone can save me. This night twelve

THE LITTLE BLACK DWARF WALKED ROUND

men will come: their faces will be black, and they will be dressed in chain armor. They will ask what you do here, but give no answer; and let them do what they will—beat, whip, pinch, prick, or torment you—bear all; only speak not a word, and at twelve o'clock they must go away. The second night twelve others will come: and the third night twenty-four, who will even cut off your head; but at the twelfth hour of that night their power is gone, and I shall be free, and will come and bring you the Water of Life, and will wash you with it, and bring you back to life and health." And all came to pass as she had said; Heinel bore all, and spoke not a word; and the third night the princess came, and fell on his neck and kissed him. Joy and gladness burst forth throughout the castle, the wedding was celebrated, and he was crowned king of the Golden Mountain.

They lived together very happily, and the queen had a son. And thus eight years had passed over their heads, when the king thought of his father; and he began to long to see him once again. But the queen was against his going, and said, "I know well that misfortunes will come upon us if you go." However, he gave her no rest till she agreed. At his going away she gave him a wishing-ring, and said, "Take this ring, and put it on your finger; whatever you wish it will bring you; only promise never to make use of it to bring me hence to your father's house." Then he said he would do what she asked, and put the ring on his finger, and wished himself near the town where his father lived.

Heinel found himself at the gates in a moment; but the guards would not let him go in, because he was so strangely clad. So he went up to a neighboring hill, where a shepherd dwelt, and borrowed his old frock, and thus passed unknown into the town. When he came to his father's house, he said he was his son; but the merchant would not believe him, and said he had had but one son, his poor Heinel, who he knew was long since dead: and as he was only dressed like a poor shepherd, he would not even give him anything to eat. The king, however, still vowed that he was his son, and said, "Is there no mark by which you would know me if I am really your son?" "Yes," said his mother, "our Heinel had a mark like a raspberry on his right arm." Then he showed them the mark, and they knew that what he had said was true.

He next told them how he was king of the Golden Mountain, and was married to a princess, and had a son seven years old. But the merchant said, "that can never be true; he must be a fine king truly who travels about in a shepherd's frock!" At this the son was vexed; and forgetting his word, turned his ring, and wished for his queen and son. In an instant they stood before him; but the queen wept, and said he had broken his word, and bad luck would follow. He did all he could to soothe her, and she at last seemed to be appeased; but she was not so in truth, and was only thinking how she should punish him.

One day he took her to walk with him out of the town, and showed her the spot where the boat was set adrift upon the wide waters. Then he sat himself down, and said, "I am very much tired; sit by me, I will rest my head in your lap, and sleep a while." As soon as he had fallen asleep, however, she drew the ring from his finger, and crept softly away, and wished herself and her son at home in their kingdom. And when he awoke he found himself alone, and saw that the ring was gone from his finger. "I can never go back to my father's house," said he; "they would say I am a sorcerer: I will journey forth into the world, till I come again to my kingdom."

So saying he set out and travelled till he came to a hill, where three giants were sharing their father's goods; and as they saw him pass they cried out and said, "Little men have sharp wits; he shall part the goods between us." Now there was a sword that cut off an enemy's head whenever the wearer gave the words, "Heads off!"; a cloak that made the owner invisible, or gave him any form he pleased; and a pair of boots that carried the wearer wherever he wished. Heinel said they must first let him try these wonderful things, then he might know how to set a value upon them. Then they gave him the cloak, and he wished himself a fly, and in a moment he was a fly. "The cloak is very well," said he: "now give me the sword." "No," said they; "not unless you undertake not to say, "Heads off!" for if you do we are all dead men." So they gave it him, charging him to try it on a tree. He next asked for the boots also; and the moment he had all three in his power, he wished himself at the Golden Mountain; and there he was at once. So the giants were left behind with no goods to share or quarrel about.

As Heinel came near his castle he heard the sound of merry music; and the people around told him that his queen was about to marry another husband. Then he threw his cloak around him, and passed through the castle hall, and placed himself by the side of the queen, where no one saw him. But when anything to eat was put upon her plate, he took it away and ate it himself; and when a glass of wine was handed to her, he took it and drank it; and thus, though they kept on giving her meat and drink, her plate and cup were always empty.

Upon this, fear and remorse came over her, and she went into her chamber alone, and sat there weeping; and he followed her there. "Alas!" said she to herself, "was I not once set free? Why then does this enchantment still seem to bind me?"

"False and fickle one!" said he. "One indeed came who set thee free, and he is now near thee again; but how have you used him? Ought he to have had such treatment from thee?" Then he went out and sent away the company, and said the wedding was at an end, for that he was come back to the kingdom. But the princes, peers, and great men mocked at him. However, he would enter into no parley with them, but only asked them if they would go in peace or not. Then they turned upon him and tried to seize him; but he drew his sword. "Heads Off!" cried he; and with the word the traitors' heads fell before him, and Heinel was once more king of the Golden Mountain.

THE BREMEN TOWN-MUSICIANS

AN honest farmer had once an ass, that had been a faithful servant to him a great many years, but was now growing old and every day more and more unfit for work. His master therefore was tired of keeping him and began to think of putting an end to him; but the ass, who saw that some mischief was in the wind, took himself slyly off, and began his journey towards the great city, "for there," thought he, "I may turn musician."

After he had travelled a little way, he spied a dog lying by the road-side and panting as if he were very tired. "What makes you pant so, my friend?" said the ass. "Alas!" said the dog, "my master was going to knock me on the head, because I am old and weak, and can no longer make myself useful to him in hunting; so I ran away: but what can I do to earn my livelihood?" "Hark ye!" said the ass, "I am going to the great city to turn musician: suppose you go with me, and try what you can do in the same way?" The dog said he was willing, and they jogged on together.

They had not gone far before they saw a cat sitting in the middle of the road and making a most rueful face. "Pray, my good lady," said the ass, "what's the matter with you? you look quite out of spirits!" "Ah me!" said the cat, "how can one be in good spirits when one's life is in danger? Because I am beginning to grow old, and had rather lie at my ease by the fire than run about the house after the mice, my mistress laid hold of me, and was going to drown me; and though I have been lucky enough to get away from her, I do not know what I am to live upon." "O!" said the ass, "by all means go with us to the great city; you are a good night singer, and may make your fortune as a musician." The cat was pleased with the thought, and joined the party.

Soon afterwards, as they were passing by a farm-yard, they saw a cock perched upon a gate, and screaming out with all his might and main. "Bravo!" said the ass; "upon my word you make a famous noise; pray what is all this about?" "Why," said the cock, "I was just now saying that we should have fine weather for our washing-day, and yet my mistress and the cook don't thank me for my pains, but threaten to cut off my head to-morrow, and make broth of me for the guests that are coming on Sunday!" "Heaven forbid!" said the ass; "come with us, Master Chanticleer; it will be better, at any rate, than staying here to have your head cut off! Besides, who knows? If we take care to sing in tune, we may get up some kind of a concert: so come along with us." "With all my heart," said the cock: so they all four went on jollily together.

They could not, however, reach the great city the first day; so when night came on, they went into a wood to sleep. The ass and the dog laid themselves down under a great tree, and the cat climbed up into the branches; while the cock, thinking that the higher he sat the safer he should be, flew up to the very top of the tree, and then, according to his custom, before he went to sleep, looked out on all sides of him to see that everything was well. In doing this, he saw afar off something bright and shining; and calling to his companions said, "There must be a house no great way off, for I see a light." "If that be the case," said the ass, "we had better change our quarters, for our lodging is not the best in the world!" "Besides," added the dog, "I should not be the worse for a bone or two, or a bit of meat." So they walked off together towards the spot where Chanticleer had seen the light; and as they drew near, it became larger and brighter, till they at last came close to a house in which a gang of robbers lived.

The ass, being the tallest of the company, marched up to the window and peeped in. "Well, Donkey," said Chanticleer, "what do you see?" "What do I see?" replied the ass, "why I see a table spread with all kinds of good things, and robbers sitting round it making merry." "That would be a noble lodging for us," said the cock. "Yes," said the ass, "if we could only get in:" so they consulted

LOUIS RHEAD.

together how they should contrive to get the robbers out; and at last they hit upon a plan. The ass placed himself upright on his hind-legs, with his fore-feet resting against the window; the dog got upon his back; the cat scrambled up to the dog's shoulders, and the cock flew up and sat upon the cat's head. When all was ready, a signal was given, and they began their music. The ass brayed, the dog barked, the cat mewed, and the cock screamed; and then they all broke through the window at once, and came tumbling into the room, amongst the broken glass, with a most hideous clatter! The robbers, who had been not a little frightened by the opening concert, had now no doubt that some frightful hobgoblin had broken in upon them, and scampered away as fast as they could.

The coast once clear, our travellers soon sat down, and dispatched what the robbers had left, with as much eagerness as if they had not expected to eat again for a month. As soon as they had satisfied themselves, they put out the lights, and each once more sought out a resting-place to his own liking. The donkey laid himself down upon a heap of straw in the yard; the dog stretched himself upon a mat behind the door; the cat rolled herself up on the hearth before the warm ashes; and the cock perched upon a beam on the top of the house; and, as they were all rather tired with their journey, they soon fell asleep.

But about midnight, when the robbers saw from afar that the lights were out and that all seemed quiet, they began to think that they had been in too great a hurry to run away; and one of them, who was bolder than the rest, went to see what was going on. Finding everything still, he marched into the kitchen, and groped about till he found a match in order to light a candle; and then, espying the glittering fiery eyes of the cat, he mistook them for live coals, and held the match to them to light it. But the cat, not understanding this joke, sprung at his face, and spit, and scratched at him. This frightened him dreadfully, and away he ran to the back door; but there the dog jumped up and bit him in the leg; and as he was crossing over the yard the ass kicked him; and the cock, who had been awakened by the noise, crowed with all his might. At this the robber ran back as fast as he could to his comrades, and told the captain "how a horrid witch had got into the house, and had spit at him and scratched his face with her long bony fingers; how a man with a knife in his hand had hidden himself behind the door, and stabbed him in the leg; how a black monster stood in the yard and struck him with a club, and how the devil sat upon the top of the house and cried out, 'Throw the rascal up here!'" After this the robbers never dared to go back to the house: but the musicians were so pleased with their quarters, that they took up their abode there; and there they are, I dare say, at this very day.

BROTHER AND SISTER

HANSEL one day took his sister Grettel by the hand, and said, "Since our poor mother died we have had no happy days; for our new mother beats us all day long, and when we go near her, she pushes us away. We have nothing but hard crusts to eat; and the little dog that lies by the fire is better off than we; for he sometimes has a nice piece of meat thrown to him. Heaven have mercy upon us! Oh, if our poor mother knew how we are used! Come, we will go and travel over the wide world." They went the whole day walking over the fields, till in the evening they came to a great wood; and then they were so tired and hungry that they sat down in a hollow tree and went to sleep.

In the morning when they awoke, the sun had risen high above the trees, and shone warm upon the hollow tree. Then Hansel said, "Sister, I am very thirsty; if I could find a brook, I would go and drink, and fetch you some water too. Listen, I think I hear the sound of one." Then Hansel rose up and took Grettel by the hand and went in search of the brook. But their cruel step-mother was a fairy, and had followed them into the wood to work them mischief: and when they had found a brook that ran sparkling over the pebbles, Hansel wanted to drink; but Grettel thought she heard the brook, as it babbled along, say, "Whoever drinks here will be turned into a tiger." Then she cried out, "Ah, brother! do not drink, or you will be turned into a wild beast and tear me to pieces." Then Hansel yielded, although he was parched with thirst. "I will wait," said he, "for the next brook." But when they came to the next, Grettel listened again, and thought she heard "Whoever drinks here will become a wolf." Then she cried out, "Brother, brother, do not drink, or you will become a wolf and eat me." So he did not drink, but said, "I will wait for the next brook; there I must drink, say what you will, I am so thirsty."

As they came to the third brook, Grettel listened, and heard "Whoever drinks here will become a fawn." "Ah, brother!" said she, "do not drink, or you will be turned into a fawn and run away from me." But Hansel had already stooped down upon his knees, and the moment he put his lips into the water he was turned into a fawn.

Grettel wept bitterly over the poor creature, and the tears too rolled down his eyes as he laid himself beside her. Then she said, "Rest in peace, dear fawn, I will never never leave thee." So she took off her golden necklace and put it round his neck, and plucked some rushes and plaited them into a soft string to fasten to it; and led the poor little thing by her side further into the wood.

After they had travelled a long way, they came at last to a little cottage; and Grettel, having looked in and seen that it was quite empty, thought to herself, "We can stay and live here." Then she went and gathered leaves and moss to make a soft bed for the fawn: and every morning she went out and plucked nuts, roots, and berries for herself, and sweet shrubs and tender grass for her companion; and it ate out of her hand, and was pleased, and played and frisked about her. In the evening, when Grettel was tired, and had said her prayers, she laid her head upon the fawn for her pillow, and slept: and if poor Hansel could but have his right form again, they thought they should lead a very happy life.

They lived thus a long while in the wood by themselves, till it chanced that the king of that country came to hold a great hunt there. And when the fawn heard all around the echoing of the horns, and the baying of dogs, and the merry shouts of the huntsmen, he wished very much to go and see what was going on. "Ah, sister! sister!" said he, "let me go out into the wood, I can stay no longer." And he begged so long, that she at last agreed to let him go. "But," said she, "be sure to come to me in the evening: I shall shut up the door to keep out those wild huntsmen; and if you tap at it, and say 'Sister, let me in,' I shall know you; but if you don't speak, I shall keep the door fast." Then away sprang the fawn, and frisked and bounded along in the open air. The king and his huntsmen saw the beautiful creature, and followed but could not overtake him; for when they thought they were sure of their prize, he sprung over the bushes and was out of sight in a moment.

As it grew dark he came running home to the hut, and tapped, and said, "Sister, sister, let me in." Then she opened the little door, and in he jumped and slept soundly all night on his soft bed.

Next morning the hunt began again; and when he heard the huntsmen's horns, he said, "Sister, open the door for me, I must go again." Then she let him out, and said, "Come back in the evening, and remember what you are to say." When the king and the huntsmen saw the fawn with the golden collar again, they gave him chase; but he was too quick for them. The chase lasted the whole day; but at last the huntsmen nearly surrounded him, and one of them wounded him in the foot, so that he became sadly lame and could hardly crawl home. The man who had wounded him followed close behind, and hid himself, and heard the little fawn say, "Sister, sister, let me in:" upon which the door opened and soon shut again. The huntsman marked all well, and went to the king and told him what he had seen and heard; then the king said, "To-morrow we will have another chase."

Grettel was very much frightened when she saw that her dear little fawn was wounded; but she washed the blood away and put some healing herbs on it, and said, "Now go to bed, dear fawn, and you will soon be well again." The wound was so small, that in the morning there was nothing to be seen of it; and when the horn blew, the little creature said, "I can't stay here, I must go and look on; I will take care that none of them shall catch me." But Grettel said, "I am sure they will kill you this time, I will not let you go." "I shall die of vexation," answered he, "if you keep me here; when I hear the horns, I feel as if I could fly." Then Grettel was forced to let him go; so she opened the door with a heavy heart, and he bounded out gaily into the wood.

When the king saw him, he said to his huntsman, "Now chase him all day long till you catch him; but let none of you do him any harm." The sun set, however, without their being able to overtake him, and the king called away the huntsmen, and said to the one who had watched, "Now come and show me the little hut." So they went to the door and tapped, and said, "Sister, sister, let me in." Then the door opened and the king went in, and there stood a maiden more lovely than any he had ever seen. Grettel was frightened to see that it was not her fawn, but a king with a golden crown, that was come into her hut: however, he spoke kindly to her, and took her hand, and said, "Will you come with me to my castle and be my wife?" "Yes," said the maiden; "but my fawn must go with me, I cannot part with that." "Well," said the king, "he shall come and live with you all your life, and want for nothing." Just at that moment in sprung the little fawn; and his sister tied the string to his neck, and they left the hut in the wood together.

Then the king took Grettel to his palace, and celebrated the marriage in great state. And she told the king all her story; and he sent for the fairy and punished her: and the fawn was changed into Hansel again, and he and his sister loved one another, and lived happily together all their days.

THE FOX AND THE HORSE

A FARMER had a horse that had been an excellent faithful servant to him: but he was now grown too old to work; so the farmer would give him nothing more to eat, and said, "I want you no longer, so take yourself off out of my stable; I shall not take you back again until you are stronger than a lion." Then he opened the door and turned him adrift.

The poor horse was very melancholy, and wandered up and down in the wood, seeking some little shelter from the cold wind and rain. Presently a fox met him: "What's the matter, my friend?"

said he, "why do you hang down your head and look so lonely and woe-begone?" "Ah!" replied the horse, "justice and avarice never dwell in one house; my master has forgotten all that I have done for him so many years, and because I can no longer work he has turned me adrift, and says unless I become stronger than a lion he will not take me back again; what chance can I have of that? he knows I have none, or he would not talk so."

However, the fox bid him be of good cheer, and said, "I will help you; lie down there, stretch yourself out quite stiff, and pretend to be dead." The horse did as he was told, and the fox went straight to the lion who lived in a cave close by, and said to him, "A little way off lies a dead horse; come with me and you may make an excellent meal of his carcase." The lion was greatly pleased, and set off immediately; and when they came to the horse, the fox said, "You will not be able to eat him comfortably here; I'll tell you what—I will tie you fast to his tail, and then you can draw him to your den, and eat him at your leisure."

This advice pleased the lion, so he laid himself down quietly for the fox to make him fast to the horse. But the fox managed to tie his legs together and bound all so hard and fast that with all his strength he could not set himself free. When the work was done, the fox clapped the horse on the shoulder, and said, "Jip! Dobbin! Jip!" Then up he sprang, and moved off, dragging the lion behind him. The beast began to roar and bellow, till all the birds of the wood flew away for fright; but the horse let him sing on, and made his way quietly over the fields to his master's house.

"Here he is, master," said he, "I have got the better of him": and when the farmer saw his old servant, his heart relented, and he said. "Thou shalt stay in thy stable and be well taken care of." And so the poor old horse had plenty to eat, and lived—till he died.

FAIRY TALES

HANS AND HIS WIFE GRETTEL

I

SHOWING WHO GRETTEL WAS

THERE was once a little maid named Grettel: she wore shoes with red heels, and when she went abroad she turned out her toes, and was very merry, and thought to herself, "What a pretty girl I am!" And when she came home, to put herself in good spirits, she would tipple down a drop or two of wine; and as wine gives a relish for eating, she would take a taste of everything when she was cooking, saying, "A cook ought to know whether a thing tastes well." It happened one day that her master said, "Grettel, this evening I have a friend coming to sup with me; get two fine fowls ready." "Very well, sir," said Grettel. Then she killed the fowls, plucked, and trussed them, put them on the spit, and when evening came put them to the fire to roast. The fowls turned round and round, and soon began to look nice and brown, but the guest did not come. Then Grettel cried out, "Master, if the guest does not come I must take up the fowls, but it will be a shame and a pity if they are not eaten while they are hot and good." "Well," said her master, "I'll run and tell him to come." As soon as he had turned his back, Grettel stopped the spit, and laid it with the fowls upon it on one side, and thought to herself, "Standing by the fire makes one very tired and thirsty; who knows how long they will be? meanwhile I will just step into the cellar and take a drop." So off she ran, put down her pitcher, and said, "Your health, Grettel," and took a good draught. "This wine is a good friend," said she to herself, "it breaks one's heart to leave it." Then up she trotted, put the fowls down to the fire, spread some butter over them, and turned the spit merrily round again.

The fowls soon smelt so good, that she thought to herself, "They are very good, but they may want something still; I had better taste them and see." So she licked her fingers, and said, "Oh! how good! what a shame and a pity that they are not eaten!" Away she ran to the window to see if her master and his friend were coming; but nobody was in sight: so she turned to the fowls again, and thought it would be better for her to eat a wing than that it should be burnt. So she cut one wing off, and ate it, and it tasted very well; and as the other was quite done enough, she thought it had better be cut off too, or else her master would see one was wanting. When the two wings were gone, she went again to look out for her master, but could not see him. "Ah!" thought she to herself, "who knows whether they will come at all? very likely they have turned into some tavern: Oh Grettel! Grettel! make yourself happy, take another draught, and eat the rest of the fowl; it looks so oddly as it is; when you have eaten all, you will be easy: why should such good things be wasted?" So she ran once more to the cellar, took another drink, and ate up the rest of the fowl with the greatest glee.

Still her master did not come, and she cast a lingering eye upon the other fowl, and said, "Where the other went, this had better go too; they belong to each other; they who have a right to one must have a right to the other; but if I were to take another draught first, it would not hurt me." So she tippled down another drop of wine, and sent the second fowl to look after the first. While she was making an end of this famous meal, her master came home and called out, "Now quick, Grettel, my friend is just at hand!" "Yes, master, I will dish up this minute," said she. In the meantime he looked to see if the cloth was laid, and took up the carving-knife to sharpen it. Whilst this was going on, the guest came and knocked softly and gently at the house door; then Grettel ran to see who was there, and when she saw him she put her finger upon her lips, and said, "Hush! hush! run away as fast as you can, for if my master catches you, it will be worse for you; he owes you a grudge, and asked you to supper only that he might cut off your ears; only listen how he is sharpening his knife." The guest listened, and when he heard the knife, he made as much haste as he could down the steps and ran off. Grettel was not idle in the meantime, but ran screaming, “Master! master! what a fine guest you have asked to supper!” “Why, Grettel, what’s the matter?” “Oh!” said she, “he has taken both the fowls that I was going to bring up, and has run away with them.” “That is a rascally trick to play,” said the master, sorry to lose the fine chickens; “at least he might have left me one, that I might have had something to eat; call out to him to stay.” But the guest would not hear; so he ran after him with his knife in his hand, crying out, “Only one, only one, I want only one;” meaning that the guest should leave him one of the fowls, and not take both: but he thought that his host meant nothing less than that he would cut off at least one of his ears; so he ran away to save them both, as if he had hot coals under his feet.

II

HANS IN LOVE

Hans's mother says to him, "Whither so fast?" "To see Grettel," says Hans. "Behave well." "Very well: Good-bye, mother!" Hans comes to Grettel; "Good day, Grettel!" "Good day, Hans! do you bring me anything good?" "Nothing at all: have you anything for me?" Grettel gives Hans a needle. Hans says, "Good-bye, Grettel!" "Good-bye, Hans!" Hans takes the needle, sticks it in a truss of hay, and takes both off home. "Good evening, mother!" "Good evening, Hans! where have you been?" "To see Grettel." "What did you take her?" "Nothing at all." "What did she give you?" "She gave me a needle." "Where is it, Hans?" "Stuck in the truss." "How silly you are! you should have stuck it in your sleeve." "Let me alone! I'll do better next time."

"Where now, Hans?" "To see Grettel, mother." "Behave yourself well." "Very well: Good-bye, mother!" Hans comes to Grettel; "Good day, Grettel!" "Good day, Hans! what have you brought me?" "Nothing at all: have you anything for me?" Grettel gives Hans a knife. "Good-bye, Grettel!" "Good-bye, Hans!" Hans takes the knife, sticks it in his sleeve, and goes home. "Good evening, mother!" "Good evening, Hans! where have you been?" "To see Grettel." "What did you carry her?" "Nothing at all." "What has she given you?" "A knife." "Where is the knife, Hans?" "Stuck in my sleeve, mother." "You silly goose! you should have put it in your pocket." "Let me alone! I'll do better next time."

"Where now, Hans?" "To see Grettel." "Behave yourself well." "Very well: Good-bye, mother!" Hans comes to Grettel; "Good day, Grettel!" "Good day, Hans! have you anything good?" "No: have

THE DOGS EAT UP ALL THE BACON AS HANS WALKS HOME

you anything for me?" Grettel gives Hans a kid. "Good-bye, Grettel!" "Good-bye, Hans!" Hans takes the kid, ties it up with a cord, stuffs it into his pocket, and chokes it to death. "Good evening, mother!" "Good evening, Hans! where have you been?" "To see Grettel, mother!" "What did you take her?" "Nothing at all." "What did she give you?" "She gave me a kid." "Where is the kid, Hans?" "Safe in my pocket." "You silly goose! you should have led it with a string." "Never mind, mother, I'll do better next time."

"Where now, Hans?" "To Grettel's, mother." "Behave well." "Quite well, mother; Good-bye!" Hans comes to Grettel; "Good day, Grettel!" "Good day, Hans! what have you brought me?" "Nothing at all: have you anything for me?" Grettel gives Hans a piece of bacon; Hans ties the bacon to a string and drags it behind him; the dog comes after and eats it all up as he walks home. "Good evening, mother!" "Good evening, Hans! where have you been?" "To Grettel's." "What did you take her?" "Nothing at all." "What did she give you?" "A piece of bacon." "Where is the bacon, Hans?" "Tied to the string, and dragged home, but somehow or other all gone." "What a silly trick, Hans! you should have brought it on your head." "Never mind, mother, I'll do better another time."

"Where now, Hans?" "Going to Grettel." "Take care of yourself." "Very well, mother: Good-bye." Hans comes to Grettel; "Good day, Grettel!" "Good day, Hans! what have you brought me?" "Nothing: have you anything for me?" Grettel gives Hans a calf. Hans sets it upon his head, and it kicks him in the face. "Good evening, mother!" "Good evening, Hans! where have you been?" "To see Grettel." "What did you take her?" "Nothing." "What did she give you?" "She gave me a calf." "Where is the calf, Hans?" "I put it on my head, and it scratched my face." "You silly goose! you should have led it home and put it in the stall." "Very well; I'll do better another time."

"Where now, Hans?" "To see Grettel." "Mind and behave well." "Good-bye, mother!" Hans comes to Grettel; "Good day, Grettel!" "Good day, Hans! what have you brought?" "Nothing at all: have you anything for me?" "I'll go home with you." Hans ties a string round her neck, leads her along, and ties her up in the stall. "Good evening, mother!" "Good evening, Hans! where have you been?" "At Grettel's." "What has she given you?" "She has come herself."

"Where have you put her?" "Fast in the stall with plenty of hay." "How silly you are! you should have taken good care of her, and brought her home." Then Hans went back to the stall; but Grettel was in a great rage, and had got loose and run away: yet, after all, she was Hans' bride.

III

HANS MARRIED

Hans and Grettel lived in the village together, but Grettel did as she pleased, and was so lazy that she never would work; and when her husband gave her any yarn to spin she did it in a slovenly way; and when it was spun she did not wind it on the reel, but left it to lie all tangled about. Hans sometimes scolded, but she was always beforehand with her tongue, and said, "Why how should I wind it when I have no reel? go into the wood and make one." "If that's all," said he, "I will go into the wood and cut reel-sticks." Then Grettel was frightened lest when he had cut the sticks he should make a reel, and thus she would be forced to wind the yarn and spin again. So she pondered a while, till at last a bright thought came into her head, and she ran slyly after her husband into the wood. As soon as he had got into a tree and began to bend down a bough to cut it, she crept into the bush below, where he could not see her, and sang—

"Bend not the bough;
He who bends it shall die!
Reel not the reel;
He who reels it shall die!"

Hans listened a while, laid down his axe, and thought to himself, "What can that be?" "What indeed can it be?" said he at last; "it is only a singing in your ears, Hans! pluck up your heart, man!" So he raised up his axe again, and took hold of the bough, but once more the voice sang—

"Bend not the bough;
He who bends it shall die!
Reel not the reel;
He who reels it shall die!"

Once more he stopped his hand; fear came over him, and he began pondering what it could mean. After a while, however, he plucked up his courage again, and took up his axe and began for the third time to cut the wood; again the third time began the song—

"Bend not the bough;
He who bends it shall die!
Reel not the reel;
He who reels it shall die!"

At this he could hold no longer, down he dropped from the tree and set off homewards as fast as he could. Away too ran Grettel by a shorter cut, so as to reach home first, and when he opened the door met him quite innocently, as if nothing had happened, and said, "Well! have you brought a good piece of wood for the reel?" "No," said he, "I see plainly that no luck comes of that reel;" and then he told her all that had happened, and left her for that time in peace.

But soon afterwards Hans began again to reproach her with the untidiness of her house. "Wife," said he; "is it not a sin and a shame that the spun yarn should lie all about in that way?" "It may be so," said she; "but you know very well that we have no reel; if it must be done, lie down there and hold up your hands and legs, and so I'll make a reel of you, and wind off the yarn into skeins." "Very well," said Hans (who did not much like the job, but saw no help for it if his wife was to be set to work); so he did as she said, and when all was wound, "The yarn is all in skeins," said he; "now take care and get up early and heat the water and boil it well, so that it may be ready for sale." Grettel disliked this part of the work very much, but said to him, "Very well, I'll be sure to do it very early to-morrow morning." But all the time she was thinking to herself what plan she should take for getting off such work for the future.

Betimes in the morning she got up, made the fire and put on the boiler; but instead of the yarn she laid a large ball of tow in it and let it boil. Then she went up to her husband, who was still in bed, and said to him, "I must go out, pray look meantime to the yarn in the boiler over the fire; but do it soon and take good care, for if the cock crows and you are not looking to it, they say it will turn to tow." Hans soon after got up that he might run no risk, and went (but not perhaps as quickly as he might have done) into the kitchen, and when he lifted up the boiler lid and looked in, to his great terror nothing was there but a ball of tow. Then off he slunk as dumb as a mouse, for he thought to himself that he was to blame for his laziness; and left Grettel to get on with her yarn and her spinning as fast as she pleased and no faster.

One day, however, he said to her, "Wife, I must go a little way this morning; do you go into the field and cut the corn." "Yes, to be sure, dear Hans!" said she; so when he was gone she cooked herself a fine mess and took it with her into the field. When she came into the field, she sat down for a while and said to herself, "What shall I do? shall I sleep first or eat first? Heigho! I'll first eat a bit." Then she ate her dinner heartily, and when she had had enough she said again to herself, "What shall I do? shall I reap first or sleep first? Heigho! I'll first sleep a bit." So she laid herself down among the corn and went fast asleep. By and by Hans came home, but no Grettel was to be seen, and he said to himself, "What a clever wife I have! she works so hard that she does not even come home to her dinner!" Evening came and still she did not come; then Hans set off to see how much of the corn was reaped, but there it all stood untouched, and Grettel lay fast asleep in the middle. So he ran home and got a string of little bells and tied them quietly round her waist, and went back and set himself down on his stool and locked the house door.

At last Grettel woke when it was quite dark, and as she rose up the bells jingled around her every step she took. At this she was greatly frightened, and puzzled to tell whether she was really Grettel or not. "Is it I, or is it not?" said she as she stood doubting what she ought to think. At last, after she had pondered a while, she thought to herself, "I will go home and ask if it is I or not; Hans will know." So she ran to the house door, and when she found it locked she knocked at the window and cried out, "Hans! is Grettel within?" "She is where she ought to be, to be sure," said Hans; "O dear then!" said she frightened, "this is not I." Then away she went and knocked at the neighbors' doors; but when they heard her bells rattling no one would let her in, and so at last off she ran back to the field again.

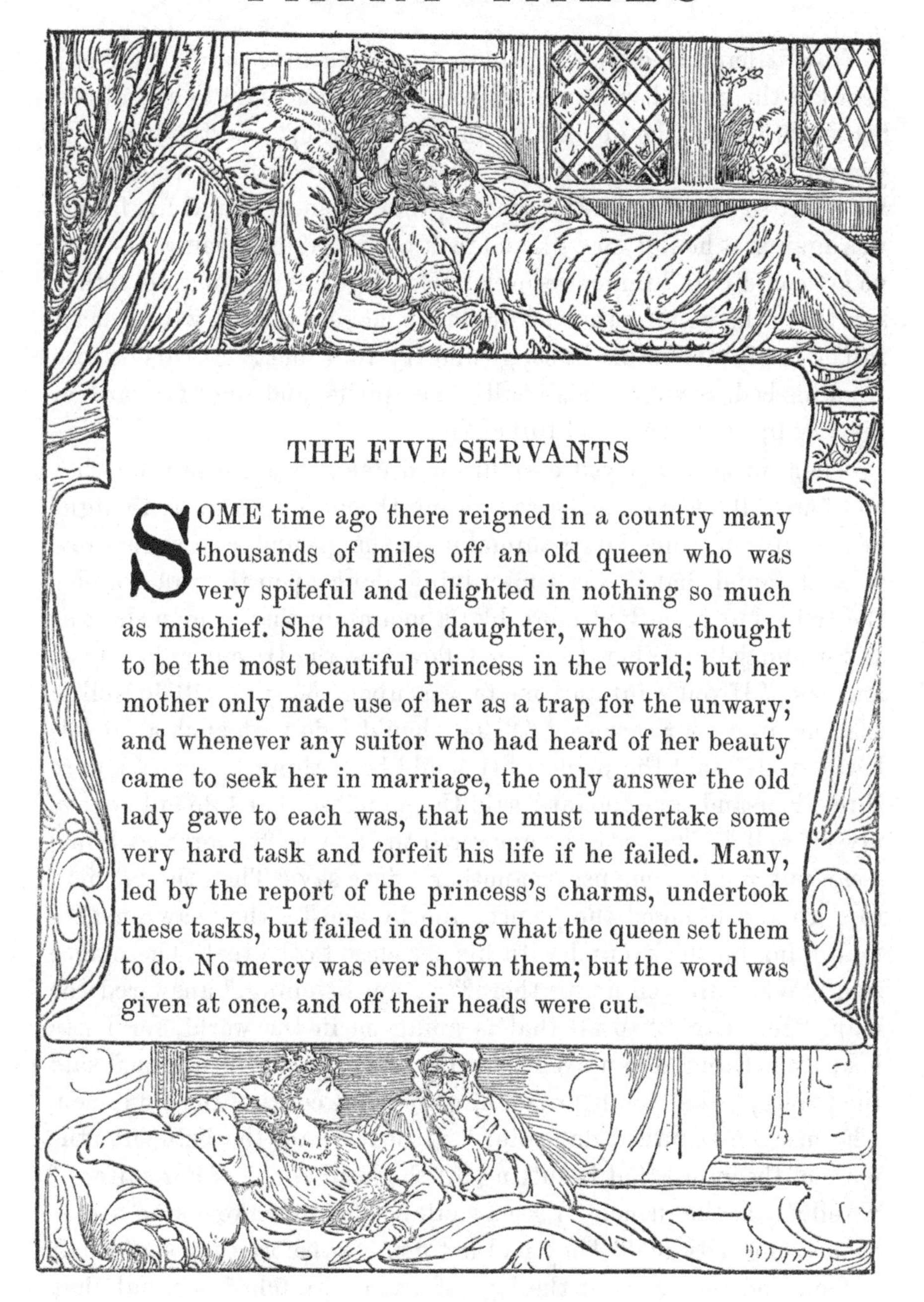

THE FIVE SERVANTS

SOME time ago there reigned in a country many thousands of miles off an old queen who was very spiteful and delighted in nothing so much as mischief. She had one daughter, who was thought to be the most beautiful princess in the world; but her mother only made use of her as a trap for the unwary; and whenever any suitor who had heard of her beauty came to seek her in marriage, the only answer the old lady gave to each was, that he must undertake some very hard task and forfeit his life if he failed. Many, led by the report of the princess's charms, undertook these tasks, but failed in doing what the queen set them to do. No mercy was ever shown them; but the word was given at once, and off their heads were cut.

Now it happened that a prince, who lived in a country far off, heard of the great beauty of this young lady, and said to his father, "Dear father, let me go and try my luck." "No," said the king; "if you go, you will surely lose your life." The prince, however, had set his heart so much upon the scheme, that when he found his father was against it he fell very ill, and took to his bed for seven years, and no art could cure him, or recover his lost spirits: so when his father saw that if he went on thus he would die, he said to him, with a heart full of grief, "If it must be so, go and try your luck." At this he rose from his bed, recovered his health and spirits, and went forward on his way light of heart and full of joy.

Then on he journeyed over hill and dale, through fair weather and foul, till one day, as he was riding through a wood, he thought he saw afar off some large animal upon the ground, and as he drew near he found that it was a man lying along upon the grass under the trees; but he looked more like a mountain than a man, he was so fat and jolly. When this big fellow saw the traveller, he arose, and said, "If you want any one to wait upon you, you will do well to take me into your service." "What should I do with such a fat fellow as you?" said the prince. "It would be nothing to you if I were three thousand times as fat," said the man, "so that I do but behave myself well." "That's true," answered the prince, "so come with me; I can put you to some use or another I dare say." Then the fat man rose up and followed the prince, and by and by they saw another man lying on the ground with his ear close to the turf. The prince said, "What are you doing there?" "I am listening," answered the man. "To what?" "To all that is going on in the world, for I can hear everything, I can even hear the grass grow." "Tell me," said the prince, "what you hear is going on at the court of the old queen, who has the beautiful daughter." "I hear," said the listener, "the noise of the sword that is cutting off the head of one of her suitors." "Well!" said the prince, "I see I shall be able to make you of use;—come along with me!" They had not gone far before they saw a pair of feet, and then part of the legs of a man stretched out; but they were so long that they could not see the rest of the body, till they had passed on a good deal further, and at last they came to the body, and after going on a while further, to the head; "Bless me!" said the prince, "what a long rope you are!" "Oh!" answered the tall man, "this is nothing; when I choose to stretch myself to my full length, I am three times as high as any mountain you have seen on your travels, I warrant you; I will willingly do what I can to serve you if you will let me." "Come along then." said the prince, "I can turn you to account in some way."

The prince and his train went on further into the wood, and next saw a man lying by the roadside basking in the heat of the sun, yet shaking and shivering all over, so that not a limb lay still. "What makes you shiver," said the king, "while the sun is shining so warm?" "Alas!" answered the man, "the warmer it is, the colder I am; the sun only seems to me like a sharp frost that thrills through all my bones; and on the other hand, when others are what you call cold I begin to be warm, so that I can neither bear the ice for its heat nor the fire for its cold." "You are a queer fellow," said the prince; "but if you have nothing else to do, come along with me." The next thing they saw was a man standing, stretching his neck and looking around him from hill to hill. "What are you looking for so eagerly?" said the prince. "I have such sharp eyes," said the man, "that I can see over woods and fields and hills and dales;—in short, all over the world." "Well," said the prince, "come with me if you will, for I want one more to make up my train."

Then they all journeyed on, and met with no one else till they came to the city where the beautiful princess lived. The prince went straight to the old queen, and said, "Here I am, ready to do any task you set me, if you will give me your daughter as a reward when I have done." "I will set you three tasks," said the queen; "and if you get through all, you shall be the husband of my daughter. First, you must bring me a ring which I dropped in the red sea." The prince went home to his friends and said, "The first task is not an easy one; it is to fetch a ring out of the red sea, so lay your heads together and say what is to be done." Then the sharp-sighted one said, "I will see where it lies," and looked down into the sea, and cried out, "There it lies upon a rock at the bottom." "I would fetch it out," said the tall man, "if I could but see it." "Well!" cried out the fat one, "I will help you to do that," and laid himself down and held his mouth to the water, and drank up the waves till the bottom of the sea was as dry as a meadow. Then the tall man stooped a little and pulled out the ring with his hand, and the prince took it to the old queen, who looked at it, and wondering said, "It is indeed the right ring; you have gone through this task well: but now comes the second; look yonder at the meadow before my palace; see! there are a hundred fat oxen feeding there; you must eat them all up before noon: and underneath in my cellar there are a hundred casks of wine, which you must drink all up." "May I not invite some guests to share the feast with me?" said the prince. "Why, yes!" said the old woman with a spiteful laugh; "you may ask one of your friends to breakfast with you, but no more."

Then the prince went home and said to the fat man, "You must be my guest to-day, and for once you shall eat your fill." So the fat man set to work and ate the hundred oxen without leaving a bit, and asked if that was to be all he should have for his breakfast? and he drank the wine out of the casks without leaving a drop licking even his fingers when he had done. When the meal was ended, the prince went to the old women and told her the second task was done. "Your work is not all over, however," muttered the old hag to herself; "I will catch you yet! you shall not keep your head upon your shoulders if I can help it." "This evening," said she, "I will bring my daughter into your house and leave her with you; you shall sit together there, but take care that you do not fall asleep; for I shall come when the clock strikes twelve, and if she is not then with you, you are undone." "Oh!" thought the prince, "it is an easy task to keep such a watch as that; I will take care to keep my eyes open." So he called his servants and told them all that the old woman had said. "Who knows though," said he, "but there may be some trick at the bottom of this? it is as well to be upon our guard and keep watch that the young lady does not get away." When it was night the old woman brought her daughter to the prince's house; then the tall man twisted himself round about it, the listener put his ear to the ground, the fat man placed himself before the door so that no living soul could enter, and the sharp-eyed one looked out afar and watched. Within sat the princess without saying a word, but the moon shone bright through the window upon her face, and the prince gazed upon her wonderful beauty. And while he looked upon her with a heart full of joy and love, his eyelids did not droop; but at eleven o'clock the old woman cast a charm over them so that they all fell asleep, and the princess vanished in a moment.

And thus they slept till a quarter to twelve, when the charm had no longer any power over them, and they all awoke. "Alas! alas! woe is me," cried the prince; "now I am lost for ever." And his faithful servants began to weep over their unhappy lot; but the listener said, "Be still and I will listen;" so he listened awhile, and cried out, "I hear her bewailing her fate;" and the sharp-sighted man looked, and said, "I see her sitting on a rock three hundred miles hence; now help us, my tall friend; if you stand up, you will reach her in two steps." "Very well," answered the tall man; and in an instant, before one could turn one's head round, he was at the foot of the enchanted rock. Then the tall man took the young lady in his arms and carried her back to the prince a moment before it struck twelve; and they all sat down again and made merry. And when the clock struck twelve the old queen came sneaking by with a spiteful look, as if she was going to say, "Now he is mine;" nor could she think otherwise, for she knew that her daughter was but the moment before on the rock three hundred miles off; but when she came and saw her daughter in the prince's room she started, and said, "There is somebody here who can do more than I can." However, she now saw that she could no longer avoid giving the prince her daughter for a wife, but said to her in a whisper, "It is a shame that you should be won by servants, and not have a husband of your own choice."

Now the young lady was of a very proud haughty temper and her anger was raised to such a pitch, that the next morning she ordered three hundred loads of wood to be brought and piled up; and told the prince it was true he had by the help of his servants done the three tasks, but that before she would marry him some one must sit upon that pile of wood when it was set on fire and bear the heat. She thought to herself that though his servants had done everything else for him, none of them would go so far as to burn themselves for him, and that then she should put his love to the test by seeing whether he would sit upon it himself. But she was mistaken; for when the servants heard this, they said, "We have all done something but the frosty man; now his turn is come;" and they took him and put him on the wood and set it on fire. Then the fire rose and burned for three long days, till all the wood was gone; and when it was out, the frosty man stood in the midst of the ashes trembling like an aspen-leaf, and said, "I never shivered so much in my life; if it had lasted much longer, I should have lost the use of my limbs."

When the princess had no longer any plea for delay, she saw that she was bound to marry the prince; but when they were going to church, the old woman said, "I will never consent;" and sent secret orders out to her horsemen to kill and slay all before them and bring back her daughter before she could be married. However, the listener had pricked up his ears and heard all that the old woman said, and told it to the prince. So they made haste and got to the church first, and were married; and then the five servants took their leave and went away saying, "We will go and try our luck in the world on our own account."

The prince set out with his wife, and at the end of the first day's journey came to a village, where a swineherd was feeding his swine: and as they came near he said to his wife, "Do you know who I am? I am not a prince, but a poor swineherd; he whom you see yonder with the swine is my father, and our business will be to help him to tend them." Then he went into the swineherd's hut with her, and ordered her royal clothes to be taken away in the night; so that when she awoke in the morning, she had nothing to put on, till the woman who lived there made a great favor of giving her an old gown and a pair of worsted stockings. "If it were not for your husband's sake," said she, "I would not have given you anything." Then the poor princess gave herself up for lost, and believed that her husband must indeed be a swineherd; but she thought she would make the best of it, and began to help him to feed them, and said, "It is a just reward for my pride." When this had lasted eight days she could bear it no longer for her feet were all over wounds, and as she sat down and wept by the wayside, some people came up to her and pitied her, and asked if she knew what her husband really was. "Yes," said she; "a swineherd; he is just gone out to market with some of his stock." But they said, "Come along and we will take you to him;" and they took her over the hill to the palace of the prince's father; and when they came into the hall, there stood her husband so richly dressed in his royal clothes that she did not know him till he fell upon her neck and kissed her, and said, "I have borne much for your sake, and you too have also borne a great deal for me." Then the guests were sent for, and the marriage feast was given, and all made merry and danced and sang, and the best wish that I can wish is, that you and I had been there too.

THE END

Made in the USA
Monee, IL
20 November 2024